Retribution

Other books by Patrick J. O'Brian:

The Fallen
Reaper: Book One of the West Baden Murders Trilogy
The Brotherhood
Stolen Time

For more information about Patrick or his works, visit
www.pjobooks.com

Retribution

Book Two of the West Baden Murders Trilogy

Patrick J. O'Brian

iUniverse, Inc.

New York Lincoln Shanghai

Retribution

iUniverse, Inc.

For information address:
iUniverse, Inc.
2021 Pine Lake Road, Suite 100
Lincoln, NE 68512
www.iuniverse.com

Cover design by Kendrick L. Shadoan from KLS Digital. Visit
www.klsdigital.com for more information.

ISBN: 0-595-28061-7

Printed in the United States of America

I owe many thanks to my usual crew for
helping out, and especially to Troy Lobosky
and John Leach for their insight.

1

Standing in the living room of his new country home, Paul Clouse took in the view of stacked boxes, clean carpet, and a fresh start for himself. Miles outside of town, he could begin anew, with the house serving as a template for his life.

In August he had proposed to Jane Brooks, and she accepted. The house was their first step in solidifying the idea of being married, particularly since Clouse's first wife had been murdered almost one year prior.

After surveying the packaged organization in the form of two dozen cardboard boxes, Clouse stepped from the living room into the kitchen, hearing the sound of his brown cowboy boots clop against the linoleum floor. He stared at the large room, looking forward to cooking breakfast for the family when he was off weekends.

He crossed the room, then walked through the open front door to the large porch, which wrapped partway around the two-story home.

"Not bad," he said of the mid-October weather.

Living almost two miles from Bloomington, Indiana, where he and Jane both worked, Clouse enjoyed having no visible neighbors, and room for his animals to run. She ran a medical clinic, while he worked for the city as a firefighter once every three days.

He loved his schedule, and worked a second job as a design consultant for Kieffer Construction, a company in nearby Bedford that always seemed to have new work for him. He could pick his own hours, sometimes doing designs at the fire station, and he felt as though his college degree wouldn't go to waste.

Wearing jeans and a flannel shirt to accompany his boots, Clouse looked more like a logger than anything else with his brown hair loosely parted, and a thick mustache he planned to trim later in the day before he attended an inaugural dinner that evening.

His blue eyes scanned the empty, tanned fields surrounding his property, and the old barn not far away, which housed his boat, his horse, and occasionally, a vehicle. It reminded him of the barn on his old property, except he no longer had space enough to keep his father's seasonal farming machines for winter storage.

Clouse broke away from the scenery just long enough to pour himself a cup of coffee inside.

As he returned to the porch, he took in the new, bare wood. He had yet to pick a color, so he decided to leave it until spring. A few old rocking chairs and some flower pots were all that adorned the outdoor retreat.

A small tan car pulled up the long drive to the house, and Clouse smiled as he saw Jane return with his son, Zach, and her daughter from a previous marriage, Katie. Part of what made their relationship seem perfect was how the kids, both five years of age, seemed to get along so well. They had both longed for a sibling to identify with, and finally found one.

"Hello," he said, planting a kiss on Jane's lips as she stepped from the car.

She looked as beautiful as ever, taking a bag from inside the car as the kids rushed inside the house to play with whatever toys she had bought them. To him, Jane never looked bad, even on her worst mornings when she dreaded going into public because she felt flawed.

Her hair flowed in the wind as though she was a supermodel at the edge of the sea, and her slender form might have landed her some parts on television if she lived out west. Clouse suspected Jane was perfectly happy being a mother and a doctor.

If there was imperfection in her personality, or beauty, he would have to find it later, because he had spent the past year mesmerized by everything about her. She felt the same about him, but Clouse never took to the compliments about his looks.

"You're not going to the dinner like that, are you?" she teased as they walked toward the house.

"I was going to wear a baseball cap too," he kidded before a sip of coffee. "Believe it or not, I do have my tux hanging upstairs, and I'll even take a shower before I get dressed."

"I'm impressed," she said with an easy smile. "So I'm taking the kids over to my parents' house to change before meeting you at the hotel?"

"Yup. I dropped their clothes off there this morning to make it easy on you."

"What are you doing this afternoon?" she asked, apparently forgetting what he had stated the night before.

"I've got to see Mark, then I'm taking the boat out one last time before we put it up for the winter."

"Don't be late," she warned. "You've been waiting almost three years for this night."

"I wouldn't miss it for the world," he said sincerely with a crooked smirk. "I'll take my stuff with me and get ready at Ken's house once I'm finished with the boat."

Ken Kaiser was Clouse's high school pal, who worked for the county police in the area of the hotel, and lived fairly close to West Baden. Clouse was no stranger to Kaiser, or the man's family, because he often dropped by when working in the area.

Kieffer Construction had begun work on the West Baden Springs Hotel several years prior, when the National Preservation Society stepped in to save Indiana's first self-supported dome structure, built just after the turn of the 20th century. Bought by Dr. Martin Smith, the hotel was funded for renovation, and eventually redone completely, from the grounds to each individual room.

Clouse took great personal interest in the project, particularly since he had drawn its new set of blueprints for his graduate work at Indiana University. His prints proved quite useful to the company during the reconstruction, and his advice was heeded by the first project manager, and now his replacement.

Tonight, a dinner marked the completion of the hotel and the impending grand reopening of the building, after decades of use for purposes other than its primary function.

"I'll finish with the boat, change, and meet you at the dinner around seven," Clouse said as the couple walked inside. "They won't start serving and announcing the guests of honor until about seven-thirty."

Clouse pulled Jane in for a kiss, wrapping both arms around her slender form. They locked lips several seconds until the children ran into the kitchen, anxious to be seen and heard.

"Where are you going, Dad?" Zach asked.

Many relatives felt Zach was a spitting image of his father. Others could see images of Angie from beyond the grave, thinking much of her rested within her son.

"I've got to take the boat for a spin while it's nice out, son."

"Can I go?"

"Nope. You've got to stay with Jane until the party tonight." He knelt beside his son. "Give Dad a kiss?" he asked, despite Zach reaching an age where such an act was no longer kosher.

Zach shook his head, indicating a refusal.

"Oh, come on," Clouse chided him. "Your friends aren't here."

His son finally gave him a hug and a kiss so he could be left alone to play again.

"I'll see you at the dinner, okay?"

Zach nodded an affirmative. In Clouse's opinion, he took to his father's new love interest quite well. In many ways, Jane was like Angie had been. She was beautiful, led a professional life, and acted cordially toward everyone she knew.

Clouse quickly replaced his boots with tennis shoes for the boat outing, and left in his Chevy four-wheel-drive truck, which he considered a must when living outside of town. Since his parents lived on a farm, and his new property was of similar nature, keeping the big truck seemed practical, despite its appetite for fuel.

He pulled out of the driveway, leaving a slight trail of dust behind.

2

Clouse stopped at a red light several blocks before Bloomington Hospital, seeing its familiar form loom beneath the afternoon sun. He hated visiting his friend every week at the hospital, but only because it conjured up bad memories from the depths of his mind.

When Clouse's first wife, Angie, had been murdered the year before, Detective Mark Daniels was the only one who gave Clouse the benefit of the doubt in his plea of innocence. When it turned out his former employer, the first project manager for Kieffer Construction, was primarily responsible for Angie's death and half a dozen others, Clouse and Daniels were already trapped by Dave Landamere's evil scheme.

Though Clouse escaped the incident without serious injury, Daniels wasn't so lucky. He was shot in the spine while scrambling to retrieve a loose weapon. The injury left him paralyzed from the waist down, and a year later he continued to battle in rehabilitation for full use of his legs.

Once a week Clouse made the trip to the hospital, feeling obligated to visit the hapless police officer in his personal fight. Ironically, Clouse had never met the man before he was accused of murdering Angie. Now they were on a first name basis and knew each other quite well.

Clouse figured guilt kept him visiting Daniels every week because the man had shown undying devotion to find the truth when no one else tried. Until the detective walked, Clouse would never truly put his mind to rest. It made him feel horrible that his

life had taken such a great direction while Daniels' had basically
fallen apart, and Daniels never spoke a negative word toward the
fireman about how he had attained his condition.

He was just that sort of person.

Confined to a wheelchair, the detective was now relegated to dispatch duty. Clouse imagined it ate him up inside, but Daniels never
lashed out at him.

Nor did he seem to enjoy the firefighter watching him fail week
after week in his attempts to walk, but he seemed glad someone
aside from his wife cared enough to help him through his burden.

Within a few minutes, Clouse parked his truck and found himself on the fourth floor of the hospital, heading toward one of the
therapy rooms where Daniels made his attempt in vain, once a
week, to walk again.

As he approached the room, he saw Susan Jameson, the officer's
doctor, walking out.

"How is he, Doc?"

"His state of mind just isn't positive, Paul," she answered. "He's
getting more and more pessimistic about his chances of ever walking again."

"Do you still think his problems stem from his head?" Clouse
asked.

She hesitated, glancing into the room as though Daniels might
see them speaking.

"Let's sit a moment," the doctor said, leading him to a set of
chairs across the hall. "His wife has been working with him daily,
conditioning his legs. He should have enough strength to take a
few steps, and he's even told me he has most, or all, of the feeling
back in them."

"But he can't or won't walk," Clouse summed up the situation.

"I've seen this before," the doctor commented. "Sometimes
there's a mental block preventing the patient from fully recovering.
Whether it be a deep residing fear of returning to active duty, or
some trauma left from the shooting incident, I don't know," she
said with an air of frustration. "Most mental blocks don't last this

long, but most are usually taken care of through psychotherapy, early in rehab."

"And he won't go, will he?"

Susan shook her head.

"No, he won't. He knows there's nothing physically wrong with him, so he thinks he can do it on his own."

"Can I talk to him?"

"Sure," she said. "He's about to attempt a walk with the support railings."

Clouse and the doctor walked into the therapy room as Daniels supported himself with two parallel braces nearly six feet in length. Susan kept the door from slamming shut for the sake of her patient's concentration as the two watched from behind. Daniels slowly dragged one leg forward, showing slight use. Concentrating fully, he wobbled a bit, jerking his right shoulder forward before dragging the left leg up to him.

"That's good," the therapist by his side commented. "Are you ready to try full weight on it?" she encouraged, despite the fact he could barely steady his feet beneath him.

Daniels did not answer, but simply steadied himself on the braces, bringing both feet to a standing position as his upper body trembled from supporting all of his weight. He slowly let go of the braces, appearing surprised he could stand at all without them. Subconsciously licking his lips in anticipation, the officer lifted one foot to take a step as the therapist moved to the inside of the bars for a better spotting position.

With his left foot off the ground, Daniels attempted to move it forward for his first step, but fell forward instead, his fall broken by the therapist. Luckily, she was accustomed to catching everyone from elderly ladies to burly construction workers, so any bumps and bruises she received from the officer's fall were expected.

"Damn it," Daniels said to himself as she helped him back to his chair.

He shook his head in disgust.

"You're doing better," Clouse commented, walking into the officer's view.

"I just can't get it," Daniels said with a discouraged tone, his eyes showing the hurt he felt inside.

"Let's get out of here a minute," his friend suggested, leading the way to the door before opening it for Daniels.

Both left the room silently, opting for the sunlit hallway outside, with an unusual warmth about it.

"Dr. Jameson still thinks your problem lies up here," Clouse said, pointing to the side of his own head for reference.

"She's right," Daniels admitted. "I want to do it, I've been physically able for eight months, but I just can't get it done."

Clouse took a seat at the edge of the hallway, across from the disgruntled police officer. For a moment he looked Daniels over, noticing a few things different about the man he'd met the year before.

For his rehabilitation Daniels had quit smoking.

That, coupled with confinement to a chair, led him to put on a few more pounds and become a bit more crotchety. He had also grown a full beard thicker than his head of dirty-blond hair.

Other than occasional minor lapses of depression, Daniels still seemed the determined, genuine person Clouse recalled meeting under unimaginable conditions.

"You know, you don't have to come watch me fuck this up every week," Daniels said as he sometimes did.

"I owe you my life," Clouse said. "The very least I can do is support you through this, so quit trying to get rid of me."

Daniels grinned.

"I really do appreciate it, but you've got a life to live. Don't put it on hold for me."

"It's no trouble, Mark. So, tell me what's troubling you this week. Why do you think you're not making progress?"

Daniels shrugged from his wheelchair.

"Dr. Jameson keeps trying new drugs on me every other week. One's for my mind, one's to help my muscles, another's to relax me. All I know is my hair is falling out in clumps, and I go through these mood swings, worse than I've ever had before."

Daniels had lost some hair over the past year, but Clouse attributed it to male pattern baldness. He never suspected the drugs might be responsible.

"She's switched prescriptions three times, and every one seems worse," Daniels revealed.

Clouse simply shook his head, suspecting the medical staff knew what was best, and Daniels was just grumpy about the side effects.

"Overall, are you holding up okay?" Clouse decided to ask.

"Yeah, I suppose. It sucks going to work and being a dispatcher when I used to bust the bad guys. No one talks to me because they feel sorry for me."

Clouse nodded in understanding, and hesitated a moment before asking a favor of his ailing friend.

"I want you to come to that dinner tonight," Clouse told the officer, speaking of the hotel's grand reopening gala.

Daniels sneered at the idea, looking to the wall.

"You *know* I don't want to go near the damned place after what happened."

"I know, but it might do you good to see the source of your problem," Clouse said, knocking on the wheelchair. "You're too damn stubborn to see a shrink, and whatever's plaguing your mind isn't just going to work itself out."

"Why can't I just go down there with you sometime?"

"Because you and Cindy need a night out, and we're both too busy to set a common time. Come on, Mark. You're already invited. You can just sit with me and Jane."

"I don't know," Daniels hesitated.

"It can't hurt, you know. I doubt anyone down there will know you, and if they do, they'll want your autograph."

"Why's that?" Daniels asked, finally drawing a smile.

"Ah, come on, Mark. You won officer of the year," Clouse said, playfully punching Daniels' left arm, still solid despite the chair. "There are thousands of cops in this country and you won."

Daniels rolled his eyes. He had remained extremely noble through the entire process, though Cindy once informed Clouse of how proud the officer acted toward the award, away from other people.

"I still think you were instrumental in that."

"A letter here, a letter there," Clouse said with a disarming wave of his hand. "The only thing I did was tell every committee that would listen about the guy who saved my ass, and probably several other lives."

Daniels seemed relaxed enough to debate with Clouse about the evening's plans.

"Is this a formal thing?" he asked.

"Tuxedo, buddy," Clouse said.

"I don't have one of those handy," Daniels countered.

"Yes you do," Clouse informed him, standing from the seat. "I asked Cindy to go pick one up for you."

Daniels lunged at him with a half-hearted punch from the chair, missing as Clouse dodged.

"I am going to kill you for this," he said, followed by a sigh.

"Fine, but you'll have to show up to do it," the fireman said, pointing both index fingers at the officer, stepping backwards toward the elevators. "See you tonight, Mark. I've got to go play on my boat."

"Sure," Daniels said, realizing he was outvoted by his wife and a good friend.

Like it or not, he would have to visit the place that cost him the most important position he had ever held, and a year of his life he could never take back.

3

Across Lake Monroe, tiny ripples bounced atop the water as a gentle wind passed through the reservoir. Clouse's boat easily glided across the lake, leaving a foamy white trail behind the outboard motor as he captained the craft.

A large boat, it was designed for overnight stays on the lake, rather than fishing. Beneath the deck, a comfortable living area provided room enough to sleep, cook, or relax when the boat was idling or stopped. A collapsible canopy could be rolled over the helm to protect the captain and his controls.

No one else dared challenge the wind and quickly cooling water on the lake. Clouse merely wanted to give the boat one last run before winter weather hit the area. He usually ran it almost completely out of gas before toting it home for storage. During the season the boat remained docked at the marina until he felt the urge to take it out.

Jane was not as enthusiastic about boating as Clouse's first love had been. It used to be a tradition for them to take Zach out overnight, or sometimes leave him with relatives if they wanted time alone on the lake.

He planned on taking the boat home after his next workday at the fire station. His work at the hotel was functionally complete, and he had no major projects pending with Kieffer Construction.

In the back of his mind he hoped Dr. Smith might give him a chance to run the day-to-day operations of the hotel, but suspected the doctor probably wanted the opportunity to do that personally, at first. There were many people to meet, and so many compliments to receive about the hotel's striking appearance.

Clouse would not pass up the opportunity either.

Noticing the gas meter drew close to empty, Clouse decided to return to the marina. He wanted just enough gas left to load the boat onto his trailer in a few days.

For a few minutes the craft skimmed across the center of the lake with the greatest of ease, then it hit something that stopped the motor. The outboard sputtered a moment, then died as the boat gracefully coasted along the water, slowly drawing to a complete stop.

"Shit!" he exclaimed, steadying himself once the boat rested, floating in the middle of the lake completely alone.

Even the nearest shore was too far for Clouse to contemplate swimming without a risk of hypothermia setting in. He looked in every direction, seeing no one around, and no way to signal for help.

If the engine failed to restart, he would be alone for some time.

Looking over the back of the boat, Clouse saw a bit of lake vegetation trickling from the back of the outboard motor. This surprised him only because the water's surface was completely clear of debris, the ripples carrying most of the plant life to shore, and the motor's blade reached nowhere near the bottom of the lake.

"What in the hell?" he asked himself, studying the plant life attached to his motor, wondering if it had actually stopped his boat.

Walking to the helm, Clouse turned the key in an attempt to start the vessel. It tried to start, but fell short of actually turning over.

"Damn," the fireman told himself, knowing there was no additional aid because his cellular phone was in the truck, and the boat coasted far too slowly to return him to shore by the dinner's start.

Also, not a soul could be found on the lake.

Returning to the rear of the vessel, he looked over the side, questioning how long he could stay in the water to fix the motor before his body began to freeze. At best, the water temperature stood between forty and fifty degrees. Without adequate covering he would feel the effects of the cold within minutes. A severe cold would be the lowest form of punishment he might receive for such a foolhardy action.

Unwilling to take a chance in the water just yet, Clouse took up an emergency oar from one side of the vessel. He returned to the rear of the boat, using the oar to prod at the underside of the motor, slowly removing debris from its blades.

While he worked, the craft's captain felt the boat shift slightly to one side, but attributed the motion to the ripples striking the other side. He fought the motor housing a moment more, noticing the rocking motion stop suddenly.

Knowing the ripples in the lake would not simply cease without a good reason, Clouse tensed, suspecting he might not be alone. It seemed far too coincidental the boat got tangled in debris during a season where the plants and brush were gone, or submerged far beneath the surface.

His boat had *never* struck anything in all the years he had taken it on the lake.

Without turning around, Clouse took a few steps back, casually reaching for the second oar as he knelt down, fearing he might need it for additional self-defense. His hand fumbled momentarily for the wooden tool, finding nothing in its usual housing.

Suspecting he was in deep trouble, now hearing the distinct dripping of water along the boat deck behind him, Clouse bolted upward, pivoting away from the potential attacker at the same time.

His action failed to distract his attacker, however, because someone wearing a black wetsuit waited until Clouse was done parrying before swinging the second oar like a baseball bat toward the firefighter's head.

Too slow to react, Clouse felt the oar impact the side of his head, which whirled him around into a defenseless position, allowing his assailant to land a second blow against the side of his head, right beside the temple.

Never able to see his attacker's face, Clouse was knocked into the water, where he struck the surface limply. His body turned as it bobbed, his clothes quickly filling with water.

Every bit of consciousness he had left went to hold his breath while viewing the dark form looming at the side of his boat from beneath the water's surface. Ripples and air bubbles along the surface obscured his view of his assailant, who looked mysterious and black in the wetsuit, with no visible face.

Everything grew dark as Clouse slipped further beneath the surface, feeling his consciousness waver as he entered a liquified oblivion. The only sound entering his ears was that of moving water before he blacked out, unable to keep the aquatic environment from entering his lungs.

4

"Goddamn it!" Daniels exclaimed as his wheelchair hit one of the chairs around the kitchen table.

Usually mild-mannered, Daniels found himself a bit more emotionally turbulent with each failure in his rehabilitation.

"What is it, Mark?" his wife, Cindy, asked as she ran into the kitchen from the living room.

"Nothing," he replied with a sour expression, forcefully shoving the chair out of the way.

His entire morning was mired in frustration, especially since he was practically being forced to attend the formal dinner.

As much as he tried, Daniels could not always avoid hurting the most important woman in his life.

He had spent his entire police career sheltering her from the occasional horrors he witnessed, and the everyday aggravations his job brought to him. Now he forced her to deal with a husband who seemed to take out his frustrations on no one except her.

Daniels went to work at the dispatch center, came home, and avoided public contact as much as possible. Even most of his old friends were shut out of his life. She often told him she was tired of him feeling sorry for himself and giving up on so much of life.

Rearranged to accommodate Daniels' condition, the house looked a bit different, especially after several friends from the police department volunteered to build an entirely new front walkway, complete with a ramp, for his chair. He slept and lived downstairs, by himself most of the time, while Cindy was at work or in bed.

He found strength in the family pictures hung along the living room walls, and lining the shelves closer to him on the ground. Though tidy because he couldn't afford any wheelchair accidents, the house seemed a bit disheveled because of the modifications made specifically for him.

Though Daniels was completely functional, he chose a lonely direction, afraid his performances in bed would not satisfy his wife, though she had urged him to try several times since the shooting.

His fears went far beyond paralysis.

"Why did you volunteer me for this dinner?" he asked Cindy, complacent to wheel himself beside the table and stare at her.

"You need to get out of the house, Mark. You're so close to walking again, and you need to keep your mind occupied. It's not like you to brood so much."

"Brood?" he questioned, raising an eyebrow. "I get shot in the back, receive a great prognosis that I'm supposed to walk within a few months, and I can't live up to my end of the bargain. How should I feel?"

"There you go again," she said, raising her voice to match his. "Something's keeping you from walking, Mark, and it isn't your legs," Cindy added, showing her frustration. "I spend over a dozen hours every week conditioning your legs and feet, keeping them strong enough so you can walk when the time is right, and something keeps holding you back. It's time you faced your fears and moved on."

"I haven't been back there in a year," he said in a solemn tone, settling down. "Every night I see that damned hotel in my dreams."

Some nights, Daniels dreamed he walked along his street, joined his daughter on the playground, or patrolled a beat at work again.

Simple things like dancing with Cindy or in-and-out use of the bathroom eluded him too.

Usually he woke up, instinctively trying to swing his legs out of bed, but it never worked. They teased him with occasional twitches, and sometimes he actually swung them out of bed halfway, before realizing it. Daniels never brought himself to stand on his own when his legs swung out, and if he tried, his legs simply buckled from beneath him. It tortured his mind, knowing everything was ready except his mind.

He never told his wife about those failures.

Cindy knelt beside him, taking his hand.

"All the more reason to face this and put it behind you," she encouraged, speaking of the dinner. "Paul moved on with his life. He's getting married again and leaving the past behind. We've got a baby boy who needs his daddy."

Daniels knew he hadn't been a model father lately. His girl, Renee, was almost three, and his son, Curtis, was only four-months-old. Doctors and friends all told him to concentrate on himself and getting well, but perhaps he had taken it a step too far and left too many friends behind, and more importantly, his family.

Before, his family meant the world to him. He remembered how many costs he cut to provide for Cindy and the kids, and to save for his children's eventual college. He realized his self-involvement tore apart his relationship with Cindy and distanced him from the children who needed more than just a mother. He was too good on the inside to realize otherwise.

"All right, I'll go," he said, knowing he was doing the right thing to be with Cindy in public if nothing else.

Perhaps his fears had gotten the best of him for too long. He would do anything to walk in front of the people who cared for him once again.

And get back to his job.

*   *   *

As Jane Brooks ascended the main stairs of the West Baden Springs Hotel toward the double glass door entrance, she took in the view of the six stories above her, and the dome topping off the old building. It still amazed her how the hotel remained so sturdy after years of decay and the eventual rebirth of the grounds.

She knew the grounds well after being a volunteer tour guide for nearly two years. Her mother lived in Southern Indiana, so Jane decided to play into her mother's interest. Giving tours was also where she had met Clouse while he helped design the building, appearing on the grounds several times a week, catching her eye.

Several selected rooms had lights on, giving the hotel the appearance of actual use for the night's visitors. It was the first time everything was complete and actually able to be used. It was Dr. Smith's way of letting everyone know the hotel was functional and ready for everyday use so they could spread the word to their thrifty friends.

"Where's Paul?" a voice asked Jane, catching her attention as the kids stopped on the steps beside her.

"Hi, Ken," she said to Clouse's friend Ken Kaiser, a local county police officer who happened to be working a security detail for the evening, dressed in a tuxedo of his own. "I didn't see your car anywhere."

"Got a different ride tonight," he said, nodding toward an older, maintained Harley-Davidson just off to the side of the steps below.

Kaiser had recently purchased it from a fellow officer.

"I see," she said.

Clouse had mentioned his friend's recent motorcycle fetish, but wrote it off as an early mid-life crisis phase. Looking the part, Kaiser had grown in a full goatee since the last time Jane recalled seeing him. His hair was buzzed short, just like usual, and she knew why. Clouse revealed his high school buddy had curly hair, and absolutely hated it, so he buzzed it short whenever it started growing in.

"Paul should be here by now," she said after a few seconds. "He said he was going to shower and change at your house."

"Never saw him," Kaiser said. "And I just got here about ten minutes ago."

Jane's perplexed look showed, because nothing would keep her fiancé from attending the dedication of the project he had worked almost three years on, not to mention the hours spent blueprinting before that.

"You know Paul," Kaiser said without any outward concern. "He's probably just running behind. The guy has the worst luck of anyone I know."

"But he usually calls, Ken," she stated.

Kaiser shrugged, unsure of where his friend might be.

"I'd better get the kids inside," Jane said, shaking off the notion anything bad might happen to her future husband.

Two doormen pulled the beautiful double glass doors open for the partial family, then the next set of doors leading to the lobby. Inside the lobby the children were awe-struck by the array of bulb lights across the overhead balcony and the stained glass windows lining the walls of the room. The room was designed to impact guests by giving them a taste about what sort of hotel they were entering.

It worked, time after time.

A circular hallway surrounded a central atrium where all of the inside rooms owned a view downward, into the social center, while the outside rooms overlooked the gardens and red brick walkways outside.

Jane paused a moment, seeing Smith with a few of his guests. They seemed to be speaking to him about the marvelous job he had done with the hotel, but as always, he was modest, giving credit to his designers and the construction workers.

"Hello, dear," he said upon seeing Jane. "So good of you to attend."

"A pleasure," Jane said, putting forth the best smile she could, considering Clouse ran fashionably late.

"Where is your future husband?" Smith inquired.

"Running late, I suppose. I'm sure he wouldn't miss this for the world."

Smith cracked a smile, though his age showed through the lines in his face and the pale nature of his skin. He seemed as happy as a deteriorating man could be. Jane suspected his health had gone downhill after the death of his wife, and if there was more to it, Smith wasn't telling.

He seemed weak, almost frail, compared to the man she met several years before, when she first started doing tours at the hotel. Still, she took his hand and gave a reassuring smile, hoping her fiancé would arrive soon.

"You've outdone yourself as always, Dr. Smith," she noted, peeking into the atrium, which looked gorgeous, despite the low lighting.

"It would never be possible without the help of people like Paul and Rusty Cranor," Smith said. "Paul was quite a find when he showed up with his blueprints all those years ago. It's a shame he had to endure all of those hardships last year."

Smith's concern showed.

"I can't imagine how he ever got through it," Smith added, "but I'm sure you were about the best therapy he could have ever received."

"Thank you."

To this point, the children had remained patient, but they were beginning to get antsy with the party calling to them from within.

"I guess we'd better get inside so you can tend to your guests," Jane said quickly.

"Thank you," Smith said, giving a reassuring grin. "I'm sure Paul will love what we have planned after this inauguration."

Jane nodded, making her way inside the atrium through a large arch.

As always, Jane was impressed with the hotel's splendor, especially when they were led into the atrium where a sea of round tables provided much of the room's lighting from the candles centered on their white, lacy tablecloths. An array of saucers and silverware adorned the tables with various colors.

Nearly as long as a football field in any direction straight across, the round atrium held beautiful colors of gold, green, and red trim that the candlelight failed to reveal. With so many tables present, the caterers would be hopping all night long.

She was amazed at the turnout, and how formal the event appeared, with tuxes and gowns everywhere. Her profession brought her to many galas, but few so grand as this.

Apparently Smith had spared no expense.

Above, a select number of the rooms were lit, teasing with pieces of their beauty inside, now that they were finished. Jane heard people speculating about what the rooms contained. Would the massage rooms return, or the saunas? Would the suites contain luxuries in the form of hot tubs, or would they be traditionally maintained?

Even Clouse refused to tell.

A new designer carpet replaced the pattern Jane saw on her last tour. She knew Dr. Smith detested the look of the old carpeting and ordered a new pattern to replace it. To her, this design of vines and various colored roses seemed no more appealing, but the primary colors of gold and forest green matched the colors of the atrium's wall and trim work.

Far above the crowd, a chandelier spread some light from its nest in the center of the glass dome. Supported by a dozen pairs of thick, steel ribs, the mammoth dome remained safe from weather and the elements. During daylight hours light streamed into the atrium, lighting various artwork and statues at different intervals. At night, the low light hid most of the supporting structure, leaving only a clear view of the stars above through the large glass panels.

Jane, like Clouse, grew to love it more every time she visited.

"Hello, Mark," she said once the officer and his wife drew her attention with a discreet wave. "I see Paul didn't sneak in."

"He's not with you?" Daniels asked.

"No, and I'm worried. He took the boat out on the lake and I haven't heard anything from him in a few hours."

"Paul won't miss this," the officer said. "He knows better than to drag me here and not show."

As most of the chairs filled, waiters and waitresses dressed nearly as nicely as the guests rolled trays filled with covered dishes into the atrium. She looked to the itinerary, noticing the guests of honor would soon be introduced with a brief ceremony and announcement before dinner.

Jane looked to the entrance, wondering where her fiancé might be. She pulled out her cellular phone before the meals made their way around, trying Clouse's number, and getting no response.

"Where's Dad?" Zach asked from beside her.

"He'll be here, Zach," she answered, not wanting to worry him.

She refused to outwardly show her concern because of the children.

Jane considered walking outside to ask Kaiser for his home phone number, or to call his wife and see if Clouse ever stopped by, but she spied him walking inside with a uniformed officer.

Daniels seemed to recognize the uniform of dark green adorned with tan patches because he raised a skeptical eyebrow.

"Who is that?" Jane inquired.

"He's a conservation officer," Daniels replied. "They work in the state parks and patrol the lakes."

The last part about the lakes concerned Jane a bit, since Clouse had taken the boat out. She figured there had to be a reasonable explanation why a conservation officer showed up unannounced to the dinner.

"Do you know him?" she asked Daniels.

"Nope."

Both continued to stare at the duo beside the door until Kaiser pointed toward their table, and Jane in particular.

"Oh, no," Jane said as the two motioned for her to join them outside the atrium in the hallway.

"Go ahead," Cindy told her. "I'll watch the kids a minute."

Collecting herself and her purse, she stood, walking as discreetly as possible toward the exit. As Jane drew closer, she saw Kaiser look away toward the floor beside him as the conservation officer took a deep breath with a grim look in his eyes. He appeared a veteran of his department, and most conservation officers with seniority transferred to the southern part of the state because it was an ideal retirement area. Regardless of his experience, the officer seemed unable to contain the unhappy emotion painted across his face.

"What is it?" Jane asked, looking back and forth between the two.

"Ma'am, I'm afraid I have some bad news for you," the officer said.

Above the crowd of people in the atrium, Lucas Rexford made use of the mirror inside Room 204. As a descendant of Lilian Sinclair and Charles Rexford, the hotel's husband and wife management team after the turn of the 20th century, he was invited by Dr. Smith to attend the hotel's ceremonial dinner and reopening as a guest of honor.

Though he owned no direct ties with the hotel or grounds, his name was important to anyone who knew its history. Smith wanted the ceremony to be much more than just a focus on the new hotel. He wanted historical value added, and with that in mind, he invited numerous descendants of various figureheads from the hotel's past. Smith paid for their travel and hotel fare just to bring them to Southern Indiana for his gala.

A dentist in Chicago, Rexford found it easy to make time for the dinner. He knew about the hotel and his link to it from childhood, when his mother told him stories. Though not a direct descendent of Charles Rexford, the dentist was the best Smith could come up with for a relation. It gave him an excuse to take a week off work to travel to the hotel he heard so much about growing up.

Most of the rooms were completely bare of furniture, though sinks, tubs, and mirrors were installed, waiting for the larger pieces to come. Rexford marveled at the detail given to each room in the trim. From below, the people never saw the completed product they were missing. That was part of Smith's plan to sell them on spending a night to see for themselves. The reopening would not take place for another few weeks, and by then, everything would be in place.

Outside the room stood a balcony painted dark green to match the wall trim. Select rooms had balconies, once used for guests to appear and wave, or simply look down upon the atrium's nightly events. In its day, the hotel drew events every evening. Circuses, seminars, large group meetings, concerts, and many other events convened within its walls.

Rexford peered into the mirror, adjusting the black bow tie to his tuxedo. He could have used the downstairs bathroom, but Smith had a plan for each special guest to appear on a room balcony for all to see before dinner. He had a few minutes before the doctor took the microphone, giving his guests their cues.

Being in a large, empty room felt creepy, especially with no furniture, and an echo from every little noise he made. He looked around, seeing nothing but the closet door opened just a crack next to the curtains. The curtains, currently wide-open, could be drawn to cover the glass window and the door to the room's balcony.

As Rexford returned his attention to his tie, they did exactly that.

*   *   *

"Please tell me what is going on," Jane demanded, more than asked, of either officer standing at the threshold of the atrium.

"This is Bill Schrader," Kaiser informed her, trying to stall for time.

Jane gave a perplexed sigh.

"Was your husband boating at Lake Monroe this afternoon?" the conservation officer asked.

"Yes."

"We had a lakeside resident report the sinking of a boat late this afternoon," the officer informed her. "By the time we arrived the boat was nearly completely beneath the surface but we were able to identify it before it sank." He paused a moment, letting Jane absorb the notion of what she knew was coming. "There was apparently foul play because the boat had several holes punched in the bottom."

"Paul's boat?" she asked nervously, not sure of what to expect. Schrader nodded.

"Where is he?" she asked.

"He's missing," Kaiser said, trying to soften the words, his expression showing he felt Schrader had been too insensitive.

"We believe someone may have sunk the boat to cover up-"

"No," Jane stopped Schrader short. "If there's no body, you can't believe that," she said frantically, beginning to break down.

As their conversation drew the attention of more than a few guests, Kaiser led Jane further down the hallway, followed by the conservation officer.

"They're looking for him, Jane," Kaiser stated. "But it doesn't look good. Paul's truck was still parked at the dock with his cell phone and briefcase still inside."

"I won't believe it," she replied, ignoring most every spoken word now. "I can't believe it."

"I'm not giving up either," the county officer said. "Paul's tough. He's been through a lot before. They'll find him."

At the bottom of the lake, Schrader seemed to think by the strange expression on his face.

"What can you tell me?" Jane demanded of the officer.

"I was patrolling the lake when I received a call about a sinking boat," Schrader began. "I was able to don my scuba gear and examine the boat before it fell beneath the surface."

He seemed to hesitate.

"And?" Jane insisted.

"There were punctures on the boat's underside. They looked intentional."

Jane sighed nervously, trying to steady her jittery hands by cupping her mouth.

"Was there any trace of Paul? Any at all?"

"No," Schrader said slowly. "But we consider that a good thing. Several divers relieved me so I could come out here, and so far as I know, they've found nothing."

Everyone stood awkwardly a moment, apparently unsure of what to say next.

"What's going on?" Daniels asked, finally wheeling himself out of the atrium, apparently to see where Jane had disappeared to.

He likely suspected a conservation officer was out of place at the dinner and wanted to know exactly what they were talking about.

"Hey, Mark," Kaiser said quickly, since the two had met through Clouse. "Paul's boat sunk in Lake Monroe and he hasn't been seen since he left home."

"Oh, no," Daniels gasped. "What do we have to go on?"

Before Kaiser could answer, Schrader shot him a questioning stare.

"It's okay," Kaiser told the conservation officer. "He's Blooming-ton Police."

"Oh."

"Both the county police and state organizations have divers combing the lake in search of clues to the boat sinking or, God forbid, a body. All of Paul's belongings are still in his truck, and it was found near the marina."

Daniels drew a deep breath.

"Not good," he said before looking to Jane beside him, his wincing face making it obvious he regretted the statement immediately.

Jane, however, felt shock settling into her body, knowing Clouse might very well be settled at the bottom of the lake near his boat. She could not think of any reason he would not contact her unless he felt her life, or perhaps his own, was still in danger. No one came to mind who would want to sink his boat or bring harm to Clouse.

She felt completely helpless as she walked away from the group to think a moment.

*   *   *

Rexford stopped fidgeting with his tie, turning around to find the curtains almost completely drawn. With his cue coming in less than a minute, that would not do. He needed an open path to the glass door to step onto the balcony. He also wished to remain obscured from view below until his cue came, per Smith's instructions.

Wondering why the curtains seemed to change positions, or if he was just imagining it, Rexford walked along the back wall toward the draw string, located near the closet door. As he approached the string, hidden far enough behind the curtain that no one inside the atrium could see him, Rexford heard the first guest of honor called.

"Damn," he thought aloud, trying to hurry his pace.

As he reached for the string, the closet door sprung open, revealing a spray nozzle shoved only inches from his face before a stream of gasoline squirted forward, squarely embedding itself in his eyes and face, burning as it blinded him. Rexford screamed aloud when the gasoline struck, his cries muffled by the applause and laughter of the people in the atrium. One of his fellow guests of honor took a bow, amusing the crowd, across the atrium at a different balcony.

He stumbled back to the center of the room, unaware of how many times his attacker went about spraying him as his body became drenched in the chemical liquid. Rexford moaned and whimpered, giving the occasional verbal obscenity during the process. The sting in his eyes was unbearable, and there was little hope of finding his way to the bathroom to wash the chemical from them, even if he felt safe enough to do so.

What seemed an eternity of blindness played out in less than a minute as Smith kept the guests distracted outside, calling various names as the guests of honor each took a turn from their balcony, waving and smiling for the dinner guests below. As the floor and Rexford wreaked of gasoline, the attacker struck a match, setting the hapless guest ablaze, giving him a swift kick toward the glass door leading to the balcony, ironically as Smith called Rexford's name.

*   *   *

An agonizing scream pierced the soft music in the background, and any noise the guests made as they whispered at their tables.

Everyone swiftly looked around the atrium, then up, in an effort to discover the disruption's origin.

To the surprise of the crowd below, Redford smashed through the glass door as all eyes turned his way. Everyone gasped as a living ball of fire burst through the glass, onto the balcony. Instantly, horror fixated itself in the guests as they realized the inferno would not stop there. Rexford stumbled toward the edge of the balcony, toppling over the railing.

He fell a short distance through a table where he continued to incinerate. The sizzle of his body reminded many of morning bacon, but the odor of burning flesh nauseated everyone nearby until several guests regained composure enough to grab a fire extinguisher and put him out.

"Oh, God," Kaiser said, rushing in on the scene too late, looking up to Room 204 and the broken glass before charging back into the hallway.

He assessed the situation quicker than anyone else, noticing what happened to Rexford was no accident. He also knew whoever caused the damage might still be on the second floor, or trying to escape. The county officer took the closest flight of stairs, rushing upstairs to search for the perpetrator, or a witness.

Along the hallways to either side of him Kaiser found nothing.

"Shit," he said, knowing how easily someone might have used a different stairwell downstairs, easily fitting into the crowd, who were all standing and surrounding the body below. Drawing his duty weapon, he began a necessary, but futile search through each hallway and room.

Kaiser looked for any rooms with an open door, starting with the room where Rexford had been preparing himself. Taking a quick peek inside, Kaiser felt a strong, horrid odor cross his nose, and retreated to the hallway, realizing the killer had not remained inside.

He heard a noise down the hall, ran down to check it, and found the conservation officer reaching the top of the stairs, thinking along the same lines as Kaiser. Both realized their search was futile, and over, because the killer had already slipped into the crowd of hundreds below.

6

Daniels felt groggy the next morning at work. He continually yawned from the lack of rest two hours of sleep had provided. After Lucas Rexford was pronounced dead at the hotel, guests were stuck there until local and state investigators questioned everyone. In the meantime, Jane Brooks grew more discontent dealing with her fiancé's disappearance. She wanted to head to the lake in case of any new developments.

Fortunately, nothing more of Clouse was found, leaving the dim hope he might still be alive. Last he knew, Jane planned to take the day off from work and remain at the lake in the hope of an answer, good or bad. She made arrangements during the long wait for the kids to stay with her mother. Daniels thought she performed magnificently with them, not letting on for a moment that anything might be wrong. She left several times, however, to be alone and out of their view.

So far as Daniels knew, the investigation into Rexford's death led nowhere. The murderer might easily have been an uninvited guest, who came in the correct attire, killed the man, and slipped into the crowd, escaping later without notice. Daniels knew of no one missing from the party, although several people failed to show for the dinner. The police would check them for alibis later.

Luckily the morning proved more mundane than usual. Daniels occasionally fielded a call, then found time to daydream about returning to work on the streets. Already, he felt forgotten by his old mates. Seldom did they stop in to joke with him like they used to, his name was never mentioned in the circles it once was, and the chief was already talking to his assistants about filling Daniels' position on the force if he didn't show improvement. All that after the man nominated his detective for officer of the year and grabbed all the kudos when Daniels won.

"I'll be right back," the officer said to one of the other dispatchers before wheeling himself toward the restroom.

Overall, things looked bad for Daniels.

Taking the trip to the hotel didn't seem to help in the least. While he was there, Daniels fell asleep during the early morning hours, waking an hour later to the recurring dream of being shot in the back. Nothing troubled him more than waking in a cold sweat, with heavy, uncontrolled breathing, and the knowledge that he was still disabled.

Clouse, the only person who had stuck with him through his ordeal, was nowhere to be found. Daniels refused to envision him turning up dead, but at the same time there seemed little alternative, given the circumstances. It harrowed him to think Rexford's death and the fireman's disappearance might be connected, but after what he'd experienced the year prior, nothing was impossible.

His thoughts wandered to Clouse, and where the man might be. Throughout the night he watched Kaiser and Jane fret about where he might have gone, while overhearing others speculate how Clouse might have somehow been involved with Rexford's murder. Daniels knew better, but kept quiet, numbed at the thought another murdering spree might be in its early stages.

Daniels struggled to pull the bathroom door open and wheel himself inside. He still faced the battle of lifting himself from the chair to the toilet, pulling down his pants without complete use of his legs, then reversing the process before returning to work.

Somehow he managed to complete the task within a reasonable amount of time, hearing someone else step into the bathroom somewhere in between.

Whoever took up the stall beside him sneezed uncontrollably several times, sniffling deeply, intermittently. Daniels listened a bit more intently than usual, hearing no unzipping of pants or drawing of toilet paper to blow a nose. Being confined to a wheelchair made him much more aware of his surroundings. He often found it damaging if he wasn't.

And it appeared someone was waiting for him.

Unsure of exactly what to do, Daniels hesitated a moment before opening the stall door, deciding no one else was going to come into the seldom-used restroom. Whoever waited in the neighboring stall probably noticed his indecision, but the officer planned to wheel clear of the person and avoid contact if possible.

He failed.

Before he could even clear his own stall, a solid hand cupped around Daniels' mouth as someone yanked his chair back far enough to tip it back, landing him on his back, though his assailant cushioned the fall with his other hand.

"You know, the last twenty-four hours I've had nothing to do but think," Paul Clouse said, looming directly over the officer, before releasing a sneeze to his side, keeping one hand over Daniels' mouth a moment more. A hint of temporary insanity seemed to gleam from one of his eyes, which were bloodshot from a lack of sleep. "Gives a guy a lot of time to think about who he really trusts and who might want him dead. I don't know who I can trust now," he said, slowly releasing his hand.

"What the hell happened to you, Paul? Everyone thinks you're at the bottom of the lake."

"I was," the fireman admitted. "I got whacked twice upside my head, fell in, and woke up later, around dark, on the shore beside the lake," he relayed the story in as monotone a voice as Daniels could ever recall, as though the events still crucified the corners of his mind.

"Why did you wait so long to let someone know?" Daniels asked with his usual tone of interrogation.

Clouse gave Daniels a look of distrust.

"Mark, you were one of two people I told about the boat yesterday. I doubt Jane told anyone I was out there, and I hope to God you didn't."

Daniels propped himself to his elbows, knowing Clouse refused to let him up by the way he remained directly over the officer. He was happy his friend was alive, but not about the man's doubt in him.

"I may have mentioned it to Cindy," Daniels admitted. "I'm not even sure I did that."

"You sure?"

Daniels nodded.

"I'm positive."

Clouse sneezed again to the side, showing the effects of the lake on him. Daniels noticed how ragged he looked, though fully dry. His hair appeared far more disheveled than usual with a dried blood spot on one side matting some of it. A foul smell accompanied Clouse with his return to civilization that only the murky lake might have provided.

"So where have you been?" Daniels asked as the fireman helped him into his chair, standing it upright.

"Well, my keys are fifty feet under water so I had no truck," Clouse replied. "So I had no cell phone, or change for a payphone. I wanted to question both you and Jane before I let anyone else know I was alive, because obviously I'm not supposed to be."

"How did you wind up on shore? Lake Monroe doesn't exactly have tides and beaches."

"Someone had to have pulled me out," Clouse said. "I don't know who or why, but someone got me out of there."

Daniels felt one of his legs twitch involuntarily. He wondered if the fall had prompted him to accidentally kick. It sometimes happened to him when he lied around in bed.

"So how do you know your boat sank?" he asked.

"The fact that it was gone when I woke up, and this morning's paper," Clouse replied, wheeling his friend toward the door. "I found a lot of time to read this morning, and to think. I understand I missed quite a dinner last night."

"Well, the main course wasn't quite what we expected," Daniels replied as Clouse held the door open for him.

"Do you think it's happening again?" Clouse asked the inevitable question.

Daniels said nothing, just shaking his head.

"I'm going to find out who's investigating the case and see if I can get some answers. Maybe they'll let me help as a consultant because of last year."

Clouse shrugged.

"Can't hurt to try. We need to know what's going on because it's no coincidence I get whacked in the head and that guy winds up dead at a hotel function."

"I'll take the rest of the day off and see what I can dig up," the officer said. "You better fetch Jane from lakeside and let everyone know you're still among us."

Clouse rubbed the side of his head, sneezed, and quickly recovered.

"Yeah. Then I'll sleep for a couple days."

7

After talking to a friend of a friend, Daniels discovered a state police detective by the name of McCabe was assigned the case of finding Rexford's murderer. He was from the Bloomington district, so it was easy for Daniels to arrange a meeting with him by that evening. He learned the detective had a favorite haunt after work every night in a predominantly Irish bar called Kelley's, where the nationality was also the theme.

He wheeled inside the door, finding the pub filled with lively music and chatter. He counted more men with red hair than he'd ever seen in one building. Many owned the shining eyes the officer had read about in fable, but he figured most of those were from too many import ales. He knew Kansas City and Chicago had bars dedicated to nationalities, but he never dreamed it in Bloomington.

For some reason it worked.

Constructed of old wood, the tavern looked somewhat like a hunting lodge with a mounted deer head along one wall, and torches set about shoulder level along the sides. They were lit by bulbs that looked like flames, to avoid any fire hazards, but the fireplace, and candles on each table were certainly real.

Daniels' eyes panned the pub for a man who fit the profile of a police detective. Daniels knew too well how to play the part after his stint in Bloomington's investigative division.

Before the shooting.

He felt his right leg twitch again as he looked, and quickly held it down forcibly with both hands. The involuntary movements showed his legs were ready to move again, but he wanted to look completely in control when he met McCabe.

Just as he spied a man drinking alone at a table set near a window, the man looked up from his green bottle, smiled, and waved Daniels over.

As he wheeled up, the officer quickly assessed the detective.

With a full head of rustic-brown hair and brown eyes of a creamed coffee tint, the detective remained in dress pants with a plain white dress shirt and loosened tie. His shoulder holster cupped his armpits, looking rather tight against the wrinkly dress shirt. Barely average in height, the man looked stocky, almost like an immovable tank of a man. What little beer belly he owned remained tucked beneath the shirt. McCabe did not appear grossly muscular, but his natural size was enough to keep even remotely intelligent pests away from him.

"Turlough Casey McCabe," he said, standing to introduce himself boisterously. Daniels assumed everyone in the bar already knew him by his outgoing nature as the two quickly shook hands. "Friends call me Terry or Tug."

"Mark Daniels," the chaired officer countered, unsure of which to call the man.

By the look in the detective's eyes, Daniels assessed he was past his first beer. There was also a slight stagger in the way he stood, but McCabe held liquor remarkably well from what friends told Daniels that morning.

"So I understand you might be able to help me on this new case I've got," McCabe said in a more reserved manner once he sat down. Daniels wasn't positive, but he thought he perceived a hint of Irish tongue in the way the man spoke.

"Have you read the reports about the incident last year?" Daniels asked.

"I have. Most interesting it was," the detective said before finishing off the mug. He motioned to a server for another. "Make it two," he said when she arrived, nodding toward Daniels. "Keep the change," he said, tucking a substantial bill into her change pouch.

"What sort of name is Turlough?" Daniels felt compelled to ask.

McCabe flashed a toothy smile.

"If you haven't guessed, I'm big into my heritage," he said. "Turlough is a Celtic name meaning 'broad-shouldered.' In English, it's translated Terence."

"And it reads Turlough on your birth certificate?"

"Yes, sir," McCabe answered. "My mother says she nearly beat my father to death for it, but he wanted his son to have an authentic Irish name on that piece of paper. Even my middle name, Casey, has a meaning of watchful or vigilant. That came from my uncle. I guess Dad knew how to pick fitting names, even at the risk of his own life."

Daniels grinned. He already took to McCabe's outgoing personality, though he personally remained reserved around other people. He also realized the man possessed brains enough to sell anyone on what he believed.

"How far up does the family tree go in America?" he asked, now curious about the man's heritage, since he was, in essence, surrounded by it.

"Been here five generations. Great-great-grandfather was a cop in New York City in the early 1900's. Now a couple thousand miles away and a century later I'm doing the same thing. You could say it runs in the family."

"That's neat," Daniels said with a genuine nod.

He sat back in his chair, taking in the sounds of violin, accordion, and drum beats that combined for a unique Celtic melody. He understood why people wanted to visit this bar once they discovered it. The atmosphere was authentic and unblemished. There was no distracting television, no blaring juke box, no parlor games in the background.

Only food, conversation, and drink made up the atmosphere, and everyone he saw truly seemed content being there.

"You know, you seem familiar," McCabe noted. "Without the beard you look like the guy I saw in a publication last month."

"Officer of the year?" Daniels asked, like it was no big deal.

"Yeah," the detective said, a smile of realization crossing his face. "Goddamn, I never put it together. You're the one who investigated that ordeal last year and got shot. The reports don't mention very much of that. They focus more on some guy they were investigating the whole time who got cleared." McCabe stopped a moment to take it all in. "Wow."

"That's what I thought too."

"I heard you lost your partner," the alcohol prompted the detective to say. His expression showed he regretted the statement before the words finished coming out. "I didn't mean to, uh…"

"It's okay," Daniels said. "Let's just say last year will never make my top ten."

"Let's get down to business before I say something else stupid," McCabe suggested. "So exactly how do you want to help me on this thing?"

"If what happened to that man last night has any relation to what occurred last year, it needs to be stopped now before more people get slaughtered."

McCabe sipped his beer, his expression showing he wasn't convinced by words alone.

"That seems like a bold statement based on one single murder that wasn't done in the style of those perpetrated last year."

"I'm just saying *if* it has any ramifications from last year. I was in your shoes at the time, and it's not something I care to ever do again."

"What do you suggest?"

"Right now I'm stuck dispatching until I finish rehabilitation on my legs. I want out of there in the worst way, and I can be a fantastic information source for you."

McCabe thought a moment, tapping his beer bottle with two fingers.

"I want your help unofficially if nothing else," he finally said. "I'll talk to my supervisor and see what we can do. From the sounds of it, your department won't have trouble loaning you out."

"Is it possible to see the room where it happened?"

"Sure," McCabe shrugged. "There's really nothing to see though. We know he was doused with gasoline by someone, set afire, and shoved off the balcony. Not much to it."

"Any ideas why it was him in particular?"

"We're checking into it. Seems someone went through his hotel room and his belongings. The only thing odd was a small jewelry case with nothing inside. We sent it to the lab for analysis but there was nothing in the room or on Rexford that might have been inside that box. He wasn't wearing anything but a watch, and there were no loose articles in the hotel room."

Daniels thought a moment, taking a drink of the unusually strong brew. His eyes widened as his throat tingled. Since starting his rehabilitation he hadn't touched a drop of alcohol, so his body was a bit unprepared for McCabe's choice in drink.

"Could it have been something other than jewelry?"

"Sure, but we won't know what until we get lab results or his family tells us something. We couldn't reach his wife from the office today. We think she's out of town too."

Daniels finished off his beer rather quickly, deciding it best to get home. He needed rest from the night before, and driving with his condition was no easy task. Using hand-controlled metal bars was far worse than any driving simulation game he'd ever played. Though his feet were mobile, Daniels could not count on his legs to respond in time for emergency braking, or even to keep consistent speed with the gas pedal.

Professional installation of such bars in his car kept Cindy free to be with the kids, rather than taking Daniels everywhere he needed to be. He drove to work, the hospital, or any fast food drive-thru alone. They were also removable if she needed use of his vehicle.

"Give me a holler tomorrow," he told McCabe, handing him a business card.

"Will do. Either way, you'll hear from me."

Daniels headed for the door, taking in the sounds of musical melodies he would only hear at such a tavern. He rather enjoyed the change of pace there.

While Clouse lay in bed, his fiancee tended to his wounds, particularly the gash on the side of his head where blood matted his hair, dried into one clump. The warmth of the sheets and two blankets that covered him felt good, but his body shivered, sometimes going numb from so much time spent in the water and cold air.

After leaving city hall, he called her cellular phone and told her just the basic facts before she picked him up. Jane gave him what limited outward affection she could without hurting him when they reunited. For the last several hours Clouse had slept as best he could under Jane's orders.

"You should have called me sooner," Jane scolded him. "I prayed and prayed you weren't at the bottom of that lake."

"I had to protect you," he said. "Whoever wanted me dead might come after me here if he thought I was still alive."

Luckily Jane had put off the authorities until the next morning, but the county police kept close watch over the house until Clouse was healthy enough for an interview. Clouse was excused from work until he felt able to return. His disappearance was everywhere in the news, drawing speculation from everyone who knew about the past year's events about what might happen. Everyone assumed he was dead, and Clouse might have thought the same if not for some anonymous help.

"I can't believe someone wanted to kill you," Jane said, carefully washing the matted spot in his hair, treating the dried sore with peroxide on a cotton ball.

"Ouch, Doc," he told her, feeling the sting of the medicine. "It's kind of cool not having to leave the house for a doctor's excuse," Clouse added, chuckling a bit until it literally hurt.

"Take it easy," she told him. "You're going to need lots of rest to fight off the effects of the lake. Don't even think about leaving this bed until I say you can."

"Yes, ma'am," he replied with a weak smile, growing more tired every second. Jane left the room a moment, probably to fetch something for him.

Sleep had almost overcome him when Zach tiptoed into the room, as though doing so behind Jane's back. It was the first time he had truly seen his son since returning home, and he felt somewhat uncomfortable letting Zach see him bedridden.

"Jane says you're sick," his son informed him.

"I am," Clouse said with an uncontrolled yawn. "I went for a swim and I shouldn't have."

"It's kinda cold, Dad."

"Yeah, I know." Clouse rubbed a hand through Zach's hair. His son quickly replaced it with a swipe of his own hand. "Were you worried about me?"

"I knew you'd be okay. Something cool happened at the dinner last night."

"I heard. Better not let Jane hear you talk about that."

"About what?" his fiancee asked, returning to the room, carrying a bowl of soup.

"Nothing," both replied simultaneously.

"Good night, Dad," Zach said, scurrying out of the room before he was told to.

"Night, Zach," Clouse called an abbreviated closing to his son.

Jane sat on the edge of the bed again, pushing Clouse's head back lightly. He recognized the smell of homemade chicken broth, then saw actual chunks of breast meat.

"My mother made this and brought it over while you were sleeping," Jane informed him. "She says to get well soon."

"This will help," he noted. "Please thank her for me."

He shivered as the broth warmed his insides, making him feel even colder externally. His body ached for rest and warmth. Clouse hoped to feel better in the morning, but the chances of that were slim.

He would wait and see.

*   *   *

After managing his way inside, Daniels wheeled quietly through the kitchen, trying to remain quiet. He suspected Cindy and the kids were all asleep, though the baby occasionally kept them up at night.

Daniels despised his modified driving, but it beat keeping Cindy from being his personal servant. Neither of them wanted that, and the officer made the best of his situation. He never wanted to fully adapt to being in a chair for fear that adaption meant complacency. Daniels never wanted to feel comfortable being in the chair, knowing he was physically capable of walking.

As he entered the living room, one of the chair's wheels hit a doll left beside the doorway, which acted like a doorstop, hurling Daniels forward, out of the chair.

"Damn," he cursed under his breath after an initial cry of pain.

Positioned on his arms and knees, the officer remained perfectly still a moment, assessing something new to him.

He looked down at his knees behind him, realizing the few times he'd fallen out of the chair, he landed sprawled out. As though unsure of what to do, Daniels stared at his knees a moment, wondering if he dared chance standing the rest of the way.

Without taking his eyes off it, he drew his right knee toward his torso slowly, as much as it would freely move. It took several minutes, but he drew it close enough that he finally placed the foot flat on the ground, in a position prepared for standing.

Daniels felt his right leg going numb from being bent for so long, so he decided to hurry the process along, taking in a few deep breaths before attempting to move his left leg for a wider base, before he tried standing.

He gained the wide base, felt his muscles tense for the first time in months, and pushed upward with what little muscle strength his right leg had. He grunted and groaned from pain as the underused leg attempted to straighten, but he only gained a few more vertical inches before the leg gave out and he collapsed to a sprawled position on the floor, just as he was accustomed to.

Though he tried to contain himself, Daniel let out several curse words under his breath. He was beyond sick and tired of failing at walking. Nearly ready to sell his soul to walk again and return his life to normal, the former detective balled one hand into a fist, then thought better of beating down his floor.

Almost in tears from sheer frustration, Daniels dragged the chair over to him, hitting it squarely in the seat before deciding just to crawl to bed. He could brush his teeth and take care of other hygiene essentials in the morning. For now, he just wanted to sleep and dream about walking again.

After lying in bed several minutes, Daniels quit berating himself, realizing what a significant leap he had found toward his recovery. Though still angry with himself, he felt for the first time in a long time walking might prove possible.

He fell asleep with a sense of hope lingering over him.

9

Daniels found himself in the break room, pouring himself a cup of coffee on his first break. A specially ordered desk held all of the snacks and condiments, assembled at just the correct height for employees confined to wheelchairs.

The former detective had noticed several new modifications made in city hall and dispatch since his return to work. He vowed to never complain about special disability privileges again.

"So you met Tug," Deputy Chief Randy Collins said, walking into the room.

"That I did," Daniels answered with some indifference.

A moment passed while the deputy chief poured himself a cup of coffee, adding sugar and cream before drinking some.

"I worked with him several years ago on a homicide," Collins noted. "We had a murdered girl found in a swamp."

The deputy chief paused a moment, looking outside the window at the parking lot below. Daniels figured the man was thinking back to the days when he wasn't confined to a windowless office, dealing with criminals rather than internal problems.

"She was a mess, covered with algae and fly shit, but we identified her based on missing persons reports. It took us a month or two, but we tracked down her scumbag ex-boyfriend and arrested him."

"What was his story?" Daniels inquired.

"A lover's quarrel I guess," Collins said with a shrug. "She didn't have any money or insurance, so it had to be a spur of the moment thing."

Daniels sat quietly a moment, wondering where this was leading.

"Quite a flighty guy," Collins commented.

"How do you mean?" Daniels inquired.

"You talked to him, didn't you?"

"Sure."

"Tug has a tendency to change a subject faster than you can blink."

Daniels gave a perplexed stare that told he knew nothing of what Collins spoke.

"Oh, he must have been drinking," the chief corrected himself. "If Tug drinks, and he does often, you'll see a cool, collected side of him."

"Sounds like you know him well," Daniels said, understanding the situation now.

"Six months we worked on that case. You get to know people pretty well that way."

Collins paused.

"Been married three times, Tug has."

"He's my age," Daniels commented, a bit surprised.

"He's just carefree about life in general except his job. His work *is* most of his life, and it consumes him. I don't think he's meant to settle into anything."

Daniels wondered exactly what Collins meant, but ignored the remarks, figuring he would find out for himself in due time. He picked a donut from a box, toying with it a moment before speaking.

"Anything else you want to tell me about him?"

"Terrible sense of direction," the deputy chief said with a squeamish look. "Once he's been somewhere, it's etched in his mind, but the first time getting there is rough."

"Interesting," Daniels commented, "but I take it you're not here to talk about old times."

"No," Collins said. "Tug called the chief today asking to borrow you for his latest assignment."

"And?" Daniels inquired with an unblinking stare.

"And, based on your experience with the West Baden Spring Hotel last year and a push from myself to get you doing some real police work again for your own betterment, he reluctantly agreed. You're free to work with him as soon as he's ready for you, but only as a consultant, so don't be carrying a firearm or wearing your badge."

Daniels nodded, failing to outwardly show his happiness.

"You're on the bubble, Mark," Collins warned, unable to look the former detective in the eye. "The chief isn't happy that your condition hasn't improved, and he's talking about adding a man from the new recruit list."

"Mandatory retirement in the form of permanent disability?" Daniels asked with a raised eyebrow, suspecting what the deputy chief had in mind.

"That wouldn't necessarily be the case," Collins said, waving off the notion. "But we've been down a man nearly a year now. If you don't get any closer to walking, you may be finding a more accommodating career."

He walked to the door, stopping just long enough to turn with a few parting words.

"I bought you some time, Mark, and the chief has nothing against you, but even the Board of Public Safety has limits to how long they'll allow the city to pay for a police officer who can't carry out his duties."

"I understand," Daniels answered, though obviously displeased.

Giving a dismissing wave, the deputy chief departed, leaving the echo of his footsteps down the empty hallway as he went.

"Damn," Daniels said, sighing heavily, looking to the ceiling above before resting his head atop his open hand. "Damn, damn, damn!"

*   *   *

Within two hours McCabe had called Daniels, picked him up, and taken him down to the hotel. Daniels found what the deputy chief warned him of completely true as he fought to stay awake, guiding McCabe to West Baden, then the hotel.

McCabe had no sense of direction.

"You're a trooper?" Daniels commented halfway through the trip.

"Nobody's perfect," McCabe retorted. "I've never patrolled this area before."

Upon their arrival, Rusty Cranor, the project manager, unlocked the hotel's main entrance and led them to the room where the homicide occurred.

"I should probably just give you a key," Cranor commented to Daniels, remembering him as the detective who investigated several murders at the hotel the year before.

"I certainly know my way around," Daniels replied.

Daniels followed the detective inside as McCabe held the door open for him. He recalled a bit of information Clouse had shared with him about the project manager.

Cranor drew near a retirement age, but an offer to manage projects for Kieffer Construction, the same company Clouse worked for part-time, kept him working at the job he loved. Helping to rebuild the hotel was his career highlight.

Both his full head of hair and beard were red, peppered with gray hairs. He wore blue jeans, steel-toed boots, and a thick, gray sweater like sailors wore to keep the wind from chilling them. It turned out to be a perfect day for such attire.

Though not a scholar, Cranor's intellect in his field gained him the respect of everyone around him. He talked little about history or world events, and seldom much about anything relating to his hometown. But when it came to his business, no one carried the vocabulary he did. The men working under him learned quickly or found themselves looking for work elsewhere.

"I'll be downstairs putting some stuff away if you need anything," the older man informed them before leaving the room.

Remaining at the doorway, Daniels looked over the room. He could see several charred spots where carpeting and curtains caught fire from the spray of gasoline. The smell of burnt flesh lingered in the room despite efforts by the hotel's remodeling crew to air it out.

"We recovered the gasoline spray can and sent it to forensics," McCabe noted aloud. "Doubt anything will come of it."

He stared at what little damage the room had suffered, but Daniels eyed it both warily and curiously.

"There's really nothing to see in here."

"I didn't expect there to be," Daniels said.

"Authorities in Rexford's hometown spoke with his wife and asked her about what might have been in that case. She wasn't sure, but said she'd look into it."

"I'd imagine she's pretty upset," Daniels commented, looking around the room. "I wonder what he would possess that someone might want."

McCabe looked toward him with a perplexed look.

"Almost as though someone knew he was bringing whatever it was from home."

Daniels agreed, but remained quiet a moment.

"So you've been married three times?" he asked as they concluded their inspection of the room.

"Yeah. Guess I'm not one who likes stability."

Daniels grunted to himself, wheeling into the hallway toward the elevator.

"So how about those Pacers?" McCabe asked, changing the subject, living up to his notorious nature.

"There may be another angle to this case," Daniels suggested as McCabe pushed the down button.

"What's that?"

"There's a myth about this hotel and a Jesuit priest named Father Ernest."

"I've heard of it," McCabe said with a nod. "The papers reprinted the shit out of it last year."

"What if burning Rexford was somehow tied into that?"

"Could be sending a message," McCabe deduced. "If they simply wanted to steal something from him, they could have broken into his hotel room. As a matter of fact, they did."

Both entered the elevator doors as they opened.

"That's bad news," Daniels said with a blank stare toward the closing doors, his memory filled with horrifying images of the past year.

"How so?" McCabe asked as they were greeted by a first floor view a moment later.

Daniels refused to answer. He recalled the year before when nearly a dozen people paid the ultimate price in the name of sending a message. He hoped no one would ever carry that agenda again.

"The guy who let us in here," Daniels started, then hesitated. "His daughter."

"Oh," McCabe said, letting the tragic end go unstated.

As the two officers passed the office where Cranor filled out paperwork, he gave a wave, which they both returned.

"Thanks," Daniels called. "We'll let ourselves out."

Cranor nodded, then returned to the paperwork at his desk.

*   *   *

While the detectives exited the hotel, Cranor found himself too engrossed in his work to care.

His office, filled with shelving, contained lots of the hotel's memorabilia, blueprints, and photographs, several of which contained his deceased daughter. Family problems after her death led he and his wife to part ways, leaving him an empty house to return to every night.

Lately things were getting worse for him. The Indiana Department of Environmental Management had fined his employers nearly one-hundred-thousand dollars for illegal dumping of paint chips along several rural roads outside of West Baden. The chips, from old paint which contained high levels of lead, were also transported without a legal permit, adding to Cranor's woes. Two of his trusted employees were responsible for the act, though without his permission. Still, he answered for the actions of his subordinates.

Rubbing his head, Cranor worked on a report to his supervisors. Though troublesome for someone who considered himself limited in the English language, the report was better punishment than filling out a resignation.

For two decades he worked with Kieffer Construction under three generations of ownership. He worked his way up from laborer to foreman, then to project manager within the past year. Apparently the company held as much loyalty toward him as he provided them, since he still had a job.

As he fought for the correct wording in a sentence, Cranor heard the door to the adjacent room slam shut. This startled him, considering he was supposed to be the only person left inside the hotel.

Bolting from his seat, he scurried to the door, looking both ways for someone down the rounding hallway. Seeing no one, he walked to the office beside his, opening the door.

"Paul?" he called aloud, seeing the lights were on as he peeked inside. Clouse occasionally came in to work on blueprints, but he always greeted the project manager first.

As Cranor stepped fully inside, a knotted rope fell over his neck, tightening before he finally reacted. From behind the wooden door someone standing high above on a wooden stepladder, hidden behind tall shelving, dropped down to the floor. The assailant pulled the hangman's noose with him, hoisting the project manager almost two feet off the ground.

While his hands instinctively clutched the rope, already embedding itself into the soft flesh of his neck, the unidentified man tugged harder as the rope shifted over the gas line near ceiling level. Cranor kicked for dear life, gasping heavily for breath as the noose tightened and the additional pull of the rope nearly crushed his windpipe.

Now croaking desperately for breath, Cranor aimed a few kicks toward the killer, missing badly both times, and expired several seconds later as the last bit of oxygen inside his lungs forced its way out. His body fell limp as his struggle for death ended tragically, the killer coldly looking over his prize as it swung from the rope.

10

After ordering Clouse to remain in bed for the duration of the day, Jane proceeded to pick Zach up from school, arriving earlier than Clouse usually did.

She checked with the main office, discovering that Zach had a gifted class on the second floor where he would finish in a few minutes. Unsure of whether Zach would be looking for her or not, she decided to venture into the classroom and tour the school in the process, since her daughter would start there the following year. Though Katie was considered the same age as Zach, she barely missed the cutoff birth date for kindergarten.

Considering how much Clouse worked with his son at home, and how much his mother had taught him before her death, Jane was not surprised to discover Zach was in gifted classes so soon. Reaching the room number given by the office, Jane knocked, finding a smiling teacher on the other side of the door.

"Hello," Jane said. "I'm here to pick Zach up."

"We haven't met," the woman said. "You must be his mother."

Jane simply smiled, taking a step inside.

"He's just finishing up in there with one of our teaching aides," the teacher said, pointing to a room with a closed door. "I'm Judy Parker," the teacher said, introducing herself.

Jane shook hands, revealing herself as Zach's expected stepmother. While Judy worked with several students, Jane took time to look around.

Several other children were at a table, working on group projects which appeared fairly complex. She wondered what sort of task Zach was given.

When the door finally opened, she noticed the room behind the emerging Zach encumbered in darkness. Only the outlines of a desk, computer, and someone cleaning up after the activity were visible. Zach smiled when he saw Jane, because his father seldom came upstairs to pick him up, fearing he disrupted the class by showing up unannounced.

"Dad still sick?" he asked her immediately.

"Yes, and I told him to stay in bed."

"Come and look, Jane," he said, taking her hand, pulling her into the main part of the classroom.

He immediately began showing her some of the completed activities on display, the toys, and several of his friends.

Jane was overwhelmed by the amount of student-created projects hanging on the wall, and covering the tables. It seemed unfair that gifted children had all the fun projects to work on.

Between all of this, Jane snuck a peek behind her, seeing a woman leave the darkened room where Zach had been, cutting out the main door. Without so much as a look back or a goodbye to the other teachers, the woman left, as though trying to leave the school before the flow of students streamed into the hallway.

Perhaps her womanly intuition got the best of her, but Jane suspected the woman was more than running late. Most teachers and aides openly greeted parents while this one seemed to avoid contact with her altogether. Perhaps it was simply a bad day, or maybe the woman just wanted to get home.

"Look at the fishes," Zach said, regaining her attention, leading her to the room's aquarium.

"They're beautiful," she commented, not taking time to correct him on his plural word usage.

She was too curious about exactly what Zach was working on separately from the other children, and who his hurried instructor was.

*   *   *

Following Jane's orders, Clouse remained in bed all morning and afternoon, despite feeling much better. Occasionally cold chills ran through his body, along with a light feeling in his head that came with viruses. He suffered from either a bad cold or flu, or perhaps pneumonia as Jane figured, but he hated being so inactive. With two jobs that kept him occupied regularly, this seemed too mundane to tolerate.

He spent much of the day on the phone, fielding calls from concerned friends and family, along with several from the press seeking interviews about his experience, undoubtedly so they could exaggerate the final product. He declined until he was well enough to see them in person.

Dr. Smith called him, wanting to know how his favorite designer was coming along. Smith, growing more idle with every year that passed, still took the time and effort to contact his employees and check on their well-being. It impressed Clouse that a man rumored to be worth several billion dollars took it upon himself to save a historical landmark in the West Baden Springs Hotel, and keep tabs on the employees there, in a good way.

Smith seemed to understand just how much Clouse had suffered the year before because the experience was partly shared by both men. He said he wanted Clouse healthy to witness and share in the grand reopening of the building. None of the employees ever dreamed it was possible to see such a day, but Smith continued to surprise them all, spending millions of his own dollars to assist the National Preservation Society in rebuilding the only hotel of its kind.

Half an hour passed while Clouse glanced through a public safety catalog, finding a few items he considered ordering, partly to pass the time. He knew eight-hundred numbers meant long waits. He sneezed three consecutive times to the side of the bed, causing a headache while adding to the dizzy feeling he already had swirling inside his head.

"Damn," he commented to himself, placing a bookmark in the magazine as the phone rang again. "Hello," he answered with a stuffed nose.

"You sound good," his buddy Ken Kaiser said sarcastically from the other end.

"Thanks. Are you calling to let me know you recovered my boat from the bottom of the lake?"

Kaiser chuckled aloud.

"You can dive for the rust deposits in a couple years, pal," the county officer said. He turned serious for a moment. "The divers did find something weird, though, Paul."

"What's that?"

"The boat's ignition key was still in place. Did you say your other keys were on a ring with it?"

"Yeah, Ken. It was a pretty solid ring. They should have all been together," Clouse replied, hoping to get his other keys back.

"They were gone."

Silence filled both ends of the line for several seconds.

"They could have broke off on impact," the officer suggested.

"No, Ken. They were on there pretty snug."

Both knew what the implications were if the keys were missing.

"So someone could have my keys," Clouse said it aloud, knowing that 'someone' would probably be his attempted killer.

"Might want to change your locks," Kaiser suggested.

"Thanks," Clouse said with a sharp tongue, already knowing it was a must. Despite his position, Kaiser was little help to him.

"One other thing," the officer noted. "We found evidence in the propeller that your boat didn't get tangled up. Someone basically made certain it ran into a cluster of thick plants, as though a whole patch of that shit was deliberately set there."

"How so?"

"The divers found traces of what was either tape or some sort of strap used to keep the plants together until they housed themselves into your motor."

"No wonder it stopped so quick."

"Hate to cut you off, pal, but I've got to get to work," Kaiser said. "I'll call you later."

"Okay. Thanks, Ken," Clouse said slowly, realizing how badly someone wanted him stranded in the middle of the lake.

He hung up the phone, picked up his catalog, and read only a few minutes more before the phone rang again.

"Now what?" Clouse wondered aloud before answering. "Hello?"

He instantly recognized the sound of traffic in the background.

Pay phone.

"Paul Clouse?"

"Speaking," the fireman answered, figuring another reporter wanted a scoop, though the man on the other end sounded nervous.

"I have to speak with you," the man said in a matter-of-fact tone.

"About what?"

"I have information about who tried to kill you."

Clouse's attention belonged to the caller.

"What sort of information?"

"Who wants you dead and why. I know who laid an oar upside your head."

For a moment Clouse thought it might be a joke until the caller mentioned the specific nature of how he was knocked overboard.

"When can we meet?" he asked.

"Soon," the man answered nervously. "I'll find you when the time is right."

"How do I know you're not putting me on?" Clouse questioned.

"I'm the one who pulled you from the lake," the answer came, followed by a click.

Clouse held the phone, staring at it. Even after the buzzing sound and dial tone followed, he stared at it, stunned by what he had learned. Several things flooded his mind to ponder, but it felt like too much. His headache worsened, and Clouse decided to lie back, letting the world around him pass by until Jane returned.

*   *   *

As the late afternoon sun blazed a trail for his Chevy pickup to follow, Tim Niemeyer stayed along the dirt trail leading to the property he alone took responsibility for maintaining. Though few of the landmarks remained, Beverly Hilton paid him a token wage to check on the property when he saw fit, and to keep trespassers away.

Money was not the issue, nor was a deep loyalty to the widowed woman who asked such a favor of him.

For years Niemeyer had wanted to buy the land, or at least part of it, from her. She refused to sell, partly he believed, because he continued to mind it for her. Sometimes he felt like the only person who cared at all for the property, mostly from a sense of ownership. He was confident it would someday be his own.

Owning a small construction business between Bloomington and Bedford gave him the option of calling the shots and making his own hours. In the past three years, several key bids doubled his business, forcing him to hire more employees and put in more hours. He knew missing some of the little things with his family would pay off when he eventually took an early retirement, or let his kids take over when they were old enough.

Niemeyer felt thrilled to be close to his friends and family after watching so many of his high school friends leave for college, or simply for better jobs, and never return. He enjoyed the neighborly things, like plowing driveways in the winter, or helping kids by occasionally speaking at a church school class.

Just off Highway 37, before the turn to West Baden and French Lick, the grounds he sought were overgrown and mired with decrepit buildings. They were a ghostly testament to what once drew visitors to the property.

A red brick drive, now overgrown with weeds, gave way to a parallel muddy path just several feet away, created by off-road truck tires. Several guest cottages barely stood, their splintered wood clinging to their frames by rusty nails. One of the roofs revealed several holes from rocks thrown by unwanted trespassers.

Just the types Niemeyer sought out.

With his favorite shotgun nestled in the extended cab behind him, he looked straight ahead, spying a foreign truck parked just past the guest cottages as the old retreat came into view. He stopped short of the old driveway, pulling out his cellular phone. He hoped Ken Kaiser was working the afternoon shift.

"Orange County Police," a female voice answered on the other end.

"This is Tim Niemeyer," he told the woman. "I'm at the old Hilton property and there are some trespassers here."

"Have you seen them?"

Normally Niemeyer spoke softly with just a hint of Southern drawl that stemmed from years on the farm around his grandfather, who came from Tennessee to live with his parents during his youth. He could turn it on and off at will, except when he got angry.

"No, but Ah'm about to go and look."

"Stay put, sir. We'll send a unit out."

"Okay," Niemeyer answered with no intent of obeying the order as he clicked the phone off, placing it back in its charger.

Stepping from the truck, Niemeyer pulled the shotgun out, wanting to make a point if he found someone. A burly man, he took jokes easily about his beer belly, and even the ones about protein drinks and steroids causing his brown hair's recession to the point of just a fringe, though he never actually took steroids.

Average in height, he had a barrel chest matched by his stomach, because he liked to eat heartily after working out.

After befriending several police officers, he often worked out with them and took it quite seriously after seeing significant improvement in the size of his upper body. He learned to take their teasing in good nature, and returned fire when chances arose.

Niemeyer was sick and tired of telling teenage punks to stay away from the property. Occasionally, curious adults came to see what became of the old retreat, once home to so many rich and famous residents of Southern Indiana, but usually trespassers were the bad kind.

Kids shot at the buildings, left trash, got high, drank, and rode motorcycles around the property without regard to its heritage or the fact that someone still owned it. He hated it when they made excuses for being there, despite all the signs warning against trespassing, or the fence they so recklessly threw aside every time.

He hated liars.

With his steel-toed boots already covered in mud, Niemeyer trudged forward, feeling warm in his thick brown leather jacket as sweat dripped down his forehead. Usually a fairly reserved person, he attended church and feared God just as much as the next man, but something about others violating his property, or that of others, lit a fire beneath him. Perhaps being a victim of theft in the past, or a heightened sense of security that came with being a family man hardened him, but there was no changing his nature.

Seeing no one around, he snuck a look at the old truck parked near the old resort. A temporary license plate stuck inside the back window revealed as little as the cab of the truck did. His sharp blue eyes scanned the area like an eagle, seeing no movement. No strange noises sounded around him either.

It was his nature to remain more calm, collected, and cerebral than even his closest friends realized. He thought of all sorts of topics they had no idea he was versed in.

Right now he focused on only one of those topics.

"Your truck's about ta get towed!" he yelled a warning, losing his accent through the top of his lungs.

His friends also knew of his temper, how difficult it was to get him mad, and to stay clear when he reached that point.

Steaming, Niemeyer examined the near skeletal frame of the resort, scarred badly by fire so many years before. By all rights it should have been torn to the ground, he thought, but Ms. Hilton wanted it in place to reclaim some of her memories, despite the danger of a lawsuit from anyone hurt inside.

Even if they were technically trespassing.

Parts of the wooden walls clung to the frame of the long, two story house. Most of the remaining wood retained its charred appearance, though the smell of fire had long since blown away with the winds that howled through the vacant wreck of a building.

The mix of gray and black wood occasionally gave way along several walls to the view of the dead, overgrown grass behind the building. Seeing streams of daylight through the building still gave Niemeyer chills, just as it had in his younger days.

Knowing his gun was loaded, the independent contractor stepped forward, finding two young men completely dressed in black emerge from the building, not spying him until he was unavoidable. Standing beside their vehicle, Niemeyer simply held the shotgun in one hand, burning holes through them with his stare until they were within several feet.

Neither looked the druggie part he expected, but one had a snake tattoo wrapped around his neck. Niemeyer referred to that as 'trouble.' Dressed in black pants, black turtleneck shirts, and dark military-type boots, the two looked like members of some cult, probably practicing their religion in a secluded area.

Taking a quick glance, Niemeyer looked for any signs of what they might have been doing on the property, or evidence of weapons or drugs.

He could see no trace of any foul play.

"Problem?" the taller of the two asked.

"You're trespassin'," Niemeyer informed them hostilely.

"We had no idea," the other said, doing his best to appear genuine.

"No idea?" Niemeyer retorted, pointing his gun toward one of few remaining signs not victimized by gunfire and run over by four-wheelers. "You two know you're not s'posed to be back here."

"We're sorry," the taller one said without sincerity in his voice. "We'll leave."

"And don't be comin' back," the property manager said before they could turn to go.

Though Niemeyer failed to hear it coming, the two younger men spied a county police car at the edge of the drive. Unsure of exactly what might be coming, they instinctively turned on Niemeyer.

"What's this?" the taller one asked, pointing in the direction of the drive.

"Protection," Niemeyer answered without looking, suspecting Kaiser, or another officer, was on the way.

Timing it perfectly, the same man shoved Niemeyer as he turned to see the progress of his friend down the drive. Caught off-guard and unbalanced, Niemeyer reacted in the manner most natural for him in such a position. Perhaps it was how he saw his grandfather settle farm scuffles as a kid, or the insurance of having a number of local police friends to back him, but Niemeyer stepped out of character.

He struck the taller man with the butt of his shotgun just as Kaiser's patrol car reached the open area of the property, giving him full view of his high school chum's perpetration.

"Get back, Tim!" Kaiser called as he stepped out of the patrol car.

Niemeyer slowly obeyed, putting down the shotgun. He felt stunned concerning his actions, like everything was part of a bad dream.

"He went ballistic!" the struck man shouted immediately. "He smashed my jaw!" he added, pointing to the blood oozing from his mouth, though the county officer appeared skeptical of the injury's severity.

"What happened?" Kaiser asked, stepping beside his friend.

"I told them ta leave, they saw you comin', and the one shoved me," Niemeyer explained. "I just went off and hit 'im with the gun."

"Are you two wanting to press charges?" Kaiser asked with a tone implying it would not be in their best interest.

Niemeyer started to speak, but the county officer silenced him, holding a foreboding hand up. "I don't have a choice, Tim," he said aside to his friend. "I saw what happened and you never know these days when someone's hiding in the bushes with a video camera. I can't risk my job like that."

"He shoved me," Niemeyer complained just above a whisper.

"I didn't see it," Kaiser insisted.

Niemeyer reluctantly nodded in understanding. Kaiser obviously had too many years on the force to risk his career. He would likely figure out some way to get his friend off the hook later.

"Damn straight we do," the taller one finally answered, much to the amazement of his friend. "Can we do this at the station so I can get this looked at?"

Kaiser hesitated a moment, looking from the two young men to Niemeyer.

"Sorry, Tim. I've got to put you in cuffs."

Niemeyer bobbed his head slowly, understanding, but hoping there was a way to avoid being formally arrested. He knew he had overreacted, but this was going a bit far considering he was in the right.

"Frisk him," the taller one insisted. "I don't want him pulling anything else out on us."

Numbed by the fact his best friend had to arrest him, Niemeyer sighed as Kaiser led him toward the patrol car, instructing him to place his hands on the hood and spread his legs. Niemeyer felt terrible putting his friend in this position, since he had first called it in. Now he was helpless to do anything but accept whatever hand fate dealt him.

"Ah'm sorry, Ken," he said between the two of them as Kaiser's hand ran up and down each leg, then through his jacket and flannel shirt. "Ah'm so sorry. He shoved me and-"

"You can't go whacking people with shotguns," Kaiser said, equally hushed, cutting off Niemeyer's last statement. "I don't know how I'm going to get you out of this, Tim."

Partly from the embarrassment of the situation and putting his friend in such a predicament, emotion overwhelmed Niemeyer as mist filled his eyes. He refused to show any emotion in front of the lying punks, so he let Kaiser hurry in cuffing him. He wondered how he would tell his wife and kids, and how would they take the news. In the past, his friends were there to stop him when anger took over, but this time Niemeyer realized it was different.

His frustration turned to fear when he saw the young men from the corner of his eye reaching for the discarded shotgun. As the last cuff wrapped around his wrist, Niemeyer began to warn his friend too late as the taller of the two darted toward him, knocking him upside the temple with his own gun, as the other apparently went for Kaiser.

Blue sky whirled around the contractor a moment before everything went completely black. His fear of being arrested became the least of his worries in one bleak moment.

11

Clouse awoke to find the confining room around him closing in. Between the flower wallpaper, the vase with the plastic red rose, and the facial tissue holder that displayed its stitched design of a kitten playing with a ball, Clouse felt like he was in a maternity ward.

He looked outside at the Indian summer day, thinking how nice it would be to play with the kids in the afternoon sun. Any number of things sounded better than being confined to a bed, sick as he had ever felt, wishing to get better.

Still staring out the windows, he saw Jane pull into the driveway.

As his son joined Katie outside to play a few minutes later, his fiancee sat on the edge of his bed with a concerned look. Sleepy-eyed, the firefighter took hold of her hand.

"What's the matter?"

"Do you know what kind of project Zach is working on in his gifted class?"

"Not at the moment. He usually doesn't talk about it."

Jane put her free hand up to her chin, tapping it a few times.

"I asked him and he wouldn't give me a good answer," she told Clouse. "I don't know if he can't or won't tell, but they've got him in this dark room by himself with just a computer, while the other children work on group projects, Paul."

"That's strange," Clouse agreed. "I'll ask him later."

"So, are you feeling better?" she asked, appearing glad he agreed with her about Zach's school situation.

"Somewhat," he answered, not about to reveal the conversation of his last phone call to her. "I'm still getting cold chills, with just a bit of a headache."

Jane quickly stood.

"I'll get some Tylenol," she said before leaving the room.

Before Clouse could tell her to avoid the drowsy type, the phone rang from beside him. Hesitantly staring at it the first two rings, Clouse decided to answer before someone else in the house did.

"Hello?"

"Paul?" a familiar, mild Southern drawl asked.

"Tim? I haven't heard from you in forever."

"Sorry about that. Listen, I need your help on something," Niemeyer said with the sounds of iron bars clanking behind him.

"Tim, where are you?" Clouse asked curiously.

*   *   *

Almost an hour later, completely against Jane's advice, Clouse arrived at the Orange County Jail in Paoli. Though he felt and looked horrible, Clouse refused to let his friend sit in jail for reasons neither of them truly knew. Niemeyer sounded scared, and even confused, because the police were questioning him heavily about Kaiser's whereabouts. The last thing he remembered was being knocked unconscious, then waking up in the jail.

Through a screen separating them in the visitation area, Niemeyer relayed the story to his other high school buddy. The three of them were country boys in their younger days, and a bit of that remained in each of them, though in different ways. They were all raised on farms, forming a pact as early as grade school that they would never part ways. In some ways they had, but all three resided in the area and loosely kept in touch. There was nothing they wouldn't do for one another.

Nothing.

"These two men," Clouse said after his friend's narrative. "Have you seen them before?"

"Can't say I have," Niemeyer replied. "God, Paul. What could they have done with Ken? They had me dead to rights for arrest. Why would they do that?"

"I don't know, Tim. One of the officers told me his patrol car was still there, you were lying unconscious in handcuffs, and there was no sign of any truck. The last report they had from Ken was when he reached the property. They sent backup when he didn't respond to radio calls and found you there."

"But I didn't do anything," his friend pleaded. "They're just holding me because they don't know what I did. And they won't believe a word I say 'bout those two guys in black."

Clouse felt drained and sicker than ever with the world around him occasionally spinning from an uncontrollable dizziness. He needed rest, not more worries.

"I'll talk to the shift commander and see if I can get you released until something comes up. Either way, I'm going to look for Ken."

"Where would he be?"

"I don't know. You've given me a description of the truck and the two men who took him. I have some ideas."

Clouse was about to stand when his cellular phone rang from inside his jacket pocket. The guards knew him well enough that they let him walk in with it. He was close enough to an external wall for it to work, so he quickly pulled it out, pressing the talk button before answering.

"Clouse."

"Hotel," a voice said before hanging up.

Stunned a moment, Clouse realized it was the same voice who called him earlier stating he knew who had attempted to take his life two days earlier. The warning was too strong to ignore, and the only lead he now had.

"Shit," Clouse said to himself. "I've got to go. I'll be back for you later."

"But, Paul," Niemeyer almost begged, not understanding the situation, unable to finish before Clouse exited the visitation area.

Clouse stopped outside the visitation area to take a final glance at his friend, who simply slumped back in his chair, waiting for the guards to return him to his cell. Though he felt guilty for leaving Niemeyer, Clouse had grave concerns about Kaiser's situation.

*   *   *

Few lights illuminated the inside of the West Baden Springs Hotel when Clouse unlocked the front door, taking a step inside. He had already alerted the county police and EMS to head toward the building, but he waited until he was almost there before doing so. The fireman wanted to be the first to see what the caller meant.

When he rounded the first corner, Clouse saw a dim light from inside the atrium brighter than he or Rusty Cranor left it when they closed the building. He also heard a dripping sound, like a bathtub faucet slowly releasing droplets into an already filled basin.

Nothing in the atrium contained running water, or even the capacity to hold fluid.

Clouse slowly approached the closest entrance to the grand center, apprehensive about what might be inside. He stood on the opposite side of the doorway, not looking in, just listening to the drips as long as he could bear it. Finally, Clouse stepped through the doorway, finding what appeared to be a work of art set up just for him.

A message.

"God, no," he muttered, taking in a view of the cleared atrium, a pool of blood surrounding one of the statues on the other end.

Drawn to the horrid spectacle, Clouse recognized the pale form of his high school friend laid across the statue, still in his police uniform.

Clouse swore immediately his friend was dead, his form tied by several crude ropes into a lying position across the statue where his left arm, left free to dangle, fed blood through an intravenous tube. Laid across the outstretched arms of the statue, the scene looked almost natural, as though the statue was holding a fallen child in its arms.

Unfortunately, the child happened to be tied helplessly in place with a heavy abundance of straps. The only way Clouse thought his friend might have escaped from the bonds would have been to physically break the statue's arms by thrashing himself around, if even that was possible.

Apparently that never happened.

He stared at the reddish puddle, thinking back to his first responder runs on the fire department, positive his friend had lost too much blood to have survived. His heart sank at the thought of losing a childhood friend so soon.

As he reached the edge of the bloody pool, Clouse saw the needle stuck inside the pale wrist of his friend, feeding blood through the tube, which leaked the fluid into a massive puddle on the floor. A tight cloth strap assured the needle remained in place, even if Kaiser had shifted positions. A clothespin slowed the progress of the blood, assuredly to prolong the suffering Kaiser went through before dying.

Immune to the sounds of the EMS personnel and police officers entering the atrium behind him, Clouse stared at the form of his friend closely. Kaiser's eyes were closed, his uniform torn and ragged as though a struggle ensued before he was drained of his lifeblood. Visible cuts and bruises showed along his face and arms, probably from various weapon strikes to subdue him.

Missing, were Kaiser's gun and belt. From the looks of the marks, they might have been used against him. Though damaged, every other part of the man's uniform appeared to be on him.

Clouse knew how tough Kaiser was, after watching him in action several times. He now understood what Niemeyer and the officer experienced was much more than a simple trespassing, but he wondered why.

"Why?" he asked aloud, looking at his friend's pale form, as though Kaiser had already undergone embalming. He couldn't help but wonder if Kaiser had been conscious for any of it. The thought of being slowly bled to death mortified Clouse.

Without realizing it, Clouse stepped back from the scene, letting the medics do their job. They carefully pulled the needle from his arm, checking his vitals as they did so. Avoiding the puddle of blood around the statue, they laid Kaiser down in a clean part of the carpeted floor, quickly checking for pulse and blood pressure as Clouse turned away.

"We've got a pulse," one of them announced, as though his experience told him victims of this nature were usually found lifeless.

Clouse whirled around, equally stunned.

"We've got to move him now!" the senior medic ordered, apparently stunned by the discovery too.

As the group placed Kaiser on a stretcher and rushed him past Clouse, the firefighter looked to the sky, thankful for such a miracle, though he knew the ordeal was far from over.

"Thank you, Lord," he said uncharacteristically before rushing toward the atrium exit, taking one last look back at the gargantuan puddle of blood before heading out.

12

McCabe milled through the photos on his desk, wondering exactly what to make of the Rexford murder. He spent the night at home alone, except for the companionship of a beer, which showed signs to those who knew him that an important case had come his way.

He told his mother he would call her back later.

He hadn't.

He promised a buddy at work he would attend his daughter's baptism.

One less person witnessed a Catholic tradition.

His friends at the bar expected him as usual once his shift was over.

They might worry a while, then get too drunk to remember what they fussed over.

Entering what he called the zone, McCabe put pressure on himself to develop a lead, despite the lack of necessary components.

Witnesses.

None that helped.

Motive.

None apparent.

Promising leads.

A big fat zero.

Usually McCabe entered the zone when he merely lacked a clue, or perhaps a shred of evidence that slammed the door shut on the case. Now he did it from desperation, realizing how quickly murder cases grew cold without solid leads to begin pecking away at.

Daniels gave him a few ideas to work with, but nothing that put him any closer to solving the case. McCabe felt somewhat like a stranger to the case because he knew little about the hotel's history or what happened to Daniels and Clouse the year before.

He wondered if anyone truly knew aside from the few survivors.

As unusual as it was for the detective to avoid socialization, it was equally unusual for him to begin a case with so little information. Everything about it felt strange. McCabe thought it eccentric to murder someone by lighting him on fire. He believed the victim was shoved onto the balcony, thus calling attention to the crime.

Also unusual.

Cross-checking the other names of those on the balconies helped very little. Most were descendant relatives of hotel patrons from years past, making them no more or less likely to be murdered than Rexford. He hoped the stolen property might shed some light on the case if its identity was discovered.

"McCabe," the detective said, scooping his phone up after one ring.

"Tug, it's Denny. We've had another situation at the hotel you're investigating."

"Not another murder," he stated more than asked, hoping his reply was true.

Denny Mason, a fellow trooper, had a history of delivering bad news to McCabe from his past marital problems to the cases that gave him nightmares.

"Not yet. County cop ended up in the hospital, drained of most of his blood."

McCabe sat silently a few seconds, wondering what on earth the curse on that hotel had to be. He would question Daniels more about it later, no matter how much the man felt personally plagued by it.

"Did they take him to Bedford?"

"There was no time," Mason replied. "Clinic in Paoli. Need directions?"

"No," McCabe said promptly, not yet ready to swallow his pride. "I'll find it."

After all, Paoli wasn't that big a town.

"There's something else."

"Oh?"

"The Illinois boys called back with some info on your case. The wife remembered him packing a piece of the hotel's old tile floor. She said they asked all the guests to bring something relating to the hotel with them for the dinner."

"What the hell?" McCabe wondered aloud.

"Was there a tile piece in his belongings?" Mason couldn't seem to help asking.

"No, but why would anyone want that?"

His friend chuckled.

"That's why you're the detective, not me."

"Thanks, Denny. See you tomorrow."

"Anytime, buddy."

As he hung up, McCabe wondered where the clinic was in Paoli. He figured he could reach the town in less than an hour with lights and siren, and radio dispatch for specific directions while en route. There was no shame in asking the whereabouts of buildings.

It seemed the missing piece of his puzzle was a piece of tile floor. He would spend the next hour questioning how a piece of tile might be at all important to someone, and if it was the reason Rexford had to die. Though it seemed unreasonable, McCabe's experience told him sometimes things just lacked rhyme or reason.

*   *   *

When the detective arrived, a man fitting Clouse's description spied him while rolling his sleeve up with a discontent look on his face. Apparently recognizing the detective's mandatory shirt and tie immediately, the man shot him a look, stating any questions would have to wait.

"You Clouse?" McCabe asked anyway.

"You O-negative?" was the reply.

"Yeah," the detective replied, seeing where the conversation was going.

"Donate a pint or two and I'll answer any questions you want."

McCabe inquired about the officer's condition, quickly learning that Kaiser's situation looked grim, his only hope being a massive transfusion, which the clinic was not equipped for. He was the type of person who would volunteer regardless.

Paramedics from Bloomington were on the scene, ready to transport once the transfusion peeked. Several local volunteers rushed to the clinic to donate once they heard. To ensure Kaiser received no foreign particles or unknown diseases the volunteers needed to meet certain criteria.

Despite his illness, Clouse gave over a pint, looking more pale than some corpses the detective had viewed over his career. McCabe saw him call someone after his donation, apparently arguing about leaving the house in his condition, and why he needed to do so. McCabe understood how women could be, despite not having a steady relationship in over a year.

While McCabe remained on the table, he saw Clouse take two county officers aside, asking them to question Niemeyer officially and release him, since he obviously had nothing to do with the incident. After radioing their commanding officer, they received permission to take Niemeyer's statement and inform him of what happened to Kaiser only after they finished.

After McCabe finished donating, the clinic staff appeared confident Kaiser could safely be transported to Bloomington, receiving any remaining transfusions along the way. Two volunteers were shuffled into the ambulance with him as Clouse helplessly looked on.

"Care for a ride to the hospital?" McCabe asked Clouse, rolling his sleeve down.

"Sure."

Five minutes later both were settled in the unmarked police car and on their way to Bloomington. Clouse thought about nothing except his friend until McCabe broke the silence.

"So what happened?"

"I was talking to my buddy Tim in jail when I got a weird call."

Clouse spent about five minutes explaining the entire situation to the state trooper, shivering most of the time, sneezing between sentences. McCabe had spoken with Daniels about Clouse's attempted murder, so the trooper understood what the man was probably going through.

"You should be in bed," McCabe said after a few minutes of silence.

"I can't sleep with everything going on," Clouse said with a forced laugh.

"Sounds like I want to talk with your buddy too," the trooper added.

With no reply the trooper looked over to find Clouse dozed off, his body too exhausted to remain awake, even during such dire times.

"I don't blame you, man."

13

Clouse awoke in a hospital bed the next morning when light peeked through the window blinds, hitting him squarely in the face. Feeling better, he threw the sheets aside, finding himself fully dressed.

"What happened?" he asked Jane after darting into the hallway.

He remembered little from the night before because the couple had stood nearby, monitoring Kaiser as closely as the hospital staff would allow. Clouse had fallen in and out of sleep in the uncomfortable waiting room chairs.

"He's stable," Jane answered, seeming to know exactly what his thoughts were. "And the staff was kind enough to provide a room for you, so you wouldn't catch cold."

Jane used her connections, in other words.

"But Ken's okay?"

"He's stable, Paul. It'll be touch and go the next few days."

"Has he woken up?"

"No. His body is extremely weak right now. Even his family isn't allowed to see him."

Clouse paced a moment, still feeling light-headed. Even with nearly a dozen hours of sleep he still felt unhealthy.

"Your friend Tim came by after I got you the room. He wanted to thank you."

"I'm glad he's free."

"Why have I never met him?"

Clouse gave a funny smirk.

"Tim and I just run into one another often enough that we don't usually call one another. We were both always tighter with Ken than we were each other. Besides, he lives south of Bedford."

"So does Ken," Jane informed him.

Clouse shrugged for lack of a comeback.

"Mark's upstairs if you want to see him."

"What's he doing here?" Clouse questioned quickly, afraid his friends were all being brutalized.

"He has an appointment with the physical therapist."

Clouse thought a moment. Kaiser's condition was not subject to change in the near future, and there was a possibility he might help Daniels if he went upstairs.

"I'll come get you if anything changes," Jane said, apparently reading his thoughts.

"Okay," he said, giving her a long kiss. "You know I love you."

"I know. Now go get Mark on his feet."

Clouse smiled, then headed for the elevator.

When he reached the appropriate hallway he spied Dr. Susan Jameson walking from the rehabilitation room, shaking her head as she clutched her clipboard.

"What's the matter, Doc?" Clouse asked when she saw him coming.

"Your friend seems to be getting worse. He wasn't cooperative toward our techniques today," she said, cupping her hand over her chin. "Has he been doing anything on his own?"

"I'm not sure," the firefighter answered. "I'll talk to him," he added, seeing the therapist leave the room.

Clouse found Daniels staring at the floor, as though he thought about trying something on his own. The officer shot a strange look his way once he spotted him.

"I hear you're being unruly."

Daniels ignored the remark, looking past Clouse toward the door.

"Paul, I want you to get behind this chair and dump me on the floor."

Now Clouse gave the odd look.

"I suppose you want me to kick you once you're down too?"

"Seriously," Daniels said, growing agitated. "I may be onto something."

Reluctantly Clouse walked behind the chair, grabbing the chair's push bars.

"Do it," Daniels ordered, noting the hesitation.

Clouse looked toward the door reluctantly before pulling up on the bars, lurching forward to spill his friend on the floor.

Landing hard, Daniels wasted no time in pushing himself up with his arms before slowly picking up his right leg, trying to position it for standing. Clouse watched in amazement as his friend showed limited use of the appendage for the first time in his presence.

"I've been able to do this before," Daniels spoke in labored breaths.

"That's cheating."

"So sue me," the officer said, reaching for one of the support rails to help pull himself up. Clouse started toward him. "No. I'll do this myself."

Clasping the rail, Daniels managed to pull himself to one knee, straining to reach a standing position.

"It's in your mind, Mark," Clouse coached. "Put it all behind you and stand up. Get your job back. Your life."

Daniels placed his other foot to a ready position.

"Stand up, Mark. Stand up, dammit."

With several strained, painful sounds, Daniels made his tensed muscles fight for enough energy to stand him up. Giving it one final push, Daniels fought to bring the back leg forward.

"Come on, Mark," Clouse encouraged. "While you've still got the energy."

Daniels pushed himself to stand, pulling the rail as he did so. Within a moment, and without realizing Clouse took up his side, Daniels managed to stand enough to lean himself against the railing. He was not walking, nor was he fully under his own power, but he was using both legs.

Both watched as Susan walked in, gasping with shock as she witnessed the spectacle. What she had fought with Daniels for months to accomplish, he managed to pull off by himself.

Leaning back against the railing, Daniels casually folded his arms, smiling from ear to ear. It was the first time she recalled seeing that expression from him.

"I'm impressed Officer Daniels," she said. "I won't ask how you did it, but I'm very impressed."

A few minutes later, Clouse walked from the therapy room nearly as happy as his friend. Walking down the hall, he smiled, giving one look back to the room before a hand cupped him around the mouth, pulling him down a side hallway.

Spinning around defensively, Clouse saw who he thought was his attacker back away, motioning for him to settle down and keep quiet. The man, dressed in black, was several inches shorter and carried nowhere near the muscle to harm the rugged firefighter.

He appeared typical in nature. Free of tattoos or piercings, he could be any young man just out of college. The black attire fit the description of what Niemeyer spoke of the night before. He appeared too harmless to be involved in anything so vile as what happened to Kaiser at the hotel.

Clouse knew too well how appearances were sometimes deceptive.

"Who are you?" he asked, complying with the man's wish for quiet conversation.

"I'm the only one who might be able to save you and everyone around you," the man said nervously, peeking past Clouse's shoulders.

"I suppose I owe you thanks for pulling me from the lake."

"We don't have time for that," the man said. His dark hair appeared wavy throughout, as though not properly combed. Clouse wondered if it might be a current style. "You're still in considerable danger."

"From who?"

A negative shake of the head was the answer.

"I'm part of a group instructed to carry out a list of objectives," the man confessed. "Our leader goes by the name Jacob."

Clouse flailed his hands in frustration, watching the dust float through the rays of sunshine streaming in through a nearby window.

"Jacob what? You aren't giving me much here."

"I can't tell you what I don't know," the man said. "I got into this group for the wrong reasons, Mr. Clouse. I no longer believe what they're doing is right. We are called the Coven, our leader's name is simply Jacob, and what you must know and understand is that a list exists which contains your name and the names of others I believe are involved with the hotel. Everyone on this list is to die, and your name was the first."

"Can you tell me who else is on it?"

"No. I only find out as they're scheduled for execution. I managed to save you and your friend Kaiser."

Clouse was taken aback. Systematic execution and a specific list. It sounded like a conspiracy plot, but he was living it.

"You call that saving him?" Clouse complained.

"Who do you think put the clothespin on that tube to keep him from bleeding to death? I managed to prolong the process long enough for you to get there, didn't I?"

"All right," Clouse admitted, realizing the true purpose of the clothespin. "You did. But what's the point of this list? The agenda?"

"I'm not privy to that information either. I know your friend Cranor was killed because they wanted something from him."

Clouse took a moment to let the words register.

"Rusty? Dead?"

He started to turn around but the man tugged his arm, getting him to stay.

"I can't believe it."

"I'm sorry," the young man said with a sincere expression. "There was nothing I could do for him, man. They'll know I came to you," he added, rubbing frustration from his head. "Jacob will have me killed when he discovers we spoke."

Clouse sighed aloud, trying to make sense of it all. One moment ago he was thrilled his high school friend was alive and a newer friend could walk again. Now his joy was crushed by the news his colleague was murdered, and he still had no idea why.

"We cannot meet again. I have to leave," the man said suddenly, pushing past Clouse who clasped his arm with a solid grip.

"What do I call you?"

"Call me Stephen," the man replied.

"And how can I get a copy of this list?"

"I'll get you one. Somehow, I'll get you one."

Clouse let go. As the man scurried away, he wondered what to do next. If what his informant said was true, it seemed prudent to inform the police. Clouse had no one to trust or contact who might begin to understand. Daniels was still in no shape to go chasing down leads with him.

"McCabe," Clouse decided aloud, walking down the hallway.

A strange feeling he was being watched by another party entered his mind, but he put the sensation aside, deciding he would do little good by dwelling on his paranoia.

14

After a search of the hotel resulted in nothing, Clouse traveled with McCabe to Cranor's house outside the city limits of Bloomington. Under the detective's blanket of request, Clouse had searched the man's office for anything that might be missing.

He found nothing out of the usual.

Because it seemed rather odd to him, and he felt clueless about its significance, McCabe questioned Clouse about the tile floor piece on the way to Cranor's house. He had a suspicion it might somehow be related.

"I'm not sure what he was doing with it, but when the company started reconstruction they auctioned off the pieces for money to aid in the rebuilding," Clouse answered as they rode toward Cranor's house.

For the first time, he noticed the odor of a car freshener in the unmarked car, wondering why officers with take-home cars always had those.

"How would Rexford, a dentist from Chicago, obtain one of those pieces?" McCabe asked, keeping his eyes on the road.

"Mailing list, probably. The hotel has a number of volunteers who keep track of all sorts of things. One list is dedicated to descendants of the hotel's former owners and major contributors."

List, Clouse thought, missing whatever question McCabe asked next. His thoughts about those around him being systematically executed haunted him. He prayed it was all one big lie. Though there was no answer when he had called, Clouse hoped they might find Cranor at home, alive.

If that was the case, he could theoretically dismiss the boat incident as a trapped thief fighting his way out, and the Rexford murder as some sort of revenge killing.

If only it would prove so simple.

"You okay?" McCabe asked, raising his voice.

"Sorry. I'm just preoccupied with this encounter."

"You didn't say much about that, aside from what he told you about Cranor being dead. Did he give any names, or anything else that might be useful?"

"Not really," Clouse answered quickly.

He felt no urgency to tell McCabe details of the meeting. State police proved of little use to him the year before, when he was accused of killing his wife. Clouse also wanted to keep his friends and family from panicking, because he knew the police were sometimes excessively protective. He also wanted to avoid a local media circus.

Clouse would handle it his own way.

He planned to confide in Daniels, because the two shared a bond in such circumstances. Whether his friend shared information with McCabe or not would be up to him. Clouse simply refused to fully trust anyone he didn't know.

Anyone.

"Can you find out who those tiles were sold to?" the detective asked.

"I'll see. Finding who has the record will probably take awhile. Getting a copy will be another task altogether."

"I'll give you whatever assistance you need," McCabe encouraged. "Did Cranor have any of those tiles?"

Clouse covered his mouth, exhaling through his nose as he thought.

"Pretty much anyone who worked on the hotel that long ago has at least one. But I still can't imagine what value they are to anyone. You really think that's motive enough to kill someone?"

McCabe shrugged.

"I don't know. It's my job to ask the dumb questions."

He paused a moment as Clouse indicated a direction to turn.

"You have any of those tiles?"

"One," the firefighter answered. "Stays inside a curio cabinet at our house."

"Must be quite the display piece," McCabe said. "Rexford kept his inside a jewelry box."

Clouse folded his arms.

"The tiles were imported, but they're pretty much worthless in such small pieces. They're more of a sentimental value than anything."

Unlike McCabe, Clouse did not feel like talking. He realized the detective was probably hardened enough that he didn't mind eating or talking through any situation, but the thought of seeing a friend dead harrowed Clouse.

"Why were the tiles brought up?" McCabe asked as they neared Cranor's residence.

"Some were stolen or damaged over the years. Enough that piecing together replacements became either too costly, or just impossible artistically," Clouse forced a quick answer. "I'm not sure which."

Once the lone country house with no neighbors for a mile in any direction came into view, Clouse tensed. As they came upon the driveway, chills shot up the fireman's spine. He felt no urge to step inside the house, or investigate the property, knowing he might see another person he cared for in a state of death.

Over the past year Clouse had mentally recovered from the torment laid upon him by David Landamere. Seeing Kaiser so close to death flooded his mind with memories he wanted only to forget. Finding another friend in such condition would only add to the heavy burden weighing on his mind.

"You staying in here?" McCabe asked, once parked in the driveway.

Clouse nodded an affirmative.

"I'm going to knock," the detective informed him. "If I don't get an answer, I'll look around and probably go inside."

Clouse watched the next several minutes after no answer came to the front door, and the detective looked around the property, including the back yard and all of the windows.

When he returned, McCabe walked to Clouse's side of the car, forcing himself to contain his initial excitement in his discovery.

"The back door is unlocked," McCabe told Clouse before starting toward the back for the second time.

"Damn," the firefighter said, tired of the detective's tinkering.

He knew McCabe wanted him to look for those damned puzzle pieces, and Clouse wanted the experience over. Opening the car door, he looked to the detective, who seemed to be smiling inwardly like a big kid.

He had gotten his way.

"I knew you couldn't resist," McCabe said, opening the back door.

"Like I had much choice."

Much to his surprise, Clouse saw the house exactly as he remembered it. Since Cranor never stayed home, the house usually appeared tidy, with all sorts of remembrances of years past.

In the living room, several photos of his deceased daughter lined a shelf. Photos of the hotel, and other major projects the man worked on, were displayed in a staircase manner, hanging along one wall.

Knowing what McCabe wanted him to look for, Clouse set about the rest of the living room, searching for several tile pieces he knew his friend usually kept on display. Several shelves and glass display cabinets lined the living room, so the firefighter carefully examined each one as McCabe explored the rest of the house.

*   *   *

After finding nothing downstairs, the detective tried the second floor, opening each bedroom and closet door with caution, his service weapon already drawn. Finding nothing in either bedroom, McCabe tried the bathroom, thinking Clouse's source of information was a big hoax. Like the fireman, he hoped it was.

McCabe peeked around the bathroom door, finding nothing disturbed. From what little light followed him inside, he noticed the shower curtain drawn shut. Shielding himself behind the door, the detective flipped the flourescent light on, watching it flicker to life as he took hold of the curtain, yanking it to one side.

Nothing.

McCabe turned around, squarely hitting someone who had come up behind him.

"Shit!" the detective exclaimed, relieved it was Clouse.

"I thought you might like to know I couldn't find those tile pieces Rusty had," he reported. "There's a bare spot in one of the glass cases, and dust surrounding it, implying something was there until very recently."

"You're doing my job," McCabe said almost defensively. "I've looked everywhere and I can't find anything."

He looked up to the ceiling, beyond Clouse.

"Except there."

Down the hallway, a draw string served to bring down a collapsible ladder leading to the attic. It was the only thing left untouched in the entire house, since there was no full basement. Clouse dreaded the thought of looking up there, preferring to keep what little hope remained for Cranor's safe return.

"Stand back," McCabe ordered, placing a hand behind him, keeping Clouse far enough away that he would be at a safe distance if something fell from the attic.

Taking hold of the string, McCabe gave it a tug.

The ladder tumbled downward, and with it, the stiff carcass of Rusty Cranor. As though placed intentionally to do so, the body slid down the ladder like processed meat, bumping every rung as it went, hitting the floor with a thud, like a sack of groceries, when it landed backside down.

"Ah, shit," Clouse said, turning away from the sight.

He wasted mere seconds before bolting downstairs to collect himself as McCabe examined the bluish form of the dead project manager. McCabe hadn't expected a man so accustomed to death to avoid the sight.

Firefighters see death almost as regularly as police officers, and McCabe sensed Clouse would be hardened after so many traffic wrecks and bodies seen on first responder calls. That, coupled with the vicious murders around him the year before should have prepared him, but then the detective also understood these were his friends dying around him.

Cranor's lifeless face had a somber expression, his eyes wide open, his mouth partly ajar, as though he refused to put up much of a fight in death.

Rope burns around the neck were outwardly apparent. Without touching the body, McCabe did a visual examination, finding nothing aside from the rope burns that might give any clues. It was time to call the coroner's office and begin the second phase of his investigation.

Based on the condition of the body, McCabe figured the time of death to be within twenty-four hours, probably soon after he and Daniels had left the hotel the day before.

Perhaps *immediately* after they left.

"Damn," he cursed under his breath, looking down the stairs at Clouse, who sat on a bench, his head buried in his hands.

McCabe wondered what motivated the killings, and how much good Clouse was to him after suffering another loss.

Time would tell, but time was something McCabe found sparse.

15

Clouse arrived home hours later to find Jane cleaning upstairs with no kids to be heard or found. Disheartened and still unhealthy, he felt discouraged about life in general. He was powerless to stop the mysterious list from being carried out, and his friends were dying around him, much like they had a year before.

Running was no option. He might save himself, but it did nothing to help those around him. Since he had no idea who Jacob might be or who he might target next, Clouse decided to speak with Daniels in the morning. He hated the idea of ruining the happiness his friend had just found, but chances were strong his friend's name was on that list.

"What's the matter?" Jane asked, turning from making Zach's bed as her fiancé entered the room.

"Rusty's dead," Clouse simply said, slumping on the bed.

"My God," Jane gasped. "What happened?"

Clouse held up his right hand, throwing a dismissing wave indicating he wasn't ready to speak about it.

"Everything is so wrong," he said, grasping the back of his head with both hands in frustration. "It's just so wrong," he continued, sniffling.

He never let Jane see him this emotional. Usually Clouse seemed calm, cool, and rational. She never saw a temper, and he was perfect around the kids, even when he felt bad, or had a rough time at work.

She had to know some things he saw as a firefighter, like dead children or the misery families suffered, tormented him. As a doctor she likely witnessed similar scenarios on a regular basis. Never had Clouse let his fiancee see him lose control. On one hand she would probably feel relieved, seeing a new, vulnerable side to the man who tried too hard to be perfect to everyone around him, but at the same time she would likely wonder what demons were running through his head.

Clouse vowed never to tell her, because no one needed to endure the pain he went through.

"The kids are with my parents for the night," Jane said, sitting beside him. "It's okay. You don't have to be tough for me."

"It's just not fair," Clouse said between heaved breaths from emotion.

"I'm sorry, Paul," she said, carefully wrapping her arms around him, pulling him close to her warmth.

Feeling too much like a consoled child, Clouse collected himself, looking down at the floor, beyond the carpeting. His thoughts stretched to the hotel and Cranor's house, seeing only horror in each. He wondered why he didn't just quit work on the hotel after the past year. His life might have returned to normal and he might have enjoyed moments alone with Jane.

"Sometimes I just want to leave," he told her. "I can't believe I ever went back to work there."

"How could you have known?" she asked a question with no answer. "You can't blame yourself for what's happening."

"But somehow I'm always the center of it," Clouse said, frustrated. "Last year I was the suspect. Now everyone close to me is dying."

"Do you want to leave?"

"No. That's not an option. Too many people are stuck here with no way of knowing who's behind it."

"And you think you can find out?" Jane asked skeptically. "You're not a detective, Paul."

"But who knows more about the hotel than me? Or you for that matter? We have to be strong, Jane, and hope to God we catch whoever's doing this before he strikes again."

She seemed to take comfort in his strength with her unblinking eyes and forced grin. If there was one complaint Jane sometimes had about Clouse's personality, it was that he refused to show her every dimension of himself. She had just witnessed his weaker side, and now his ability to pull himself together.

"We'll get through it," she said, pulling him close. "Just be careful."

"I've got too much to lose if I'm not," he said before giving her a kiss on the cheek. "There are a lot of possibilities, but Mark and I will figure it out somehow."

Somehow, he mentally assured himself.

*   *   *

Without the benefit of full lighting, Stephen left the West Baden Spring Hotel's atrium carefully, so as not to disturb the off-duty state trooper providing security. Though the combing of evidence for Kaiser's attempted murderers was done, the yellow tape remained, sectioning off part of the atrium where blood stained the intricately-detailed carpeting.

After ensuring Clouse had a realistic chance of finding the list he took so much risk in stealing, Stephen felt better. He knew his position within the Coven was now endangered, even to the point that Jacob might order him dead.

Luckily Stephen kept one step ahead of the group and its leader.

If not for his foresight in taking Clouse's keys from the boat before it completely sank, Stephen never would have gained access to the hotel. It was one place Jacob could not follow because of security and a lack of entry. Stephen entered and immediately locked the doors behind him.

Stephen participated in the attempted murder of Kaiser, though he foiled it in the end. Up to that point he felt his trust in the group was earned because he was the shorter of the two men Niemeyer encountered, and ultimately the one who knocked the county officer cold. This allowed them to transport him to the vacant hotel where he spied Jacob coldly toting Cranor's body out of the building.

He felt positive someone ratted on him for lingering behind, which would probably lead Jacob to ultimately discover a traitor in his camp. It showed in his cold eyes.

Unsure of where the guard wandered off to, Stephen left the atrium as quietly as possible, glad the carpeting replaced the old tile floor. Footsteps, like any sound made in the open area, echoed throughout the six story dome and served to alert anyone around. At least his footsteps would go unheard.

Soon after joining the Coven, Stephen realized what a terrible error he'd made in deciphering their motives. What he thought was a relatively dark religious sect turned out to be a group with a much deeper, darker purpose than he ever imagined. Rebelling against the common practices of society was one thing, murdering a slew of people in the remembrance of one slain long ago was another.

Cautiously looking for the guard as he exited the atrium, Stephen made his way down the hallway toward the exits, looking to see if the man might be positioned in the lobby window where he could view most of the grounds. Occasionally the guards did rounds, which this one seemed to be, based on his absence.

Stephen breathed a sigh of relief, seeing a clear path out. He walked past several rooms on the way. One of the last was Paul Clouse's office, where Cranor was killed. It was the one murder he was unable to prevent because it was planned in such a way that Stephen had no access. Jacob carried out the murder himself, taking the body directly to Cranor's residence, where he claimed he would search for something "necessary to the cause."

A flicker of light from beneath the office door caught Stephen's attention. Like a moth he was drawn to the odd, orange flicker. Clouse's keys included a master key which opened any door in the hotel, but the door was already unlocked when Stephen tried it.

When the door swung in, Stephen was shocked by an eerie jack-o-lantern set atop Cranor's desk, not because it was out of season, but because it meant death for anyone who saw it.

He knew the Coven's calling card all too well.

Beside the jack-o-lantern came flickering shadows along the walls, looking like black specters prepared to grab Stephen at any moment.

"So nice of you to join me," Jacob's voice whispered as he clasped Stephen's mouth, holding him completely still by threat of breaking his neck from behind, following a brief struggle. "I have quite a little surprise in store for you."

Stephen objected through muffled cries.

"Believe me, Stephen, your treachery hasn't gone unnoticed. You aren't the only one who acquired keys to this place."

Held helplessly still by Jacob, Stephen could barely resist as his taller, stronger captor pried his mouth open, using a dropper to place several drops of clear liquid on Stephen's tongue. Held a moment longer until the drug's effects began to kick in, Stephen quit resisting, feeling quite a bit more relaxed. Jacob let him go, where he soon fell to the floor, seating himself against the wall in an almost fetal position.

Stephen knew the calm before the storm had set in. Soon his mental journey would take a winding road, because he knew what was happening to him through Jacob's previous threats. The potent brew of modified LSD was already sending Stephen down a road of madness, allowing Jacob to be the driver.

As Stephen began to shake and shiver, his twitches indicated he would soon be seeing things no one else could. His eyes began to take in everything around him, factual or not. The real world called it a bad trip, and it set in rather quickly.

"What's the matter, Stephen?" Jacob asked, kneeling down beside him.

Even in such close proximity Jacob's form was obscured by shadows. Stephen always wondered exactly who he was. Where did he fit into normal society, and as whom?

"I see bugs everywhere," the apprentice answered nervously, seeing them everywhere above him. On the ceiling, on the walls, around the jack-o-lantern on the desk.

"There's one," Jacob said, pointing to Stephen's arm.

"Ah! Get it off me!" Stephen cried.

"One just crawled inside your neck," Jacob said with remarkable calm, pointing toward Stephen's face.

"No!" Stephen defied, clawing at his cheeks and neck intensely, drawing blood.

"You'll never get them that way," Jacob informed him. "Dig harder. Deeper."

Stephen did so, madly drawing more blood, feeling nothing as he tore strips of skin and blood from his face. Beneath his fingernails the tissue balled up, making them useless as scraping or digging tools. His progress slowed when he saw bugs crawl up his arms, into his open wounds, stopping to feed in swarms at the blood from the gashes. He heard incessant bug chatter as they gnawed his flesh away.

"No," he moaned, rather than fight his imaginary enemy.

Fantasy and reality meshed into one setting for Stephen. Spying open cuts on his arms, Stephen saw puss ooze from air pockets. Like boiling spaghetti sauce atop a stove they rose, then burst, spilling a mix of soupy red and yellow. After each rupture Stephen saw the tip of a fly larva surface for air, then disappear beneath his skin again.

"Maggot," Stephen whispered to himself, wide-eyed, positive he felt the wiggles under his flesh. Disgusted and frightened, the thought of such creatures festering within his body overwhelmed him. Like a child he moaned and sobbed, rocking back and forth. Now he was afraid to touch or reach for anything.

"What's the matter, Stephen?" Jacob asked, feigning sympathy. "You're not digging deep enough to stop them, are you?"

After opening a thick blanket beside Stephen, Jacob placed latex gloves over his hands, snapping them into place. He turned to pull a hammer with a jagged ripping claw out from behind him.

"Let's dig together, shall we?"

16

Returning to the hotel was not how Clouse planned to begin his day, but a call from Dr. Smith and his new quest of finding who purchased or took pieces of the atrium's old tile floor forced the issue.

Using his spare key to the hotel's main entrance, Clouse let himself in. Considering the hotel was like his second house it seemed fitting he kept a spare.

While waiting for Smith to arrive, Clouse opened Cranor's office, finding everything in order. He then walked into his own office, not wanting to touch anything, pending McCabe's search for evidence, but seeking any advance notice of foul play. The detective would want to check both rooms over, so Clouse touched nothing in either.

A distinct smell of candle wax entered his nostrils when he walked in. Clouse took a moment to sniff the air, certain of the odor. He wandered into the room, seeing no sign of candle activity or anything out of place.

Remembering what McCabe told him of the visit to the hotel, and knowing how Cranor died, Clouse panned the ceiling for something solid enough to support a man's weight while he dangled, struggling for life. The visual picture of his friend dying disturbed him, but he contained his emotion, even after seeing the solid gas line above and several areas of chafed paint where friction burns had occurred.

"Knew it," he said to himself, climbing a chair for a better look. He planned to report his find to Daniels or McCabe.

Climbing down from the chair, he heard his boot clop against the floor, then nearly trip him up as its smooth leather sole slid a bit from something on the floor. Usually ice or any liquid similar to water gave his boots poor traction. It just so happened blood did the same thing.

"What?" he asked himself, kneeling down to scoop a few droplets of blood onto his forefingers, examining the substance closely.

Only several spots remained along the floor, seemingly fresh. Such small drops certainly should have dried, had they been Cranor's. Clouse could only wonder what events had transpired at the hotel during his absence, because nothing else in the room gave him any clues.

Deciding to leave the room alone, he stood and walked out the door, bumping into someone as he closed it.

"Dr. Smith," he said, regaining his composure after the initial scare.

"Paul. Nice to see you're in good health," the man his grandfather's age replied.

Smith made his fortune early, making his net worth in the billions according to many locals, supported by several magazines focused on the nation's wealthiest people. To Clouse he seemed normal, like any other local business owner the fireman knew. He put so much finance and effort into the hotel's reconstruction that it couldn't help but succeed.

Success had a price, however, as the efforts and events from the past year surrounding the first batch of murders took a toll on the doctor's health. Once as healthy as men Clouse's age, the doctor now looked much older, even decrepit to some. His walk seemed more hunched, and he brought a staff with him to aid him when his back failed.

"I'm doing fine," Clouse replied to the comment about his health. "Yourself?"

Smith simply nodded an affirmative, his dark gray hair set upon a face drawn inward from worsened health. He appeared in good spirits, but physically the doctor seemed on a downward spiral compared to the man Clouse had met a few years prior.

Clouse knew another major episode at the man's favorite land-mark would probably do irreparable damage. Smith had considered selling the property during the tumultuous period the year before.

"Is it happening again?" he asked Clouse.

"It may be," the firefighter answered. "But this time I've got some clues and I need your help, Doc."

"How can I help?" the doctor asked, walking toward the atrium where sounds of work emanated. They walked to the door then stopped, watching several workers remove the carpet from the floor and thoroughly clean the statue where Kaiser had been placed. "How is your friend?"

"He still hasn't regained consciousness," Clouse answered. "The doctors fear the worst."

He hesitated a moment, seeing Daniels make it through the front door with heavy use of crutches. Clouse was amazed his friend left his chair behind at all, so soon after regaining use of his legs.

"You were saying?" Smith asked.

"I need to know who acquired the old tiles from the atrium floor," Clouse answered as Daniels slowly made his way up, depending heavily on his right leg over the left. "Is there any record of who purchased the tiles?"

"Somewhat," Smith answered. "We had a ceremony several years back where many of the tiles were sold. Most everyone who attended put their name on a list, whether they purchased or not. Many put addresses and phone numbers down for contact purposes."

"Who has that list?"

Smith's eyes rolled as he tried to recall.

"You might check with Joan Landamere," the doctor answered. "I think she was in charge of most of the hotel's fund-raising back then."

Clouse felt a chill run through him, hearing that name, and Daniels' face seemed to take an apprehensive expression. Though she was as much a victim as they were the year before, they dreaded the idea of having to speak with her again. Daniels knew her better, after interviewing her several times in his investigation of the first series of murders.

"That's all you," Clouse said, passing the buck.

"Thanks," Daniels said with no sincerity. "Impressed?" he asked, looking down at his crutches.

"Walking involves both feet, Mark. You might try using the left one too."

"I'm working on it. Dr. Jameson said I was lucky to even think about using these so soon, but Cindy's kept my legs in great shape."

"Have you felt any cramps yet?" Smith asked, apparently familiar with how difficult walking after a layoff was from his years of experience in medicine.

"Oh, yes," Daniels said emphatically. "I still use the chair around the house."

He looked up to the second floor momentarily, as though reflecting on the tragic events from the year before.

"If you'll excuse me, I've got something upstairs to look at."

"Careful, Gimpy," Clouse playfully warned, catching a disapproving shake of the head in return. "He's loosened up around me," Clouse informed Smith, "but the guy's too serious all the time. It's not healthy."

Smith grinned.

"I know a certain firefighter under my employment who once acted much the same."

Clouse smirked, shaking his head. He did not feel he had ever acted quite so seriously on a regular basis.

"Another one of those reporters called me this week wanting exclusive rights to an official account of the events here last year," the doctor said. "I told him where to stick his exclusive."

"I know. They call me almost every week too. It'll get worse once they find out what's going on now."

Everywhere, unofficial books lined the shelves, attempting to tell the story of the West Baden Murders the year before. Most times events were completely wrong or characters were misrepresented. One account made Clouse's character sound like the fugitive from the television series, running to prove his innocence. Another placed Daniels as a determined Hispanic detective, fighting to gain the respect of his white counterparts while solving a case with their jealous eyes watching.

Neither account had any merit.

Names were always changed, and the facts completely misleading, but the newspapers provided so much public information that the books were usually correct in part, with some creative writing used to spice up the characters and details.

Only a few people knew the entire truth, but they weren't talking.

"So how are you holding up these days, Doc?" Clouse asked as they walked away from the atrium entrance.

"I'm doing fine," Smith answered. "Rusty's death leaves me at a complete loss. It just seems everyone I've cared about since this project started has either betrayed me or died in the process."

"I know the feeling," Clouse said. "I promise you I will find out who's behind this before anyone else gets hurt or the hotel's reputation gets tarnished."

"You may be too late for that. You and I are all that's left of the people who care about this place."

Clouse shook his head.

"There are others. You'd be amazed at the community spirit toward this building."

"But they didn't put it back together," Smith noted. "You and I did. Rusty and David did too, but they're gone." He lost himself in thought a moment. "But if finding who bought those tile pieces can help you, talk to Joan Landamere about some of those fund-raiser events and she will probably have some sort of list for you."

List.

Again, the word haunted Clouse. Such a simple word, used by so many people in so many ways. Quickly the word became synonymous with death.

"I'll have Mark check into it," Clouse said. "Somehow we'll figure out who's behind this."

*   *   *

Daniels felt compelled to check the Rexford murder room once more. It amazed him how close the hotel came to opening again, only to have more trouble stirred up. Being inside the building conjured bad memories for him, but he was on his feet again, and able to get around.

Sort of.

Riding the elevator to the second floor, Daniels heard a ding as the doors opened, letting him crutch his way out. For a moment he simply stared down the hallway, which was lit with lights mounted along the walls. Unlike ordinary hotels, the West Baden Springs Hotel was circular in design, so he could only see until the hallway curved in either direction.

Decorative carpet lined the floors, matching the gold and forest green decor throughout the atrium. Mostly consisting of leaves and plant life, the designs on the carpet were enchanting, keeping a person's eyes on them instead of the freshly painted walls or decorative doorways.

As he ambled toward the room Daniels rounded a hallway, seeing a glimpse of a dark flash ahead of him, like someone streaking across the hall.

Saying nothing, the officer ignored the room for the time being, staying close to the wall as he struggled toward the area where the person appeared. A perplexed look came across his face when he rounded the next bend, finding nothing. Hearing something behind him from one of the rooms he'd already passed, Daniels whirled around, nearly losing his balance as his crutches fumbled against the floor.

Someone streaked down the hall the other way.

"Paul?" Daniels called. "You know better than to fuck with me."

Clouse did know better, leading Daniels to think he was alone on the second floor with someone far less friendly.

Even so, the former detective was between two elevators, neither much closer than the other. Despite an eerie feeling someone was on the second floor with him, he decided to check the murder room anyway, because he was in no condition for a quick escape.

Daniels started back toward the murder room, feeling his muscles tense, and his breathing become heavier. He was almost a dozen rooms away from the closest elevator and stairs simply were not an option. The stairs were the only open area where sound might travel to the first floor. Even so, the hotel's vast interior would probably serve to prevent anyone from hearing the officer if he tried calling for help.

Reaching the open door of the Rexford murder room, Daniels slowly peeked inside, wondering where the streak had ended up. Leaning against the doorway, Daniels carefully peered inside the room, hearing another door fling open.

Across the hall.

Barely ducking a scythe planted in the wall where his head had been, with the sound of an ax splitting wood, Daniels fell to the floor. He lost one crutch, clinging to the other for dear life. He looked up, wide-eyed, at his attacker. Dressed in a robe befitting the grim reaper, no face was visible, nor any features. It was the same disguise used the year prior in the West Baden Murders.

Without ample means to defend himself, Daniels desperately crawled toward the elevator, boot camp style. He gained several feet, crawling without use of his legs, before the killer pried the weapon from the wall, giving chase.

Hearing footsteps behind him, Daniels instinctively rolled to one side. The scythe sliced through the new carpet like a knife through butter, sticking once again. Rolling to one side, Daniels swung the crutch with what force he could muster, striking the person's knee. As the killer clasped his injured knee, collapsing to the floor, Daniels started toward the elevator once more.

Without his footing the officer crawled at what felt like a snail's pace toward the elevator, which seemed to grow no closer. Adrenaline kept him from feeling the skin rubbed nearly raw on his elbows as they swung forward, one after another, moving him along. He failed to hear the killer resume the chase until he neared his escape route.

Knowing he would not make it, Daniels used the crutch to punch at the down button on the elevator, but missed. He quickly glanced, seeing the killer slowly rise from the floor, still clasping his knee, but having the presence of mind to retrieve the scythe, yanking it from the floor.

"Shit," Daniels muttered to himself, using the crutch to punch at the down button again.

Once more, it missed.

Now the killer was shaking his knee, trying to lessen the pain. He obviously felt confident Daniels was not going to escape, or perhaps he was playing a cat and mouse game.

Nervous, but steady enough to try once again, Daniels wriggled himself a bit closer to the elevator and held the crutch firm, finally punching the down button. He then crawled into a small waiting area, just to the right of the elevator doors. He hoped it might offer shelter or something else to defend himself with.

Wrong on both counts.

"Damn," Daniels said, realizing the killer was directly behind him as he reached a three-foot jut in the hall where a large glass window provided a view of the atrium for guests while they waited for the elevator to arrive.

It served as a tiny lobby area of sorts, because there was extra room available when a suite was converted into the elevator shaft on each floor.

Crawling as far in as he could, Daniels flipped over to his backside just as the killer reached the end of the hallway, holding the scythe. With nowhere to run or hide, Daniels used his hands to crab-walk back to the glass, leaving his crutch out of range. There was simply nothing to do except watch as the killer raised the weapon over his head, delaying a few seconds before letting it fly.

17

Daniels cringed as the weapon made its way downward. Using both hands, he pulled his head forward of the blade's intended target. He was shocked to hear a crunching sound, thankful the blade embedded itself in something other than his head. The noise likely caught the attention of Clouse, below in the atrium.

The glass cobwebbed where the scythe landed in its center, just above the former detective's head. Beyond the obscured surface, Clouse spied the reaper imposter looming above Daniels.

"No!" Daniels heard Clouse exclaim from below, virtually assuring him help was on the way.

Shocked he was still alive, Daniels lunged forward for his crutch, thankful the killer failed to hit another mark. As he snagged the crutch, the elevator dinged, indicating it was ready for him. While the killer tried freeing the weapon from the glass, Daniels used the crutch's wide end as a battering ram, striking his attacker squarely in the testicles. While the man hunched over and fell back, Daniels seized the opportunity, crawling toward the elevator.

He quickly found himself inside its serene confines as the doors began to shut. A hand jutted through, preventing their closure as the killer pried them open, now wielding a double-edged knife in his other hand, ready to end the officer's life one way or another.

Daniels forced himself back, quickly raising the crutch, striking the killer's jaw as he did so, clearing the elevator. As the doors closed, Daniels breathed a sigh of relief, unable to imagine who wanted him dead, or why. One thing appeared certain.

Last year was repeating itself.

When the elevator reached the first floor, the door opened, revealing someone racing down the stairs nearby. Tensing in fear, Daniels drew the crutch close, unsure of how many more attacks he could withstand.

"Mark," Clouse said, revealing himself from behind the stairwell. "What the hell happened?"

"He came after me," Daniels said between labored breaths, trembling as his friend helped him to his feet. "I think that was our killer."

"Let me get your crutch," Clouse said, starting for the stairs.

"Don't," Daniels said quickly. "Don't go alone."

Clouse thought a moment, then decided to take the elevator with Daniels.

"I didn't see anyone up there," Clouse said on the way up. "Where was he when you last saw him?"

"I don't know. I hit him, then he fell back. I don't know where he went."

Clouse looked discouraged, being so close to nabbing the killer, and angered that the person dared assault Daniels, just a day after the man regained use of his legs.

"How are the legs?" he asked, his hands clenched in fists from his obvious fury.

"Fine," Daniels said, using Clouse almost entirely for support. "They can't hold me up yet."

"I know it's against protocol, but you might want to keep your piece with you," Clouse warned as the doors opened.

"I plan to," Daniels replied. "Believe me."

*   *   *

"What do we have?" McCabe asked a local officer as he side-stepped down the hill toward the cordoned crime scene.

He had already completed an inspection and analysis of the roadside area.

Every track and footprint was now collectively placed in police evidence through photography.

All morning clouds had hovered overhead, threatening precipitation, adding to the gloomy feeling inside the state trooper's gut when he received the call.

McCabe planned to spend his morning investigating Cranor's death, combing through the man's office at the hotel. Things grew more eerie when a call came over his radio pertaining to a body found outside the Paoli town limits, less than half an hour's drive from the hotel.

"Hard to tell what happened," the officer said, staring down at a lump rolled inside a dark blanket. "Found this guy nude inside the blanket. Coroner's office already pronounced him. Ugly marks all over his arms, and there's basically no face left."

"Any ID?"

"Nothing whatsoever. A number of teeth are knocked out too."

"A bitch to identify him," McCabe commented, pulling latex gloves over each of his hands. "Anything else?" the detective asked, taking the final few steps toward the body, ready to examine it himself.

"A strip of his skin was removed from one arm."

McCabe lifted the blanket, partly spattered with blood, to reveal the skull containing a misty red core in some areas, tatters of skin and fleshy tissue in others. Everything appeared moist, telling him the murder was recent. Parts of the organic material looked like meat chunks from the deli, ready to be plucked off and bagged.

One eye remained, loosely embedded in a chunk of tissue, looking blankly forward at the detective, sending an uneasy feeling through him. The other hung halfway down the cheek, attached only by a few veins protruding from the eye socket. He noticed something was used to pry the man's face to the bone in some areas. It looked like a boulder randomly picked by climbers, but he assumed otherwise.

Both eyes seemed placed where they were on purpose. The face was apparently carved to give the most disturbing appearance possible. It seemed like a piece of artwork, perhaps even a message. Mafia families were known for such things.

"I'd say more than a strip was removed," he added, looking at the claw marks, apparently from fingernails, along each arm.

"Flip it over," the officer said, speaking of the left arm.

McCabe did so, finding a perfectly rectangular bloody patch along the arm where the skin had been surgically removed, probably to hide some tattoo or distinguishing mark. He decided to fetch his photography equipment and radio for some forensics experts, suspecting more than a random homicide or robbery coverup was amuck. With so little to go on, he could ill afford to miss any shred of evidence.

"Who found the body?" he asked the officer.

"Farmer came down here to repair some fence and found this instead."

"He still here?"

"No, but we interviewed him and took his information. Said he'd be home all day. We're checking with neighbors next."

"Good," McCabe said before turning to the body with a thoughtful gaze.

"What's wrong?"

"Nothing," the detective replied, thinking it too coincidental that a person turned up dead with so many identifying marks ripped away. In the wake of the other murders it didn't seem to fit, but each contained entirely separate clues to begin with. "I need the area sealed off from the road to the body and twenty feet every direction around it," he instructed the officer, since no official crime scene information was apparent.

"Okay, detective," the officer said, ready to rally several of his buddies to assist him.

Accustomed to taking charge, McCabe rather enjoyed being the only state detective in the area. It kept him busy, but also gave him a sense of purpose and phenomenal opportunity to grow in his profession.

It also frustrated him knowing how the system worked. As fast and accurately as he was able to perform his job, forensics and the brass above him often slowed the process. It often took months to a year for lab results to make their way back to him. Sure, there were alternatives like the university for lab work, or friends in the right places who might occasionally move things along, but McCabe's uses for them came few and far between.

He looked around the body, thumbing through the blanket for anything that stood out. McCabe found nothing in the blanket but dust and several hairs forensic scientists would waste their time pondering over without a suspect to match them to.

"Shit," he muttered, checking the victim's genital area for any signs of sexual activity including semen or marks, carefully shield- ing the body's area from the hoard of reporters above, in case they lacked a sense of decency.

Finding nothing, McCabe discovered the murder had something in common with the others after all.

It appeared unsolvable.

*   *   *

Seated at a local cafe, two men desperately tried to piece together the numerous leads that might inevitably help them save several lives, including their own.

"Are you sure you want to do this?" Clouse asked Daniels, con- cerned for his friend so soon after a near-death experience.

"Positive," the answer came immediately. "I want to find out who that was and chase him around with a weapon," Daniels added with a quiver in his voice that came from a controlled anger. "So who are our suspects and their motives?" he asked while Clouse tapped a pencil against the pad of paper he took from his truck.

"There's always revenge," Clouse said. "They've gone after me, Ken, Rusty, and now you. It's like unfinished business from last year."

"Motive, but who falls in that list of suspects?"

"Any of Angie's family," Clouse said, speaking of his first wife. "I haven't really spoken with any of them since her death and they never seemed to believe in my innocence last year."

"Who else?" Daniels pushed.

"I don't know."

"Who else is around you?"

"Jane, you, Ken, Dr. Smith, people from work sometimes. I don't think anyone around me would do this."

Daniels grimaced.

"That's what you thought last year. What about your pal Tim?"

"Tim? He'd never do something like that. We grew up together. He goes to church picnics, takes his family to Disneyland, works close to home."

"He was carrying a shotgun."

"Yeah, but-"

"And doesn't he work construction?"

"Damn it, Mark. He doesn't have it in him. I'm sure you're going to think it was all just a bit too coincidental that he was with Ken when he got abducted by those freaks, and all he got was a bump upside the head, but he's no killer. Speaking of which, you're not paying much attention to the possible occult aspect. What about the guy who approached me with information?"

Daniels showed his indifference about the subject by looking away momentarily.

"It may be bullshit, Paul. A Coven? Stephen? Jacob? You're throwing these names at me because they're what he said. There's no proof of occult involvement in this."

"And there's none to the contrary."

Clouse put his hands up defensively.

"All right, back to your revenge theory. What if it's someone seeking retribution for a slain relative last year?"

"Rusty Cranor's daughter was murdered," Daniels thought aloud. "So was her boyfriend. The list just goes on. You've got a point, but that's a lot of people to check out."

"I know," Clouse said. "I also want to know how these tile floor pieces tie into everything. There has to be a reason they're so important. You know what Dr. Smith said about that."

"Yeah," the officer said reluctantly. "It means I get to talk to Mrs. Landamere."

"The sooner the better," Clouse added, jotting down several more ideas for leads on the notepad. "We're running out of time."

"What do you mean?" Daniels asked after a sip of coffee.

"Have you thought about what holiday we're coming up to?"

Daniels drifted off in thought a moment of the things brought by the fall season, taking a quick look outside. Dead leaves, bare lawns, chilly breezes, and cloudy skies. They culminated for the perfect witching season.

"Halloween," he answered, realizing how significant it was the year before.

If the possibility of occult participation proved true, it became all the more important to stop the killer from striking again, especially with such a critical date impending.

"Let's go talk to Mrs. Landamere," Daniels said, reaching for his crutches.

18

Clouse phoned Jane to have her pick Zach up from school again, knowing he would not be home until after dark. He wished things could be normal again. Picking his son up from school ordinarily seemed mundane, but now it felt rather dear to him as his friends died around him or remained steadily unconscious in hospital beds.

Daniels seemed disappointed not to hear from McCabe all day, but both he and Clouse had come to realize it was up to them, and them alone, to find the killer's identity before they joined the list of casualties.

"How do you do it?" Daniels asked from the passenger seat as they neared Joan Landamere's house, which sat in the midst of abundant nature.

"Do what?"

"Go on with everyday life knowing someone is out there wanting you or everyone around you dead?"

"You're sounding abstract, you know? It's not like your situation is any different."

Daniels gave no reply.

"Truthfully, I worry more about those around me than I do myself. People can't go on living any sense of normal life thinking every corner might reveal a serial killer. I'm a big boy, Mark. I take care of myself and worry more about others."

Silence for a moment.

"Did you cry when Angie died last year?"

Clouse exhaled a sigh, letting the disturbing nature of the question show. It was out of character for Daniels to inquire about Clouse's personal life, even as good of friends as they had become. Perhaps the idea of their own mortality weighed heavily on each of them.

"Why are you asking that?"

"It's just that everyone had you made out to be some greedy son-of-a-bitch able to kill his own wife for the benefit of a life insurance policy. I want to know how the real Paul Clouse reacted behind closed doors."

Clouse nodded. Daniels' forward nature surprised him, but he felt comfortable enough to give an answer.

"All right. I cried myself to sleep that night, Mark. After you and your partner hounded me for answers that I couldn't give, I put my boy to bed and I cried my ass off. Are you happy?"

Daniels glanced over just a second, then returned his eyes to the road.

"While we're clearing the air, I'm going to ask you something, buddy," Clouse said.

"Fire away."

"You spent a year in that wheelchair. Unable to walk, couldn't go out with the wife and kids, couldn't recover your life the way I did. All this because you were the only one with guts enough to believe me and search for the truth. Do you blame me for what happened?"

Daniels thought a moment. The question apparently hit equally as hard as any he threw at Clouse.

"No, I don't blame you," Daniels answered slowly, as though not entirely sure of himself. "I don't regret sticking up for you, taking a bullet in the back, or missing a year's worth of work, or even putting a bullet in Dave Landamere's head. The only thing I regret is putting myself in such a lonely spot for so long."

"What do you mean?"

"I fell into a trap of self-pity and shut out everything important to me."

Both reflected on the answers for a moment.

"Feel better?" Clouse asked, pulling into the appropriate driveway.

"Not really."

"Me neither."

Both remained silent as the house came into view beyond a large iron gate.

"You know, I stopped taking my medication," Daniels revealed, as though Clouse was the only person he might confide in.

"Why?"

"I feel better without it. Don't tell Cindy or she'll flip, but I don't feel as tired and groggy now that I'm off it."

"Then don't take it," Clouse agreed.

As dusk overtook the gorgeous property, encumbered by rare shrubs and statues, the two men approached the door. Daniels hesitated before knocking, but gave three quick raps. Both knew they were being viewed through the peep hole in the door momentarily, then several deadbolts unlocked and the electronic beeps of a security system being deactivated were audible from their position.

"Mrs. Landamere," Daniels said, viewing the older woman from head to toe as Clouse did the same.

Conservative, short gray hair took nothing away from an unusually youthful figure. Dressed in a light blouse with dark slacks and off-white tennis shoes that worked perfectly for casual dress, a flood of yellow light emitted by the numerous ornate lamps almost silhouetted her in the doorway. In her right hand she cupped a short glass filled with what appeared to be a strong alcoholic beverage.

"Detective," she said, recognizing Daniels instantly, despite the crutches supporting him. "Do come in."

Daniels seemed a bit uncomfortable as he followed Clouse inside.

Clouse recalled Daniels telling him stories about how Joan flirted with him briefly the year before, despite being his mother's age. The former detective apparently hoped to avoid such conversation again, trying to keep his eyes strictly to himself.

"Have a seat," she said, inviting them into the living room, waving them toward any number of couches or love seats. "How may I help you two?"

"It's started again, Mrs. Landamere," Daniels said after settling into a couch, placing the crutches beside him.

"I heard," she said, slumping herself into a chair across from both of them, taking a long, stiff drink from the glass. "I prayed it wasn't true. I hoped and prayed."

"Mrs. Landamere," Daniels said. "I know this may be difficult, but we need to ask about a list that might help us stop the killer before he strikes again."

"Before you ask me to help you on this, detective, I want to explain to you exactly what the last year of my life has been like," she said matter-of-factly, much like Bette Davis might have in any number of her movies. "You both think you know what David put me through, but I've never told anyone, including the press, including the police, exactly what happened to me that day."

Daniels nodded, then sat back, making himself comfortable for the tale both men genuinely wanted to hear.

"The day everything happened, David already had Detective Daniels safely tucked in the hotel," she began, looking to Clouse. "David comes home acting as cheerful as he can be, considering he missed two weeks of work, giving me only a phone call between visits."

She shifted uneasily in her seat before continuing.

"Well, I think little of it until he says he wants to check on the hotel's condition in his absence. He wants me to go with him," she said, the glass in her hand trembling slightly. The words came uneasily and she paused before restarting her story.

"Naturally I'm a bit reluctant because he never asks me to go with him on business, and everyone there knew we were a marriage of convenience. It was no secret, and I was wondering exactly what he was up to."

She took another drink from the glass, taking time to refill it at the nearby bar.

"Care for any?" she asked her guests, both refusing with hand signals.

After settling back into her chair she prepared to continue.

"This is my strength now," she said of the drink in her hand. "Every day I live with a security system on, every night with the front gates locked. I knew it wouldn't stop with David's death."

"Why did you go with him?" Daniels asked, prompting her to return to the narrative.

"I was concerned for my safety if I didn't," she said. "After all, he made the money and left me to the life I always wanted, surrounded by the garden and tranquility I loved. Though he never said it, the ability was his to remove it all in a heartbeat. Something about his eyes let me know there would be consequences if I did not go. Or he would force me to go anyway."

"Was Roger there?" Clouse asked of Landamere's accomplice.

Roger Summers was Clouse's brother-in-law, and a fellow firefighter, who attempted to frame him for the murders.

"He didn't show up until later," Joan answered. "It was when we reached the hotel and everyone was gone that he set up the final scenario. He dragged Detective Daniels out from the back," she noted, causing Daniels to uncomfortably look anywhere except toward the two other people in the room, remembering how helpless he was for two days at the hands of Landamere, bound and gagged in a secluded room.

"The two took great pleasure in tying me up to the post, then gagged me," Joan continued. "David then told me everything he planned to do, including how he planned to kill me and pin everything on you, Mr. Clouse. Until you arrived, I was the subject of taunts and revelations even the devil might cower at," she noted, closing her eyes to block the emotion.

"At that point I realized they were both insane, and almost nothing would stop their plan. They had it worked out in such detail that I questioned how anyone would ever believe otherwise, once all three of us were dead." She quietly trembled for a moment. "I truly believed none of us were going to make it out of there alive."

"Inadvertently we all contributed to their scheme," Clouse said. "We all survived a horrible ordeal."

"What I'm about to say is the part I've never told anyone else," Joan said, putting the glass down on a small table beside her.

Both Clouse and Daniels leaned forward in anticipation.

"When David spoke of contributors to his potential purchase of the hotel, I think he spoke of some very powerful businessmen."

"I thought he was talking about investors or stock holders," Clouse said.

"No," Joan said. "A different sort of power."

"Are you speaking of mafia involvement?" Daniels questioned.

"Perhaps. He told me they were people who could get things done. That's what he said."

Daniels and Clouse locked eyes for a moment, knowing what sorts of things were getting done by the mysterious presence.

All three sat silently a moment more.

"We came to see if you might have a list," Clouse said. "A list of people who might have purchased pieces of the old tile floor, or even names and addresses of hotel visitors. People who toured and bought at the souvenir shop. Anything."

Joan held up a finger, stood, and walked into the parlor. Clouse and Daniels exchanged looks again as she shuffled through a desk drawer.

"This should help," she said, returning with a worn notebook, several of its pages clinging to life inside the wire binding.

"What is it?" Clouse asked.

"Several years ago we sold the pieces during an auction at a hotel gathering. It was before you started work with Kieffer Construction, Mr. Clouse. I hope it helps with whatever you're looking for," she said with a look of empathy, and a certain emptiness in her eyes they both related to.

"It will," Clouse said. "Could anyone else have seen this list?"

"David would have had access to it," she said, all three outwardly realizing the dire consequences of Landamere's access. "The previous secretary had that notebook, but of course she passed away. Poor thing was eighty-five."

"You've been a great help," Daniels said, balancing himself to his feet with the crutches. "Be careful, Mrs. Landamere," he added, giving her one of his old cards. "If you need anything, just call me."

"I will, detective. And I'll be sure to watch the news. With any luck at all, I'll see you apprehending the killer, instead of more senseless killings. Why that one this morning was the worst yet."

"What?" Clouse asked, looking from her to Daniels, who seemed equally clueless about the homicide.

"The young man they found outside of Paoli. The news man said his face and arms were nearly torn off."

Clouse and Daniels quickly said departing words, ready to contact McCabe and discover just what they had missed.

*   *   *

While waiting for Clouse's return, Jane sat down with a magazine after unpacking more of their belongings. After a day at the clinic, and organizing the house, she felt drained. She worried about her fiancé and everything happening around him. They met soon after his wife had died the past year, and though they did not court for some time after that, she felt close to him during the ordeal the first time through.

She heard sounds of laughter behind her from the back yard as the kids played during the last few minutes of sunlight. Soon she would put them to bed with the hope that Clouse might be home in time to read them a bedtime story. Beside her, a fire roared to life in the fireplace, countering the cold drafts their large house allowed to roam throughout its two stories.

Feeling a slight chill run through her, Jane found herself in the mood for some hot chicken soup. She walked to the kitchen, taking a few minutes to open the can and heat it on the stove top. Placing the burner on a simmering temperature, she decided to call the kids inside.

Before she reached the front door, a disturbance came from the back bedroom in the form of the stereo she had unpacked and set up just a few hours before. Sounding like one of the hard rock songs

Clouse often listened to, Jane found it difficult to tell whether it was a CD or the radio kicking on, because the stereo system's volume was so high.

She did not recall placing any compact discs in the stereo or turning it on. Whether or not she even plugged the device in was in question. Still, she made her way back to the room, wincing from the deafening tones as she turned the volume control down, then turned the stereo off completely, looking around for what might have turned it on.

From the back bedroom, one hallway led back to the kitchen while the adjacent hallway led to a bathroom, then the family room. She decided not to search that hallway.

A bit nervous, she turned all the lights on as she walked toward the kitchen. A door creaked open, causing her to rush her pace.

"Paul?" she called, reaching the kitchen, realizing the front door was closed. "Damn," she said, turning off the stove as the soup bubbled.

Turning her attention to the family room, Jane knew the creaking door had to be the house's side exit. Slowly, she stepped toward the doorway to the family room where the fire could not curtail the draft pushing through to the kitchen. Her fear was realized when she saw the door swung open from the edge of the room, feeling almost positive someone else was in the house.

Or at least had been.

Without turning her attention from the family room, she stepped back. Her destination, the front door, seemed several nervous breaths away as she frantically looked around her, feeding into the paranoia Clouse was all too familiar with. Never again would Jane doubt anything he said about creepy experiences.

Kids, she suddenly thought, oblivious the past few moments to any sounds around her except those of creaking doors. Her eyes focused on the family room and the open door, swinging lightly with the breeze from outside, thumping against the wall.

Reaching behind her for the doorknob, Jane refused to wait any longer. She turned to open it as a hand clasped her own.

She shrieked until realizing her potential attacker was her future stepson. Jane cupped her mouth to both apologize and muffle her fear as she collected herself.

"Zach, where is Katie?" she asked, still trembling.

"She's outside. We saw the side door open."

"Katie!" she called. "Come here, sweetie!"

Little Katie came running through the same side door Zach had, taking the long way around the winding hallway where the back bedroom was. If someone had turned on the stereo in the bedroom, he could have easily slipped around the back hallway and exited through the side door before Jane realized it. The blaring music distracted her long enough to keep her from finding the person, and scared her enough to keep the kids close.

She intended to keep Clouse much closer too. Someone violated her life and her house, and Jane would be damned if she let it happen again.

Taking up a knife from the nearest kitchen drawer, Jane walked into the family room, closing the door. She looked around the room, then to the bedrooms and upstairs. The kids followed her every step, wondering what the commotion was about, and why she held the knife defensively as she climbed the darkened stairwell.

The light atop the staircase was burned out, and she had no intentions of searching a darkened hallway without protection. Clasping a flashlight atop the stairs, Jane quickly checked the rooms without getting too thorough, and breathed a sigh of relief.

Satisfied the house was clear of any intruders, Jane quickly made certain each door was locked, turning each one's deadbolt to assure top security until Clouse returned.

Starting the next day, she planned to make some lifestyle changes for the better.

19

Clouse spent the next morning on the computer, searching for any ties to the Coven or his secret helper. When he and Daniels parted ways, they photocopied the notebook so each would have a copy. Daniels vowed to meet with McCabe and discover more about the murder they heard about through Joan Landamere.

He had returned home to find Jane awake by the fireplace, too upset to sleep. They talked about how she thought someone might have been inside the house, despite Clouse thinking it was the kids all along. He refused to doubt her, because experience had taught him better. Raising the security around his family seemed the logical solution, and Jane said she wanted him around the house more, instead of seeking out the killer.

A feeling of responsibility toward potential victims, including his own family, pushed him forward in the investigation. He knew hesitation usually resulted in countless deaths and put himself and those around him at risk. Jane needed to understand why he and Daniels sought out the killer.

They had lived through it once before.

Clouse had already taken several steps in securing his family, including a call to a local electronic security firm. He planned to purchase a handgun and permit in town later that day. He would probably have to wait a week to take the gun home, but he would feel more secure.

Letting his dogs stay in the house provided another layer of protection. If he made Jane feel secure again, perhaps she would feel better about him hunting the killer.

As he sat before the computer monitor, the phone rang.

"Hello?"

"Paul, it's Mark."

"What's new?"

"McCabe told me the body was unidentified and they don't have a clue who it might be. Too many teeth and distinguishing marks are missing."

"Makes it tough, doesn't it?"

"Somewhat. You have time to do some legwork on this list of ours today?"

"It seems I've been grounded."

"How's that?"

Clouse quickly explained Jane's story from the night before.

"She wants me here all the time."

"Maybe I can talk to her for you."

"Not a good idea, Mark. I'm trying to heighten her sense of security so I can get out of here. We both know sitting around won't help a bit."

"You're right about that. I'm trying to cross-reference some of the names on this list with any crimes. If these people bought pieces of that tile floor, they may have been burglarized in the past couple years, or someone might have contacted them, wanting to purchase the pieces."

"Or they might have met with foul play," Clouse suggested.

"I'll find out soon enough. So, what have you been working on?"

"Playing on the Internet to see if I can trace this Coven or anything about it down. I go back to work tomorrow, so I'll see Tony Dierker. He's a computer whiz who can probably track down stuff I can't."

"He can't do any worse than we are."

"Let me know if you come up with anything on that list, Mark."

"I will. Tug might want you to look at that body later. He thinks it might be someone you know if it's related to the hotel."

"So you two are on first name basis, huh?"

"Jealous?"

"I'll get over it. Call me if you find anything."

"Will do," Daniels said before hanging up.

Clouse spent a few more minutes searching through related websites, relying on key words to guide him. With the computer calling up any listing of "coven" or any references to the occult, the firefighter looked at a potential of spending days tracking down any realistic lead.

"You've got mail," the computer voice of his server said.

"Thanks," Clouse said more to himself than the voice, clicking out of another worthless website to view his mail.

He saw the message from StephenCov was sent as a delayed message, received only at the current time specified. The message box read: "Valuable information."

Slightly apprehensive, Clouse clicked on the message.

Paul,

After our meeting the other day I realized Jacob had me figured out. I couldn't risk sending you something in the mail for fear he would intercept it. Even this could be intercepted, so I delayed it. Unfortunately the message I leave you is somewhat encrypted because I know you will figure it out before anyone else.

At this point I am probably dead, but I won't give you any hints about myself, the Coven, or their objectives because my family would be both horrified and ashamed at what I've done and affiliated myself with.

In closing, I give you the location of your list, though you will need to think a bit before understanding it.

Look in the place where the puzzle pieces most.

Best of luck,

Stephen

"What the hell?" Clouse asked after closing the message, certain to save it for the next day in case Dierker could help him track it down.

Granted, Stephen would not make it easy for authorities to track him, but Clouse wanted to know who the man was, where he came from, and everything he could about the Coven. McCabe and Daniels could doubt him all they wanted, but he was a believer.

"Where the puzzle pieces most," Clouse repeated the riddle to himself.

What puzzle?

What pieces?

Clouse harbored urges to knock Stephen silly if he found the man again, and if he wasn't already among the recently deceased. Somehow he suspected the body McCabe busily investigated was probably that of Stephen, but it sounded like they might never know.

If what Stephen wrote was true, his family knew nothing about his affiliation with the alleged group, so perhaps his family considered him missing. If so, investigators were probably already be looking for him, perhaps under a different identity, but a match would identify him and lead Clouse closer to the truth.

He decided to call Daniels with his discovery later that afternoon, but he wanted to do some more searching on the Internet for the Coven or any missing persons between the ages of eighteen and twenty-five before he did so.

A yawn forced his mouth open, hinting that his day might be longer than he suspected.

*   *   *

"No, Mr. Barnett, you cannot see the patient unless you are with the family," the nurse scolded the unwanted guest.

"I have a story to do and I need to talk with *someone*," the local African-American newspaper reporter retorted. "It's eight o'clock and my deadline is almost here."

"No one but family is allowed to see Officer Kaiser," the nurse replied.

"Is any of the family here? I'll settle for anyone at this point."

"No. They've all left for the night," the nurse said.

Everyone in Bloomington knew Jerome Barnett from the *Bloomington Post* as a household name after his coverage of the West Baden Murders the year before. Unlike other reporters, he failed to capitalize on the events by publishing a book, but he still tried.

After failing to secure interviews with Clouse, Daniels, Smith, or any of the other key witnesses to the finale of the murders, he aggressively sought current related events, especially when the murders began again. His articles, accompanied by his photo, and his beaming, almost insincere smile, were an everyday occurrence in the *Post*.

It was as though he knew whatever words rested beside his photograph and byline were going to be exaggerations used to sell newspapers.

"Visiting hours are over," the nurse said sternly. "As you can see, no one else is here," she said, waving a hand toward the vacant hallway on either side of them. Only she and one other nurse remained on the floor for the remainder of their shift.

"But I-"

"*Over*," she repeated sternly as someone stepped from Kaiser's room, instantly catching the reporter's attention.

"He's not family," Barnett said, pointing to Tim Niemeyer, who walked slowly toward them, ready to leave after a long day of visiting his comatose friend. His eyes seemed to follow the dark lines of the floor as he walked toward the elevator.

"He has family permission to be here," the nurse said.

Niemeyer, hearing the blaring conversation, looked up. He recognized the reporter, cursed under his breath, and turned around, heading for a flight of stairs as an alternate escape route.

"Mr. Niemeyer," Barnett said, giving chase. "How do you feel about police speculation that you might be the new Baden killer?" he asked a piercing, though unfounded question to gain the attention of the stocky construction worker.

It worked.

Niemeyer turned around, readying his right hand into a fist, but stood perfectly still, knowing better than to punch Barnett or give in to the man's preposterous claims. As the nurse blocked the reporter's path, Niemeyer simply turned around, heading for the staircase.

In doing so, he passed Kaiser's room again, tuning out the taunts Barnett threw at him from afar.

Niemeyer apparently had other things to worry about, but the reporter had planted a seed that would likely help him later.

*   *   *

Inside the room, Kaiser groaned and mumbled in his sleep, showing the first signs of life in several days. Constant visits kept his mind working, even if his body refused to cooperate. Now, after hearing Niemeyer's voice so close for hours, and a disturbance in the hall, Kaiser's body decided to return to the real world.

His eyes fluttered momentarily, adjusting to the dark room, which seemed intently bright after days of unconsciousness. He could see everything around him clearly, feeling the tubes inside his nose. For a moment he simply breathed, lived, and took in the room around him, remembering the horror of being beaten and laid upon the statue, barely conscious from the intense pain.

He remembered the needle gouged into his arm, looking down at the faces of the three people attempting to kill him, almost positive he recognized one of them through the blinding pain. As the man who referred to himself as Jacob commanded the other two, Kaiser stole a glance at the list, seeing which name fell after his own.

Feeling parched in the throat, Kaiser reached for the phone, unsure of whether or not he was capable of speech. Swallowing to regain some moisture in his vocal chords, Kaiser slowly dialed the number to Clouse's cellular phone. It rang three times before his friend picked up.

"Hello?"

Kaiser tried to speak, but only muffled, chaffed groans emitted from his throat.

"Hello?" Clouse asked again, a bit more emphatic this time.

Kaiser attempted to speak again, but it took several seconds before he was able to utter a word.

"Paul," he said as a click reached his ear.

Already exhausted, Kaiser let the phone fall to the floor from his limp hand. He looked around him, trying to find the pager to summon a nurse. His hand patted down the side of the bed until he found the device, pushing on it. At last he would be free of the hospital bed, and perhaps he could help Clouse find the real killer before the person struck again.

Though it took several minutes, someone walked through the door, with several items in hand. Kaiser looked through dizzied eyes as a womanly figure walked toward him, and he saw a gleam of metal as she raised something from beside her waist.

Something that might be sharp.

"No!" Kaiser yelled, squirming away from the nurse who tried to place the stethoscope near his heart.

"Settle down, sir," the nurse said calmly. "You've been through a traumatic experience. I'm here to help."

"I need to talk to Paul Clouse," Kaiser stammered.

"There will be time for that later," the nurse assured him. "I'm going to fetch a doctor to have a look at you."

Before Kaiser could utter any defiance, a streak of darkness entered the room, clasping the nurse's mouth. To the officer's horror, the killer raised a duel-edged knife, its blade gleaming from what little light entered the room from the hallway. Despite the nurse's muffled cries, she was at the mercy of the shadowy figure. Wasting little time, he rammed the knife through the woman's backside. Its blade pierced her chest at the sternum, the tip covered in shiny blood, which trickled down her uniform blouse before her lifeless form was dropped to the floor with a thud.

Horrified, Kaiser shrunk back toward the edge of the bed, watching as the killer wiped the knife on his own dark costume. The officer recognized the grim reaper costume from past experience, but until the killer placed a knife within a sheath at his side and drew out the scythe, Kaiser did not feel sheer terror about his own mortality.

"Shit," he said, falling back from the bed, pulling the entanglement of tubes from his nose by force.

He landed awkwardly on the floor, quickly regaining his footing, despite a weak, dizzy feeling throughout his body.

Staying in a crouch, Kaiser quickly surveyed the room, seeing the killer nowhere in sight. Weaponless, and in no condition to do battle, the officer spied a vase beside him on a table. Seeing few other alternatives, he snatched it, slowly walking around the hospital bed toward the door, cautiously looking around him.

Wearing nothing more than a hospital gown, Kaiser felt even more disadvantaged. Bare feet and scanty clothing would not get him far. On sheer adrenaline he walked around the edge of the bed, carefully stepping over the nurse's body, hearing a creak from somewhere in the room.

His own nervous breathing drowned out most every other noise in the room, but he stopped momentarily, holding his breath, to listen intently.

Less than a second passed before the entire bed came springing upright from the floor toward him, pinning him against the wall. The vase fell to the floor, shattering into what seemed a million pieces. Kaiser felt the air depart his lungs as the killer's seemingly faceless form rose from behind the bed, drawing the knife from its sheath once again, raring back to stab at the officer's throat.

Using what little energy he possessed, and one free hand, Kaiser punched the killer through the faceless hood, connecting with what he thought was a real nose. With no force behind it, the bed fell to the floor as the killer stumbled back.

Kaiser started toward the door, feeling pain stream through his feet. The vase's shards of glass pierced the tender skin, making it almost impossible to walk. He gave in, falling to the floor in a quick attempt to crawl into the hallway and pick the glass splinters from his feet in the process.

He reached the hallway, attempting to crawl away as the killer reached the door, scythe in hand. Kaiser evaded one swing of the weapon, rolling himself against a wall. Using one of the shards pried from his feet he cut the killer along the ankle, trying for the Achilles heel. The costumed reaper reacted, clasping the ankle, but soon picked up the pace, taking the scythe and charging toward Kaiser once more.

Feeling a kick to his ribs that probably broke one or more, Kaiser rolled against the wall, taking another kick from some form of hard footwear. It felt military-grade, much like the police issue boots he sometimes wore on patrol. He groaned, feeling another swift kick to his kidney, rolling back over, facing the killer who loomed directly above him.

He saw the killer held the scythe behind his head, ready to swing it down upon him.

"Fuck you," Kaiser muttered, suspecting who his killer was before the blade hurled toward his chest.

20

McCabe arrived shortly after ten o'clock at the hospital. He was nearly finished at his favorite bar when the vibration from his pager took him from a card game. Since he was winning, it seemed fishy to the other players his job suddenly summoned him.

"When Lisa didn't come back after half an hour I started searching the rooms," he overheard a nurse tell one of the Bloomington detectives as he passed the nurses' station.

A camera bag at his side, he focused exclusively on Daniels and the open door ahead. McCabe knew which room it was, after several personal visits to Kaiser, but he was given no details about what to expect. Because he was already investigating several other related murders, including the first attempt on Kaiser, Bloomington officers immediately requested him.

Outside the room, a slight bloody streak became visible along the edge of the wall, only if a person studied the floor carefully. Where the trail appeared to have started before a brief cleansing, a large chunk of the floor tile appeared forcibly dislodged. McCabe knew which clues to search for, even when alcohol did some of his thinking for him.

"It's not pretty," Daniels commented as they stood at the door's threshold.

"Anyone been inside?"

"Only the nurse who found the bodies."

"Bodies?"

Daniels nodded.

"Our killer took out Kaiser and a nurse."

McCabe let out a belch, controlled by the closed fist applied to his mouth.

"You been out?" Daniels asked him, aside from the other cops.

"Yes," the detective answered the silent accusation. "Don't worry. I'm fine."

Daniels probably wasn't concerned how well the man held his alcohol, but rather how efficient he would be at performing job tasks. Any speck of evidence overlooked would never be recovered. Daniels appeared rather uncomfortable being around the Bloomington detectives he once worked with on a daily basis. He failed to fit in, wearing jeans and a hooded sweatshirt, a bulge seated beneath his right shoulder.

"You packing?" McCabe asked, noticing the protrusion.

"After what happened yesterday, I won't leave my house unarmed," Daniels replied. "I've got a family to worry about."

"Your buddies won't say anything?" McCabe inquired, knowing one of the stipulations of Daniels working with him was that he remain unarmed and carry no identification affiliating him with the Bloomington Police Department until his rehabilitation was complete.

In other words, he was to act merely as a source of information.

"They won't care," Daniels said. "I worked with all of them before my accident last year."

McCabe let out another quiet belch, looking around this time for anyone who might have heard. Most of the officers were mingling amongst themselves, or questioning hospital staff. Only a few people were even visible on the floor, although a deputy coroner was one of them.

Assured everyone was too occupied to have noticed the sound, McCabe looked inside the room.

"Any witnesses?" he asked Daniels.

"None."

"What about security cameras?"

"They tape a sequential pattern from floor to floor. We've got officers reviewing the tape, but it seems unlikely they caught the right moment."

McCabe thought a moment about his bad luck, then decided to make the best of what he had.

"Let's do this," he said, leading the way inside, where he stopped just past the door, able to survey the carnage.

Daniels appeared unmoved by the scene, but McCabe took in the chaotic mess for the first time, carefully panning the room. The overturned bed, the pools of blood, the white heeled shoes of the nurse, still attached to unmoving, smooth legs. All at once the view flooded his mind, leaving him with any number of ideas about where to begin his search for clues.

"Did you know Kaiser?" McCabe asked, looking over to the overturned body of the county officer, face-down on the tile floor, one hand placed up on the heating unit, as though reaching for something to save him.

The detective knew Kaiser's body was placed in the room from the blood he spied in the hallway. A path of blood led across the fallen bed mattress from the direction of the hallway, leading him to believe the killer again sent a message, leaving the county officer in such a prone position.

"Knew him a little through Paul."

"He was a good guy from what I understand," McCabe replied. "Never had a chance to work with him, but a lot of the guys said he was an outstanding officer."

"That I can vouch for," Daniels said, remembering the year before when Kaiser saved him from a bullet in the head at the hands of David Landamere.

McCabe further examined the room without benefit of moving. He pulled his camera from the bag, attached the flash, and began examining through the lens with each push of the button.

First shot.

Ignoring the untouched wall to the left of the door, the shot included part of the overturned, bloodstained mattress, and the lower half of Kaiser's body.

His bare feet protruded from the hospital gown. Spatters of blood speckled the gown, mostly from a weapon's impact, but some from moving the body. The tubes formerly providing Kaiser nourishment and oxygen lay to the left of his body, hastily discarded in McCabe's opinion.

He began to assess exactly what happened.

Second shot.

Finishing the view of the overturned mattress, the shot included Kaiser's torso. His left hand was placed atop the heating unit as the rest of him lay flat on the floor, face down. A cavernous, bloody pool stained the clothing. Through the blood and shredded area of cloth, McCabe saw some flesh color, including strips of skin dangling from the open wound. The weapon exited through the officer's back, thus chipping the floor as McCabe noticed in the hallway.

"Whoever did this cleaned it awfully quick," McCabe noted aloud.

"I smelled a cleaning agent of some sort," Daniels said. "I asked one of the detectives to check their closest janitorial closet, but he hasn't come back yet."

"Good thinking," McCabe noted, realizing he missed the smell, or it had diminished too much by the time he arrived.

Third shot.

Moving the camera to a completely different area of the room, directly to his right, McCabe photographed the dead nurse, hands lying open on either side of her body, as though placed in a holy position. Her head looked awkwardly angled to one side.

She was dead before she even hit the floor. From the blood stains in her white uniform McCabe deduced what happened, but the mess seemed contained compared to Kaiser's wounds.

He recalled Daniels' story of the killer pulling a knife on him in the hotel elevator. Compared to last year, the killings seemed far less predictable. Various weapons and no clear motive left McCabe wondering where to begin, even after half a dozen murders.

"I'll be right back," Daniels said as McCabe focused exclusively on the room.

"Okay."

*   *   *

Growing tired of McCabe's silent, mental calculations of the scene, Daniels stepped into the hall, finding a distraught, well-dressed man approaching the edge of the police line where several uniformed officers and detectives halted his approach, although the hospital security officer seemed to know him.

"I'm Barry Andrews," the man said as Daniels quickly looked him over, wondering why a doctor would be so uptight.

He had noticed the man's hospital identification badge pinned to his knitted gray sweater.

With brown hair, laced with streaks of gray, and a smooth face accented by greenish hazel eyes, he looked like the type of person cast for a Lifetime Channel original movie as a caring husband and father. His fluent, deep voice would nearly guarantee him a role.

"I was downstairs," he began to explain. "I heard someone was murdered and my girlfriend works up here."

Daniels crutched forward.

"Can I talk to him?" he asked the lead detective.

An affirmative nod allowed Daniels to proceed. Too busy with the case at hand, and not wanting to be bothered with an irrelevant interview, the detectives were happy to let Daniels take the man aside.

"Follow me, sir," he instructed the doctor as he looked for a place for them to talk.

A moment later he found several nearby chairs in a waiting area. Realizing he looked out of place, especially with crutches, Daniels decided to begin the conversation appropriately, with a slight lie.

"I'm Detective Mark Daniels," he said, despite his inactive role. He took out a notepad, flipping it open. "And you are?"

"Barry Andrews. I work in the surgical ward."

"Who is your girlfriend, Dr. Andrews?"

"Lisa Terrell. She was working the floor and I heard about a murder. Have you seen her?"

Daniels finished writing several notes.

"I'm afraid I have bad news for you," he said, struggling to look directly at the doctor.

"Oh, God. Is it true?" Andrews questioned, eyes wide with anticipation and fear.

"Yes. She and a patient were murdered within the last two hours," Daniels decided to reveal.

"No," the doctor muttered, shaking his head. "I just saw her at shift change."

"I have some questions I'd like to ask you, sir."

Andrews shook his head violently.

"Can it wait until tomorrow, detective?" Andrews pleaded, bolting from the chair, running his hands through his hair in an obvious frenzied state. "I really can't even think right now."

"Sure," Daniels replied, knowing none of his questions were directly related to the murder.

He suspected Lisa Terrell was by no means the actual target of the killer.

"Doc, do not tell anyone about the information I've shared with you here," he warned, knowing he should not have leaked a few of the details. "The coroner's office will have to notify the next of kin before we can release her name to the public."

Andrews nodded in understanding.

"Where can I reach you tomorrow afternoon?" Daniels asked, regaining his feet with the use of the crutches.

"At my clinic, or at home," the doctor answered as Daniels began to hobble toward the crowd.

Before the officer could ask him where the clinic was, Andrews underwent what appeared to be a nervous breakdown. Daniels decided just to call the hospital in the morning for information.

Daniels hobbled down the hall, stopping to speak with the officer he'd asked to check the janitorial closet before returning to the bloodied room.

"Find anything?" McCabe asked when Daniels returned.

"Found the boyfriend of our dead nurse. A surgical doctor here. He won't be much help tonight, so I'll interview him tomorrow."

"I doubt he can give us anything important if his alibi checks out," McCabe deduced. "I'm done with the photos, so I'm going to get some forensics people in here with the dying hope they might find something useful."

"Whoever we're dealing with knows how to cover things up. Speaking of which, my buddies found the janitorial closet and it looks like some form of bleach was used to clean up the mess."

"So we've got a killer who knows how to avoid leaving any trace of evidence, and knows the quickest way to the cleaning supplies," McCabe decided.

"It probably doesn't take a genius to find where the stuff is kept."

"Still, we're talking about someone who had at least some familiarity with this hospital and where things were."

"Kaiser was here a few days. Maybe our killer took his time and staked out the floor."

"And knew exactly where Kaiser was?"

"Follow one of his family or friends up here and it's easy. We can interview them to see if anyone strange was around, or following them up here."

"They'll be shook up for a while," McCabe said. "I'll get a list of who has been here to visit, and start interviews tomorrow. You can speak with that doctor. See if he's noticed anything strange up here, since he probably visited his girlfriend a lot."

"I'm going to give Paul a call. I don't want him finding out about this from someone else first."

"How close were they?" McCabe questioned.

"Paul and Kaiser? They went to high school together. They were pretty much best friends."

"Send him my condolences," the detective said with a look of genuine sincerity. "Somehow we'll find the bastard behind this."

*   *   *

An hour later, Clouse sat at the kitchen table alone, thumbing through his high school senior yearbook. Daniels had phoned from the hospital to inform him of Kaiser's death before the press received any information.

Clouse looked at the photos of himself, Niemeyer, and Kaiser. It was a time when Niemeyer still had hair, and shortly after the time Kaiser kept his continually buzzed. Clouse chuckled, thinking how his friend hated having curly hair so he constantly buzzed it, often nearly to the scalp, just to keep people from remembering what it looked like.

One photo depicted all three beside Niemeyer's pickup truck. Since all three were country boys, each owned a truck almost from the time they could drive. All three had no problem wearing cowboy boots to school because no one dared tease them about it.

Clouse played basketball, Kaiser was destined to be a cop from a young age, showing it throughout high school, and Niemeyer had a quick temper. Being the largest of the three, he played football, then spent his off-season working on the farm or chasing girls.

Soon after Daniels called with the tragic news, Clouse decided to use a sick day and miss work the next morning. He figured either the chief or another of the fire department brass would call and tell him to return to work when he decided to. The year before they worked around him, partly because he was accused of murdering his wife and they wanted to keep their hands clean in case he was guilty. At the same time, they were supportive by giving him time to work things out.

He hoped for the same now.

"How are you?" Jane asked, joining him at the kitchen table after making certain the kids were asleep.

"I'm okay," he lied. "I just have this overwhelming urge to find whoever's doing this and squeeze the life from them with my bare hands."

Jane took hold of his thick forearm.

"I won't pretend to understand what you're going through, but if you need anything at all, just let me know."

Clouse felt a tear slip past his right eye, dripping down his cheek. His emotions were getting the better of him.

"I'm going to need freedom, Jane. I need time to work with Mark and find whoever's behind this."

Jane appeared to feel more secure after they installed an alarm system on the house and Clouse took several other steps in raising the security of their house, including a change of locks and letting the dogs run free outside, or in the house. Luckily no neighbors were within a half mile of their property, so the dogs would know their boundaries and keep to them.

"You do what you have to," Jane insisted. "When you're stuck here, you're restless and unsure of what to do with yourself. I can't expect us to live normal lives until this is all over."

He gave her a quick kiss on the cheek.

"You know I love you."

"I know," she replied. "A week ago we were planning the final details of our wedding, and now we're living in fear for our own lives."

"Don't worry about me," Clouse assured her.

"I can't help it. Every minute you're away from here I worry someone might try and kill you again."

"I know, but Mark and I know what to expect. We keep an eye on one another."

A knock at the door interrupted the conversation, leaving both to wonder who might visit their property at such an hour.

"Tim?" Clouse asked, opening the door.

One look at his friend told him Niemeyer already knew about Kaiser. In his left hand he clasped a high school yearbook, apparently thinking like Clouse. His eyes appeared red and a bit misty. Clouse was unsure whether mourning or drinking could be held accountable for the state of his high school pal.

"Feel like getting drunk?" Niemeyer asked, giving a partial answer.

Clouse looked to Jane, then back to his friend, knowing it was time to exercise some of his newfound freedom.

"Actually, I do."

*   *   *

Half an hour later the two sat at a table, away from the bar and the televisions that caused most of the commotion inside a local bar and grill. Clouse stared at the onion rings placed before him for a moment. Like every other table, theirs held a centerpiece oil lamp that seemed to provide most of the light around them.

For a weeknight, the pub bustled with activity. Country music blared from surrounding speakers while occupants of several tables engaged in loud conversation or roared at the basketball game's results on the big screen television. Others played electronic trivia, and some simply sat off to the side, away from the noise to hold quieter talks.

"A friend of mine working security at the hospital told me," Niemeyer stated. "I couldn't believe it. I just visited Ken tonight."

"Was he awake at all?"

"No. I hope for his sake he never woke up."

Niemeyer chugged down the last of his fourth beer. His speech was noticeably slurred, and his eyes a bit more red than before. Though he was big enough to hold alcohol in bulk, even Niemeyer had a limit.

"You remember the time we all brought a pig to school for homecoming?" Clouse asked, sipping his second beer. He tried to contain himself to be a designated driver for Niemeyer.

"I thought Mr. Evans was going to shit himself," Niemeyer said with a bit of his southern accent coming through, cussing uncharacteristically with a crooked grin.

When provoked or drunk he tended to swear more, and take threats much more seriously.

Clouse picked an onion ring from the basket, biting off an edge as he thought about how the three of them were never as close after high school.

"Why didn't you and I talk more after we graduated?" he simply asked.

"We did," Niemeyer objected, looking at his empty bottle. "I guess things just get in the way sometimes."

"I guess."

Both men seemed to stay closer to Kaiser than one another, though they never became strangers.

"What can I do to help you find whoever's behind this, Paul?"

"I don't want you to do anything, Tim. I've already lost enough friends to this maniac."

Niemeyer massaged the bald area of his head while he groaned.

"What's wrong?" Clouse inquired.

"This loud music is givin' me a headache."

Clouse sighed to himself, trying to remember what he was about to say before his friend developed a headache.

"I just want you to be careful and keep an eye on your family," he finally said. "Are you still working in Bedford?"

"We're buildin' a new shopping complex at the edge of town."

"Good. Stay away from West Baden and Bloomington, Tim. I don't want anything happening to you."

After calling for another beer, Niemeyer took out a cigar, puffing it to life as he lit it. When the beer arrived, he tipped the waitress, exhaling directly above him. He returned a glassy-eyed stare in Clouse's direction.

"Since when did you start that habit?" Clouse asked.

"Ah, a couple of my weightliftin' buddies smoke stogies when we play cards or go out."

"You're giving in to peer pressure at our age?"

"I ain't givin' in," Niemeyer said defensively. "No one forces anything on me, and there ain't nothin' wrong with enjoying a good cigar once in a while," he added, letting his grammar and his drawl slip a bit.

Clouse shrugged indifferently. He didn't want the conversation taking any more of a negative run than it already had.

"What can you tell me about the two men who attacked you and Ken?"

Niemeyer spent a few minutes relating the story to his friend, giving details about the two men, including the serpent tattoo on the taller one. Clouse felt certain the other was his secret helper, Stephen, whom he feared was murdered. He felt positive a snake tattoo would stand out in public, or its owner needed to constantly wear concealing clothing.

"Who do you think is behind it, Paul?"

"I don't know. Last time it was someone closer to me than I thought, but this time I just don't know, Tim. I just hope I figure it out before more people get hurt."

"Me too."

Clouse took a sip from his beer bottle, wondering if some of the answers he needed weren't already around him. Somehow he would get the time off work and begin his own search.

21

Despite the agony of leg cramps, Daniels refused to use the wheel-chair the next morning when he found Barry Andrews' clinic in Paoli. Strangely, it was the same clinic that treated Kaiser after he was found inside the hotel. One phone call to the hospital gave him the location of the clinic, sending a strange chill through him.

It felt a little too close to home.

When he walked inside the small clinic, he saw several employ-ees walking around, tidying up the place, but no Andrews.

"How can I help you?" a young lady asked, looking up from some papers on her desk, from behind a glass shield.

Daniels felt certain she thought he was a patient, despite him donning a suit to look more the part of a police detective. His fire-arm remained holstered beneath his left shoulder, in the event that danger crossed his path again.

"Is Dr. Andrews in?" he asked.

"He's not available at the moment," she replied, glancing behind her.

"It's police business," he said, displaying his credentials.

"Oh," she said, pointing toward a door. Daniels crutched over, entering the back of the clinic. "I'll get him for you," she said, leav-ing him centered in a sea of examination tables and chairs, all empty at the moment.

Though small, the clinic obviously served a purpose, and seemed fully functional, as though an extension of the local hospital. It probably gave local residents a sense of having a family doctor around in a small town.

Everything appeared new and clean, and mostly light in color. Though he had grown to detest hospitals, Daniels felt more at home inside the clinic than in his own rehabilitation room in Bloomington.

"How long have you known Dr. Andrews?" the officer asked a young man who cleaned one of the nearby tables.

"Almost 21 years," the tall, ample employee answered. "He's my father."

"Are you studying medicine too?"

With a chuckle the young man ceased his mopping to shake Daniels' hand. He looked very little like his father with light, stringy hair that reached his shoulders. Not the type of kid one expected to work in a medical clinic.

"No, that is not my field of study. I just work here for extra spending money, and to help my father out. He's taking Lisa's death pretty badly if that's what you're here about."

"Yeah, it is."

Daniels let the younger Andrews return to his work as his father emerged from the back office.

"I know this is difficult, but we have to talk," Daniels told him.

"Of course," Andrews said, motioning the officer to follow him back to his office.

"It's nice that your clinic is a family affair."

"Have a seat, detective," Andrews said when they entered the office, giving the impression he was uninterested in small talk.

He closed the door behind him.

"My daughter, Kenya, is about to enter the nursing program after her freshman year at college, while my son, Ryan, has decided to pursue acting in his college studies."

"Is he any good?"

"Oh, he's very good, but he works here out of financial necessity while my daughter considers it a paid internship of sorts."

"I see," Daniels said, taking out a notebook and pen.

Taking a seat behind his desk, Andrews waved toward a seat, which the detective gladly took to be off his feet a moment. Daniels waited until the doctor made eye contact again before asking his first question.

"Can you tell me where you were last night around eight o'clock?"

Andrews told the detective he was in his office working on some overdue reports. He went on to state that he and Lisa Terrell had been dating almost two years. Andrews was divorced, though he assured Daniels the relationship with the nurse followed the proceedings. Daniels believed Andrews was truthful, and sincerely grieving, but the coincidence of the clinic, the hospital, and the murder of the nurse, along with that of Kaiser, plagued him.

"How familiar are you with the West Baden Springs Hotel?" Daniels asked, blazing a new path of questioning.

"Somewhat. Lisa and I used to take tours of it."

"Did you ever purchase any pieces of the tile floor when it was broken up and sold as souvenirs several years ago?"

"As a matter of fact we bought one, but it came up missing sometime last year."

"Can you give me an approximate month or time?"

"Around the holidays. I know it was after that murder spree down there, because I went to look for it and it was gone. Strangest thing too. We kept it in one of our kitchen windows with some jars and it just disappeared."

"Disappeared?"

"Well, I leave the window open sometimes when I cook. I'm not a very good cook, so I take precautions. One day I just noticed it was missing."

Daniels flipped his notebook closed.

"I guess that about covers it," he said, reaching for his crutches.

"May I ask what happened to your legs?"

"I was shot in the line of duty. I'm on a rehab assignment, assisting the state police with their investigation."

"I didn't think beards were allowed in police departments," Andrews noted, as though to test Daniels' legitimacy.

"They aren't," Daniels said, forcing a grin. "Again, I'm just assisting. I'm not on active duty yet. But we need as many legs as we can afford, to get this solved, even if they aren't one-hundred percent good."

"I see. I want you to find who killed Lisa, detective. If I can help in any other way, don't hesitate to call me."

Daniels nodded, pulling himself to a standing position.

"I'll show myself out, Dr. Andrews."

*   *   *

Daniels struggled through the front door of his house later that afternoon to find his wife holding their son in her arms.

"What's going on?" he asked, knowing she had planned to leave the kids with her mother so they could have a night together.

"He's running a fever," she replied, looking up.

"Oh," Daniels replied, looking for the cordless phone.

"It's over there," Cindy said with a tone admonishing him for paying little attention to their son's sickness.

He knew she felt he was growing obsessive about the new set of murders.

It was the same as last year, only far more dangerous. A year ago, she was outwardly proud of him for working toward solving the crime. Now he was a potential victim, not fully healthy, and in danger of losing the strong support she provided over the past year.

Forever.

She had made statements recently about her frustration, helping a man who refused to help himself. Occasionally she dropped questions and comments that implied she thought Daniels might be happier alone, but he always indicated he would not be.

Cindy paid him little attention as he spoke with McCabe, discovering the detective had no luck with the hospital's cameras, or with security officers on the double homicide. Daniels hung up the phone, unhappy with the lack of leads.

"How's my boy?" he finally asked, sitting beside his wife, feeling Curtis' forehead. "Wow, he *is* warm."

As Daniels settled into the couch, she handed the moaning boy over to him, heading for the kitchen. From her rigid walk he began to realize she was unhappy with him. He heard several pots and pans clanging from around the corner, providing further evidence of her displeasure. Apparently knowing he could not readily get up to confront her, she waited several minutes before returning to the living room.

"I thought we were going out tonight," he said.

"We were until Curt ran a fever this morning."

"Did you take him to the doctor's office?"

"I called. They gave me a prescription."

Daniels held his son close a moment, simply touching Curt's tiny fingers and watching how his baby fussed and moaned, refusing to cry. He inherited the strong will of his parents, refusing to let life's obstacles keep him down.

"Are we going to make a night of it?" he asked as she placed Curtis in the crib on the other side of the room.

"Do you actually plan to stay here tonight?"

"What's that supposed to mean? I planned to go out tonight, with you."

"I don't know, Mark," she said, exasperated. "It's almost like you use this whole murder spree to avoid me. There is absolutely no sense in you chasing down a killer when you can't even walk yet."

Daniels sighed.

"I'm in no danger–"

"No danger? You nearly got killed at the hotel a few days ago and you're in no danger?"

"Paul was there. It wasn't that bad."

"Yes, it was," Cindy said, seating herself next to him, taking hold of his hand while hers nervously shivered. "If you won't do it for me, do it for the two children who want to grow up knowing their daddy."

"Do what?"

"Give up this chase of yours. You aren't a detective anymore."

Daniels simply sat stunned as the words pierced his heart and soul. He couldn't believe his wife ever thought of him as anything less than the job title that consumed him. At the same time, he realized perhaps too much of his life intertwined with his career.

"I cannot give this up while Paul is still in danger. Until I find this supposed list, I don't know who's in danger, and there won't be any telling who the killer might be. Cindy, this is no different than last year."

"Yes, it is. Last year you were on the outside looking in. Now someone wants you and Paul out of the way for stopping Dave Landamere. I don't want to see you hurt again."

She cupped his bearded cheek in her hand as their eyes locked. He felt disheartened and vulnerable, but knew his assistance to McCabe could not stop until the case was solved. He wanted so much to promise Cindy everything would be fine, but he knew better. The memories of a bullet ripping into his backside haunted him, though he never actually saw it coming.

"I can't promise-"

She shushed him, placing her hand over his mouth, replacing it with a deep kiss. Romance had disappeared from their lives over the past year, and Cindy realized her last hope was to win him back, and keep him home.

"Can you make it upstairs?" she asked, planting another kiss on him, arousing him now that the shock was over.

A smile crossed his face.

"Oh, I think I can." He looked to the crib. "What about Curt?"

"He'll be okay for ten minutes."

"After a year that's all I get?" Daniels asked, reaching for a single crutch, knowing the baby monitor worked perfectly from hearing their son's cries most every night. He planned on making his return trip to the upstairs worthwhile.

"We'll see," she answered. "You'll have to earn it."

Daniels uncharacteristically let out a tiger-like growl as he hobbled up the stairs behind his wife.

*   *   *

Clouse walked up the stairs to his son's final class at the elementary school, feeling somewhat better after a talk with the fire chief about him taking a few weeks off until things settled down. The following day, Kaiser's calling hours and funeral would keep him busy. After that he could stay home with his family and leave the investigation to the police.

He hoped.

A feeling of helplessness overwhelmed him. Clouse tended to believe if he could confront the killer, he could overtake him. Like before, the killer was always one step ahead of him, taunting him. He picked on those around the fireman, adding to his guilty conscience by making them suffer. His entire life felt violated because someone wanted at him and everyone around him.

"If only I could find that list," he muttered to himself, reaching the classroom door.

He knocked, finding Zach's gifted and talented teacher, Judy Parker, waiting on the other side. She smiled, knowing she hadn't seen Clouse in some time, or often enough. She wondered how involved Zach's father was in his life, not realizing the strange schedule of Clouse's jobs, or that his son meant everything to him.

"Here to pick up Zach?" she asked, leading him into the classroom where several restless children were anxious for school to let out.

"Yes," Clouse answered, looking around. "Where is he?"

"He's working with Mrs. Teague on the computer," Judy said, looking toward a closed door.

Clouse recalled Jane's statement about Zach working behind closed doors, away from the other students.

"Who is Mrs. Teague?" he questioned, recalling Jane's mention of a teacher scurrying off. Clouse felt obligated to be suspicious of everyone and everything.

"One of our teaching aides. She's here three days a week."

As the bell rang and the kids dashed for the door, only to be halted by another teaching aide who insisted they walk rationally, Clouse took off his brown leather jacket. He laid it across one arm as he inspected the classroom.

"Why is Zach being kept separate from the other students?" he asked Judy without looking away from the fish tank.

"Apparently this time of year is rather difficult for your son, Mr. Clouse. The other kids have sensed it, and give Zach a hard time about certain things."

"Angie," Clouse said his deceased wife's name under his breath.

He couldn't believe other kids were so meanspirited at such a young age, but he knew children sometimes acted before they thought.

"We decided to keep Zach on some special projects until the season blew over," Judy informed him. "Perhaps if you spent more time with him-"

"I *do* spend time with him," Clouse insisted, taking a defensive tone. "This isn't exactly a great time of year for me either, but you don't see me shelled up at home. If Zach is alienated from every kid in school, every year like this, he'll never grow up normal. I don't want him thinking he needs to spend the month of October holed up like some hermit."

"I didn't mean to imply that you didn't spend time with him, Mr. Clouse. He just needs as much support as he can get right now."

"And he'll have it," Clouse assured the teacher.

"He's been doing well with the computer education so we stuck with it."

"Fine, but get him out of there once in a while, Mrs. Parker. I don't want to tell you how to do your job, but he needs normal experiences."

Any further conversation ceased as the door opened and Zach walked out, followed by Mrs. Teague, an older lady Clouse took as a retired teacher or bored grandmother. Zach immediately ran over to his father's embrace, apparently happy to see someone who understood the demons caged within him.

"How are you, sport?"

"Fine, Dad. Can we stop at the store on the way home?" Zach asked, referring to the only worthwhile drugstore on their way out to the country.

"Sure, kid. Get your coat and backpack."

Clouse stood, looking to Judy while Zach crossed the room.

"I didn't mean to get out of line, but Zach is about all I have left. I'd never let anything happen to him, or neglect him."

Judy let a smile creep across her face.

"I know. I'm sorry, too. I would just like to see you here more often so we could talk about the problems he sometimes has."

Clouse nodded as Zach returned to his side.

"I will. Take care."

They walked together outside the room, and Clouse tried to sneak a peek inside the computer room, but the door was only open a crack, and he decided not to appear nosy. He simply walked outside the school with his son, greeted by a cool autumn day and falling leaves from nearby trees.

Neighboring houses had pumpkins lining their porches, along with bales of straw, and corn stalks tied to pillars. Artificial cobwebs hung from tree to tree, and some families had gotten creative enough to place miniature cemeteries in their yards.

Clouse looked at the scenes, but Halloween would never be a chipper holiday to him again. Candy and pranks took a back seat to the haunting images burned within his mind.

He helped Zach into his truck and turned away from the yards, knowing his family life would never be as normal as the picture perfect families living near the school.

*   *   *

Almost a mile from the road they lived on, Clouse's truck pulled into the KTS Drugstore upon Zach's request.

"Why are we stopping here, Zach?" the fireman asked his son, genuinely uncertain, but more than willing to accommodate his son's wishes.

"I want to look at costumes."

Clouse pulled into the store's small parking lot, stepping out as his son dashed inside. He tried calling to Zach, but it was too late. The boy had slipped past the electronic door.

"Why the change of heart on Halloween, kid?" Clouse asked, once he found his son sorting through the costume rack.

"All the other kids are going out on Halloween. They all think I'm weird," Zach replied, a pouting look across his face.

Clouse knelt down, looking into his boy's blue eyes.

"You're not weird. I think you're a pretty cool kid."

"That's not what they think."

Clouse smirked, forcing a grin from his son.

"I know this past year has been rough on you, but I want you to know I love you, and I'm never going to leave you. You're the most important thing in my life right now."

"Even more important than Jane and Katie?"

Clouse hesitated a second, deciding to answer honestly.

"Yes, you are. And I miss your mom just as much as you do, Zach."

"Is she really in a better place?"

"It's called heaven, son. She's with God, and someday I'll tell you all about it."

"Promise?"

"I promise. And if you want to go out on Halloween, we'll go out."

Zach nodded, his childhood innocence showing through his grin. He grew up too fast for Clouse to keep up with. It seemed just a year ago he could barely speak an entire sentence, and now they could carry on brief conversations.

"Pick out whichever one you want, kid. I'm going to grab a few groceries."

Since the entire drug store was in view from any vantage point Clouse felt secure leaving his son alone momentarily, especially since no one else was visible except the store's owner and a pharmacist.

As Clouse sauntered down the aisle, he thought about what a horrible time of year it truly was for himself, and Zach. When his wife was murdered, Clouse had been at work while Zach was inside the house when his mother's blood spilled. Clouse was immediately accused of the murder and interrogated by two detectives, one of which was now a good friend.

Between the investigation, the press, and the fact that he could never properly mourn Angie while being a single father, he had a bad taste about the season in general. His faith in those around him crumpled as the murder of his wife, and every other killing around the hotel, could be traced to greed.

He sensed the same cycle recurring, but this time a hint of revenge seemed obvious, since he was apparently the first choice to die. Unfortunately, Clouse felt certain the man who saved his life had suffered the fate meant for himself.

Looking over the various potato chips for the brands the kids preferred, he considered the possibilities of those around him being the killer and how several had survived apparent close encounters with the killer, coming away with far better health than himself.

Niemeyer escaped with a severe headache from a rifle butt, after seeing the person who was, quite possibly, the killer. He was also the last person to see Ken Kaiser alive. Clouse felt his friend had no motivation to kill anyone, shaking off the notion that an old high school chum might commit such an act.

Daniels avoided what should have been an obvious death in Clouse's view. Perhaps the killer was inexperienced with a scythe, or perhaps Daniels escaped unharmed for a different reason. Clouse knew the best alibi for not being the killer would be a third person viewing that person next to the killer. He focused on the chips again, trying not to think of the coincidences thrown his way the past several days.

Even Jane had told him several odd stories, making him leery of even the woman he planned to marry. Zach's solo education was satisfactorily explained in his view, and the stereo incident in the house was probably just the kids accidentally turning it on and refusing to take any blame for their misuse of appliances. Clouse wondered about everything and everyone around him, almost constantly.

Perhaps, in part, the killer was getting what he wanted.

At one point, Clouse mistrusted Kaiser, and perhaps vice versa, when Angie was murdered, but their skepticism was later forgotten. Still, it was someone close to him committing murder the first time, and he felt obligated to be wary of everyone again.

Clouse picked up some popcorn and soda for the kids before Zach ran up to him, carrying a costume with a familiar appearance.

"Can I be a fireman for Halloween, Dad?"

"It's awfully dangerous work, Zach," Clouse said, kneeling down beside his son. "Sure you can handle it?"

"Yeah. I need a hose too."

"That can be arranged," Clouse said of Zach's request, knowing there were some old leftover garden hoses in the barn.

Clouse playfully messed up his son's hair, taking a look at the costume. He found it odd how all firefighter costumes seemed more like unfashionable raincoats of bright red and yellow than the real thing. They always came with a tacky plastic helmet shaped somewhat correctly to give the costume a minor look of authenticity.

He looked at the elevated drug store price on the costume.

"I'll need a second mortgage to pay for this," he muttered to himself as they proceeded toward the checkout counter.

22

A feeling of despondence overcame Clouse as he tugged his tie into place the next morning. His best friend would be laid to rest in a few hours while he felt certain something more could have been done to prevent Kaiser's death.

A guard at the door.

More investigators assigned to the case.

Quicker follow-up on leads.

Faster forensics.

He realized none of this was easily feasible, and that police were doing the best they could, given the circumstances. Clouse wondered what more he could do.

With the funeral drawing closer, the consequences of his best friend's death truly hit him. He would have to face the man's family and know that somehow, no matter how inadvertently, he was part of the problem.

"Almost ready, Paul?" Jane asked as she walked past the dresser where he stood, straight into the bathroom.

"Just about," he replied, dabbing the mist from his eyes, realizing all the times he and Kaiser shared were gone. Two children would grow up without a father because Clouse wasn't there to protect his friend.

"What's the matter?" she asked, returning from the bathroom, finding him sitting on the edge of the bed, his hands limp atop his lap.

"I feel like it's my fault."

She sat beside him caressing his shoulder.

"There is nothing you could have done for him. Whoever did this knew exactly what they were doing, and exactly when to do it. You know Tim had to leave when visitation was up, and he couldn't have done anything either."

"But at least Tim was there."

"And he feels the same way you do. Both of you need to realize someone with no conscience, no heart, is doing this to us. Start worrying about your family and the friends you have left."

Clouse knew why she made such a good doctor. Her spirit and general outlook on life made her one of the strongest women he had ever met. He admired her ability to shrug off the bad and continue on with life.

"Do you know Barry Andrews?" he asked, wanting to quickly change the subject.

"Of course. His clinic is a lot like mine."

"The murdered nurse was his girlfriend."

"I know. They were the talk of the hospital."

"How so?" Clouse asked, standing to find a tie clip.

"They were off and on for the longest time."

"Off and on how?" he asked, clipping the tie, then searching for his sport coat.

"Every so often they broke up and he found a new girl for a few weeks. It was mostly to make Lisa jealous I think."

Clouse grunted quietly, scoffing the idea of such a relationship.

"Don't worry," she said, wrapping her arms around him as he looked in the dresser's mirror at his tie. "I would never treat you that way."

"I think we've gone a little too far to play around now."

She kissed his neck, apparently sensing how tense he was. Jane had experienced him accused of murder, and now losing friend after friend. Understanding exactly how he felt was virtually impossible, so she supported him the best she could.

"I've got another question for you," Clouse said, satisfied with his attire. He sat on the bed again, putting his shined black shoes on. "Those tiles they removed from the hotel floor and auctioned off. Do you know anything about those things that I might not?"

Jane had volunteered as a tour guide at the West Baden Springs Hotel for two seasons, learning much about its rich history. She shared her knowledge in tours, but there were lots of little shreds of information she kept in her mind. Often the tours were pressed for time, so much of her knowledge went to waste, with no time to share it.

Her volunteer work had enabled her to meet Clouse the year before while he worked on the hotel's interior, soon after his wife was murdered. His knowledge was vast, considering he was a buff of the landmark, but Jane had access to people he did not.

"Lilian and Charles Rexford took over the hotel in 1916 and had the tile put down."

Rexford. The name caught Clouse's attention once again.

"Anything special about the tile?"

"It was imported, put in by the Cascini Mosaic Tile Company. They were Italian craftsmen out of Cincinnati."

"Probably the best available. Anything else special about the floor?"

"Not that I know of, but if you want to hear from someone who actually watched it put down, old Charlie Winters can tell you first-hand how the process went."

"Who's he?"

"He was a local teenager who did grounds work for the hotel when it came under new ownership. He's seen about everything new there since it was rebuilt. He even gave tours before the hotel was declared a landmark."

"I might want a chat with him this week."

Jane looked to the clock on the wall. Her sister had already stopped by to babysit the kids, so things were in order.

"We'd better get going," she told her fiancé. "It won't look good if we're late."

Clouse looked himself over in the mirror one last time before following Jane out of the bedroom. A tear dripped from his eye as the realization that his best friend, soon to be his best man, would never be around him again. He felt selfish, knowing how many other friends and relatives Kaiser left behind, but the officer was the closest friend he could possibly lose.

He sniffled, collected himself, and followed Jane.

*   *   *

At the mortuary Clouse found himself numbly shaking hands with old friends and people he had never met. As a pallbearer he was stuck in the spotlight, next to Kaiser's wife and two children part of the time. He stole glances at Sandra and the kids, thinking how similar his friend's situation was to his own. His own death would have left Jane with Zach and Katie, all by herself.

Throughout the course of the calling hours Clouse spied Daniels and McCabe at separate intervals. When each went by he asked them to stay through the funeral so they could talk afterward. Daniels would be able to give him a ride home, since they both lived in the Bloomington area. Clouse felt the three, collectively sharing information, might speed up the process of discovering who was behind the murders.

Since Tim Niemeyer was another pallbearer, the two spent most of their time exchanging glances until the guests began to thin out, preparing to head for the cemetery. Niemeyer gave him curious glances when he spoke to each of the officers at some length. His friend soon crossed the aisle, taking Clouse aside.

"I hate this," Niemeyer confessed. "We're not supposed to do this now. Good God, we're supposed to be grandparents before we start burying one another."

"Not fair, is it?" Clouse asked, slumping into a chair, since most of the visitors were already outside.

"I feel so responsible. Like I could have done something different."

"Yeah, I know how that goes, Tim."

"I guess you would after losing so many friends," Niemeyer said, immediately realizing how terrible his words sounded by the look on his face. Clouse gave a questioning glare. "Sorry, I didn't mean it like that."

Clouse's expression lightened as he stood and slapped his friend on the back.

"You never were much for words, Timmy. If I die before you, let someone else do my eulogy, okay?"

"No problem. I hate public speaking."

Both walked toward the casket, peering in to see their friend, a bit paler than he was in life, at eternal rest. So many memories flooded the heads of both men that his visitors, even his closest relatives, would never share. Most never truly knew Ken Kaiser and what he stood for.

They were oblivious to his undying devotion to his family and to just causes. Kaiser always fought the good fight, and Clouse felt a tear run down his cheek as he prayed his friend might see them from above, knowing they cared, loving him like a brother.

"God, I remember the day he got married," Niemeyer stated, sniffling a bit. "Kenny got so drunk he could barely stand, and we had to cover up for him so his police buddies wouldn't badger him later."

"When it came down to it, we were always the guys there for him. Like the time he got stranded in Indianapolis. Who did he call?"

Niemeyer chuckled.

"He called you because my wife thought it was a prank and hung up on him."

"Poor Ken," Clouse said with a grin. "There'll never be another."

Realizing it was truly goodbye, Clouse looked at the body of his best friend one last time, trying to contain himself. Kaiser had so much to live for, and so many people who cared about him. Unfair, Clouse thought of his death. He was young, in his prime, and died simply for doing what was right. He played by the rules.

Those rules have to change, the fireman thought. Clouse began to understand part of where the killings came from, but discovering who was actually swinging the scythe proved more difficult. No matter what it took, or how many laws required bending, Clouse vowed to find the killer before other innocent victims, himself included, were placed in coffins.

"Are you two ready?" the mortician asked, bringing the other pallbearers into the room, ready to transport the coffin.

"Yeah," Clouse answered, able to stop a flood of emotion before it began.

*   *   *

During the trip to the cemetery Clouse felt a certain numbness as lights blurred past him on the overcast day. Neither he, nor Jane, spoke during the brief trip. He replayed all of the good and bad memories with Kaiser inside his mind, ready to lay his friend to rest before setting out to find the killer.

A bit of misty rain further dampened the spirits of those surrounding the burial site as the coffin lay atop the ground and a fairly large gathering listened to the pastor give a final resting speech. Clouse heard and felt little through the proceedings until Kaiser's department members, along with a slew of various officers, gave their final respectful salutes to their fallen comrade. Each gave a salute while the flag from the coffin was handed over to Kaiser's wife as his two children sat idly by, unsure of why their father was not coming home.

Clouse lost all sense of who or what surrounded him, mourning his friend quietly, tearfully, as he dragged himself away from the group no sooner than they began lowering the casket into the ground. Thankful Zach was not part of the funeral, or witness to the lack of his father's usual strong composure, Clouse stumbled through the rainy mist toward a boulder seated at the edge of the graveyard.

By himself, he took a seat, buried his head inside his hands and cried the next several minutes, hoping everyone else was too busy to notice. Occasional glances showed he wasn't the only person openly mourning as Kaiser's fellow officers and lots of friends and family wept, walking toward their vehicles.

Jane walked among them, viewing her future husband from a distance. To her he probably looked like a person lost to the world, obviously hurt over the loss of such a close friend. It was another part of his vulnerable side she would see for the first time. She veered from the group, taking a walk toward him.

"Maybe I'm just a selfish bastard," Clouse said, sniffling and wiping his eyes dry as Jane approached him. "God, I miss him."

"You're just doing what comes natural. You're human."

"I guess so. I just can't believe he's gone."

Jane sighed to herself, at an apparent loss for words.

"Mark said he could take you home," she said, kneeling beside him, placing her hand on his knee. "Are you sure you'll be okay?"

Clouse nodded, still too choked up to speak at length.

Quickly giving him a gentle kiss on the forehead, Jane turned to leave. She would have plenty of projects to keep herself busy the rest of the day.

A moment passed before Daniels and McCabe headed toward him. McCabe let Daniels amble ahead of him to speak with Clouse first. Clouse pulled out a pair of sunglasses, putting them on to mask his grief.

"You sure you still want to talk?" Daniels asked, approaching apprehensively.

"I'm fine," the firefighter answered, wiping the remaining moisture from under the shades.

"This can wait, you know."

"No," Clouse said defiantly. "It can't."

McCabe stepped forward.

"Where are we going then?"

Both men shrugged.

"I know a place."

"No bars," Clouse and Daniels said simultaneously, looking squarely at him.

"I promise, no bars," the state trooper replied defensively, raising his hands. "I do occasionally frequent other establishments."

Clouse's attention turned from the two officers.

"What the hell is he doing here?" Clouse asked himself, seeing Jerome Barnett some distance away, overlooking the remains of the proceedings from beneath a shady tree.

Before he contemplated an answer, Clouse glanced further to his left as he removed his sunglasses, adding to his distress.

"Oh, shit," he said, rising from the boulder.

He saw Niemeyer marching in the direction of the mettlesome reporter, unsure of whether Barnett saw him, or what the burly contractor might do when he reached him.

Before the two officers understood the problem, Clouse darted in the direction of his friend, hoping to cut him off at the pass.

He made it just in time, as Niemeyer began screaming several choice words at the reporter, before even reaching him.

"You have no right to be here!" he yelled as Clouse physically restrained him from stepping any closer, fearing Niemeyer's temper might lead to a discharged fist. It took every bit of strength the firefighter mustered to keep his larger friend away from Barnett.

"I'm not here for any trouble," the reporter said defensively. "I just came to pay my respects."

"And see what scoop you could get," Niemeyer fired back. "You son-of-a-bitch! You've done nothin' but capitalize on all of us this en'tar time and you expect me to believe that?"

"I'm sorry. I'll leave," Barnett said, turning to go.

Niemeyer struggled to get at the man, virtually ignoring Clouse's physical restraint.

"This isn't the time, Tim," Clouse said sternly. "Leave it alone."

"He's nothin' but a piece of shit, Paul," Niemeyer said, letting his drawl slip into his speech through the pent up anger.

Barnett turned just long enough to get in some parting words.

"Yes, Mr. Clouse. You probably should keep an eye on him and that *killer* instinct of his," he said, inferring once again that Niemeyer was perfectly capable of murder.

Infuriated, Niemeyer lunged forward again, prompting McCabe to assist in keeping him at bay, particularly since several stragglers from the funeral watched from their cars.

"Easy, big guy," the state trooper said, grasping one of the contractor's arms until Niemeyer finally settled down, Barnett too far from his reach.

"Damn, Paul, I'm sorry," Niemeyer apologized. "It just pisses me off every t'ahm I see him after what he put you and everyone else through last year."

"He doesn't need to be pointing fingers," McCabe noted. "It's not the press's job to wildly throw out names of suspects."

Niemeyer gave a strange look to McCabe, as though asking if he was truly a suspect, or if it was a slip on the trooper's part. McCabe turned away with Daniels while Clouse took his friend aside momentarily.

"You okay now, Tim?"

"Yeah. I'm fine."

"Good. I feel like I'm playing big brother to you lately. Start worrying about yourself and your family, and leave everything else to the police, okay?"

"All right. I'll let it go," Niemeyer reluctantly agreed.

"Thanks. Now I've got to have a chat with Mark and his buddy to see what we can find out about Ken's killer. Just go home and relax a little while," Clouse said with a hearty slap to his friend's backside.

Niemeyer nodded.

"And one other thing, Tim."

"Yeah?"

"You aren't that bad at public speaking."

A grin slipped across the contractor's face as he turned to leave. Like Clouse, he probably felt a void in his life without his high school buddy. He was obviously infuriated about being publically accused of murder, twice at that.

23

While McCabe insisted on changing in the restroom of the cafe the three men stopped at, Clouse ordered coffee, catching glimpses of a peculiar grin forming on his friend's mouth every minute or so.

"What's got you so giddy?" he finally asked Daniels.

"Nothing."

"Don't give me that. You've been acting weird all day." He paused to sip from his coffee. "Mark, you're the most grim, serious person I know. Today it's like you're a kid getting a trip to the candy store."

"Thanks for the kind words."

Clouse gave a sarcastic complimentary nod.

"Despite my hallow and boring life, I got home last night and made my way upstairs for the first time in a year."

Clouse gave a puzzled look.

"You know," Daniels said in a lower voice. "Upstairs. Where my bed is."

"I still don't see where you're going with this."

"Because I haven't been able to walk for a year, I've been sleeping downstairs alone, where wheelchair access is easier. Cindy took me upstairs last night."

Clouse thought a moment before what his friend stated finally materialized in his mind.

"Oh," he said with a momentary hesitation. "You mean you've gone a whole year without it?"

Daniels nodded, the relief showing in his face.

"Guess I'd be pretty chipper too."

McCabe emerged from the restroom carrying his covered suit, wearing jeans and a T-shirt depicting the statement, *You can always tell an Irishman when you see him, but you can't tell him much.* He settled into the booth beside Daniels, draping his suit over the seat.

"Welcome back, Turlough," Daniels said, teasing the detective about his heritage, and personal obsession with it.

"At least my last name doesn't have a hundred listings in the phone book," McCabe retorted. "There's nothing wrong with a man's roots."

"And there's nothing wrong with us getting this over with," Clouse stated. "We've got a lot to cover."

Both officers looked at one another guiltily, forgetting momentarily just whose funeral they had just come from.

"Okay," McCabe began. "I'm having no luck whatsoever on this *Coven* your informant told you about," he said to Clouse. "Either the group doesn't exist, or they're so underground that no police organization has ever heard of them. And that is highly unlikely."

"It sounded regional," Clouse recalled aloud. "Local, perhaps."

"I'll keep checking, but it doesn't look promising."

"What about suspects?" Daniels inquired.

"I've eliminated all of the Summers family," McCabe said, referring to relatives of Clouse's deceased wife. "Our revenge theory is probably out the window."

"Unless of course it's revenge for someone other than Roger Summers," Daniels noted.

"Are you speaking of David Landamere?" McCabe inquired.

"Not necessarily. Maybe someone's loved one got axed last year and they hold Paul and me responsible, so they're taking out everyone else involved, saving us for last."

"So knocking me unconscious off my boat was just a strong foreshadowing?" Clouse asked his friend with more than a little skepticism.

"Who knows? Maybe they intended to pull you out so you would think you're very lucky. Maybe this whole informant thing you've got is one big lie."

Clouse shook his head.

"I don't think so." He looked to McCabe. "I think my informant is that mutilated body you found roadside a few days ago."

As their waitress returned, each quickly placed a light order, then returned to the business at hand.

"Seems we're a bit shorthanded on suspects," the state detective told Clouse. "Your buddy Tim and that reporter guy were both placed at the hospital just minutes before the murder occurred. Granted, the cameras didn't catch anyone else snooping around that floor, but it would be awfully tough to completely avoid detection, wandering hospital floors."

Daniels sipped some orange juice before speaking.

"Not that tough. After visiting hours the place is like a ghost town on some floors."

"And if it isn't Tim or Barnett, then it's probably someone who has familiarity with the hospital," Clouse said. "Maybe he works there, or had time to study it. You might ask their staff if anyone unusual has been snooping around."

"Already have," McCabe replied. "They said no one stuck out."

Daniels sipped his juice, probably thinking of what clues they already possessed, and how to further check them before speaking again.

"Assuming Paul's buddy is truthful about those two teenagers wearing black, it might be worth checking out some of the local tattoo parlors. A snake tattoo with someone's neck as a template shouldn't be too hard to trace."

McCabe nodded in agreement.

"Are you pretty certain the person who attacked you on your boat wore diving equipment, Mr. Clouse?"

"What little I saw was black and rubbery," Clouse recalled. "And it was a little chilly to be wearing normal swimming trunks."

"Okay. I'll check the local outposts and see about purchases made in the last year. Maybe I'll get lucky and snag a recent purchase that seems fishy."

"Don't hold your breath," Daniels commented with a strange smirk, knowing how scarce lucky breaks were the previous year.

"Ah, a pun," McCabe said. "I like that."

Clouse found it amusing that Daniels could only be funny completely on accident. Even before the shooting, his friend was quiet, and often emotionally detached from everything around him. He often wondered what caused the former detective to find so little in life entertaining.

"So tell me what you're both thinking," the state trooper requested.

"I think this Coven doesn't exist and Paul's informant led him down the wrong track to begin with," Daniels began. "Our killer probably has a deep-seated interest in the hotel, much like Landamere and Summers did last year."

McCabe nodded, looking to Clouse.

"I think the murders are very personal," Clouse began. "The Coven could be bogus, but I think these tile floor pieces are extremely important to the killer. If we are dealing with an underground faction, it could be difficult, but I don't think any leader is going to trust multiple people with carrying out several murders. We're probably dealing with one to three people, tops. I think the killer waited until this season, picked out the important survivors from last year, and set to it."

"And you're a fireman?" McCabe asked, eyebrow raised. "We may have to recruit you."

"Sorry. I'm perfectly content where I work."

Everyone paused until the waitress placed their food on the table before speaking.

"You might also check out campus apartments that have been vacated, or missing roommates in case my informant was a college kid," Clouse told McCabe.

"I can try," the detective noted doubtfully, "but your informant could have been from any number of towns around here. I'll glance through the missing persons reports."

"While you check out your leads, I want to go with Paul to speak with the people who bought those pieces several years ago, so we can check them out. Since Paul's an acting manager for the hotel, it'll be perfectly legit."

McCabe thought a moment.

"Good idea. Make sure you photograph each piece, front and back, so we can see if there's anything about them worth killing for."

"We can start tomorrow," Clouse said. "Mark and I need to spend a day with our families to appease the womenfolk."

"Good," Daniels said, obviously feeling better, knowing his friend took some scolding at home, much like he did.

"That's fine," McCabe said. "I'm going to do some interviews and find a good bar where I can organize my findings."

24

Most of the next morning seemed spent in vain for Daniels and Clouse as they followed a route of their own planning, trying to reach as many tile buyers as possible before dusk. By late afternoon they were on the tenth name.

Four had moved, one turned out to be a false name and address altogether, and the other four owned only singular pieces of the tile. For the most part they were happy to see Clouse, hear about the hotel, then allow their pieces to be photographed for what Clouse called "preservation purposes."

To both men, none of the pieces held any significance whatsoever. Clouse noticed the pieces were like new on their shiny side, where either forest green or white were predominantly the colors. The backs showed nothing but dull gray, and occasionally specks of the adhesive used to put it down almost a century before.

As he navigated a typical county road outside of Paoli, Clouse spied everything possible to remind him of the season at one time or another.

"I hate this time of year," he muttered.

"It's not my favorite either," Daniels replied.

"Are we getting close?"

"About another half mile or so," the officer replied, reading house numbers as they went.

Clouse spied a lit jack-o-lantern on someone's front steps, reminding him of how his first wife died, and the entire setup of the first batch of murders.

"Does this whole thing ever make you wonder about how you might die?" he asked Daniels as they drew closer to the house.

"I know none of the people who were murdered ever expected it. You and I know better, and that's why we're hunting, instead of being the hunted."

"I can't believe the killer came after you when you couldn't even walk."

"That's the whole idea," Daniels explained. "Catch people when they're off-guard, or at their weakest. If we sit around our homes thinking we're safe, we'll be as vulnerable as everyone else, if not more so."

From a distance, the two men spied an isolated farmhouse with a rickety unpainted barn in the back yard, looking close to falling in upon itself. Clothesline was strung across the back of the house to the barn, and several large toys, such as toddler peddling tricycles were strewn across the yard.

Clouse pulled into the drive, spying several pumpkins set along the porch. A scarecrow, stuffed awkwardly, sat in a chair with a large, rusted scythe resting atop his lap. A shrieking ghost, like the one he and his first wife had, swung from atop the porch, giving signs that children probably lived in this household, unaware of the suffering the Halloween season brought some people.

Though dressed in slacks and a tie, Daniels did not bring along his firearm. He simply played along with his friend's charade, revealing nothing about his police background unless absolutely necessary to attain information. To this point, it mattered little what he did, because they were no further than they had been that morning.

"Take a look," Clouse said, pointing out a sign that displayed the house was guarded by a security agency, making it difficult for any potential thieves to steal the pieces, assuming the family and the pieces resided here.

"Maybe we'll get lucky," Daniels noted.

Before knocking, Clouse took the list out from his pocket, assuring himself the address and name were correct. He found Gerald

Thompson had purchased four pieces during the sale of the tile fragments.

He knocked.

"Hello?" a man slightly older than the two visitors asked when he answered the door, figuring he was being harassed by peddlers.

A sour look of dismay crossed his face as he prepared to ask them to leave.

"Mr. Thompson?" Clouse asked.

"Yes."

"I have somewhat of a strange request for you, if we could have a moment of your time," Clouse asked of the man.

Several minutes later, they found themselves seated in the living room as Clouse explained a partly fictitious account of why they were visiting.

Considering the yard looked to be in shambles, the house's interior was quite the opposite.

A redone Victorian house, the place had a spotless interior with vast shelves and curio cabinets filled with antiques and collectable plates. Most of the house lacked carpet to display the original wood flooring. Even family photographs were framed in antique wood, continuing the look of the house's restoration.

"So you think there's something on the back of these pieces that was overlooked before they were sold?" Thompson asked when Clouse finished his explanation of why they were visiting.

"Yes, possibly the designer's name, or exactly where they were imported from."

"I have to admit I've never really examined the back of the things. Kim, can you get those out of the cabinet?" he asked his wife.

She left the room to fetch the tiles.

"Can I get you two anything to drink?"

"No thanks," Clouse answered for both.

"So you're really one of the top dogs in the reconstruction?" Thompson asked Clouse, interested in the hotel's condition, like many local residents familiar with the structure.

"I am, when I'm not putting out fires in Bloomington," Clouse explained. "I work for the city, and tend to the hotel on my days off."

Thompson nodded.

"I sell agricultural machinery to farmers," he explained. "I was a volunteer firefighter when I lived closer to city limits. Addictive, isn't it?"

Clouse agreed with a friendly smirk. He noticed Daniels perk up when Kim Thompson returned with four tile pieces in hand.

"Here you are," she said, carefully handing them to him.

Clouse examined them momentarily, finding something unique on the backside of two fragments. Daniels took up the camera, snapping shots of each side as Clouse held them in position. The former detective also seemed to notice the peculiar markings.

Marks in the form of several lines seemed to cover part of the two pieces, one of them containing part of what looked to be an "X" near one edge. Clouse set the fragments on the nearby coffee table, seeing if they formed any sort of pattern.

"How did these come?" he asked Thompson, unsure since he started the hotel project years later.

"They were in a box," the salesman recalled. "I just remember picking out four on top, trying to get the largest chunks I could. We got extras in case the kids ever got interested in the place."

Clouse noticed the two pieces containing markings fit together at one corner, but like a jigsaw, several other pieces were necessary to complete whatever map or design was meant to be studied. Even as he noticed a snug fit along a one inch surface where the lines connected perfectly, he wondered if it was truly possible the pieces belonged together, from a batch of potentially hundreds of fragments.

"Photograph that," he told Daniels, who was poised to already.

"What do you make of it?" Thompson asked, assuming Clouse had some sort of expert opinion far beyond his own.

"I'm not sure. It's a lot more than I expected to find." He stood, ready to continue his quest with newfound initiative. "I appreciate you taking the time to help us."

"It's been enlightening," Thompson said with a sincere smile. "Let me know if there's anything else we can do for you."

"Thanks," Clouse said, shaking the man's hand. "I just might do that."

A few minutes later the two men headed down the road, feeling a sense of accomplishment, as though their search was not in vain.

"What do you really think?" Daniels inquired, apparently under the impression his friend held out on the Thompson family.

"I really don't know. But at least I feel like there's some information on the tiles. Why it's worth killing for is beyond me, but it must be important."

Daniels rewound the film in his camera.

"So what now?"

"We'll drop that off at a one-hour lab and I'll get you home."

"And you?"

"There are a couple other things I want to take care of before I call it a night."

*   *   *

Most of his little cottage appeared dark as Charlie Winters read in his favorite plush chair, using only the light from a nearby lamp to skim the words of *The Scarlet Letter*.

He often read classic novels, thinking every modern book was nothing more than a mutation of previous works. Only the names and slight plot details ever seemed to change when he read such trash. To him, nothing was more frightening than the details and realism of classic horror and drama, written long before even he was brought into the world.

Over the years Winters found respect for antiques and the way the world once was. He remembered two world wars, the great depression, and the Reagan years. To him, nothing remained fonder in his memory than his youth, and how good it felt to be reckless, without a care in the world.

By today's standards, he thought, his notion of recklessness was quite tame. Kids never thought of vandalism, murder, and taking guns to school. Teenagers stayed to themselves, or in small packs, never aiming to bother or harm anyone. Things had changed, he pondered as a knock came to his front door.

"Who on earth could that be?" he asked aloud, setting his book down to see who his unexpected visitor might be.

"Hello," a young man answered from the other side, holding a notebook and pen. "My name is Paul Clouse. I'm working on the restoration of the West Baden Springs Hotel. My fiancee said you might have some information to help me in a particular search I'm conducting."

"What kind of search?" Winters asked, curious, as he waved the younger man inside.

For a man of his advanced age, Winters' voice and even his posture appeared remarkably intact.

"I'm looking for pieces to the atrium's tile floor that were sold off years ago. I think they might have a message, or something the restoration crew overlooked before selling them. I understand you worked at the hotel when the Rexfords took over?"

"I did," Winters replied. "Have a seat, Mr. Clouse," he added, taking refuge in his favorite chair again. "Would you like to take your coat off?"

"No thanks. I won't take up too much of your time."

"So, you work at the hotel, eh?"

"I've been there several years," the visitor replied. "We finished the place up this year, and were prepared to have a grand opening when a tragic accident happened last week."

"Yes, I heard," Winters replied.

"So what exactly do you do there?"

"I'm a design consultant. I created blueprints of the hotel, then got hired to help research and restore the hotel to its original appearance."

"I see. I'm glad you take such interest in that beautiful building."

"That I do."

A moment passed while Winters watched his visitor open the notebook and ready the pen.

"So, what can you tell me?" he asked at last.

"Many years ago, when I was younger than yourself, I watched them put that floor down."

"So you weren't actually part of the crew?"

"No. I was just there to do odd jobs. My job there was basically political, since my mother knew the Rexfords and wanted to keep me busy during the summer."

"What can you tell me about that floor?"

"Very little, other than the fact that it was stunning. They put it in, piece by piece," the old man recalled, running a thoughtful hand through his uncombed thicket of gray hair.

His beard looked to be about a week old, as though it slipped his mind to shave within that time.

"So you're saying each little one inch piece was placed by itself?"

"Well, most all of them."

"What?" Winters' guest asked inquisitively, setting the pen down. "Was there an exception?"

Winters groaned a moment, unwilling to automatically tell his guest the secret he kept locked inside his mind for so many decades.

"If I tell you something, will you take it to your grave as I've sworn to?" the old man asked, as though relieving himself of a deep, dark secret on his deathbed.

"If it helps me in my search, I'll make certain it never leaves this room."

Winters pondered a moment, knowing what a can of worms letting his secret out might create. For years the hotel lay in decay, with declining public interest, and even less help in its struggle to retain any of the beauty remaining from its glory days. Now, with things looking better, and near the anniversary of the murder spree, he wondered if the man before him could truly be trusted. He also realized this might be the last person he could reveal his secret to, who might have the slightest comprehension of his tale.

"Very well," Winters said, clasping his hands in his lap, deciding he had nothing to lose by telling the story to someone connected to the hotel. "Toward the end of the floor's completion, a bare spot about three feet around stood with no covering for several days.

One morning, as I was making my way around several rooms upstairs, I heard a conversation from the atrium between Mr. Rexford and several workers. I peeked from a balcony room to see the four men below, two of them carrying the last tiles for the floor, only this time they were in one solid piece, cut perfectly to fill the empty space."

Winters paused, taking a sip of water from a nearby cup.

"On the other side of the tiling appeared a detailed sketch, which I took to be some sort of map. Several lines led to a few distinct marks, almost like a pirate treasure map. It drew my attention, enough to make me follow Mr. Rexford after the conversation ended, and the floor was being finished."

Winters looked to his hands, then to his visitor.

"He returned to his room, taking a small chest out from a closet. After opening it, he removed a canvas bag, which appeared somewhat weighted. He made some comment about keeping it safe, and set about replacing it into the box, which he locked."

After writing several notes, the visitor closed his notebook, giving Winters a curious glance.

"Did you ever see the bag again? Or its contents?"

"Never on either count. But I'm sure they hid it wherever that map led them to."

"If they hid the contents, why would they leave a map to its whereabouts?"

Winters shrugged.

"I suppose, so that a later generation might find it. Perhaps it was their personal memoirs they wanted saved for later, or valuables they felt would fall into the wrong hands at the time. They were a different sort, the Rexfords."

"But you feel certain the map led to whatever Mr. Rexford possessed that day?"

"Of that I have no doubt. He gave an impassioned soliloquy about keeping its contents safe from harm and his wife's family."

"I appreciate you confiding in me, Mr. Winters. That certainly does help my cause."

"Is there anything else I can do for you?" Winters asked as his guest stood to leave.

"You've been quite a help already. Thanks for your time."

As his guest turned toward the door, Winters noticed an unusual skin marking at the collar of the man's jacket. He drew closer, seeing it partially covered by the jacket, and by a black turtleneck sweater.

"Oh, there is one other thing," his guest said, turning around as Winters made out the serpentine tattoo along his neck.

Before he thought to react, the knife blade rammed beneath his sternum with the force and speed of a charging bull. He groaned and lurched forward while blood spewed from his open mouth. His murderer heartlessly tossed him to the floor, the blood emptying from Winters' abdomen as he slowly bled out.

He listened as the door opened and the man known to others as Jacob left the residence. In all his years, he never expected such an end, and Winters supposed the element of surprise was all part of life.

One thing seemed certain.

His secret would never leave the room.

25

McCabe finished his second beer at Kelley's pub as he glanced over the paperwork from that morning. He had checked tattoo parlors with little success.

Most of the serpent design customers were bikers passing through town, or college kids. Both were nearly impossible to trace because the parlors kept no detailed records of their customers.

He called most of the major apartment rental companies in Bloomington and the surrounding area, gathering a short list of male renters who had recently disappeared, either because they found new apartments, moved home, couldn't pay their rent, or simply disappeared for no reason.

He planned on visiting existing roommates or family members, starting the next morning, to discover the whereabouts of the missing renters.

For the moment, he occupied himself by reviewing a list of people who had purchased scuba equipment the past five years, and the information they left behind. He could only search for promising names and locations initially, and if that resulted in nothing, McCabe would probe deeper, interviewing suspects in the order of apparent relevance.

Ordinarily he never brought work to the pub, but he felt more relaxed, seated at his own table with Celtic music in the background. Some regulars thought he was some sort of accountant, or in business for himself. He seldom wore his gun or badge inside, and never told people his profession unless they asked. McCabe simply wanted to fit in the best he could, and when others knew he was an officer of the law, they tended to be less accepting, and less comfortable.

Raising his hand, he motioned to one of the waitresses for another beer, tipping her when it reached his table. He took a sip, looking at the thicket of papers in front of him. Sorting through them required hours of concentration. He sighed aloud, deciding to visit the restroom before getting started.

Shuffling his papers into one neat pile, he stood, draping his sport coat over the chair to ensure everyone knew he would be right back. He sauntered into the tiny, one-stall men's room, hearing a noise from outside the window.

After zipping his pants, McCabe walked to the window, opening it further than the inch it was already cracked, looking out to the back of the pub where several cars sat in the darkness. Cold air hit his face, reminding him of why it was better indoors.

He grunted to himself before returning to the music and festivity of the tavern.

McCabe seated himself, sipping from the beer bottle before sifting through the papers, making certain everything was there. He began to look over the first inventory sheet when the pub's door opened, revealing a man dressed almost entirely in black, stepping inside. He looked around momentarily, as though looking for someone, or something.

To the detective, he appeared completely out of place. He was too young, and he didn't look the least bit Irish. His hair was black, perhaps dyed, judging by the strange gleam it seemed to produce.

His clothes, except for the turtleneck, appeared out of place. He wore heavy black boots, almost of a military issue, that were hip in some dance clubs. The young man could easily have been a model in any teen magazine with his slender build and smooth face. McCabe was about to start reviewing his paperwork when their eyes locked and the young man acted as though he'd found what he came for.

"Are you Detective McCabe?" the young man asked as he approached.

"I am."

Looking nervously around, the young man pulled out a chair beside the detective.

"May I?" he asked.

McCabe waved him into the seat.

"My name is Stephen," the young man revealed. "I've spoken several times with Paul Clouse about my involvement with a certain, um, faction. He told me where to find you."

"What brings you to me?" the detective asked with a hint of suspicion.

"It's getting too dangerous for me to keep sneaking out on the group. I'll tell you everything you need to know about these people if you'll protect me. Put me in witness relocation, give me a new identity, something."

McCabe sighed aloud, taking another sip of his beer before shifting the papers into one stack, using a paperclip to bind them.

"What can you tell me?" he asked, sitting back.

"Oh, no," the young man said, looking around. "We can't talk here."

"What did you have in mind?".

"There's something at the hotel you really need to see. Something I couldn't tell Clouse. I can't tell you everyone who's involved, but I can tell you what they're after. And I can show you exactly where it is."

McCabe pondered the situation a moment, knowing how safe a public place was compared to the outside. His gun rested in the trunk of his patrol car, allowing quick access if necessary. His tendency to trust the young man wavered against the knowledge that Clouse's informant may very well have been the mutilated body discovered outside Paoli.

"Okay," McCabe said after a moment. "I'll be right back," he said, taking his beer up to the bar with him, gulping it on the way.

Setting the half-empty bottle on the bar, McCabe tapped the bartender on the shoulder. Shawn Kelley had known the trooper several years, especially since McCabe had helped him keep the bar safe from trouble over the years.

Some locals weren't willing to accept a theme pub after it opened, but McCabe ensured Kelley's maintained peace anytime he was there. The trooper also received free drinks on occasion, making certain his patronage was ongoing.

"What is it, Tug?" the owner asked, an authentic accent acquired from his father, coming through.

"Shawn, can you call my local post and have them send a unit over here once I'm outside? My radio's out in the car and I don't want to make a scene," he said, shifting his eyes behind him without moving his head.

"Problem?" Kelley asked.

"Not at all," McCabe answered, using a slight accent of his own.

"That kid came in for a moment while you were in the restroom, acting like he was looking for something."

"That a fact?"

"Yeah. Walked over to your table like he was supposed to meet you or something. Got a confused look on his face and walked back out. Be careful, Tug."

"Always am," the trooper replied, stepping away from the bar, his feet feeling a bit rubbery beneath him.

Two beers never even phased the trooper.

Never.

Perhaps it was unsteady nerves, but McCabe's walk was not as hearty as usual when he returned to the table.

"Had to tell my friend I was leaving," McCabe lied to the young man when he reached the table, taking up the collection of papers from the scuba gear dealerships.

He snatched his sport coat from the chair, putting it on for protection from the brisk weather.

Giving a nervous nod, the young man followed McCabe's lead out the door. A wall of cold air hit them both instantly, leaving McCabe fighting for his senses. He reached for his keys, intending to retrieve his gun from the trunk, but dropped them on the ground as his fingers began to shiver.

"Feeling a bit disoriented?" the young man asked, his voice sounding much more certain than before.

The shift of control still eluded McCabe as he reached for the keys, stumbling a bit as he did so.

"Allow me," the young man said, picking them off the ground, quickly finding the key to the trunk.

McCabe shot him a confused stare, knowing somehow he was drugged or poisoned, but uncertain of how. Kelley's words echoed through his head, speaking of when the man walked into the pub, searching for something. McCabe had left his beer on the table when he used the restroom, leaving ample opportunity to slip something into it.

Suddenly the noise out back made sense.

"I know what you're thinking," the young man said, opening the trunk with ease, keeping his focus on McCabe, rather than what the trunk held. McCabe spied his service weapon, holstered beneath his briefcase.

"You want to know who I am and exactly what I put in your beer that's giving you a drunken feeling you probably haven't experienced since college. We'll have time for that a little bit later. First, I have to show you that important something at the hotel."

McCabe stumbled over toward the young man, his mind as groggy as his body. The younger man pulled the turtleneck down, revealing a marking McCabe had only been familiar with through description until now. Without much thought or provocation, he swung at the man he knew to be the mysterious Jacob, and missed. Giving a slight laugh of amusement, Jacob shoved the detective into the trunk, ready to close the lid when McCabe lunged with another fist, receiving the trunk against the top of his head as a reward for his effort, knocking him cold.

*   *   *

Russell Hinds walked the grounds of the West Baden Springs Hotel for only his third night.

One of four private security guards hired by Dr. Martin Smith, he had the graveyard shift. After the incidents the previous year, combined with Ken Kaiser's strange death, Smith decided to hire private guards, having them sign waivers, rather than risk contracting state or local police.

He wanted to ensure his guards were full-time, knowing the grounds and the hotel they patrolled like their own back yards. It took some of the liability away when they signed contracts assuring they, or their family, could not sue for loss of life, or injury, because they knew beforehand, the hotel was a dangerous assignment.

Strangely enough, Hinds was a local reserve officer from the neighboring town of Orleans, who worked mornings at a factory job. Tall, dark-haired, and strong, he looked the part of a cop with his mustache and slight gut, which coffee and donuts occasionally contributed to.

The plain blue uniform did little to inspire Hinds, and he refused to wear the cap Smith provided with its generic silver emblem. A horrid yellow stripe down either pant leg would have made the uniform completely intolerable for the guard, but he was simply in it for extra money, figuring no one would ever see him at such late hours.

He might have done regular police work if the factory didn't pay so well. Money never seemed abundant enough though.

After two divorces, the security guard had two children and little free time on his hands. Child support kept him working two jobs, though his oldest was nearly out of high school, giving him a reprieve to look forward to the next year.

As he walked the grounds, customary of the first hour every night he worked, his steely blue eyes peered through the thin frames of his glasses, over the sunken garden as his old leather holster creaked at his side. Both the holster, and the .357 Magnum it held, were gifts from his grandfather soon after his first marriage. Upon signing with Smith to guard the hotel, he was instructed never to fire the weapon unless his life appeared immediately threatened.

After signing a waiver that forbid anyone from receiving compensation for his death or injury, Hinds decided he would fire the weapon whenever his police training dictated it was appropriate. By no means was he putting himself in the path of a flying scythe.

Passing the cemetery, Hinds looked up to the bland, white markers, knowing one of them contained the legendary Father Ernest, who had been dug up for a few days the year before, during the murder spree. A grave set apart from the others, it seemed undisturbed to this point, despite the witching holiday drawing near.

Across the sunken garden, near the hotel's main entrance, Hinds spied a car pulling up the long driveway, after somehow bypassing the chain at the front gate.

"Ah, damn," he cursed, beginning the long walk back toward the hotel, ready to bark at whoever had enough indecency to barge through an obvious gate and make their way onto private property at such a late hour.

When Hinds reached the concrete steps leading up to the drive and the hotel, he found the car parked. Its rear end faced him, and as he drew closer, keys shimmered from beneath the trunk. Several of the old, antique lamp posts loomed overhead, giving him a good perspective of the car and the entire driveway.

"Strange," he said to himself, picking them up, noticing the car's red and blue lights mounted inside the car's windows.

A look at the plate confirmed it was an unmarked state police car, but where was the owner?

Using his flashlight, Hinds peered inside the vehicle, finding nothing. He shined the light around the area, seeing nothing more than trees, shrubs, lamps, and the mammoth hotel behind him. He unzipped his nylon jacket, reaching for the portable radio he'd forgotten to bring in his hurry to work.

"Shit," he said, finding nothing to grasp inside the jacket.

There was no base, or another officer for him to contact anyhow. His only use for the radio was emergency calls to local police departments, and he could do that from any phone.

"Fuck," he muttered, breathing a bit more nervously now. "Anyone out there?" he called in a controlled volume, hearing a slight echo from the grove of trees seated behind the hotel.

With no response, he decided to open the trunk, fearing something odd was afoot. Either way, it was his watch, and he needed to discover why a state police car was parked in the lot. To this point, he felt no immediate danger to his life, though the tranquility surrounding him made him feel his well-being was subject to change.

As he placed the key in the trunk, a noise reached his eardrum. Unable to decide whether it was below or behind him, Hinds placed his right hand on his sidearm, ready to draw if necessary. With his free hand he turned the key slowly, letting the trunk pop itself open as he stepped back.

*   *   *

From inside the trunk McCabe barely saw through the drug's effects to spy Jacob running up on the unsuspecting security guard, knife in hand. The wide eyes of both officers locked for an instant, shocked to see one another. His gun already drawn, the trooper fired two shots through double vision, both nailing Hinds in the right side of the chest, just missing the intended target behind him.

"Oh, shit!" McCabe cursed to himself aloud for screwing up his one opportunity for an easy escape, and hitting a fellow officer.

Hinds whirled around in pain, and in an instant, Jacob lunged forward, swung his right arm, and knocked the gun from McCabe's impaired fingers.

Certain the trooper was no longer a threat to him, Jacob ran to Hinds, jabbing him in the side with the knife, forcing a painful groan from the guard, before using both hands to launch Hinds off the concrete walkway, down the cold steps where he heard several of the guard's bones break on the way.

During the first few tumbles, Hinds grumbled and yelped in pain, but nearly halfway down, he made no sound, even as his body tumbled end over end toward the sunken garden.

Jacob watched the guard land awkwardly at the bottom of the steps, feeling certain the man was dead. Even if he wasn't, he would be before daybreak. The cold weather would do little to sooth his open wounds as his warm blood slowly leaked onto the concrete.

"See?" the young man asked, returning to McCabe. "That wasn't so bad, was it?"

"Fuck you," the detective replied as he was hoisted from the trunk with some degree of difficulty. "What did you do to me?"

"Oh, it's all about you, isn't it? You just shot and killed a fellow police officer, and you're thinking about yourself?"

"You bastard. That's not true," McCabe replied with a drunken sort of slur.

"Ah, I see your condition is worsening. I'd better get on with explaining my master plan before you completely pass out, hadn't I?"

Only a spiteful mutter came from McCabe.

"You see," Jacob said, practically dragging the detective toward the hotel entrance, "I slipped you a drug known as GHB, or gamma-hydroxybutyrate, while you visited the restroom. I'm sure you know it as a date rape drug, but believe me, I have no intention of carrying out such acts on you."

"That's a relief," McCabe mumbled, unable to bear his own weight any longer, much less put up a fight.

He knew GHB acted very much like alcohol, only much more intense, even in small doses. There was no telling how much his body took in, even though he never finished the beer. Symptoms included dizziness, difficulty focusing the eyes, slurring of speech, grogginess, and positive mood swings.

Except for a good mood, he had experienced them all.

"They say large doses can kill a person, and I did give you a rather frightful amount, but it seems you'll live, at least for the time being. Even if you had died, it would have served my purpose. We can't have you tracking me through all the local merchants, now can we?"

McCabe felt himself being dragged up a flight of stairs, probably toward the hotel's main entrance. He wondered exactly what Jacob had in store for him, or if he would remain conscious to experience it.

"And, as for that body you found, that was my former protégé, Stephen. It seems he didn't like playing by my rules. It's so hard to find team players these days," he continued, opening the glass front doors, leading the way into the hotel.

A moment later, McCabe realized he was being dragged into the basement. Despite a size and power advantage over his captor, the drug made him powerless to retaliate. Every ounce of energy he possessed went to keeping himself conscious long enough to figure out a measure of escape. His survival depended on observation, now that his best chance of killing Jacob was foiled.

"Don't worry, detective. I have far worse fates in store for your newfound friends," Jacob continued, pulling McCabe into a small corridor, separate from the supplies stored in the basement.

A stack of bricks and mortar mix were waiting nearby, and McCabe sensed his ultimate fate.

Even as shackles cupped his wrists, attached to the thick concrete walls of the hotel, he could put up no fight. His consciousness wavered over the next few hours while a brick wall grew before him, sealing him in what would become a tomb devoid of sound, and possibly air. A candle placed on his end of the new wall burned brightly, then dimmed over the course of time as the wall went up.

McCabe regretted never getting to the radio in his front seat, and accidentally shooting Hinds, but his few measures of escape seemed far out of reach as the final bricks went up, leaving the candle to die slowly from a lack of oxygen. McCabe had no way to touch the wall, call for help, or hope to escape such a predicament.

Even as the effects of the drug wore off, and he realized how dire the situation was, he could only rattle the chains, bolted tightly to the wall, and think how similar this was to a story he'd read while in high school. He never much cared for Poe, or the man's eerie horror stories, but now he was living one, realizing the cold, calculating process Jacob must have gone through to pull off such a plan.

Through the wall he could barely hear Jacob whistling to himself, obviously happy with his plan's evil result as he left the room.

26

"You know, we should probably just see about getting a couple suites at this place," Daniels commented as he pulled into the hotel's drive, no longer using any devices to help him drive. "We're certainly down here enough."

Clouse stared ahead at the flood of police cars and ambulances.

"Quit bellyaching. You getting me up at the crack of dawn isn't my idea of fun either."

What Daniels knew to this point was something about a grizzly discovery made by the supply manager, when he came to find Hinds for access to the hotel. Though few details were released to the former detective, he knew McCabe had somehow been involved, and feared for the trooper's life.

After calling for a state police escort that took him most of the way down to West Baden, Daniels made good time, allowing him to get there before he missed anything important. His limited investigative powers came with his allegiance to McCabe, and if the trooper was missing as they said, or worse, he and Clouse would be powerless to conduct any sort of legitimate investigation. The thought of having no law enforcement power, with a killer after him, worried Daniels greatly.

Both stepped from the car, greeted by a county officer who recognized Clouse. He started to hold up a foreboding hand but Daniels showed him his old badge. Though he still used both crutches, Daniels' mobility increased every day. He passed as a working detective.

"I'm working with Trooper Tug McCabe on the homicides. He's with me," Daniels said of Clouse.

"Okay," the officer said. "We don't have a homicide here, but it's pretty fucked up."

"Who's in charge?"

"Sergeant Williams," the officer said, pointing to another county officer with stripes on the sleeve of his duty jacket.

Daniels led the way, introducing himself, and Clouse, to the sergeant before asking what they were looking at on the base of the stairs, at the foot of the sunken garden.

"Luke Williams," the sergeant said, shaking both their hands first. "We had a security guard shot and busted up," the officer said. "He's not making much sense. We think he might have some internal bleeding, and possibly a broken spine. That's why they're taking so long moving him."

"Has he said anything?"

"Something about getting shot by a state trooper. We've had men searching the grounds all morning and we haven't seen a damn thing. No bodies, no state vehicle, no nothing."

"How about inside the hotel?" Clouse asked.

"We had some men check in there too, but with six-hundred rooms, or whatever it has, there's no way we're going find anyone who doesn't want to be found."

Clouse took notice of a man off to the side, standing by himself at the base of the building's main entrance.

"Who's that?" Daniels asked.

"Carl Welch, the hotel's shipping and receiving manager. He comes in early two days a week to check inventory and unlock the back gate for the supply drivers."

"He probably found the poor security guard."

Clouse nodded.

"I'll be back, Mark," he said, excusing himself.

*   *   *

"Hi, Paul," Welch said, seeing a familiar face after a bombard-ment of police questioning.

"How are you holding up, Carl?"

"Doing okay, I suppose. It's not every day you come to work and find what you think is a dead body."

Clouse understood, but knew it got less traumatic each time.

"So what happened?"

"I came to work through the front gate and found the chain down. When I got out of my truck to look, I saw it was cut with bolt cutters. Well, I knew something wasn't right, so I hurried up to the main entrance, and that's when I heard a groaning sound from the sunken garden."

He nodded toward the group of people now standing there.

"One of the guards was laying down there on his back and I saw a bone sticking out of his left arm, so I knew it was bad. I just told him to lay still and went to call for help."

"Did you talk to him at all?" Clouse inquired.

"I tried, but he was in a lot of pain. Said something about a state trooper's car up here and being shot by the trooper. He got stabbed and tossed down the landing, but he wasn't sure who did that to him."

Clouse felt completely lost. All attempts to locate McCabe that morning had failed. He failed to respond to telephone calls, pages, or even his radio unit. Clouse worried something might have hap-pened to the trooper, especially if he drew too close to the truth.

Something terrible.

"But there was no sign of any other vehicle, or other people, when you got here?"

"No," Welch answered. "Like I said, the chain was cut, but other than that, everything else seemed in order."

Clouse was about to inquire about the front doors when a noise from behind the two men startled them. A loud diesel engine roared at the back gate as a truck parked at the locked structure, its driver impatiently stepping on the gas while it was in neutral to attract attention.

"Asshole," Welch said of the driver. "Figures he'd show up an hour late and still be as much of a prick as always."

"Who is it?" Clouse asked, unaccustomed to being on hotel grounds so early.

"One of our two supply delivery drivers. His name is James, and he's quite a piece of work," Welch answered, leading the way to the locked gate.

"What's his problem?" Clouse asked, following.

"The world, I think. Just watch."

Welch approached the gate as the driver of the truck, donning a stained, tan college baseball cap of some sort, looked down on the two men.

"About time you got over here," he said to Welch.

"It's not my fault you're two hours late," the supply manager replied, unlocking the gate.

Grunting, the driver noticed the commotion inside the hotel grounds.

"What's going on over there?"

"An accident," Welch said.

"Damn, this place is cursed."

Welch stared at the driver a moment, indicating he wanted no further mention of the hotel's checkered past.

Both walked with the truck as the driver backed it to the cafeteria doors, which provided a short route to the basement, where supplies were delivered and stored.

"No partner today?" Welch questioned when the driver stepped down from the cab.

"Nope. Small shipment."

Clouse decided to test whether or not the driver was as much of a jerk as his colleague described.

"Paul Clouse," he said, extending his hand as the man walked toward him.

"James Hartley," the driver replied, simply walking past, his eyes never wavering from their gaze at the hotel's cafeteria entrance.

Clouse spent a moment observing the man, noticing his navy blue shirt, nylon back support, steel-toed boots, and tattered blue jeans. His brown hair made way for flecks of gray, and his eyes seemed fixed a bit closer together than those of most people Clouse met, but he seemed ordinary enough. There was no wedding band on his left hand, and Clouse had some ideas why, but he wondered what made some people miserable toward everyone they met.

Probably no older than the firefighter, Hartley seemed to even walk with an arrogant stride that resembled a hunched gorilla with his protruding belly and thick arms. Clouse observed him for a moment at Welch's side as he shoved a mechanical lift like those used in retail stores, beneath a stack wrapped in heavy plastic. He wasn't about to do any more work than necessary.

"When he does make a joke, it's always bad," Welch noted aloud.

"There's too much stuff here to fit in the storage room," Hartley complained, pulling the cart out from the truck, rolling it down a ramp.

"It'll fit."

"You're wrong. I'll come get you when it doesn't, so you can tell me where you want it."

"Asshole," Welch muttered.

He noticed a strange bundle settled toward the edge of the truck, wrapped in heavy plastic atop a strong skid.

"Did you order bricks?" Welch asked Clouse.

"I've never personally ordered *anything*, Carl. Why?"

"Probably a shipping error. I don't feel like dealing with James again today. Let's see if they've made any progress with the security guard."

Clouse snickered, walking beside his co-worker, then remembered why he was there to begin with as they approached the scene. He noticed the guard now atop the stairs at the sunken garden, strapped into a stretcher. Daniels was speaking with the guard, despite the anxiety on the faces of the emergency medical technicians.

"Hold on just a second," Daniels said to the paramedic in charge. "What I need to ask him concerns life and death for someone else."

All eyes fell upon Hinds, who appeared fully conscious, despite the brace around his neck.

"Hurry it up," the paramedic replied. "He's got several broken bones, possibly including his pelvis."

The medics had determined his back and neck were probably fine, but the arm and pelvic bones were definitely in bad shape. Despite several things Hinds had forgotten to bring to work, a bulletproof vest was not one of them. His vest stopped both slugs from hitting anything vital, and actually stopped the knife from gaining full access to his ribs.

"What happened, Russ?" Daniels asked, using the man's first name now that he knew it.

"I swear to God there was a state police car parked in front of the hotel," the man said. "The keys were at the base of the car, so I opened the trunk slowly. Before I could draw my revolver he fired two shots, and I spun around."

Hinds took a few labored breaths before continuing.

"Next thing I know is I'm getting jabbed with a knife and tossed off the walkway where I lay unconscious most of the night."

Daniels scribbled mental notes as he went, trying to think of vital questions.

"Do you think the man in the trunk was the state trooper?"

"I think so."

"Is he the one who tossed you down the steps?"

"I don't know. It happened so fast, I never saw who it was. Thank God I've got insurance for this."

Before Daniels could invoke any further questioning, the paramedics rolled Hinds off to the ambulance, where he would likely be transported to a larger medical facility than the Paoli clinic.

"Damn," Daniels muttered.

"What do you think?" Clouse asked, leaving Welch to join his friend.

"I think either way we look at it, Tug is in some major trouble."

"You don't think he-"

"No," Daniels halted the question. "I think Tug was locked in his trunk, fired his weapon, and for some reason, missed the intended target."

Clouse sighed heavily, rubbing his chin.

"Where could he be?"

"I'd like to know that myself," Daniels replied. "He must have been too close to the truth, and someone wanted him silenced, but I have no idea what happened here."

*   *   *

Taking the final load into the basement, Hartley placed it, lowered the cart's fork arms, and took one final look around the area, satisfied he was correct.

"Told him it wouldn't all fit in the storage area," he muttered to himself.

A faint jingling sound caught his attention, as it had several times earlier during the unloading process. At first Hartley dismissed it as noise from workers upstairs, but he remembered no further work was being done at the hotel until after its official grand opening, whenever that happened. This time the noise seemed closer to him, almost from an adjacent room.

But there were no adjacent rooms.

About to dismiss it and leave the creepy hotel, he heard a jingling noise once more, almost like chains clanging against concrete.

"What the hell?" he asked himself, stepping toward where he believed the noise originated.

Hartley thought the storage area looked somewhat smaller, but failed to notice one particular area bricked up.

Until now.

He approached the wall, examining it from top to bottom as he did so. The type of bricks used were smaller than any other concrete blocks used in the hotel's basement, giving the impression they were older or newer. Feeling almost positive it was new, he touched the mortar, discovering it wasn't fully set.

Part of it rubbed off to the touch, showing it had yet to cure. A sudden rattle of chains behind the fixture caused Hartley to jump back, startled at the thought of someone being inside.

Using the fingers on his right hand, he gently pushed one brick, watching it give almost a centimeter. He pushed a bit harder, causing the entire brick to fall back into the wall, leaving him to wonder how solid the rest of the wall remained.

"Help me," he heard a voice murmur from inside, as though dehydrated to the point there was barely a voice left.

"Help yourself," Hartley said, ready to bolt from the room and leave the hotel grounds for fear of his life.

Bumping into a solid body halted him as he looked up into a faceless mask, held in place by someone wearing a grim reaper costume. He felt his breathing come in heaves.

Death itself had come for him.

Both hands, covered in the same black nylon as the rest of the costume, wrapped themselves around Hartley's neck, squeezing momentarily before launching him face-first into the stack of bricks he had just delivered, breaking his nose, stunning him, and setting him up for the kill.

Moaning in pain, and too shocked to move, Hartley slumped against the covered bricks until the reaper came forward, grasping him by the back brace, yanking him to his feet. This time the killer hurled him toward a solid wall, letting his face hit first, cracking his jaw. His ankle twisted on the fall downward, leaving him no chance of running away.

Hartley nearly lost consciousness, staggering to regain his footing with what little sense the killer hadn't knocked from his head.

Taking a moment to collect himself, the driver looked through mildly blurred vision around the room, seeing no one. Several stacks of bundled goods loomed around him, each potentially hiding someone. He heard his nervous breathing as his eyes darted around the room, looking for any possible hindrance to his escape.

Hartley wanted nothing more than to hop in his truck and get out of the hotel forever, and let the police deal with whatever psychopath lurked in the basement.

Mentally mapping the safest route out of the room, Hartley regained his footing the best he could, and headed for the entranceway to the storage area, looking around him as he gingerly limped toward daylight and the cafeteria above.

In his haste, he looked behind him for anyone lurking behind the bundles, distracting him momentarily from the entrance where a large, curved blade swung upward, making a swoosh sound as it did so.

No, Hartley thought as he turned around too late, the blade already in motion toward his abdomen. He caught a glimpse of the steel as it pierced his soft muscle tissue and organs, creating a gap too big for even modern medical miracles to heal. To ensure quicker death, the killer tugged the blade to the side, opening the wound further. Blood and intestines leaked from the driver's stomach, unrolling like a small carpet sample.

He looked upward, seeing the empty black of the mask staring back at him, almost certain he saw a smile in return. Death was not as he expected. It was cold and hallow, and no light, or family members from the other side were there to greet him. His life ebbed quickly as the pool of blood grew along the concrete floor, and soon his lifeless eyes stared at the wall he had accidentally punctured just moments before.

The very reason he died.

*   *   *

"It's about time," Welch said as the delivery truck drove away several minutes later, a dusty trail rising from the bare back lot of the hotel.

Welch and Clouse stood in the sunken garden. Daniels had left to search the ground for clues while the other two talked momentarily.

"Guess he had enough room," Clouse noted.

"That or he was too big of a prick to tell me," Welch replied. "God, there's times I just wish he would fall off the face of the earth."

Clouse turned his attention to Daniels, who knelt over where the concrete steps met the grassy edge of the garden. He walked over, wondering if his friend might have found something important.

"Nothing yet," the former detective noted, still examining the ground. "You know, I would have expected to find a spent casing or something."

"When they get those bullets out of the guard, won't you be able to do a comparison?"

"Not without Tug's weapon, unless the state police have a ballistics record for his service weapon already on file."

Without McCabe's car or weapon, and without any trace evidence in the form of blood, bullet casings, or fingerprints, Daniels would have little trail to follow.

For the sake of covering bases, he had asked one of the local police officers to scrape samples of the blood atop the walkway and the stairs, where Hinds landed, for DNA testing, though he seemed to feel positive it all belonged to the security guard.

"I guess I should lock this place up," Welch said, ready to depart.

"Go on home, Carl. I'll lock up for you."

"You sure?"

"Positive. We'd like to take a look around first, anyway."

A few minutes later, Daniels crutched behind Clouse while he locked the back gate, then headed for the cafeteria entrance.

"I should probably check downstairs and make sure the delivery guy left us an invoice, and left everything he should have."

"That's not your job, is it?" Daniels inquired.

"No, but someone needs to do it."

Clouse soon made his way down the basement stairs while Daniels waited in the old dining area. Most of the hallway was dark, as most of the overhead light bulbs were smashed.

"Ah, shit," Daniels heard his friend say from below in the darkness.

"What?"

"Son-of-a-bitch," Clouse cursed from the entrance of the supply room.

"What?" Daniels insisted more intensely this time with a concerned tone.

"That asshole spilled an entire shipment of bricks all over this room," Clouse yelled down the hall, staring at a pile that scattered across most of the room, nearly half his own height. It would take some time to clean up such a mess. "And he smashed almost every overhead lightbulb down here. I almost fell on my face twice."

Clouse cussed under his breath, turning to leave the storage area. The mess could sit another day or two until the company returned with the next shipment. Infuriated, Clouse had no intention of forcing his own people to clean up the bricks, or replace the bulbs.

"I'm going to give his supervisor such a bad report the guy will have to leave the state to find work," Clouse spouted on his way up the stairs, keeping Daniels' attention.

Simply shaking his head, the officer made it clear he had no idea what his friend was talking about.

"You don't need to be worrying about the little things right now," the officer said.

"I know," Clouse replied. "It just seems like whenever it rains, it pours."

27

While Clouse went to check on some leads at the hospital, Daniels managed to derive enough courage to step into city hall, and Deputy Chief Randy Collins' office. He barely used his crutches at all when the secretary showed him in.

"Mark, looks like you're doing well," the deputy chief noted upon inspection of the former detective.

"Doing better these days," he replied, taking a seat across from Collins, who stood to fix himself some coffee.

"How do you take yours, Mark?"

"Cream, please."

Collins set the coffee down for Daniels, noticing the concerned look across the man's face.

This was no social visit.

"Something the matter, Mark?"

Daniels hesitated a moment, unsure of how to place his words, or ask the favor he desperately needed.

"It seems there was an accident last night at the West Baden Springs Hotel," Daniels began. "A guard was shot, and it appears Tug may somehow be involved."

"You mean, in the shooting?" Collins questioned skeptically.

"Well, perhaps, but not intentionally. I think someone set Tug up, and he's nowhere to be found. We've called, paged him, talked to his post, spoke with his commanding officer, and tried his radio. Hell, I even tried his favorite bar. Nothing."

Collins sat a moment, thinking with a poker face. Daniels said nothing, patiently waiting for the deputy chief to speak.

"Any idea why he would have disappeared?" the question finally came.

"I think he was close to discovering who the murderer is. My guess is he's either dead or incapacitated. We were in pretty close contact and he hasn't made any attempt to reach me."

"And I suppose you want my blessing to let you continue the investigation without Tug if necessary?"

Daniels nodded slowly.

"Some form of credentials would be nice," he added.

Bobbing his head in thought, the deputy chief arrived at his only feasible conclusion.

"I can't give you clearance to investigate, much less use departmental equipment of any kind," Collins said.

Daniels began to object, but refrained when a foreboding finger raised before him.

"Furthermore, only a doctor can release you medically to active duty, and it doesn't seem to me that you've been very consistent in your rehabilitation appointments."

"But, sir, I have to-"

"I know what you're up against, Mark, and I know there are some demons in your past holding you back. But it sounds to me like you're looking for a legal way to protect yourself because you're scared for your life. Am I at all correct?"

Daniels swallowed his pride along with a sip of coffee.

"You're partly correct, sir. I've already been attacked once, and barely lived to tell about it."

Collins acknowledged Daniels silently.

"I don't know what else to do, Chief. I won't sit at home and let myself be a target for this asshole. Too many people have already died, and like it or not, I may be one of the few people left who can stop this maniac before any more innocent people get hacked up," Daniels said emphatically, showing a rare sign of both heated emotion and confidence in his abilities.

"Legally, there's nothing we can do, Mark. The chief filled your spot in detectives officially this week with Brent Jones."

Daniels gave a disgusted face.

"Jones is a fuckup, and a lackluster patrolman to begin with. I wouldn't let him investigate missing pets," he said with a frustrated wave of his hand. "He's a lawsuit waiting to happen the way he handles people."

"Apparently the chief saw the same thing in him that he saw in you a couple years ago," Collins retorted.

Grabbing his crutches, Daniels pried himself up from the seat. Perhaps the chief was suffering an acute blindness when it came to his personnel.

"Even the chief makes mistakes."

He headed for the door, unhappy with his current situation in every way.

"Mark," Collins called, stopping him at the doorway.

"Sir?"

"Do what you have to, but don't go dragging the department into it, or you won't have a job left to come back to. Understood?"

Daniels nodded.

"Perfectly."

*   *   *

Clouse walked up to a particular office in the hospital, finding the door closed. He read the name "Barry Andrews" on the metal nameplate, knowing he was correct. After a few knocks and no answer, he decided to move on.

He wanted to ask Andrews several questions pertaining to the man's care for Kaiser in Paoli, under the guise of a concerned friend. Discovering where the doctor had been the night before would also satisfy Clouse's nagging doubt about his potential involvement in the murders. Andrews' timing and placement felt a bit too coincidental to dismiss.

A walk down the hallway left him at an office he knew even better, and it was his other reason for visiting the hospital that morning.

"Hello," he said, calling to his fiancee from the doorway while she filled out several papers across her desk.

"Paul," Jane answered, her face outwardly showing the joy of seeing her husband, since their paths had never crossed that morning. "Where have you been?" she asked, rising to hug him.

"It appears my problems with the killer just got worse. We had a security guard attacked at the hotel last night."

Jane's expression changed.

"What happened?" she asked with concern.

"We're not quite sure. Is Barry Andrews here today, by chance?"

"Haven't seen him. Did you try his clinic?"

"Mark and I tried this morning, but he wasn't in. I'm beginning to wonder about him."

"Barry's good," Jane stated. "I don't think he could ever hurt anyone."

Clouse nodded, knowing how people were sometimes deceptive. He considered his brother-in-law a good man the year before.

"Where are the kids?" he asked.

"Your mother picked them up. She said they could stay with them for the night."

"That's fine," he said with an uncontrollable yawn.

"God, you look tired," she said, rubbing his face, staring at the dark patches beneath his eyes. "You need some rest."

"Are those doctor's orders?" he asked, giving her a flirtatious kiss on the cheek.

"Those are," she said, pushing him away gently, with a smile while she looked around her. "Not at work, Paul," she scolded him in a hushed voice. "It's hard enough keeping respect around here."

He took hold of her hand.

"You know I love you," he said, like so many times before. "When this is all over, you and I will spend a week together. I don't care where, I don't care how much it costs. You will be treated like a queen when this is over."

Jane laughed, apparently already knowing he would reward her for her patience.

"So let me get this straight," she said. "I'll have choice of where and how we spend this alleged week?"

"You will."

She flung her head back with a chuckle. Clouse figured she was thinking of the various ways in which she could spend a week with the only man who meant anything to her.

"I think I see dollar signs."

"Oh, no," she replied, fingering his chest, certain no one was looking. "I have some very intense ideas for you and I."

"Oh, do you?" he stated more than questioned, pulling her close, though the timing was nowhere near right.

Not caring if anyone was looking or not, he gave her a long kiss, knowing it might be some time before they could spend any time alone.

"I've got to go track down Dr. Andrews," he said afterward.

"Are you planning to talk with Charlie Winters anytime soon?" she inquired.

"Maybe tonight. You want to go?"

"Sure," she said, valuing any time she had with her future husband.

He kissed her goodbye before starting down the hallway.

"Good luck," Jane called after him.

"I'll need it," he replied, turning only for a second.

*   *   *

"Ouch!" Cindy Daniels heard from the bathroom as she walked upstairs.

"What are you doing, Mark?" she asked, reaching the doorway.

Dressed only in his underwear, Daniels ran a razor along his cheek, finishing off the stubbly remains of his beard, heading toward a completely clean-shaven appearance. Several thin, bloody cuts lined his chin and cheeks, indicating how tender the skin was after months without shaving.

"I decided it's time to shave the rug, now that I'm recovering."

"Does that mean you'll be back on the force soon?"

Daniels hesitated momentarily before answering.

"Not exactly."

"Then what does that mean?"

"It means I need to look that part."

Cindy took a seat on the bed, watching him finish before he put peroxide on his wounds and toweled his face dry. He looked completely different without a layer of hair along his face. She preferred him that way.

"You aren't planning on investigating this under false pretenses, are you?"

"If I have to."

"Mark, you could lose your job altogether," Cindy noted with obvious concern.

He had fought too hard, and too long, to throw away his career.

"It beats losing my life," he said, walking slowly without crutches to the bed, in great discomfort, then sitting.

He awkwardly placed his right leg to one side, pulling up a pair of dress pants within a few minutes.

"Is Paul putting you up to this?" Cindy asked, afraid her husband had lost his mind, or at least his common sense.

"No," Daniels answered sternly, buttoning his shirt. "This isn't just about me, Cindy. And it isn't about Paul either. It's about me protecting you, protecting Renee, and protecting Curt. This is just like last year. You know how badly I wanted to stop that madman and keep all those innocent people safe. You know the consequences if I don't do anything."

Cindy scooted over beside him.

"I don't want our children growing up without their dad," she confessed, clasping his arm. "You're finally walking again, Mark. Everything looks so right, yet you're willing to toss it by the wayside and chase this madman by yourself."

Daniels squeezed her hand.

"I'm not by myself," he said in a calmer voice. "Paul isn't going to let anything happen to me, and I'll be damned if I let any homicidal maniac get to him. We're so close to finding the killer, and I can't just stop now."

"But you could. You could let someone else do the searching."

"Yes, I could, but I would be letting Paul down. I'd be letting myself down." He kissed her cheek, caressing it with his hand. "Cindy, I'm too damn close to stop now, and if we put pressure on this bastard he'll make a mistake. Then he'll be mine."

Cindy took a deep breath, then sighed aloud. Knowing there was no changing his mind, and unwilling to put undue pressure on him by threatening separation, or something more drastic, she simply gave in.

"Please, just be careful," she pleaded.

"Always," he said, grabbing his crutches from beside the bed. "I'm starting to feel like a new man."

*   *   *

Clouse entered an auditorium on the Indiana University campus, finding a rehearsal of *Caesar* already in progress. He observed momentarily as the climactic scene of Caesar's death unfolded. He watched as the actor portraying the great leader took several dagger shots from other actors around him, a shocked look crossing his face as his pretense friends and allies murdered him.

Echoes of the actors' voices boomed through the vacant auditorium as the visitor strolled down the row between the seating columns toward the stage.

Everything was dark except the stage itself, and the actors were too busy in their work to notice him at first. Even the director, off to the side, was consumed by the college kids playing out their roles.

Clouse watched Caesar's violent death on stage, feeling familiar with stabbing and the way in which people died, but goose bumps still crawled up his arms. Flashbacks from so many deaths the past year flooded his mind, and he felt his hands tremble subconsciously.

Feeling a sudden urge to leave and separate himself from the scene, Clouse turned as the director took notice and called for him.

"Sir, can we help you?"

He turned, deciding to finish what he came for.

"I'm looking for Ryan Andrews," he stated, hoping the trip proved worthwhile.

"Right here," the young man said, dressed in a toga and sandals fashioned in the era of Caesar.

The director ordered everyone to take a five minute break since the students were already beginning to disperse.

Ryan placed a dagger down, alongside a script, before sliding off the stage to Clouse's level. "How can I help you?"

"My name is Paul Clouse. I need to speak with your father as soon as possible. It concerns the murder of his girlfriend," Clouse told a partial fib.

"Have you tried the clinic, or the hospital?" the son asked, apparently assuming Clouse was part of McCabe's investigative crew.

"Both. No sign of him at either."

"If he's not home, there's only one place he might be. We have a cottage down by the lake. Sometimes he'll go there for time alone, or if we have a family outing."

Clouse nodded.

"You make it sound like you don't have too many family events."

"Not much anymore," the younger Andrews answered. "Things have changed since my sister and I left home."

Clouse glanced at the stage where most of the actors were parting for their break, carrying their scripts and props with them.

"Who do you play?"

Andrews looked at his own script, and the dagger sitting upon the stage. He chuckled a moment.

"I play Marcus Brutus, the man who forms a conspirator legion and betrays his ruler," he said with a laid back air of knowledge. "He acts with no thought for his own safety, and without any hope of gaining widespread power. He puts men and country before his own well-being."

"Does he die for his treachery?"

"You'll just have to buy a ticket and find out."

Clouse grinned.

"Maybe I will."

He gave a wave, turning to leave.

"Need directions to the cottage?"

"I'll be all right," Clouse said, already prepared to let Daniels search for the doctor.

He had other leads to follow.

*   *   *

A few hours later, Clouse picked Jane up from work, prepared to get some answers from Charlie Winters about the tiles and their significance.

"I can't believe I'm actually helping you on this," Jane commented, rather excited about the notion of aiding in something so important. Her everyday life as a doctor grew rather tiresome in its routine.

"You're only helping because this is a safe trip," Clouse replied. "Most of the time I go somewhere wondering if I'll be jumped from behind, or find a corpse."

"We're almost there," Jane said, changing the subject as they neared the small residence.

As the words came out of Jane's mouth, rain began to pour from above, drenching the windshield of Clouse's pickup truck. He flipped on the wipers, surprised at the sudden nature of the weather.

"I didn't even know it was that cloudy," he noted. "Did they say rain in the forecast?"

"Unfortunately," Jane replied. "Didn't you notice how windy it was, or the difference in the humidity?"

"I'm not noticing much these days," Clouse said in a somber tone as he pulled into the driveway, following Jane's pointing finger. "Life isn't as much fun when you find all of your friends dying around you."

Despite the pouring rain, both emerged from the truck seconds later, dashing through the merciless onslaught toward the small cabin where a light glowed from inside several windows surrounding the residence.

Clouse knocked as Jane took his side, cringing beneath the small eave above them, which provided little protection from the rain. Waiting several seconds with no answer, he knocked again, prompting Jane to look over to a window, despite getting drenched doing so. It was too late to save her from the involuntary shower.

"No answer," Clouse said as she stared through steamed windows, which made it impossible to see inside.

"His car's in the drive, Paul," she noted. "I can't see inside, but the lights are on."

Without much thought to it, Clouse tried the doorknob, finding it unlocked. He slowly pushed the door in, wondering what to expect once inside.

"This is creepy," Jane said, stepping in first.

The lights flickered as lightning flashed outside, startling them both.

"Mr. Winters?" she called with no answer.

Noticing a kerosene lantern on the table, Clouse darted over to it as the lights flickered again, sensing the power might go out any moment. He found a book of matches near it, and brought it to life momentarily.

"This feels weird," Jane said, looking around the abandoned house, which, for all intents and purposes, should have revealed its owner by now. "Oh my God," she said, kneeling down where several drops of blood sat atop the stained wooden floor.

"What?" Clouse asked, coming over.

"This," she said, fingering the blood from the floor, still somewhat moist in the form of large droplets.

"Great, just great," Clouse said sarcastically, looking around himself a bit more frantically, wondering just what to expect.

Before he contemplated his next move, his cellular phone rang from its holder on his belt.

"Hello," he answered quickly as the lights flickered again.

"Paul, it's Tim. You got a minute?"

"That's about all I've got," Clouse said a bit impatiently. "What do you need?"

"I've been thinking about Beverly Hilton's old estate and how I found those two punks screwin' around out there. They might have been lookin' for something, so I wanted to go out and explore the grounds, but since the buildings are so crumbly, and well, you know…Paul, I don't really want to go out there alone."

Any other time, Clouse would have taken time to badger his friend about acting like a frightened school girl, but this was not the time for joking around.

"All right, Tim. I'll go out there with you, but I've got somewhat of a situation on my hands right now. Can I call you back when this storm is over?"

"Sure, Paul, sure. Talk to you later."

"Bye," Clouse said, clicking the phone off, looking to Jane, who seemed more interested in moving on than hearing his conversation.

"You want to go outside?" he asked, offering her a way out.

"Not a chance," she replied, looking out at the downpour, knowing all too well what they might find within the small cabin.

"I want to know how in the hell everyone knows my cell phone number, hon," Clouse complained vehemently. "Is it listed in the phone book or something? It's not like I leave it up at either job anymore."

"You didn't give it to Tim?"

"I don't remember giving it to him," Clouse said, starting toward the back of the house. "And everyone from friends and family to psychotic killers get the number, then call me. It's a bit strange, don't you think?"

"Maybe Ken had given Tim your number."

"Could be," Clouse said as he opened several closet doors.

He could not see inside as the lights went out for good.

"Ah, shit."

He held the lantern up to the closets, expecting a ghostly white face to meet his, from inside, but only clothes and several small trunks lined the interior.

"Here, hold this," Clouse requested, handing the lantern to Jane while he looked around the kitchen for a flashlight.

While he searched, Jane backed into a wall where objects were stored above in a low-budget storage bin, created by the house's owner to keep memorabilia he seldom viewed. Spying several small boxes above, she reached for one, as something smacked against her head from the other side.

Clouse saw and felt it too, turning to observe the action taking place through the dim light of the lantern. Whirling the lantern toward the source of the hit, Jane found an arm dangling from above her, obviously dislodged from her attempt at viewing the box. Jane shrieked, then screamed, experiencing her first corpse outside of the hospital, especially since this one was brutally murdered.

Clouse took hold of the lantern while his fiancee shrunk back, shining the light up into the rafter where Charlie Winters' pale face stared back at him, eyes wide open, completely void of life. Though much of the body was obscured by boxes, Clouse noticed that blood stained much of the man's shirt, showing the murder was no different than any other slaying the firefighter recalled from the past year.

"Damn," Clouse said, pulling his cellular phone from its holder once more to phone the police.

*   *   *

As thunder rolled outside and lightning occasionally gave his house better lighting, Daniels sat on the couch downstairs, feeding his son, who cradled himself in his father's lap. With power lines down, there was no television, and little else to provide entertainment.

Candles burned in the living room, and on the kitchen table, providing just enough light for him to find his way around. Seldom did the power go out during storms, but there were times the lines actually snapped, or a tree fell on them, breaking the circuit.

With little else to do, the disabled officer simply replayed the recent events of his case through his mind.

Speaking with Barry Andrews, as Clouse had asked of him, provided little information. Andrews' alibi was suitable, though not perfect. It seemed the man spent much of his time to himself, or at the clinic. His work apparently took a back seat to his mourning.

In reality, the alibi mattered little. After speaking with people at Kelley's, Daniels felt convinced the young man with the snake tattoo was responsible for McCabe's disappearance, and possibly the murders. He might have requested a sketch artist, but placing a sketch would automatically tip the man off that Daniels was close. He felt extremely close to discovering who the man was, so Daniels opted to hold off a bit longer.

After speaking with Hinds, Daniels knew the officer's shooting and McCabe were tied in somehow. He pieced together a fairly accurate scenario of what had occurred, though uncertain of where McCabe or his unmarked car might be.

In the meantime he discovered Smith had canceled all security measures at the hotel, opting to lock up every gate and suspend all activity there until further notice. When he last spoke with Clouse, Daniels discovered his friend had a meeting with Smith in the morning to finalize a plan to suspend the hotel's opening indefinitely, if not permanently.

Good, Daniels thought. He would sleep better knowing the cursed grounds were sealed off, unable to invoke more deaths.

As his son finished off the bottle and began moaning, the officer gently placed Curtis over his shoulder, patting his back solidly for a belch. While he waited, a vehicle pulled to the front of his house in the pouring rain, prompting Daniels to stand agonizingly.

"Who the hell could that be?" he wondered aloud.

"Want me to get it?" Cindy called from the kitchen.

Daniels sensed the visitor was probably there to see him. He decided he wanted to keep his wife from his affairs, or danger, if that was still possible.

"No, just hold Curt, please."

While she took their son from his arms, Daniels grimaced as he hobbled toward the door. He expected to see someone familiar on the other side, but found a denim-clad, burly man he felt certain was a biker. His reddish beard looked overgrown and unkept while black boots with square toes kept the rain from soaking his feet. A black Harley-Davidson shirt peeked through his thick, faded denim jacket as the man waited for the officer to say something.

"Can I help you?" Daniels finally asked, figuring the man needed directions.

Noticing Cindy holding the baby, the man appeared a bit shy about speaking his intent. He looked behind him, since the rain had begun to dissipate.

"I need to speak with you about Detective McCabe's disappearance," the man said.

"Oh, okay," Daniels replied, recalling the man from the tavern where he had asked questions that morning.

He had probably raised a few eyebrows when he asked about a certain snake tattoo from the few patrons inside the pub.

"Outside," the man insisted, holding the door for Daniels, who motioned to Cindy that everything was fine.

"What can you tell me?" the former detective asked of the man, not asking for a name, because he doubted a truthful reply would be forthcoming.

Daniels stepped down the front steps gingerly, his legs cramping more with every second of use. He felt the dissipating rain peck at his head and shoulders as it refused to completely subside.

A few minutes outside, and he would probably be drenched.

Pacing a moment, the larger man seemed to contemplate what he wanted to say, as though carefully choosing the correct words to use, probably to keep himself out of danger, or trouble with his peers.

"First off, I wasn't at the bar last night when McCabe disappeared. They say that guy with the snake tattoo came in and acted like he was looking for the trooper. They also say he probably slipped something into the man's drink."

"Who is '*they*'?" Daniels felt compelled to ask.

"Just people at the bar."

"Do *they* all know he's a state police officer?"

"Some do. Most just think he's a business man of some sort."

Daniels knew from talking with the owner the basic story of what occurred the night before. The part about the man slipping something into his drink was new.

"What else do you have?"

"That guy with the snake tattoo might be someone I've met before."

"Where?"

"About six months ago we had a rally up near Indianapolis and this younger guy came into my buddy's tattoo parlor looking at the displays on the walls. Well, he kept looking at the snakes and touching his neck, like he was wondering how one of those might look wrapped around it."

"Did he give any information about himself, or get any work done?"

"He didn't get anything done, but he did say he was passing through, heading south."

To Daniels that made sense. It also opened up the possibility that the killer was not local, or part of Clouse's alleged Coven for that matter. Things were possibly about to get much more complicated.

"Did you see what he drove, or remember what he wore?"

"I was getting some work done on my posterior," the man confessed with a crooked grin. "So I wasn't in a position to see a whole lot. I don't remember him really looking the part of a biker, though. He wore jeans, an old long-sleeve shirt, and what looked to be hiking boots. Almost like he'd been in the woods doing something."

Burying a body maybe, Daniels thought, only half serious.

"Let me know if you think of anything else," Daniels said.

The man nodded, starting to leave when Daniels thought of something else.

"Hey, did you know McCabe or something?"

"Not very well. But he's a great guy, and I hope you can find him."

"Me too," Daniels said to himself, returning to the comfort of his house.

28

Several birds, too stubborn to head south, let Clouse know he was not entirely alone on the hotel grounds as he waited for Smith to show up the next morning. He knew what the meeting concerned, and he felt both depressed and relieved at the same time.

Closing the grounds ensured no more innocent blood was shed, but it would close off a historical chapter of the town for an indefinite amount of time. It was also an important part of the last three years of his life.

At the foot of the entrance stairs, Clouse waited, looking around him at the beauty of the trees, and the six story building looming over him in all its colorful splendor. He fished his key ring from his pocket, picking out a particular golden key from the set. He wondered if he would have to surrender it to Smith, or if the hotel would still be like his own property.

His thoughts abruptly ended with a chill piercing his unzipped jacket. Though sunny, the morning was cool enough to keep him from waiting outside.

He ascended the stairs toward the hotel, thinking of all the good and bad times over the past several years. Several of his closest friends died there, all as a result of greed and manipulation, though never on their part.

A moment later Clouse walked into his office, looking at the list of phone numbers along the wall, looking for the distribution center where Welch's supplies came from. Finding the number a moment later, he dialed.

"Carson Distribution," the man answered on the other end.

"Hello, can I speak to the distribution manager, please."

"This is Billy Carson. I'm the owner."

Clouse introduced himself and explained the situation as he saw it from the day before. He inquired about the driver's ethics and courtesy.

"Well, Mr. Clouse, James never came back from that run. After calling your hotel and getting no answer there, I alerted authorities because I thought something might have happened to him. They said they'd keep an eye out for his truck, but it didn't sound promising."

"Do you think he took off?"

"No, no," Carson scoffed over the line. "James is probably the most reliable driver I have, and he's actually a very good guy when you get to know him. I guess he had a rough upbringing. You know, teased a lot by other kids and stuff. So he's a bit rude, and maybe backwards in some ways, but he would never just disappear like that. In fact, he missed his final two runs yesterday."

"So this was the last run he actually made?"

"Yes, sir. And he never checked in afterwards, so this is the first I've heard of him even being there. Like I said, I tried calling, but there was no answer."

Clouse's mind raced, beginning to worry that the driver met with foul play on the hotel grounds. It happened the year before with an unwitting electrician.

"Well, things have been a bit slow here," he explained. "We're dealing with a few internal problems right now. But if I hear anything, I'll let you know."

"I'd appreciate it."

Clouse hung up the phone, wondering about the mess downstairs. He felt negligent not checking the bricks or the storage room more thoroughly. Locking his office as he stepped into the hallway, he decided to look downstairs when a plea for help on one of the floors above caught his attention.

Frozen, he listened a few seconds more, then another cry for help came, this time sounding more familiar to him.

"Dr. Smith?" he questioned aloud, wondering when the doctor had slipped in, and what the problem might be.

Forgetting about the business of the hotel, Clouse sprang toward the nearest stairway, listening for further cries. He started up the stairs, hearing another terrified cry from what seemed to be several floors above.

Echoes rang through the vacant hallways, so he could only take an educated guess where the noise was originating.

"Doc?" he yelled up the stairs. "Is that you?"

He heard nothing as he ascended the stairs, spiraling his way up. Each floor came and went without utterance, or any sign of life. Clouse finally reached the sixth floor, peering in every direction as he might have in a search and rescue routine. With nothing in sight, he chose the hallway on his right because more openings, including the access to any of the four towers, and two restrooms, would be accessible.

Clouse started down the hallway, unsure of whether he even had the right floor, much less which rooms to check.

"Dr. Smith?" he called down the hall, continuing his walk.

As though in answer to his query, he heard a door shut further down the hall. Most of the rooms were locked on the higher floors, which left only the restrooms or the towers, where Clouse truly feared visiting after the results of the previous year. It was where he confronted his brother-in-law for the last time.

Four towers rested along two sides of the hotel, each with only one hatch leading up to its top area, which looked much like a gazebo from anywhere but within. Each tower barely held four people, and the drop down to the main roof would hurt to say the least. Clouse knew the towers were a dangerous place to be, particularly on a windy day.

Cautiously opening the doorway into a small room with a metal ladder mounted to the wall, Clouse peeked around, certain no one hid behind the door before proceeding up the ladder, unsure of what sort of trap or predicament he might be rushing into.

With experienced quickness the firefighter scaled the ladder, finding the hatch above already open. He looked above him, then around the tower once his head pierced the surface, finding a horrifying sight, just beyond his control.

Climbing up the roof ledge, Smith used his last means of distancing himself from the reaper pursuing him with a scythe. Clouse saw a bloody slash along the doctor's side as the elderly man stumbled onto the ledge, possibly unaware that only a foot of ledge stood between himself and a six-story drop.

"Doc!" Clouse yelled, catching the attention of both his employer and the faceless killer.

Both looked at him, but as the firefighter went to climb the last few steps, his boot slipped, allowing the killer to return his attention to his prey. Clouse stumbled up to the tower's top, and sprawled out along the roof, forced to watch an action that threatened to haunt him the rest of his life.

Taking a final swipe with the scythe, the reaper missed, but Clouse was forced to helplessly watch as his employer lost his footing, realizing too late that nothing except air was behind him. Clouse watched the doctor's horrified face as he began a six-story plummet, hearing the terrified scream for a second or two until the dreadful impact came, silencing the man. Clouse scrambled to his feet, beginning to rush toward the ledge for a look.

His eyes met the blank, drooping mask of the killer, and Clouse quickly changed his mind as the reaper pulled a knife from a sheath along his side, holding it out for Clouse to see while he turned it threateningly.

"Bastard," Clouse muttered, blinded with fury toward someone so cowardly.

He wondered how anyone could attack someone as kind, giving, and defenseless as the doctor.

Wary of the blade, but fearing little for his own safety, Clouse kept both eyes fixated on the murderer. For what seemed a minute passed with both men staring one another down, before the killer charged him, forcing Clouse to dodge the blade or be stabbed through his internal organs.

Whirling to face his adversary, Clouse quickly realized the attack was nothing more than a feign to get him out of the way for an easy escape. He watched as the killer slid down the ladder hatch with incredible ease, forced to choose between giving chase or viewing the unsightly body of Smith.

He ran to the edge, seeing the twisted corpse six stories down, a pool of blood draining beside the body. For a moment, his body felt numb. His heart sank, but his mood quickly returned to a different level. Infuriated, he bolted toward the hatch, streaking down the ladder in pursuit of the killer. Once he hit the floor, Clouse darted out the roof entry into the sixth floor, listening for any sound leading to the killer.

He heard an elevator ding in the distance.

"Shit," he said under his breath, taking the closest staircase down.

Clouse flew down the stairs, reaching the bottom just as the elevator car arrived, opening on the ground floor. Waiting several seconds, Clouse poised himself outside the elevator until the door opened, revealing nothing. There were any number of staircases the murderer might have taken, and Clouse was too late to check any of them.

Desperately searching around him, he looked for any sign of the killer, hearing a slight hiss from one of the tension springs on the ornate glass doors on the other side of the atrium. He sprinted to the other side of the hotel, taking in every angle of the hotel grounds once he reached the cold outdoors, finding no trace of the reaper.

"Damn it," he said, reaching for his cellular phone.

He would call for police, and in turn, the coroner.

*   *   *

Daniels crutched himself into the third floor of the newspaper office, finding a bee hive of activity as people darted from desk to desk, typed, answered phones, and did a bit of horse play in between.

He already felt grossly negligent, and somewhat corrupt, using his old badge to gain access to the news room where an impending deadline for the morning paper had reporters, photographers, and editors scrambling in the late afternoon to make all the pieces become one cohesive unit.

Daniels understood pressure, and working under a deadline. He knew how homicides worked, and how putting off any work might result in the killer going free. To this point, he had no fantastic leads, no real suspects, and the only person of any official, real help to him had disappeared.

"I'm looking for Jerome Barnett," he told a female reporter, obviously too busy to help him as she shrugged haplessly, talking on the phone and typing as she did so.

Daniels felt a bit rude after interrupting her, but carried on nonetheless, panning the room for the reporter. When he saw Barnett emerge from a conference room, Daniels quickly hobbled over to the man's desk, tossing several papers down as Barnett took a seat.

"Yes?" the reporter asked, viewing the headlines he had manufactured the past year.

"I'd like to have a talk with you about some of your recent headlines," Daniels said, taking a seat across from the stunned reporter.

"Are you feeling left out of my stories?" Barnett inquired. "I've been meaning to include some pieces about your investigation into these murders, despite the lack of departmental backing."

"I've had departmental backing," Daniels retorted. "I've been working with state police as a consultant."

"And carrying a gun," Barnett noted.

Daniels gave an irritated sigh.

"Where exactly do you get your facts, Barnett? I'm very curious about the source from which you draw conclusions."

"My sources remain anonymous."

"You know, you would be a lot more help to the public if you'd focus on the real issues at hand, rather than trivial facts that no one will give a rat's ass about."

Barnett held up one of the papers from the previous year announcing Paul Clouse as the main suspect in his wife's murder, despite little more than circumstantial evidence. Daniels fully remembered investigating the case and giving very little to the press.

"It's the little things the public likes to hear about, Mark. May I call you Mark?" Barnett asked without waiting for an answer before setting into his next discourse. "See, it's much like a soap opera. We provide little hints and clues to keep the public interested. In a manner of speaking, you, Paul Clouse, Tim Niemeyer, and Detective McCabe are simply bit players in this story I unfold for public consumption."

"Speaking of which, you seem awful quick to point fingers at Niemeyer for no apparent reason."

Barnett flashed an exaggerated smile, similar to his photo in the newspaper.

"I accuse no one. The facts speak for themselves. Tim Niemeyer was there the night his friend and that nurse were murdered. He also lacks a solid alibi for every other murder to this point."

"*You* were there the night they were murdered too, but I don't see you mentioning that in any of your articles."

"But I can account for my whereabouts during the Rexford murder, Cranor's murder, and even this morning's latest slaying."

Daniels' face registered his ignorance on the latest slaying.

"Oh, you didn't know Dr. Martin Smith was thrown off the West Baden Spring Hotel this morning, detective?"

"I had no idea," Daniels replied slowly, unsure of how to take the news.

"Strangely, your friend was there and witnessed the entire thing. Sounds like deja vu, does it not?" Barnett added, knowing how the killer teased Clouse the year before, allowing him to view parts of the murders in order to lure him in, then frame him for the killings.

"So how can I be sure you weren't at the hotel, pushing the good doctor off to add some much-needed drama to your soap opera?"

"Because I was at work, detective," Barnett said with a grin. "Oh, I keep slipping with that title, don't I?" the reporter added, acting sarcastically apologetic. "What is your working title these days? Is disabled police officer politically correct?" he asked, trying to push the right buttons.

"I prefer *recovering* police officer, myself," Daniels said before taking up the newspapers he brought. "You can jack with Niemeyer all you want, but you're not going to get me to play your media games. I've got useful work to do."

That said, Daniels hobbled from the room to carry on his investigation as Barnett shot a strange stare toward the former detective.

*   *   *

Clouse sat at his kitchen table with papers strewn everywhere, trying to figure out where to begin with his former employer's funeral plans.

Actually, he had little to plan because once the coroner pronounced Smith dead at the scene, he informed the firefighter of the man's friendship with a local funeral director out of the Bedford area. One call later, Clouse discovered Smith had sense enough to pre-plan his funeral, since he left no living relatives, a wife, or children. It was up to Clouse to inform everyone important in the doctor's life that a visit to Bloomington was necessary in two days.

He felt bad for Smith after losing his wife several years back, and leaving behind a legacy, along with a fortune, to no one in particular. Toward the end, the doctor led a truly sad and desolate life, living only for those around him with nothing left to spend his fortune on.

He dedicated much of his time and money to the hotel renovation, though his motivation never shone through. Perhaps the doctor had a childhood connection to the land, or he was a closet history buff, or maybe he held a fascination for the hotel itself. Either way, Clouse would never know why Smith chose to devote his finances to the landmark.

Clouse wondered what would become of the hotel. It could become state property, or be fully taken over by the National Preservation Society, or perhaps transformed into a tourist attraction. None of the options sounded healthy, but he saw no other way for the hotel to see completion.

In between phone calls, Clouse had touched base with Niemeyer, assuring his friend he had not forgotten to inspect the resort ruins along Highway 37 with him the next afternoon. He also planned on visiting the hotel the next day, once the task of calling everyone in Smith's book was complete. Fearful of what he might find there, Clouse planned to ask Niemeyer to return the favor and tag along with him.

As he skimmed the doctor's old address book for phone numbers and acquaintances he hoped might be able to attend the calling hours, the phone rang.

"Hello?"

"Paul, it's Mark."

"What's up?"

"Nothing here. Is it true about the doctor?"

"Unfortunately."

"I'm sorry, man. Anything I can do?"

"Just attend the calling hours and funeral in a couple days. Maybe we'll get lucky and dig up some clues."

Daniels seemed to hesitate before his next question.

"Is it true that you saw it?"

"Yes," came the equally hesitant answer.

"What did the killer look like?" Daniels asked for comparison sake.

"Same as last year. Grim reaper outfit. I couldn't see the eyes or face at all."

"Any ideas?"

"Nothing more than before."

"Don't take this the wrong way, but could it be your pal Tim?"

"No, Mark. Tim is neither thin nor nimble enough to chase people around a hotel."

"That disguise hides a lot, you know."

"I'm aware of that, but no. You're starting to sound like that reporter."

No reply.

"You didn't go talk to the man, did you?"

"Well, I did it on my own terms."

"And?"

"I'm not convinced he's innocent either."

"How so?"

"I have a feeling every alibi he gives will be work-related. You know reporters are in and out of their offices all the time."

"As are detectives," Clouse noted.

"Yes, but detectives usually lack motive to go on killing sprees. Barnett is thinking newspaper prizes, a book deal, maybe a movie of the week."

"You know what they say. Fact is stranger than fiction. He could write an accurate account a lot easier if he was in on the action."

"You got it. And by the way, detectives don't sit around all day doing nothing like firefighters."

"No, they only have eight hour shifts to sit around their offices and complain about the rest of the world," Clouse said, deciding to give his friend a ribbing. "In between bitching and complaining, they call home to check on the kids. After that, they get to go home and sit around griping about what a rough day they had at work."

"Hey, be nice. We're like you, when we have to work, we really earn our paycheck."

"Okay, I'll give you that much, Mark." Clouse looked down at his booklet of names and numbers. "I hate to cut this short, ol' buddy, but I've got about a hundred phone calls to make tonight for this funeral."

"All right. I'll call you when I have something new."

"Okay, bye," Clouse said, clicking the talk button on his phone, wondering just what it might take to prevent anyone else's death before examining the contents of the address book.

29

Clouse spent much of that night and the next morning calling people listed in Smith's book, surprised by the ratio of success to failure. He contacted nearly everyone, despite the book's age, and most were not surprised Smith had died, but all seemed shocked about how he met his end.

He put off his search with Niemeyer once more, realizing it was too late into the afternoon to make the trip to both the resort ruins and the hotel. He phoned his friend, assuring him they would make the trip the next day after the funeral. Niemeyer seemed unhappy about waiting yet another day, but reassured Clouse he would not make the trip alone after what happened to Kaiser.

After a quiet supper with Jane and the kids, Clouse felt confident he had contacted everyone possible from the book, and from his memory. Every employee at the hotel, including construction crew, had been contacted, and most would attend the calling hours. If anyone had been excluded, he knew he had tried his best to invite everyone in Smith's life.

Once the table was cleared and the kids ran off to play outside, Clouse started the dishes without saying a word. Jane seemed to sense he was somber after Smith's death. As he washed a bowl, she wrapped her arms around him from behind, leaning tightly against his back.

"Want to talk about it?"

"What's to talk about?" he replied. "I can't keep anyone around me alive."

"You're being too hard on yourself. It's not like you're the cause of all this."

"Not directly, but I keep wondering if all this would have happened if I had just died in the lake."

She spun him around to see the look in his eyes. He sounded fairly serious about the notion, which seemed to greatly disturb her.

"Blaming yourself, or wishing you had sacrificed your life to help everyone else is not going to solve your problems. Whoever keeps killing these people has an agenda. And he's going after everyone who survived last year's attacks."

"That's why I'm going to visit Mrs. Landamere tonight, Jane," he said with a tone that indicated he could do little good. "She's one of the last remaining people who made it through that ordeal last year. After that, it's basically just Mark and myself."

Jane tapped his chest a few times.

"Aren't you forgetting something?"

"What?" he asked, genuinely unsure.

"Zach has parent-teacher conference tonight. You signed up to be there."

He closed his eyes, shaking his head in mild defiance.

"I can't go *now*."

"I'll go for you," his fiancee volunteered. "I want to see the school again, and I can get the scoop on Zach for you."

Clouse forced a grin.

"You sure?"

"Of course I am. Maybe I can get some ideas on what to start teaching Katie for next fall. I don't want her to be behind the other kids."

He planted a kiss on her lips, knowing he could not ask for anything better at home, even if the rest of his life's story read like a Shakespearean tragedy.

"Are you going to take the kids with you?" he asked.

"I can drop them off at my sister's house. I don't think an hour with Cassie will hurt them. In fact, they love her rabbits."

He turned to place a bowl in the drainer.

"Speaking of domestic animals, have you been taking my horse out lately?"

"Bucky? You lied about that horse. I've worked with him the past two weeks and he's as docile a ride as any horse I've ever been on."

"You sure we're talking about the same horse?" Clouse asked skeptically.

"Positive. I just don't think you know how to work with animals," she chided.

"That, coupled with the fact I'm never home long enough to train them."

"Well, you'll just have to try him again sometime."

Clouse chuckled, a first for the day.

Once a weekend cowboy, he had let that part of his life slip away because his first wife enjoyed different kinds of recreation. Bucky became more of a pasture horse than a pleasant country ride on Sunday mornings.

"I'll take him out when I get the chance," Clouse said. "But for right now, I need to get started if I'm going to catch Mrs. Landamere at home," he said, giving her a quick kiss. "Thank you."

"For what?" Jane inquired.

"For being here with me. For putting up with me, even when I act like a complete moron."

"You're welcome. Just be careful out there."

"I will, and you do the same. There's no telling when and where this asshole might strike next. As long as you're around me, you and the kids could be in danger."

Both looked out the window momentarily as the kids pushed one another on the swing set, content to enjoy the fall sunset, unaware of all the grownup dangers around them.

*　　　*　　　*

Somehow the school seemed less like an elementary school. Encumbered by adults, as Jane walked through its quiet hallways, it seemed overly peaceful. Passing several other parents as she made her way upstairs, Jane headed toward the gifted and talented room where Zach finished each day.

She was over the dead body, but the encounter forced her to realize the mortal danger Clouse put himself in, every single time he went to the hotel alone.

Putting any negative thoughts behind her, Jane walked down the hall, remembering her own schools days with the lockers and bland floor tiles everywhere around her.

Zach's primary teacher had nothing but praise for the way he carried out activities and finished his work ahead of most students, but pointed out his interaction with other children still seemed shaky. Perhaps, Jane thought, Clouse set an accidental bad example by straying from several of his friends, and seldom having company over to the house. Both seemed most comfortable at home, and who could blame them?

Jane wondered if the gifted program was the best thing for Zach, considering the way he behaved around others. Most gifted classes involved self-awareness and independence, which it seemed Zach needed little of at this point. She suddenly questioned her fiancé's involvement in his son's life and studies, for allowing him to enroll in such a class. Perhaps Clouse only saw the positive attributes of the program, and not how they might harm Zach as he matured.

Like most others, the gifted class's door was ajar, welcoming any parents inside. Paintings, drawings, simple writing tasks, and art projects lined the walls, displaying the achievements of every child in the class. As she walked inside, Jane noticed a cluster of parents speaking with the teachers in the opposite corner. Off to her left sat the room where Zach seemed to work by himself, the door closed.

Quickly deciding to investigate the room, Jane tried the door, thinking she would say she was looking for her child if anyone was inside.

No one was.

Certain no one spied her movements, she scurried into the room, shutting the door behind her, before turning on the computer without benefit of an overhead light. She hoped leaving the light off served to keep anyone from entering the room, though she knew it would appear terribly suspicious if anyone did walk in.

Her finger nervously trembled as she turned the computer on, waiting for what seemed an eternity for it to boot up. As the screen slowly showed signs of life, laughter and brief chatter passed by the door as the parents and teachers walked into the hallway.

As the computer finalized its load sequence, she clicked on the hard drive directory, reading the available files as she went.

"Simulator, Spelling Bee, Fun with Benny the Hamster, Games, Math Master, Spanish Translator, Reading with Lady Bug. Oh, boy," she commented, noticing how many directories were before her.

Deciding to wade through some of the jargon, she clicked over to the recent documents folder, trying to see which programs had been utilized the past few days.

Finding only text and photo files fell into the appropriate category, she decided to do a search through the find command by most recent date, getting several responses for the past week. Most appeared to be games or educational software. Two stuck out on her in particular because they sounded like they had nothing to do with school.

"Lock," she said, clicking to open the file.

After a few seconds of loading, then reading the file before her, Jane felt horrified, even sickened at what she read. *Behind Locked Doors* was apparently the title for an adult book. From the first chapter she read, Jane deduced it was written by one of the teachers in her spare time. An obviously steamy, and poorly written text, Jane saw little chance of its success, except in a fantasy store alongside sex toys and blowup dolls.

"Maze," she said, trying the other file, simply because it was not attached to a childish title and seemed to be more of an actual program than the other files had.

As it loaded up, using a larger program to run the program called "Maze," Jane saw a computer animated cavernous opening before her. Using the arrow keys on the keyboard she followed the entrance in, finding several choices in caverns, noticing something strange along one side of the cavern entrance that stuck with her as she progressed through the program.

It was small, perhaps even insignificant, but a small strip of gold and forest green stuck in her mind as she walked through the computerized cavern, unsure of where it was leading, or why there seemed to be no variance in the walls.

"Good Lord this is boring," she said under her breath, deciding the journey led nowhere in particular.

A sudden absence of light from underneath the door and the locking of the main door outside led Jane to believe her time to leave had definitely come.

"Oh, no," she said, rising from the chair toward the entrance.

Waiting a moment for all other noises to cease, she quietly stepped into the hallway, looking both ways before darting for the nearest stairwell as the lights shut off around her. Forced to wait a moment for her eyes to adjust to the darker setting, she ventured toward the stairs, finding a railing just as she spied the steps.

Once she reached the bottom, voices were audible at the other end of the building as teachers left for the night, probably anxious to get home after such a long evening. Spying an exit door, Jane pushed on it, only to realize an inner security bar held the doors in place, foiling any attempts to levy the bar down from the outside. Only janitors typically had keys for such devices, and Jane could not budge the system.

"Damn," she cursed uncharacteristically, heading in the opposite direction for another door.

She found herself partly down the school's main hallway when the sound of footsteps echoed behind her, with no voices or any other form of comfort remaining.

Hoping a teacher had simply run late in leaving, Jane spun around, expecting to see a friendly face.

Instead, there was no face, almost the distance of two cars away. A shadowy figure stood behind her silently, perfectly still a moment, until a gleam of metal caught her attention.

It shimmered as a single beam of light from down the hallway caught it. To her it looked like nothing except a knife.

Gasping, Jane darted toward the opposite door, fearful for her own life for the first time since Clouse's ordeal had begun.

She rounded a corner, seeing the means of her escape straight ahead as she burst through the double metallic doors, into the waiting arms of a dark figure.

"Whoa there, miss," a local police officer said, holding her at a distance from himself.

He was a brawny black man who wasn't about to let her go. Jane felt nervous being outside the building, but still in potential danger.

"You get lost in there?"

"No," she said quickly. "There was someone behind me."

"Probably my partner Darren," the officer said, looking beyond Jane toward the empty hallway. "Darren, you there?" he called.

For a moment nothing happened, then a figure emerged from around the corner and Jane saw the gleam of metal one more time. The person hesitated, then stalked forward toward the two. Jane felt her body tense with fear. Oh my God, she thought, unsure of whether this was the partner or someone far more diabolical.

"Lady, you had me scared to death," the second officer said as he came into view.

Jane was relieved her imagination was working so hard, and that she was out of the school.

"Why did you run like that?"

"I had no idea who you were," Jane said. "I got caught up in looking around the school and the next thing I knew the lights were getting shut off," she told a partial fib.

"I'm glad we checked it over," the first officer said. "You could have been stuck there all night if the custodians secured all the exit doors."

"Thank God for small miracles," she said, hoping her fiancé had better luck and fewer scares than she had.

*   *   *

In the darkness, Joan Landamere's rural paradise looked far less appealing compared to the times Clouse visited during daytime hours. The garden, statues, and beautifully trimmed bushes failed to show at night, but the landscaped front yard and iron gate before the house were prominent as the off-duty firefighter pulled up to the front gate, seeing that some lights were on.

Surprised the front gate was open, he drove up the paved driveway, slowly exiting his truck as he looked around the grounds, listening for any strange noises.

He knocked on the door a moment later, greeted by several deadbolts unlocking, then a hesitantly opened door.

"Mr. Clouse," Joan Landamere said, instantly recognizing him through the small opening from behind the door. "What brings you out here?"

"I believe you might be in danger, Mrs. Landamere. Can I talk to you a moment?"

"Certainly," she replied, opening the door. "Come in."

A moment later she fixed them both coffee and Clouse found himself seated across from her, still amazed by the size of the house. Though a participant in mass murder, David Landamere had taken care of his wife by building a sizable house, nearing mansion status, before his death. Much of the work reminded Clouse of the man he once respected and worked for, but the manner in which Landamere betrayed him left Clouse skeptical of fully trusting anyone again.

"What makes you think I'm in danger?" Joan asked, stirring some cream into her coffee.

"All of the verified murders seem to be people who survived last year's attacks. I've been attacked, and Mark Daniels nearly got killed. The two of us, and yourself, are about the only people left who survived."

She shook her head sadly.

"I heard about Dr. Smith."

"It's been rough on everyone, ma'am. Will you be at the funeral tomorrow?"

"Yes. And I'm curious what will become of his estate."

"Did he have any distant relatives who might stand to inherit?"

"I don't believe he did. He never had children, and no one really knows much about him. Still, Dr. Smith must have drawn up some sort of will."

Clouse shrugged.

"I'm sure we'll find out soon enough."

Joan took a sip from her coffee mug.

"I appreciate your concern for my health, but I can't do much else to protect myself. I don't go outside after dark, I leave my security systems on constantly, and I keep my dog out back to prevent anyone from sneaking in."

"Are you sure you're fine out here?" Clouse asked, not wanting to leave until he felt certain she was safe on her own.

"I'm fine. No one can get in here to get me, and I have no plans on leaving the house until this whole mess is resolved. Well, aside from the funeral tomorrow, of course."

Clouse stood, setting his coffee cup on the nearby table.

Guilt plagued him for leaving so soon, but his objective was accomplished, and there were any number of things he needed to prepare for the next morning. The funeral, from the number of people he confirmed were coming by phone, would be a rather large event. Clouse had to stop by the funeral home before heading home to finalize details with the funeral director concerning the casket, flowers, and the arranged final resting place to see if there was anything he needed to do.

His overnight rest would be limited.

"I have to go plan for the funeral," he revealed as he stood. "If you need anything, anything at all, just call me or Mark."

"I will do that," Joan assured him. "And I appreciate everything you two have done for me."

Clouse nodded, then headed awkwardly toward the front door. Joan stood to open it for him, and as he stepped outside, he heard the locking of several deadbolts from within. He hoped it might be enough to keep her safe until some sort of resolution was reached concerning the murders.

30

Similar to most of his nights, Clouse ended up sleeping very little before the calling hours the next morning. When he found a rare opportunity to sleep, he never could, and even a usual night of full rest never seemed to restore him to full strength.

"How do you feel?" Jane asked as he finished tugging his tie in the bathroom.

Feeling sluggish, he took an unusually long time getting dressed.

"I'm okay," he said, not feeling like talking.

If the choice was his, he might have slept into the afternoon and spent the day around the house with his fiancee and the kids.

Clouse picked his sport coat up from the bed, ready to start what was certain to be one of the worst days of his life. Strangely, he sensed things were about to look up. No rhyme or reason, just an instinctive feeling nagged him that something good would happen soon. He hoped more than anything the killer's identity would come his way.

Jane had already taken Katie to stay with her parents, and Zach to school, which Clouse constantly thought about. He hated leaving the kids out of his sight one moment, especially with Halloween only a day away. Things looked more dangerous for Clouse, Daniels, and their families with each passing day.

"Is Mark going to be there?"

"Yeah," Clouse answered in short.

He made it obvious he felt rather bad in spirit. She drew close to him, placing a hand on his shoulder.

"It's okay. I know you must be dead tired, Paul," Jane noted, wrapping her arms around him momentarily. "Take the day off after the funeral. You don't see Mark running to Paoli every day checking for clues. Do what he does and stay home with us."

Clouse winced, partly from a building headache, and partly because he was tired of hearing how many things Mark failed to help him with, when he knew full well his friend was covering every angle he wasn't.

"Mark is putting his career on the line by investigating these murders, Jane. If he wasn't checking the leads he had, I couldn't check most of the ones I've got. We feed off one another to get closer to the truth."

"Which is?" she demanded.

"What do you mean?"

"Is it a truth you're actually seeking? A person? A justification for what's going on around you? I'm starting to lose track of exactly what it is you're after. I know you've lost a lot of friends, but instead of protecting them and your family, you track this ghost of a killer. This damn reaper who haunts your soul."

Clouse simply burned a hole through Jane with his stare, stunned she finally called him on his obsession with finding the killer.

"That's it, isn't it?" she prodded further. "You're actually caught up in the fact that you're chasing this spectral figure, as though no one else in the world can do it."

"No one else in the world seems to be trying, or they're dead," he said sternly, still in control of his emotions, despite the whirlwind of thoughts dancing through his mind. His head hurt too much for the start of any day, particularly this one. "And I realize I'm making personal sacrifices by leaving all of you here so much, but it's only because of my concern for your safety. Don't think for a second that you and the kids aren't on my mind every time I step out of this house."

"I don't want to argue about this," Jane said after a moment.

"Then please don't bring it up. This funeral is important to me."

"I'm sorry. I realize Dr. Smith meant a lot to you."

Clouse put his sport coat on, adjusting the fit.

"Yes, he did. And I'm actually hoping to see if the killer shows up. Mark and I are going to watch everyone carefully. Last night the funeral director gave us permission to place a camera inside the funeral home for the calling hours."

Jane started to speak but he put a foreboding finger between them.

"Let's just go."

*   *   *

On the way, Jane related the story of the night before at the school to Clouse, letting him know about the strange program she encountered, and how much part of it looked like the architecture at the hotel. He asked if it was the program Zach might be using, but she was uncertain, though the dates indicated it had been used more often, and more recently, than most other programs.

Clouse nodded, thinking it odd that Zach was learning from a program that seemed to give endless tunnels that never changed. If he had time, he would go to the school and question the teacher on what type of program it was, and if Zach was actually using it.

At the funeral, Clouse immediately met up with Daniels, leaving Jane to mingle with Cindy and several other acquaintances. His friend was without crutches, but noticeably suffering the effects of labored walking, and the cramps that accompanied it.

"You okay?" he asked the former detective.

"Sure. It gets a little easier every day."

Clouse panned the room, seeing a flood of people waiting to pay their respects to the late doctor. The room contained lawyers, doctors, construction workers, cops, and people from nearly every walk of life. More importantly to Clouse was something he spied in abundant numbers he did not expect.

"Notice how many women are here?" he asked Daniels.

"Some are particularly young, aren't they?" the officer observed.

"And strangely enough, I don't remember calling too many women on the phone."

"You're about to get married, Paul. That could get you in trouble."

Clouse grinned. After his bout with Jane he wondered just how blissful their relationship remained. Still, she was looking out for him, and that seemed healthy enough.

"See anything else unusual?" he asked Daniels.

"Nothing noteworthy, except for this one fella who keeps eyeing you every so often."

Clouse's glance followed his friend's. He spied a suited man leaned against a corner post, simply staring his way, distanced from everyone else in the room. He appeared very professional, and probably old enough to be Clouse's father, though he could not recall ever having met the man.

He seemed to have a deeper purpose than paying respects to Smith. He also appeared oblivious to the stream of people walking up to the coffin for a final look or to say a prayer. Clouse was amazed they had pieced enough of the doctor together for an open casket after the fall had reportedly shattered nearly every bone in his body.

"He does seem to be staring our way," Daniels noted. "Maybe he's a secret admirer of yours."

"Doubtful," Clouse replied, noting the man's gaze was not especially friendly.

"Maybe he's interested."

"Hardly," the firefighter said, smacking his friend's arm, not enjoying his unusual display of bad humor. "I think perhaps it's time I have a talk with our friend," he said, starting to walk across the room.

"Don't get too chummy. We still have work to do."

Clouse looked above his friend at the hidden camera.

"That's what we have that for."

As Clouse drew closer, the man did not shy away or even look in another direction. He appeared as though his wish had finally come true, grinning slightly as the firefighter stepped up to him.

"Harold Simms," he introduced himself, arms folded, still leaning against the corner post. "I already know who you are."

"And how is that?" Clouse asked, snagging the other edge of the post, leaning a shoulder against it, enabling a view of the crowd while he spoke to Simms.

"I'm Martin Smith's lawyer."

Giving a questioning stare, Clouse ignored everything around him, wondering what interest Smith's lawyer might have in him, other than a pending lawsuit for mishandling the funeral arrangements.

"What can I do for you, Mr. Simms?"

"Actually, I was hoping to talk to you after everything was over today, but since you approached me first, I feel obligated to tell you. Can we step outside a moment?"

Clouse looked over to Daniels, giving a wave as he followed Simms toward the door, indicating everything was fine, and his conversation would be brief. A wisp of cold air hit the two men as they reached the outdoor balcony of the funeral home, taking in a view of the city block as they did so.

Clouse would not have held the funeral processions in Bloomington, but he followed the doctor's wishes to the letter, including the burial later that day outside of French Lick.

"So how do you know who I am?" Clouse asked, breathing the cool morning air, noticing patches of fog stretching to the next block.

An eerie gray sky loomed overhead, setting up the witching holiday perfectly.

"Martin told me lots about you, Mr. Clouse. He was very fond of you, and your work. So much so, that he named you in his will."

Clouse's attention was captured.

"He named you *alone* in his will, sir," Simms said, shaping his forefinger and thumb like a gun, aimed at a stunned Clouse, who stood there almost a minute in disbelief, fumbling for the balcony railing to steady himself.

A certain realization hit him with Simms' words.

"You're telling me he had no living relatives anywhere?" he asked, a straight arm clasping the railing to support his buckling knees.

"I'm telling you it doesn't even matter. He named you the executive heir to everything he owned, including a theme park, hundreds of acres of land, a hospital ward, and even the hotel you both worked on together. This is all unofficial to this point, of course."

"Of course," Clouse said numbly, wondering if this might be a dream, or some sort of cruel hoax. "Can you prove any of this to me?" he asked Simms.

"Not right now. Come to my office at your convenience and I'll show you the paperwork," Simms said, flipping out a card which Clouse took and examined. "I know my timing is bad, but it was important to talk to you in person."

Clouse regained his composure.

"That's fine. I'll probably see you in a day or two."

Simms turned to go inside.

"I'll pay my respects and make a brief appearance at the funeral," he informed Clouse. "Stop by my office when you're ready."

As Simms stepped inside, Daniels brushed past him onto the balcony. He noticed his friend appeared a bit befuddled.

"What's up?"

"I'm not quite sure."

"What does that mean?"

"I was just informed that Dr. Smith's estate falls into my hands."

Daniels blinked several times, seeming unsure of what he heard. He had always trusted Clouse wouldn't lie to him, but apparently needed to clarify what his friend's words meant.

"You mean you inherited everything the man owns?"

Clouse nodded slowly, leaning uneasily against the balcony rail.

"It appears so. I'll get the proof in a day or two."

"Smith's lawyer?" Daniels asked, thumbing back toward the room where Simms had just returned.

"Yeah."

A smile crossed his friend's face.

"Wow, Paul. So I'm going to know the wealthiest man in the state?"

"We'll see about that," Clouse quickly offset his friend's assertion. "Even if I do stand to inherit Dr. Smith's estate, the taxes will probably eat me alive."

"Still, that's incredible."

Clouse gave a dismissing wave, still not sold on the fact he stood to inherit millions, perhaps billions of dollars from his employer's estate.

"We better get back inside," he told Daniels, ready to proceed with his day as planned, if that was still possible.

Niemeyer still wanted to see the land he oversaw with the security of companionship. Not one to break promises, Clouse would go because he felt the lives of his friends were very much his responsibility.

His high school buddy had waited long enough to look at his land, and Clouse felt an urgency to check the hotel, especially now that it might be his own.

*   *   *

An hour after the funeral, Clouse pulled into Niemeyer's driveway, deciding to let his friend drive, considering his mind was racing with any number of pending matters. Niemeyer took a scenic route to the resort ruins, giving the two an opportunity to talk. Both noticed the number of colorful leaves fallen alongside the untended road, creating a perfect fall day. With little sun and continued brisk temperatures, both wore sweatshirts beneath their jackets.

Clouse neglected to mention his potential inheritance until he received absolute proof. He dreaded telling people about his good fortune since it could be false, or the will could be contested in court by some unknown relative coming forward.

"Your week been pretty bad?" Niemeyer asked, taking a winding curve.

"Not entirely."

"Mine hasn't been worth mentioning," Niemeyer noted with enough frustration to bring out his drawl.

Clouse couldn't help but chuckle.

"What's so bad about it?"

"We're behind schedule on my new project, and your buddy who did your hotel landscaping couldn't make it, so now the owners are wantin' to sue me for a breach of contract, just because I missed a tentative deadline, even though it wasn't in the contract."

"Sounds like fun," Clouse said sarcastically. "So Brian canceled on you?" he asked, knowing Niemeyer referred to Brian Kern, the landscaper contracted to do the sunken garden and surrounding plant life at the hotel.

Most of the landscaping at the hotel was complete, so Kern had moved on to other projects, recommended heavily to Niemeyer by Clouse.

"At least he's good enough to call," Niemeyer said. "Most of those guys just show up when they feel like it and don't think you'll have the balls to call anyone else in."

"That's what contracts are for, Tim," Clouse said evenly, trying to get a rise from his friend.

"Don't even talk to me about them damn things. That's going to be my sore spot for quite a while, Ah'm afraid."

Clouse observed the resort ruins from half a mile away in the form of the burned hull of the main building and the surrounding buildings in their desolate form. It was a reminder of what neglect sometimes did to even the most beautiful of grounds.

"What exactly is this place's history?" Clouse asked as Niemeyer pulled into the makeshift drive, merely a muddy trail where trucks had come and gone, beside the overgrown brick drive that once provided elegance leading up to a gorgeous resort.

"Beverly Hilton owned it back in the '50s," Niemeyer began as they stepped from his truck.

He took the lead toward the hull of the building, its boards creaking with the morning wind as the fog lifted from behind. The scene unnerved both men, though neither would confess it.

"I guess it rivaled some of the great hotels in the area, including yours down in West Baden. Take a look back here," Niemeyer said, leading Clouse around the huge remains to the back where the ruins of the large indoor pool and its surrounding villa stood a short distance behind.

Clouse noticed ornate designs through the charred surface of several stones along a path leading toward the pool. They paralleled those of the hotel he worked on, and now possibly owned. With the fog lifting, Clouse saw the few remaining details of the villa walls surrounding the pool, and the intricate detail put into the wood and glass surviving the fire and vandals who plagued the resort. Beyond all of it, he spied a sizable body of water he considered to qualify as a lake, though he had never taken it in from this angle.

"Guests had a pool, game rooms, a cigar room," Niemeyer noted, taking out a cigar of his own and lighting it before continuing the tour. "They even had access to the lake back here by boat, or they could swim along the beach. Hell, a lot of guests even fished I guess."

"So this was a fully functional grand resort, huh?"

"It was. And Beverly expanded it after her husband's death in the '80s. It burned down just a few years ago during a summer renovation," Niemeyer said, leading Clouse around the front, where several boards swayed and creaked overhead, threatening to break loose and land on their heads as they passed. "Luckily no guests were around."

"So what actually happened?"

"With the fire?" Niemeyer asked before taking a moment to think, thumbing the cigar at his side. "Well, I heard one of the caretakers was doing some work late one night, got a little tipsy, and accidentally burned himself, and the entire resort up with a cigarette dropped on a mattress. They found his remains a couple of days later in the ashes. Happens all too often, doesn't it?"

"Yeah," Clouse honestly replied after seeing several such incidents where discarded cigarettes sent apartments or houses into fully developed blazes. "But you're telling me this entire place caught fire because of that, and no one got here in time to save it?"

"This building is close to a century old, Paul. They didn't have fireproof materials when they built it."

"I thought you said Mrs. Hilton owned it in the '50s."

"Sure, but she bought it from someone."

While his friend thoughtfully puffed on his cigar a moment, Clouse looked at the rickety boards above them, noticing the frame of the main doorway they stood beside. Like part of the villa near the pool, the wood showed signs of artistic detail. No paint survived the fire, but Clouse recognized the decor of the frame as similar to that of the hotel. He wondered if the same architects were used for both projects, since they would have been erected around the same time.

"Can you check some history on this place, Tim?"

"What do you want to know?"

"Who designed and built it? And the dates of construction if possible."

"That shouldn't be too difficult," Niemeyer said with a shrug. "Let's get inside and get this over with."

Clouse followed his friend through the doorway as the door hung awkwardly to one side on a single hinge, unable to perform its function ever again. Despite the daylight streaming through the broken boards of the resort, the inside remained fairly dark. Clouse noticed the remains of divider walls where rooms once stood, and sensed the size of the lobby, even though it was nothing but gray ashes and a charred block where the reception desk once stood.

Above were boards and support beams clinging to the walls where several floors once stood high above. The two could see all the way up to the roof, and in the distance one of the staircases remained just intact enough to decipher what it was. By all rights, and probably in a legal sense, the place should have been torn down immediately after the fire in Clouse's estimation. For Niemeyer's sake, he hoped his friend could talk Mrs. Hilton into demolishing the building, or she potentially faced a lawsuit when someone got killed or injured inside the structure.

"What about the insurance?" Clouse inquired. "Surely she had a sizeable policy on a resort this size."

"She collected, but she put the money to other uses," Niemeyer replied. "I think she was uninspired to rebuild the lodge and run it at her age, so she just left it this way."

He knocked against a support beam with his knuckles.

"It's still solid," the contractor noted, looking around at the walls before drawing on his cigar. "It was a beautiful place, Paul."

"But you're more concerned about the land, aren't you, Tim?"

"Hell, yeah. This resort was a great place, but this is where I wanna come home every night, buddy. When I retire, I'll be sittin' on the porch of my dream house, lookin' out at that lake. You can even fish here if you want."

Clouse didn't plan on being in any boats again in the near future. Any fishing would be done from solid ground.

Holes in the roof revealed bird nests in the few remaining rafters. Clouse felt uneasy beneath a flat roof, knowing they usually gave rather quickly once their support beams were burned, but apparently the boards above were strong enough to keep it intact. The three stories of flooring that had burned and fallen to the ground, now crisp debris all around him, were what concerned him. If they had disintegrated, the roof probably wouldn't be far behind.

"What are we looking for?" Clouse asked, starting to step forward, the wooden remains nearly up to his knees in some areas. "Glad I wore my old boots," he thought aloud.

"I'm trying to figure out what those two punks were doin' in here," Niemeyer said. "Whatever it was, they came out empty-handed."

Clouse's eyes panned the room.

"And you think *we're* going to find it?"

"Sure," Niemeyer said, optimistic as possible.

Clouse doubted that seriously as he began stepping through the debris toward one of the room hulls, seeing nothing but an endless trail of ash and burned wood. Ignoring the wind howling through the holes, and the empty streams of light entering the building's weak points, he quickly changed direction, heading for what was the main hallway stemming from the lobby.

"Can't you get some sort of injunction to have this place torn down?" he asked his friend.

"Mrs. Hilton would never speak to me again."

"Do it anonymously," Clouse suggested. "Then her fading memories are history and she'll sell you the land."

"You're devious, Paul," Niemeyer said as they waded through the debris toward the back of the building.

"I just have your best interest in mind, pal. And by the way, where are we heading?"

"Toward the basement."

Clouse stopped, staring at his friend with a curious stare.

"There's a hatch leadin' to the basement, but I doubt those creeps found it," Niemeyer stated, chomping his cigar.

"And I doubt we will either."

Niemeyer chuckled a moment, knowing he was close, but not positive where the basement door might be.

"When the hotel was operating, according to Mrs. Hilton, the hatch was flush with the floor, hidden 'neath a large carpet."

"You can't expect us to find this hatch without shovels, Tim," Clouse said. "There has to be a foot of this shit in here, and we're going to get busted up if we dig by hand."

"Any ideas?"

"Let's go to the hotel. I can get us some tools there, and do my stuff, then we can come back and dig around."

"We will come back, right? I don't want you doin' your thing, then denyin' me the chance to help you find out what the hell is goin' on around here."

Clouse looked at the debris surrounding his feet, and throughout the room. It was a battle he would not win under present conditions.

"I promise, Tim. Let's go."

31

Clouse unlocked the front door of the hotel, stepping inside with his friend close behind. As gray clouds loomed outside, the inside of the domed building seemed dark and imposing.

Both men stepped in, cautiously looking up to the ceiling and one of the balconies above, as though sensing they might not be alone.

Though no evidence showed otherwise, such as a car outside, or strange noises, the two detected a peculiar difference in the building. Even Niemeyer, who had only visited the place a few times, seemed to feel something odd in the air. He stepped in carefully behind Clouse, jumping slightly when the door closed behind him.

"Nervous?" Clouse asked.

"A bit."

Lightning flashed outside, providing them with an even worse feeling. It seemed fitting so close to Halloween, but a bright sunny day might have made the trip more tolerable. His boots clopped against the floor, echoing throughout the large hotel, as he crossed the lobby to a light switch, flipping it upward.

Nothing.

"Shit. Power must be out."

"No backup generator?"

"Not yet," Clouse said. "It's on our 'to do' list."

He looked around, then down the winding hallway toward the offices. He started toward his office, Niemeyer quickly following.

The contractor seemed to fear remaining in the lobby by himself, given the circumstances.

Clouse barely found his way to the office as the hotel grew darker with each step away from the daylight in the lobby. Niemeyer followed unusually close behind, even stepping on Clouse's heel at one point.

"Sorry, Paul."

"Hang on a second, Tim. I'll get in here and get us some flashlights."

Niemeyer waited in the hallway as Clouse fumbled around inside the office, finally reaching the cabinet where several flashlights, and other pieces of equipment, were stored. He emerged a moment later, handing his friend a light while turning his on.

"What exactly are we here for again?" Niemeyer questioned.

"Two things. First off, someone gave me a riddle to solve, and I've had time to think about it with a clear head the past couple days."

"A riddle?"

"This supposed list of victims can apparently be found where the puzzle pieces most."

"What in the hell does that mean?" Niemeyer asked skeptically, his accent showing through.

"Now that I know what the pieces are, Tim, I may have an idea where to look."

Niemeyer followed Clouse's lead toward the atrium with a perplexed look on his face. Keeping up with his friend's life had apparently become a major chore.

"What pieces are you talking about?"

"The tile pieces that used to be in the atrium. They got sold when renovation began, and now I'm finding out they have some kind of weird puzzle on the back."

"Puzzle?"

Clouse shook his head, shining his flashlight into the atrium entrance as they reached it. Above them, the dome allowed some gray light to enter, but shadows predominantly covered the atrium's new carpet floor and the statues placed neatly around it.

"I'll explain later."

Clouse looked around him, knowing the pieces of the floor came from the atrium, where they were all originally concentrated. Even so, he was unsure if Stephen had meant the atrium, or wherever the pieces now resided. Considering the pieces resided in several hundred different homes, he hoped he stood close to the answer.

"If you were a list, where would you be?" he asked Niemeyer.

"Probably hidden where two people idiotic enough to come in when there's no power would come lookin' for me."

Clouse ignored his friend's ill humor, looking around the room until he thought he spied the answer in one of the statues. Suddenly everything made sense to him.

"I think I've got it," he stated, envisioning how Stephen might have returned to the room in his efforts to save Kaiser, leaving hastily out another exit.

One of the exits contained a statue beside its arch, twice the size of either man. It had an elongated horn just above Clouse's field of vision. To be precise, it looked like some sort of leprechaun holding a horn while on the lookout with a great purpose. Clouse approached it, sizing it up and staring at the horn, which appeared to be the only area on any statue where the potential for stuffing a piece of paper might have existed.

He reached up, finding the horn too deep for him to reach on his own. No chairs, or other lightweight objects were around, leaving him only one way to extend his reach.

"Give me a boost," he told his friend.

"Ah, damn," Niemeyer replied, clasping his hands together for Clouse to step up on.

His weightlifting strength was about to be tested.

With considerable ease, he boosted Clouse another couple feet off the ground, enabling the firefighter to feel around inside the horn until his index finger received a paper cut. The joy of finding his objective outweighed any pain he might have felt as he carefully tugged the paper from its cubby hole.

"Find it?" Niemeyer asked, the strain of hoisting his friend's weight residing in his voice.

"Yeah," Clouse no more than said before he felt his friend let go of the support.

Landing on his feet, Clouse tucked the piece of paper into his jacket pocket, finding a shocked look on Niemeyer's face.

"You ain't even gonna look at it?"

"Not yet. I have to check on something downstairs first."

"You have another revelation or something?" Niemeyer asked, half joking, still unsure of where Clouse suddenly came up with all the answers.

"I've been up some late nights, Tim," Clouse said, starting toward the basement access door. "When you have nothing to do but think, all sorts of possibilities start coming to you."

Momentarily, Clouse led the way down the stairs to the basement, following the row of broken bulbs above him, shining his flashlight toward the room at the end where all the bricks lay in a heap. Drawing closer to the room, both men noticed an odor growing more intense. What might have been the smell of a dead animal now seemed much larger in proportion.

"Good Lord," Niemeyer commented as his friend stepped into the room, making his way around several bricks toward the back wall. "What in the hell is that smell?"

"I don't know, but it's a lot stronger in here," Clouse said, stepping on several bricks, hiking toward the top of the hill. "Hey, Tim, do you want to go down the hall and pick out some shovels and equipment for our trip back to your resort?"

"Sure," Niemeyer said, turning to head down the hall. "I'll be right back."

Clouse quickly reassessed the situation.

"Tim, wait," he called while his friend was still within earshot.

A moment passed with no sound, or visual contact with his friend. Clouse started down the hill of bricks when his high school pal rounded the corner.

"I saw some red marks along the wall," Niemeyer reported.

"Blood?"

"That's what I thought, but they're some sort of rust drips from the I-beams. What's the matter?"

"Nothing. I just changed my mind about having you run off by yourself."

"They're just down the hall," Niemeyer stated, ready to head that way again.

"I know," Clouse said with genuine concern. "I've already lost enough friends and I'm not taking any chances with those I have left."

Niemeyer chuckled at the notion of Clouse's overprotectiveness.

"I can take care of myself, Paul."

"I know, Tim, but Ken was a cop and look what that asshole did to him. When we're alone is when we're the most vulnerable. You can help me by keeping your light aimed up here so I can find my way around."

Niemeyer shrugged, keeping his light beam aimed into the room where his friend walked, able to help Clouse find whatever he was searching for. Occasionally he peeked around the pile, wondering if there was anything important to see. The secondary flashlight beam seemed to follow his friend's eyes, so Clouse relied primarily on his own light.

He chose an edge to start with on the other side, walking down to it, then around the pile until something strange caught his attention. Along with the rustic color of the bricks, two bluish pipes seemed to emerge at one edge, too close to the wall to be in any light but that of Clouse's flashlight. Kneeling down, he shined the beam across the objects, discovering they were human fingertips, protruding from the stack of masonry, discolored from days of decay.

"Got your cell phone?" he asked Niemeyer.

"Yeah, why?" his friend asked, peeking around the bricks, unable to see what Clouse had discovered.

"Call the police, and tell them we need the county coroner down here," Clouse said as though it was second nature to him.

He hated thinking another death had come at the hotel he cherished rebuilding.

"Damn it," he said under his breath.

"What do I tell them?" Niemeyer asked as he dialed, obviously clueless about what his friend had found.

"Tell them we have a buried body in the hotel basement, and I think it might be a missing delivery man," Clouse said as he continued to circle the edge of the bricks, hearing a faint noise from one side, though he couldn't tell where. "Hear that?" he asked Niemeyer, who asked his friend to shut up with a hand motion while turning away to hear whatever the 911 operator was saying.

Letting his friend complete the call, Clouse turned completely around, then around again, trying to determine where the noise might have originated.

Again the noise echoed throughout the room, sounding like shackles, or some sort of chain to the firefighter. Clouse looked up to the solid ceiling above him, made of concrete and steel, knowing no sound ever pierced it. Anything outside the room Niemeyer would have heard before he did. Solid concrete enclosed the room except for one brick side, which appeared much more fresh to the designer, and it struck him that the wall seemed out of place, even if he wasn't in the hotel's basement enough to be familiar with it.

"Police are on their way," Niemeyer announced, putting his phone away.

He saw Clouse feeling along the wall with his hands, beginning to think his friend had developed psychic powers after he made several amazing discoveries, possibly working on another.

"What on earth are you doing, Paul?"

"I keep hearing this noise. Sounds like shackles or something."

"There's a brick loose on your right," Niemeyer said, pointing to the brick sticking out several inches with his flashlight.

Clouse walked to it, tugging on it until it broke free of the wall, allowing air to rush into the sealed makeshift room. The sound of jingling chains grew louder as he placed his flashlight up to the hole, trying to look inside.

"Oh, God," he said, finding a familiar state trooper close to death. "Tim, call 911 again, and tell them to send EMS. We've got a live one."

32

After hours of intense questioning from authorities, as usual, Clouse and Niemeyer drove to the hospital to check on McCabe's condition. Other than severe dehydration and some weight loss, the trooper appeared fine once the local volunteer fire department dug him out of the makeshift wall, careful not to throw bricks on him. The trooper's ability to talk and think straight came soon after he was hooked to some intravenous fluids.

Strangely enough he asked if Russell Hinds, the security guard he had accidentally shot, was still in the hospital. When he found out the guard's wounds, primarily the stab wound, had kept him there, McCabe asked to be wheeled to his room.

Clouse and Niemeyer walked with him to Hinds' room, then met up with Daniels, who had been there when the trooper arrived, thanks to a phone call from Clouse. The three stood outside to talk a moment and finally reviewed the list found in the statue. Inside the room, McCabe, weak as he was, smiled when he saw the security guard sitting up in bed, grinning the same way, obviously happy the detective had survived to give him an explanation.

Both men were dressed in hospital gowns, so there was no shame in them being wheeled around, or feeling like invalids.

"I can't tell you how sorry I am for shooting you," McCabe began. "That son-of-a-bitch had me so drugged up I couldn't see straight."

"Your buddy Daniels told me what probably happened," Hinds said. "I didn't figure you were aiming for me."

"How are you coming along?"

"I'm healing pretty well except for the knife wound. They said it came close to some vital organs. Got a broken arm, and a disc in my back got screwed up, but they say I'm healing pretty quick. I was lucky I didn't have a broken pelvis like they first thought."

"Sounds it."

"They still don't know who that guy was that stabbed me."

"No, but we may be getting closer," McCabe said, glancing out to the hallway where three of his acquaintances talked.

"I can't believe you got the list," Daniels said with contained excitement. "So, what's it say?"

"Oh," Clouse said, realizing he had yet to even read its contents. "I haven't even had time to look."

Taking it out from his jacket pocket, Clouse unfolded it, looking at several scribbled names, as though Stephen had jotted them down hurriedly before Jacob might have caught him. He sensed his informant was always in a hurry to avoid detection, and therefore, always in grave danger.

Both of his friends looked over his shoulder while he read the list to himself. In order, the names read:

Paul Clouse
Lucas Rexford
Rusty Cranor
Ken Kaiser
Martin Smith
Brian Kern
Tim Niemeyer
Mark Daniels

"Glad to know I'm not excluded," Daniels commented, seeing his name.

"What the hell am I doing on there?" Niemeyer exclaimed, never thinking his voluntary assistance to Clouse would land him on a list, ignorant of the fact it was created long before his actual involvement.

"I don't know, Tim, but it seems to be in order of who was supposed to die."

"You sure?" Daniels questioned.

"Pretty sure. If you don't count my miraculous survival, that is chronological order."

Daniels studied the list again.

"Then Brian Kern would be next," the former detective noted. "Who is *he*?"

In reply, Clouse gave a worried look, glanced at the detective and security guard inside the room, and plucked his cellular phone from his side.

* * *

A leafy blanket covered the spacious lawn of the Kern residence. An old white farm house with a majestic picket fence enclosed the front yard while a gray barn guarded it from behind, accessed by a winding driveway. A mailbox in the shape of a barn stood at the edge of the driveway for the mailman to place letters into every afternoon before gazing at the beauty of the property the landscape contractor had made the talk of the neighborhood.

Ordinarily the leaves were already raked and mulched, but the owner left them just long enough for the Halloween season, with plans to dispose of them the first day of November.

Despite the cooler fall climate, shrubs and flowers bloomed around the house while a front porch encompassed two sides of the two-story house. Several jack-o-lanterns sat along the porch, their carved faces staring into the country road out front.

A large maple tree stood between the house and the road, providing shade in the summer, and a place to hang decorations during the holidays. To the side of the house an old Ford tractor sat with a hay wagon hitched to its back. All the fields had been hayed during the early fall, leaving it little to do except lead occasional tours around the farm.

Beside it, several large fir trees began a wooded area, domesticated by the owner and his family to become a pretense haunted woods during the fall, with signs leading to it from every highway and town within a twenty-mile radius. Every year, Brian Kern took time off from his construction work to provide Bedford and several surrounding communities a good time around Halloween.

With only tonight and Halloween left, he worked on repairing several key locations in the haunted woods which had either failed or broken the prior evening.

The morning thunderstorm came and went rather quickly, Kern thought, but gloomy gray skies remained overhead, threatening to bring more of the same.

His usual work involved planting shrubs, flowers, and trees, but it sometimes meant excavating with a bulldozer, or even laying down entire brick walkways to suitable houses. A tall man with a strong build, Kern could usually be found wearing steel-toed boots, jeans, and one of his blue T-shirts. His summer tan had yet to fade, nearly as golden as the thick wedding band on his left hand.

His brown hair, as well as the blond-colored mustache and eyebrows that accompanied it, had also faded with summer sunlight, but Kern took care of himself by wearing suntan lotion after hearing reports about skin cancer. Most people would think of him as a lumberjack before they considered him a local businessman who might relocate flowers in their yard.

Always wanting to be outside as a kid, Kern built his own tree house at a young age, planted shrubs and plants with his mother, and made certain the area animals had plenty to eat while he was growing up.

He never dealt with computers or business classes until he had decided what his profession would be. Though he might have been perfectly happy working in a park, or as a conservation officer, he never would have been satisfied with the income.

His job allowed him to help people, making them happier with their living conditions, while saving enough money to beautify and expand his own place.

With his kids in school and his wife picking up several vital supplies in town, Kern worked on repairing a hangman's noose where a dummy strategically fell during the haunted woods tour.

Depending on the age of the visitors and size of the tour, Kern sometimes let them walk through, or used the tractor to pull a large group.

Alone, and involved in his work, he had left his portable phone inside the house to avoid being disturbed. While the dummy stared at him blankly from its resting spot on the ground, Kern tightened the noose to his own specifications, ready to test it out.

While he went to work on another nearby display which triggered the noose, Kern heard several cars pass along the road behind him, then he heard one slow down. Through the trees he looked out to his driveway to see if he had company, but no car was visible.

"Huh," he said to himself, returning to the mechanical triggering device.

In the next few minutes everything around him and the house seemed to grow more quiet. No birds or insects made any noise, prompting him to quit tinkering with the mechanical device on the ground momentarily. He checked his watch, knowing his wife would be gone at least half an hour more, and no one he knew of would be visiting.

He looked out toward the house one more time, seeing no activity whatsoever. What sounded like a branch, snapped behind him, causing him to whirl around, again finding nothing. Kern took up the claw hammer he had been using on one of the repairs, clasping it in his right hand.

"Anyone there?" he asked out loud, giving someone a final chance to show themselves before he searched further.

Few men he knew matched his size and strength, but even Kern was reluctant to go searching his own haunted woods. Still, he stepped forward to investigate.

*   *   *

"Getting anywhere?" Daniels asked Niemeyer as he tried the number to Kern's house one last time.

"No. It just keeps ringing and ringing. Brian has an answering machine. It should click over, like I told Paul."

Clouse had left for Kern's house after the first failed calling attempt, fearing the worst. Daniels, especially, had a sense of dread, knowing they were the final two on the list, with only half a day left before Halloween, the anniversary of last year's first brutal slaying. One by one the survivors had been hacked down, along with a few other people in between, leaving only a handful of suspects, which he wanted to pursue the remainder of the day.

Standing at the edge of the hallway, out of earshot from Hinds and McCabe, the two men spied Jerome Barnett speaking with the doctor who had treated the trooper.

Like a bull, Niemeyer saw red.

"He's *dead*," the contractor declared to the former detective, surging forward.

"No, no," Daniels said, holding the contractor back. "Let's see what he does."

Niemeyer obeyed, knowing the reporter could not see them because he appeared too involved in conversation with the doctor. He took down several notes, then headed for the room where McCabe and Hinds were still talking. The doctor quickly told him he was not permitted to enter that room and pointed in the other direction. Both watched as Barnett hesitantly obeyed.

"I truly *hate* the man," Niemeyer stated.

"Hate is a strong word, my friend."

"I'm not takin' it back if that's what you want. He's nothin' but a snake in the grass who thinks only about himself."

"I agree, but he's doing a job, just like we do."

Daniels eased up a bit after Niemeyer settled down, then both headed back to the room to check on McCabe. Daniels felt more strength in his legs than before, and cramping came a lot less often. Though his steps were slow and gingerly, his improvement was obvious.

"Now that I know he's going to be okay, I'm headed home to be with the wife and kids," Niemeyer said when they reached the room, referring to McCabe. "I wish Paul wouldn't have insisted on goin' out there alone."

"He knows what he's doing," Daniels said. "Paul won't do anything too dangerous."

"He's not afraid to take chances, and that's what worries me the most," Niemeyer said with obvious concern. "Take care," he added with a quick wave, heading for the elevator.

*   *   *

On the ground level, Jerome Barnett talked with an interested fan and her son, who had just been released from the hospital for a gash on his arm, suffered on the playground at school. Her son remembered Barnett from school, where his teacher spoke highly of him, especially during black history month.

"So you don't plan on releasing your own book?" the woman asked. "It seems a man of your talent would almost have to."

"I don't want to publish anything less than the facts, and the witnesses from last year's ordeal have been reluctant to speak about their trauma," Barnett replied.

"Can't blame them," the woman replied.

In his thoughts, the reporter disagreed, but he nodded affirmatively.

"So you've been reporting on the new set of murders?"

"I have," Barnett said. "It seems quite a bit like last year's set, but there might be some random killings they have yet to pin on the killer."

"Oh, really?"

"Yes. Several murders have yet to be tied directly, but I believe the police are holding back information."

Nodding anxiously, the woman seemed delighted about the opportunity to speak with the local reporter.

"It's so nice to know people like you are a fixture in our black communities, doing such a great job for the public. Tyrone just kept talking about what an influence you were on his class when you came and spoke last year."

"I appreciate that," Barnett said, looking from mother to child. Her son simply smiled, affirming what his mother said in the reporter's opinion. "It's good to know I have a few fans."

"Oh, our whole community has always loved your work. You're about the only one who tells it the way it is anymore."

Barnett realized he had several errands to run before his deadline. One included some personal research at his house. He quickly excused himself and headed out the hospital to the parking garage.

Fifteen minutes later he slid through his front door, quickly closing it behind him. Everywhere around him looked the part of a normal house.

Beautiful leather furniture, antique cabinets and desks, a new computer, and a modern kitchen that would make Martha Stewart green with envy. He made a fair living, and with his wife working as a vice president at a local bank, they more than made ends meet.

With his wife at work and daughter halfway across the state at college, he could do as he pleased with his time.

He chose to play the part of a killer.

Darting into his bedroom, Barnett reached beneath his bed, pulling out a flat trunk containing several black garments and a rather long weapon. Feeling a tingle shoot throughout his body, he slowly pulled the black robe over his head, feeling the hood snugly caress his face while keeping it from the view of anyone who might spy him.

He then donned a pure black mask, just like Roger Summers had worn the year before to keep his face from any possible detection. The mask, made of pure black, had woven, plastic threads sewn over the eye slots allowing limited visibility out, but none inside. He wondered how Summers had managed to stalk and kill so many people when his eyes received less than half the normal amount of light through the mask.

A complete feeling of secrecy and power overcame him as he took the scythe from the box, knowing exactly how a serial killer might feel, chasing around hapless victims, or whacking unsuspecting townsfolk in the abdomen before they were able to react. He could kill at will beneath a cloak of secrecy, no one ever seeing his face, much less guessing his identity.

He wanted to understand the power the killer felt before he began his next piece. Knowing how that person felt would aid Barnett in creating some of his best work yet. Still, one thing was missing in the reporter's perception of the killer that he never quite grasped. The one emotion about to bring about his downfall.

Killer instinct.

Barnett heard a creaking noise from the floor behind him. Yanking off the mask and hood, he whirled around to find the true killer standing there, immediately embedding a sharpened, deadly scythe upside down at his waist, yanking it upward without hesitation. He saw no eyes, and no emotion on the killer's face because the mask concealed his identity perfectly, just as Barnett always suspected. As the killer gave one final jerk of the weapon, rubbing steel against bone, the reporter had few thoughts left.

He felt his organs sever as the blade journeyed to his sternum, and blood drain from his lower torso like a leaky carton of milk. His final gasps traveled with the blood running up his throat, flowing out of his mouth as his eyes glazed and he realized he would soon be one of the highlights he relished writing about the past year.

*   *   *

Clouse pulled into Brian Kern's driveway to find nothing indicative of foul play. He saw the tractor beside the driveway and recognized the man's pickup truck parked behind the house. Slowly climbing from his own truck, Clouse looked around, hearing only the wind rustling the leaves of the nearby grove. He walked up to the house, ringing the doorbell and knocking several times before trying the knob, finding it locked.

Finding no indication of anyone staying inside, he went around back and tried the other door, finding it locked as well. Sighing as he stepped from the porch, he noticed the signs pointing toward the haunted forest, wondering if Kern might be working on something inside the natural thicket.

"Brian?" he called. "You around?"

No answer.

Hesitantly, he walked into the entrance of the grove, spying what he figured were spooky decorations for the nighttime run through the haunted woods. Several scarecrows, a reaper, jack-o-lanterns, and what appeared to be a pile of fake intestines beside a witch took up the first main drag of the tour, distracting Clouse until he rounded the corner, tripping a wire.

From above, the sound of heavy rope rounding a pulley drew his attention as something large descended quickly, jerking beside him as it came to an abrupt end of its line. Clouse spied the steel-toed boots beside his head first, slowly looking up to see what dangled from the rope as he stumbled back.

"Oh, shit," he said, thankful the victim was simply a dummy constructed for the haunted woods.

He exhaled a sigh of relief, backing into a solid object.

Whirling around, he found the land's occupant smiling from ear to ear.

"Brian. What the hell?"

"Gotcha good, didn't I?" the landscape contractor replied. "My favorite part of the whole show, Paul," he added, tugging the dummy's leg to make sure everything remained intact after the plunge. "Happy Halloween."

Upset, not from the scare, but rather his friend's ignorance of the recent danger surrounding them both, Clouse shook his head.

"I've been trying to call you almost an hour now," he said. "No one answered, and the machine didn't pick up."

Kern gave a puzzled look.

"It always picks up after three rings."

"It didn't."

Kern started toward the house, wondering how that could be.

"Did you leave both doors locked?"

"I did," Kern replied.

"Then I think I know what happened," Clouse noted, heading for the house's front, then around to the far side. "Where is your phone line out here?"

"Over there," Kern said, pointing to a line, painted over as though part of the house's original construction.

Before reaching it, Clouse could tell it was cut clean through, probably by a knife or wire cutters. Kern noticed the cut as well, but still seemed unaware of what danger he might be in.

"Shit," Clouse said, happy Kern was alive, but curious why someone made the trip out to the man's house just to cut a line. "When your family gets home, keep them inside, Brian," he warned.

"But I've got the woods running tonight. I can't just hole myself up and skip it."

"I understand. Just be careful, Brian. The same person who cut your line is probably the same one who's been killing people at the hotel these past few weeks."

"Paul, you've got to give me some idea of what's going on here," Kern stated. "You came all the way out here to check on me and you haven't said one word about what you think might happen to me."

Clouse wondered why someone bothered to cut the line unless they suspected he had freed McCabe, or knew he had the list. Either scenario jeopardized the killer's identity and plan to some extent. He thought about who might have seen either situation, then realized more importantly, he was squarely between the hotel and his own residence, unable to reach either before the killer might.

As Clouse thought about his own situation, Kern's expression showed he began to realize what his former colleague was worried about.

"You think this wacky son-of-a-bitch might come out here again?" Kern questioned as Clouse pondered the danger his own family might be in.

"I don't think so, Brian," he said numbly, knowing what his next move had to be.

"Why not?"

"Because I think he's coming after my friends and family now," Clouse answered, starting toward his truck. "Be careful!" he called

back, praying he was wrong in his theory, knowing what a dangerous game he might be playing.

33

Standing on the side of a hill, Daniels watched as a crane hoisted the dripping wreckage of McCabe's patrol car from a large pond just outside of Paoli. Ordinarily the discovery of a vehicle beneath water failed to create major local headlines, but when divers discovered it was a police vehicle from the license plate, and it was later verified as McCabe's, the state police wasted little time in getting a local crane operator to the site to extract possible evidence in the attempted murder of one of their own.

Moments later, the car was examined, and the trunk opened. Every shred of paper appeared waterlogged, and any equipment left inside would be rendered useless. Daniels realized what the state investigators would soon discover. No evidence remained inside the vehicle of value to them, and any documents would now be impossible to read.

Monitoring his scanner was about the only way Daniels knew about such events. He retained several ties at the local and state level who occasionally fed him information, but putting himself too close to the events too often would lead him into trouble.

"What do you make of it?" one of the investigators asked him, apparently seeing his opinion of some value.

Daniels knew the man's last name as Hansen, only because they had taken the same class about basic forensic science few years back.

"I doubt you'll find anything of use. Our killer hasn't left anything yet."

"It must be weird having to go through this stuff all the time," the man said, fidgeting with his tie, something Daniels often did while a detective. "Do you ever get used to it?"

"You mean the gruesome killings, losing people I care about, or the fact that the killer never leaves me any clues?" Daniels answered with his own question, sprinkled with sarcasm.

"Well, death is never easy. It just seems like the motives are crazier than ever," the detective commented. "I mean, kids kill because their parents piss them off, or because they saw it in a movie and decided to go experiment. The worst part is, they get away with it. Go to court and blam-o, you're free as a bird when the defense pleads temporary insanity, or blames society for the kid's upbringing. Makes you wonder."

"Yeah, it does," Daniels said, watching as officers searched the trunk, pulling a firearm from the sludge lining the trunk, all dripping wet.

"We found McCabe's gun," one of them announced, recognizing the issue as that of state police troopers. The serial number instantly proved true possession of the firearm.

Phased little by the discovery, Daniels watched a moment more before heading back to his car, stopping halfway as the officers made another discovery, this one more profound.

"A knife," one of them said aloud as the former detective hobbled down the hill to see them holding up a peculiar weapon by latex glove, which he believed would only be a weapon with the right intent.

"Actually, a scalpel," Hansen said, apparently the detective in charge of the scene.

"Actually, a post-mortem knife," Daniels corrected him.

"What's the difference?"

"Ever been to an autopsy?" Daniels asked.

He had attended over a dozen as a detective before growing tired of seeing bodies treated like meat. Most investigators left the autopsies entirely to the coroners and their technicians. His desire to be the best investigator possible had constantly kept him curious about the workings of the human body.

"Never one in progress," Hansen confessed.

State police often missed out on the fun stuff, Daniels thought. Hansen tossed Daniels a latex glove, noticing the inactive officer wanted a closer look at the blade.

Daniels took hold of the potential weapon, looking it over on both sides. He made mental notes during his examination of the blade, finding some modifications that made an ordinary knife into a deadly weapon.

"Your typical scalpel isn't a very large blade," he finally said, pointing to the length and width of the blade, screwed into a die-cast handle. "During an autopsy you need a larger blade to cut rib meat and small bones with. This one has been modified to accommodate two blades, reversed from one another, giving it a double edge. I think the reason our security guard pulled through, aside from luck, is the fact that this knife couldn't enter his side far enough to reach any vital areas. The handle is too thick to allow penetration beyond the blade."

"So did someone from the medical field abduct McCabe?" the detective deduced aloud, trying to save face in front of his peers.

"Possibly. With Internet sales and the possibility someone stole the blade, it's hard to tell. It's likely someone modified the blade for another purpose, such as scraping or dissection, then found himself forced to use it. A lab might be able to find traces of something on there."

"How was it modified?" Hansen asked Daniels, getting the weapon back.

"Ordinarily the blades work like those of a utility knife. You can screw one in, and it stays pretty snug. If you look at this closely, you can see the edges where someone grinded down the securing ends, kind of like key makers might do if a key is too thick for a lock."

Nodding in agreement with the assessment, Hansen probably saw the ends were thick enough not to break while providing stability enough to carve, stab, or scrape. Made of heavy-duty carbon steel, the blades were meant to last with fairly rugged use.

With such a smooth handle, it made for an impractical weapon, backing Daniels' theory that it might never have been intended as a weapon, until necessary. Besides, the killer's main weapon of choice was a scythe, which provided much quicker death than an enlarged scalpel.

Daniels felt he had seen enough to satisfy him. He turned to walk away when Hansen's voice got his attention.

"You think our killer left this here as a calling card, or by accident?"

To this point, the killer, or Jacob, whatever people wanted to call him, had left nothing to chance. Daniels knew whoever was behind the murders, and the assault on McCabe and Hinds, if indeed the same person, was no fool.

"Calling card," he said before trudging up the hill.

*   *   *

Feeling a chill run through the barn at her new property, Jane pulled the saddle down from Bucky, Clouse's horse, straddling it across a nearby partition as she led the animal into his stall. Each time she rode him the horse grew more tame from being around a human being, proving her fiancé wrong about its behavior.

Covered in a colorful wool pullover, Jane felt protected from the wind and cold, though the tingling of her face and runny nose told her otherwise. She wore lace-up boots when she rode because they were easily freed from the saddle in a hurry, and comfortable to walk in if necessary.

She glanced at her watch, noticing she had almost half an hour before Zach finished school. A hot cup of coffee would revive her, then she could make a trip to the school to pick up her future stepson while his father searched what seemed like all of Indiana to find the reaper.

Jane had gone all morning without seeing or hearing from Clouse. Under ordinary conditions he was the best father and future husband she could ask for, but the murders changed him, taking him away from her. She hated being alone so much, especially when the kids kept wondering where he was, and Jane could not explain the situation to them.

As she scooped some feed from a nearby bag, a creaking noise from the hay loft above her caught her attention. Freezing a moment, Jane heard nothing, then proceeded to line Bucky's trough with the feed.

Winds picked up outside, causing several doors along the barn to flap in and out, banging against the solid structure. She heard howling as the winds darted through the open cracks of the old barn. Several broken windows let in the cold chill, and sounds seemed to come from everywhere in the old building.

Another strange noise came from above, this time sounding like a heavy footstep along the bare, wooden floor.

Without a word, Jane took a hatchet down from the selection of farm tools along one wall. A rake dropped to the ground, tumbling toward the open entrance door. She climbed a stationary wooden ladder which she guessed was part of the farm's original construction, because it was solidly mounted to the hatchway above. With no hatch to hinder her progress, Jane reached the top, sticking her head up through the square opening, keeping the hatchet ready for action.

After a quick glance around, she found no one in the loft. The only available hiding place was beneath a dozen hay bales. Deciding not to pursue her search any further, Jane climbed down the ladder, prepared to pick up Zach. She took out her cellular phone, to try calling Clouse, which someone hiding from her might have interpreted as a call to the police.

As she headed for the door, phone cupped to her ear, a cloaked figure emerged from the shadows, cupping her mouth from behind as the phone dropped to the concrete, breaking on contact. Her attacker's other arm wrapped around her free arm, keeping her close to him, entangled enough for him to pull a knife from a sheath along his waist, much to her dismay as her muffled cries went unheard.

Spying the gleam of the knife above her, fearful of where it might plunge, Jane drew close to a wall, kicking with both feet against the solid surface. Both Jane and her unknown assailant tumbled backwards, the cloaked man taking the fall for both of them as he landed neck and head first against the barn's cold, concrete foundation. Jane regained her footing much quicker, darting for the open door of the barn.

Far ahead of the dark figure, Jane looked back to assure herself she could make it, but tripped over the fallen rake at the foot of the doorway. She landed hard, knocking the wind from her lungs and cracking a bone in one wrist.

Regaining her composure, Jane turned herself over, staring into what looked like an empty hood, dripping black cloth all the way down to her legs. She drew a horrified breath as the stalker held up a long knife, tracing the blade with both his index finger and thumb. Wasting no time, Jane attempted to stand up, but the figure stepped on her ankle, threatening to snap it with his industrial-grade black boot if she made any further moves.

Knowing escape was nearly impossible, Jane stared upward, uncertain of what her fate might be as the assailant stared a moment, then swooped down on her.

*   *   *

Clouse reached the top of the stairs at his son's school, unsure of what to believe was happening. His cellular phone rang twice during the ride there, but died suddenly. When he tried the automatic redial function, it dialed Jane's number, but he got no answer, only seconds after the initial call.

Unsure of what move to make next, Clouse had contacted Daniels, telling the detective to check on his own family before meeting him. The two quickly exchanged their findings, deciding their course of action for the remainder of the day would probably determine how many people might be saved from certain death.

Concerned for both Jane and Zach, he stopped by the school first, knowing it was closer. He decided to check on his son's whereabouts first, rather than backtrack, wasting time and miles if he found nothing wrong at the farm.

Finding the school recently abandoned of all activity, most of the doors remained open as teachers gathered their notes and ungraded assignments before heading out for the evening.

Clouse walked in as one of the gifted and talented teachers was about to lock her door and head out. He startled her as she closed the door, prepared to lock it. She appeared young, as though just out of college, with cheeks the color of fall apples.

"Sorry," he apologized for startling her. "I'm Zach's father."

"Oh, I recognize you," she replied. "When neither of you showed to pick Zach up at three, Mrs. Morgan called your house."

Clouse's surprise showed, for good reason.

"Jane didn't show up?"

"No, but she asked Mrs. Morgan to take Zach home."

"Who is Mrs. Morgan?"

"She's one of our teaching aides. A very sweet widow who dedicates herself to our class three times a week, especially with your son."

A chill shot through Clouse.

"Did you talk to Jane on the phone?" Clouse asked, genuinely concerned at this point.

What he was hearing of his fiancee sounded very much unlike Jane's behavior.

"Yes, I verified it. And Mrs. Morgan said it was right on her way home."

I'll bet she did, Clouse thought, beginning to realize what might be happening.

"What's going on?" Daniels asked, walking up on the situation.

He was dressed in slacks and a tie with his shoulder holster, just as Clouse had requested, in case they needed some official police access. Daniels had already made it clear he would rather lose his job than see anyone, including himself, lose his or her life.

"Do you have any photos with Mrs. Morgan in them?" Clouse asked the teacher, who seemed perplexed by the entire situation.

He turned to speak aside to his friend.

"Jane never came to pick up Zach."

"Shit," Daniels muttered as the teacher unlocked the door.

Once inside the room, Clouse requested his friend boot up the computer while he and the teacher searched for any photos containing the mysterious teaching aide. Digging through a stack of photos buried in a desk drawer, the teacher seemed to sense Clouse's urgency, though she probably failed to understand it.

"Mrs. Morgan isn't very much for photos," she commented. "She just likes to be in the background helping the kids. Is that man a police officer?" she asked Clouse a virtually rhetorical question.

"Yeah. A friend of mine."

"I don't think you have much to worry about," she commented, continuing to flip through the stack of photos. "Mrs. Morgan is a very sweet lady."

Clouse reserved his judgment.

"Here we are," she said, pulling out a mildly out of focus picture, taken outside the Indianapolis Zoo about a month earlier on a field trip.

Singling out Mrs. Morgan in the photo, Clouse took a hard look, finding his fears confirmed instantly, despite the woman in question turning from the camera, as though trying to avoid being photographed altogether. Clouse would not be fooled, and he began to sense exactly what the scheme might be.

"Mrs. Landamere," he said, drawing a confused look from the teacher.

He stormed off toward the computer room, ready to grab Daniels and head toward his farm. Knowing better than to expect to Jane and his son to be safe and sound at home, it was much closer than the West Baden Springs Hotel. By default, he needed to check there first.

"Come on, Mark," he virtually ordered, standing in the doorway of the small room.

"Take a look at this real quick, Paul," Daniels said, intrigued by whatever he had found on the computer.

Clouse swung around the desk, finding the same program Jane had viewed just a few days before. Daniels reset the program, causing the hotel's blueprint designer to take an interest in the virtual reality grate located at the forefront of a tunnel system. It appeared filled with intricate designs Clouse instantly recognized after the painstaking renovation at the hotel.

"That's the hotel's emblem," he said, pointing to one particular pattern as Daniels traced the tunnel to one end.

"I keep taking different routes," Daniels commented. "Every time I can only get so far, regardless of what path I take, then it seems to suddenly end, as though it isn't complete. This one is complete," he said, reaching the end of the fourth of four paths, finding only an empty space for his trouble. "It's as though the program isn't complete."

"It wouldn't be if you didn't have all the puzzle pieces to finish it," Clouse commented, motioning for the seat. "This program looks awfully familiar."

Daniels complied, letting his friend sort through the program, exiting the simulation until he reached the main program itself. There, he discovered a familiar copyright symbol, along with the name of the designers and title. In the lower right-hand corner he found exactly what he thought he would. The program, *Trailblazer*, was created at Indiana University in the exact same architecture building he once attended as a student, and later as a graduate student. It looked as though the program hadn't changed since he used it.

He thought of only one person he knew who might have access and knowledge enough to correctly use the program, though he hoped he was wrong.

Suddenly everything fit.

It would take a phone call or two to verify his theory on who was behind the murders and why, but it could be done. He could ask the man beside him to stretch his pretentious credentials just a bit further.

Daniels looked at Clouse as though he spied the wheels working inside his friend's head while Clouse stared at the computer monitor.

"What are you thinking, buddy?"

"I'm thinking I know exactly who's behind this and why, Mark. And we need to get going right now."

34

Niemeyer burst through his front door, disrupting both his wife and two children, who were watching television. He stepped inside, only socks on his feet, not bothering to unzip his thick leather jacket, despite the heat cranked inside the house. All three realized the look on his face was not that of a happy man.

Not the least bit chipper.

"Where are your boots?" his wife, Vicky, asked as she stood from the couch, referring to the pair of work boots he usually wore on the job.

"Outside," he replied in short. "They're muddy."

He stepped past the kids without a word, which seemed unusual for the family man. Heading straight for his gun cabinet, he unlocked it and took out a riot gun, similar to the shotguns used in police or security work, which one of his police buddies had encouraged him to buy. Throwing it over his shoulder, Niemeyer freed one arm to snatch a box of shells, which he dumped into his jacket pocket, letting a few carelessly fall to the floor.

Picking the loose shells up from the floor, he stuffed them into the other pocket, not looking to Vicky or the kids even a second before crossing the room toward the closet. Vicky stood, obviously concerned about her husband's irrational behavior. Never had he entered the house in such a hurry, or hostile mood. He never hunted without his brother, so this was not a quickened search for wild game.

"Tim, what on earth are you doing?" she implored as he swung the closet door open, his eyes wildly searching for some new footwear.

"I can't talk about it," he answered abruptly.

Given the choice between hole-ridden tennis shoes or the pair of cowboy boots he sometimes wore to church, he chose the latter. He put the shotgun down just long enough to pull them on, then stood, ready to leave again.

Vicky stood in his way, glancing to the children. Niemeyer looked, seeing the confusion in both his son's and daughter's eyes. Despite his hurry, he decided to take a moment with his family, uncertain of what his future held. For all he knew, he could wind up in jail or worse before the day was through.

"Come here, kids," he said, kneeling to pull them into a hug. They ran over, each grabbing one of his thick arms. "Daddy has something to take care of," he told them, feeling a tear coming to his eye. "Remember, I love you both, and I always will. Now go watch the television and don't worry about me."

Both slowly responded, allowing him to confront his wife at the front door.

"What is going on, Tim?" she demanded quietly enough that the kids would not hear.

"I have to do something," he said, clutching the shotgun. "An old friend and I have some business we need to finish. If anything happens to me, you call Randy," he instructed, speaking of his younger brother. "I love you," he added before heading out the door toward his pickup truck.

He pulled out of the driveway, knowing he had never let his wife and kids see his aggressive nature at its worst. Niemeyer hoped to see them again after taking care of some business.

*   *   *

At dark, Clouse pulled into the hotel's long brick path, leading up to the hotel. He saw no other vehicles outside the building, but the two jack-o-lanterns sitting on the grand staircase left little doubt he had reached his final destination.

"Looks like the party's just starting," Daniels noted from the passenger seat.

"If they hurt Jane or my son, someone is going to die," Clouse said, anxious to get inside the hotel.

"Whoa there, Paul," Daniels said, physically keeping his friend in the truck once it was turned off. "Remember, we can't go running in there with both guns blazing. We've got a plan, remember?" His words made sense, and Clouse settled into his seat for the moment. "You *sure* you don't want to call the police on this?"

"I'm not risking the lives of my future wife and child, Mark. Besides, what if this is another false alarm? What if police sirens tip off the killers and let them escape, or worse yet, they hurt Jane or Zach? I'm not taking any risks. We've got the plan, so let's do it."

Clouse had taken Daniels with him to the house, finding no sign of Jane or Zach, as he suspected. Jane's car remained in the driveway, and everything else seemed in order. Even the mail had been left on the table, and the dogs fed in their pens. It was almost as though his fiancee had left and never returned.

Both decided to head to crucial locations they knew of, beginning with the resort Niemeyer looked after. Clouse found similar design patterns in the charred remains of the building, leaving him to think the trap door his friend spoke of might have been the answer, since the hotel's basement had no obvious tunnel system beneath it. Though it seemed plausible the hotel kept a few secrets from him, Clouse could not think of anywhere the tunnel entrance might be hidden, though someone had managed to put a brick wall up without him immediately realizing it.

After traveling to the hollowed resort, where Clouse expected to find the center of criminal activity, and finding nothing but a cleared area where the trap door seemed to be, he felt absolutely disappointed and anxious.

Someone had beaten them to it.

When he and Daniels descended a ladder from the trap door into an elaborate tunnel system, remarkably similar to that of the computer system, they quickly found why a child had been selected to learn and carry out the details of the mission.

Four distinct directions were evident, but each quickly narrowed, leaving an adult only several feet of walking or crawling space before he or she would be stuck in the shrinking walls. Along the settled dust in the tunnel floors he saw footprints heading in and returning to where he stood at the narrowing edge.

He felt certain Zach had been there.

The tunnels were made of dirt, but the years, and the destructive fire, had baked them into a hardened clay that would take a man and his tools literally years to dig through.

A child seemed the only possibility of getting to the end of the system. After seeing so many of his friends and colleagues die around him, Clouse knew why his child had been chosen. It was simply the climax to the personal hell the killer put him through.

Clouse called several times for his son with no response, wondering if Zach had been forced inside, never to return. He desperately tested the walls with his fist, drawing blood on several knuckles as he shined a light inside, able to see nothing. It paralleled any number of fire scenes he had worked on, where sight and hearing were sometimes little use to him. Often instinct got firefighters by, and he sensed this was a waste of time.

After several minutes of calling with no reply, and with urging from Daniels, the two decided to move on to the hotel with the hope that Zach and Jane would turn up unharmed, even if it meant confronting the source of their investigation head on.

"You know how to use this?" Daniels asked, handing him a semi-automatic pistol, similar to his police department issue.

"Yeah, but it's been awhile. My aim is terrible."

"With any luck we won't need them," the officer said, checking his own firearm. "I still can't believe Mrs. Landamere has anything to do with this," he commented, shaking his head. "You sure she wasn't being a protective guardian or something?"

"I'm awfully sure," Clouse replied sternly. "I don't see why else a person would force a kid to learn a maze, have him risk his life getting some sort of box or book, and abduct him from school unless their motivation was at least a little bit evil."

Daniels nodded.

"All right, let's do this. You said it yourself there might be two of them, so watch it, Paul. I'll go around back and try getting myself on a higher floor in case anything happens. I'm not going to be too mobile if something goes wrong, so be careful."

"Good luck," Clouse said, climbing from the truck, wasting little time as Daniels looked around cautiously before letting himself out. If he was spotted, their splitting up would be pointless. If he made it, he could begin to look for Joan Landamere or the person Clouse suspected of being her partner.

While Daniels made his way around back, as quickly as possible with rehabilitating legs, Clouse climbed the stairway, eyeing the gutted vegetables as he passed them. The candles inside flickered, and he knew what their symbolism entailed. A jack-o-lantern was one of the last objects his wife had seen on Halloween night the year before. Moments later, she was ripped apart with a scythe, left mutilated across his kitchen floor for his son to find the next morning.

He felt no desire in sharing her fate.

Stepping inside the double glass doors a moment later, Clouse felt the firearm tucked into his belt at his backside, concealed by his jacket. He wondered if he possessed skill enough to save his own life with it if necessary. The last time he recalled firing any sort of pistol was long before he joined the Bloomington Fire Department.

He entered the lobby, seeing a light down the hall, probably from the atrium where he expected to find the center of the action, like he had the year prior when his brother-in-law revealed himself as the murderer, and David Landamere as his partner. Clouse still had nightmares about the ordeal, and how he allowed himself to be tricked by two people he trusted so much.

Not this year.

Careful to step quietly so his boots would not give him away, Clouse found himself at a crossroads in the hallway, unsure of which direction to take. The entire hotel was rounded, so it did not matter in the sense of a destination, because he could reach any-place in due time by walking around the circular hallway. He wondered where he might gain an advantage over the abductors of his son and fiancee before they could do him harm.

Before he decided, he heard the glass doors close behind him as air rushed into the compression springs meant to keep the doors from slamming.

Taking a deep breath, Clouse turned around, finding a shotgun held by its butt, with the barrel aimed straight at his chest.

"I didn't expect you so soon, Paul," Niemeyer said in a voice somewhat above a whisper, to keep from gaining unwanted attention.

Clouse swallowed, unsure of whether his assessment about Joan Landamere's potential partner was entirely accurate, particularly after he had called the contractor to help him.

"I don't like wasting time, Tim," he decided to say. "Let's say we get on with this."

"Okay," his friend said, lowering the riot gun, which he had simply used to point, and assure himself it was Clouse before proceeding.

To this point, Niemeyer knew only as much as Clouse and Daniels, but the firefighter felt a bit more secure knowing his high school buddy had made an effort to arrive so quickly.

"It makes perfect sense why I'm on that list now," Niemeyer commented. "I stood between them and whatever they were looking for on the property."

"I know it isn't safe to do this, but we need to split up, Tim," Clouse deduced in a whisper. "I think there's two of them, and hopefully three of us can somehow overtake them before anyone else gets hurt."

"Only two?"

"I hope," Clouse said with a shrug.

Niemeyer gave a short, parting wave, heading down the hallway on the left, while Clouse opted to head the other way, hoping to sneak a peek inside the atrium.

*   *   *

Niemeyer found a set of stairs down his hallway, deciding to get a view from above, much like Daniels had. Quietly as he possible, the stocky contractor rounded the stairway until he reached the second floor. Finding it dark, he carefully looked both ways before stepping out to the carpeted floor.

He only heard his nervous breaths as his eyes panned the floor. He tried several of the closest doors, finding every room closed and locked, except one. A few doors down on his right, Niemeyer saw a door open just a crack. He wondered if it might be a setup or his only chance to overlook the atrium from above.

Approaching the door cautiously, Niemeyer held out his shotgun, opening the door the remainder of the way, finding a trickle of dim light from the hallway follow him inside. He could not turn on the room's light because he risked revealing his position to anyone down the hall, or in the atrium below.

He found it easy to check the room because no furniture had been placed inside yet. Without benefit of the light, Niemeyer checked behind the door, then crept over to the closet, which had a sliding door.

Holding the shotgun with one hand aimed at the closet, he slowly slid it open, breathing nervously with the few breaths he dared take. Making just a little noise, the door slid open, revealing complete vacancy inside.

Niemeyer silently sighed relief, walking over the curtains, peeking through a small space between the adjoining sets to the atrium below, finding a scene worse than he hoped.

"Oh, no," he whispered, hearing a step behind him, allowed by his momentary lapse of caution.

Niemeyer whirled around, allowing his cloaked adversary to grasp his shotgun, ramming the length of its steel and wood up against his forehead. A loud thwack sounded as his head met the stock of the weapon, nearly knocking him unconscious in one swift motion.

Too stunned to retaliate against his much quicker opponent, the contractor was grasped by his jacket collar and rammed head-first into the far wall with a running start, his shotgun falling to the ground, too far away to aid him.

Blood trickled from the center of his fringe, but he was too close to unconsciousness to realize it. His footing wobbled momentarily as the shadowy figure regained his grip on the jacket, leading Niemeyer toward the window.

There was no balcony to this room, which left only a two-story drop to the atrium below. The decorative carpet below provided little cushioning as the contractor was hurled through the large window, landing hard on his back, sprawled along the atrium floor. An audible moan stemmed from his mouth as his head fell limp to one side as he remained motionless.

*   *   *

From one of the four entrances to the atrium along the ground floor, Clouse observed his friend's ill fate, disturbed because a member of his team had already fallen prey to the evil he meant to stop. He was more upset about his wife and child sitting tied up and gagged in the middle of the atrium while a cloaked figure stalked the other side of the mammoth room, keeping another victim close by, hands tied behind his back.

He could not tell who the person was because he faced the other way. After assessing the situation, Clouse knew entering the room meant putting himself at the mercy of at least one conspirator.

He looked to Jane and Zach, thankful both were alive and unharmed for the most part. His eyes moved to Niemeyer, who lay motionless across the room, blood oozing from the cuts on his head. It was impossible to tell whether or not he survived the fall.

"Oh, shit," he told himself, momentarily uncertain of what to do.

A completely nervous state overcame his body as he paced the hallway, out of sight and earshot of anyone else. He could not risk putting himself in danger if he was their last chance at survival, and he refused to stand around waiting, hoping for Daniels to come through.

"Fuck it," he concluded suddenly, marching into the atrium to confront whoever was behind the mask at the other end of the circular chamber.

Either way, this would end very soon.

35

The clop of Clouse's boots announced his arrival to the atrium before the dark figure even spotted him. He purposely left his jacket unzipped for easier access to the gun, unsure of where Daniels might have gone. His eyes stared straight ahead as they locked with the mask of one of the conspirators.

As though instinctively, the cloaked person pulled out a knife, taking up the nearby hostage, holding Barry Andrews in front, a knife to his throat. Clouse made some quick, keen observations about the knife's wielder. Andrews was definitely taller, as the killer had to pull him back like a bow to threaten his throat area. Clouse knew who the person was immediately, but waited until he drew closer before engaging in conversation.

"Give it up, Mrs. Landamere," he said without hesitation, drawing as close as possible. "I know it's you, and you're the brains behind this operation. I want some answers before we settle this."

"You're in no position to order me around," Joan Landamere's voice said as she pulled the hood back on her black cloak, removing a solid black mask from underneath.

The mask explained why no one ever saw a face beyond the cloak, making the wearer incredibly mysterious and intimidating, but Clouse knew only ordinary people like himself were behind the killings. No longer would he be intimidated.

"It's over," he said, stepping closer.

"Stay back," she ordered with a vicious sneer he never imagined the widow possessing. "I'll slit the good doctor's throat in a heartbeat," she added, positioning herself to walk back toward Jane and Zach, who were tied helplessly in the center of the atrium.

Clouse started toward her, then viewed her up and down, searching for any signs of vulnerability, or any other weapons. She seemed to take note of his keen observations.

"Are you wondering?" she asked, pausing for an answer.

When none came, she continued.

"Do you wonder if the good doctor might be my partner, just posing as an innocent victim like David did last year?"

Clouse refused to answer, remembering how easily he had been duped by the duo of killers before. It haunted him still.

"Can you take that chance, Paul?" she asked, an evil smile forming along her lips.

Somewhere along the line, Joan had snapped, or she was extremely good at containing her psychotic tendencies the entire time Clouse had known her.

She drew dangerously close to his fiancee and son, making him want to draw the gun and blow her away, but he wasn't convinced of the doctor's position. Andrews appeared to be drugged, or in shock. His eyes looked glazed, and he responded little to the fact his life was in danger.

A trick?

Or worse, the real thing?

Clouse felt he was in a battle he could not win.

"I know who your conspirator was, Mrs. Landamere, and it is not Dr. Andrews," he said without falter, daring to call her bluff as she stopped at the feet of Jane, who was too terrified to do anything but look up from the insane widow to her future husband.

Joan's face showed little emotion as she pondered what he said, thinking of her next move. She wanted to shock Clouse, to show she meant business. At the same time, she did not want to exhaust all of her cards in this human game of poker.

"Then you won't mind this a bit," she said callously, drawing the blade across Andrews' throat, leaving a trail of red in its wake.

Gurgling a moment before he died, Andrews slumped to the floor, convulsing as the life and blood ebbed from his body. Hands bound, and quite possibly doped up, he never stood a chance against the psychotic woman. While Clouse watched in horror as the doctor met a cruel end, blood pooling on the floor from his opened throat, Joan snatched up Zach from the floor, holding him in a similar position before Clouse called her several adjectives her senseless murder brought to mind. She simply grinned, apparently satisfied she had shocked a man accustomed to death and trauma.

He looked from the dead doctor, to his fiancee, to his son, held close to the blade dripping of Andrews' blood.

Few choices remained.

"Don't do this," Clouse pleaded. "What is it you want, Mrs. Landamere?"

"I want my husband back, Paul. I can call you Paul, can't I?" she said more than asked with a knife pressed against his son's throat, assuring no objections would be sounded. "Let me tell you a little story about exactly what happened last year, and how things should have gone."

Clouse stood a safe distance from her, keeping his eyes focused on Zach, knowing the gun was accessible, but of little use to him if he reached for it under the circumstances. He would never draw and fire quickly enough to keep his son from harm, even if his aim was true.

"It's time for a little story, Paul," she said, keeping herself moving in a pattern that kept Clouse at a safe distance from her and both of her hostages. "I'm going to tell you exactly why I want everyone in your life dead, because you and your fucking detective friend killed my husband last year. Kind of a shame," she said, as though feeling a bit of regret. "That Daniels is rather cute. That's why I wanted to save him for last."

"Your husband wanted to kill you, Joan," Clouse said, trying to reason. "Why on earth would you want to avenge his death?"

"Because you don't know the whole story," she said bitterly, as though he should have. "David's coverup was only part of the plan, my dear," Joan began, waving the knife in front of Zach, terrifying the kindergartner further. "David had told Roger Summers they were partners until the end, splitting the money from my life insurance policy between them. In reality, David and I planned to kill Roger, our simple pawn, blame him for everything, be the sole survivors, and destroy Martin Smith in claims court, taking everything he had, including the hotel. After all, it was his ultimate refusal of closing down the West Baden Springs construction that led to so many murders, and would have nearly cost my husband and I our very lives," she said with a bit of artistic license. "Smith was weak, and he would have settled out of court, giving us everything we wanted."

"So exactly what *are* you after?" Clouse insisted, wanting a concrete motive.

"This time, I'm after revenge. And I also want those jewels buried by Charles Rexford oh so many years ago. I think they would make it worth my trouble."

"You mean you don't have them?"

"No, my partner has the loot. He saw fit to leave me your son before heading off to dispose of any other snoops."

Everyone looked over to Niemeyer, who remained motionless where he originally landed.

"What makes you think he won't run off with the prize and leave you hanging like you did your husband?"

"Fuck you!" she exclaimed, gnashing her teeth. "When your friend shot my husband, my heart nearly stopped, but I knew at that very moment I would carry out our plan. I would own this hotel and Dr. Smith, and I would have complete ownership of the tile pieces. See, David and I did some research when we found a few of those pieces a couple years ago, and we found out what they led to and where they might be."

She smiled, waving the knife in front of Zach again, disturbing his father greatly. Clouse thought of ways to continue the conversation, to distract Joan.

"So you knew about the tiles that long ago?"

"Oh, yes. We only had a few by this time last year, but with ownership of the hotel we planned to buy the others back at any cost and make our fortune with the lost Rexford jewels. Every account I've ever read says they were imported, and quite valuable. They were merely hidden away because of Rexford's overbearing nature, and his impending divorce. He stood to lose a great deal in the divorce proceedings, including the jewels."

"And you figured out the Rexford family owned a retreat not far down the road, and where the jewels were hidden below?"

"It wasn't easy, but we secretly retrieved enough of the pieces to make a map, no matter the cost," she said with a wry smile. "So you see, between the hotel and the jewels, David and I had it made. We would have become one of the richest couples in the country, retired early, and led happy lives in seclusion after selling our new-found goods at a hearty calling price. Everything was perfect until you and your detective friend murdered my husband."

"Pardon me for surviving," Clouse said, knowing full well he was forced to participate in the final charade the year before, just as he was now.

At the moment, his chances looked worse, considering the scenario.

Clouse glanced around, seeing no sign of her partner, or his own for that matter. He felt as though he knew, and to an extent, understood Joan's motive, but he wanted to know for certain if he was right about the partner, and if so, what his motivation was.

"Where are you, Mark?" he wondered under his breath, glancing around the atrium and its surrounding facade.

*   *   *

From across the atrium Daniels surveyed everything below, including the hostage crisis and Niemeyer's condition, which seemed shaky at best. Unlike the contractor, he had picked the lock of a room, closing the door behind him. Careful to leave the lights off, he spied the scene below, unsure of what his best move might be.

It felt like watching a movie where he was helpless to determine the outcome, but he decided a move closer to the action might change that.

His legs felt rubbery, partly from so much use. Nerves had an impact on how well he functioned as well. He carefully opened the door, looking around outside before stepping, his gun drawn for both threat and protection. He needed to watch every step with caution, but something instinctive alerted him that he was already being watched.

Perhaps even stalked.

To his right, a streak of black seemed to zip by. He turned, but it was already past, perhaps into another corridor, perhaps a figment of his imagination. The last time he experienced such a feeling, his head had nearly lost a permanent fit with his neck. Assuring himself the safety was off, he took careful hold of the gun, looking in every direction before advancing up the hallway.

Again he thought something moved behind him.

Again he turned.

"Damn it," he muttered, seeing nothing.

He returned his attention to the hallway and the barrage of doors before him. As though he paddled down a winding stream, they were his shore, showing him where to go. He quickened his pace, despite the discomfort in his legs. He would literally have to walk nearly a quarter of a mile to help his friend, considering how big the atrium and its surrounding hallways were. Getting there presented more of a challenge than just the walk.

Rounding the first set of rooms, Daniels felt halfway home, but a gut feeling told him something dangerous drew near. He stopped his walk, turning around completely to look at the dimmed hallway he had just come from.

Nothing visible.

He had nearly shaken off the notion of anyone pursuing him when a door burst open to his side, revealing a black shape too fast for him to shoot before it rammed him against the wall, knocking the wind from his lungs.

And the gun from his right hand.

Larger and stronger than his foe, Daniels could not match quickness with the cloaked figure as he grasped the person's throat, only to receive several knees to his groin for the effort. Daniels slumped to the floor, taking several more kicks to his ribs, each hurting more than the one before.

He audibly hurt, seeing his gun only a few feet away through dizzied vision. The thought of reaching it died as the figure pulled him to his feet, pulling a knife in an attempt to finish his work.

Seeing well enough to detect the shine of the blade, Daniels clasped the stalker's hand at the wrist, preventing any action from the blade. With his other hand, the former detective struck the figure's head, spinning him back.

The cloaked figure immediately retaliated with a charge led by the blade. Daniels dodged, hurling the killer forcefully into the wall as he dove for his gun. His legs failed him as he fell short of grasping the weapon he so desperately needed. He began to crawl toward the firearm, but felt a sharp pain in one leg as the killer plunged the knife into the back of his calf muscle. The weapon immediately pulled free, but Daniels rolled over, grasping his new wound while the killer took up his gun.

Knowing he was unarmed and at a heavy disadvantage, the officer struggled along the floor toward the shadows, hoping to make some sort of defense for himself. He nervously wiped his head once, streaking it with the blood from his wound. Within seconds, the killer loomed over him, fully masked, entirely unknown, and holding his own firearm. Daniels drew in a horrified breath, knowing what mortal danger he was in.

He could only watch as a shot fired, aimed at his abdomen. His hands reacted before his thoughts, clutching the area in question, taking up a pool of blood in each palm as he stared at his hands, a combination of a gasp and moan emitting from his open mouth. His eyes panned the cloaked legs up to the faceless mask of the person wanting him dead. In the shadows, neither could really see much expression from the other, but the stalker was apparently in no mood to fool around.

He watched a moment as the detective gasped for breath, which came in heaves due to his abdominal wound. Blood appeared to trickle out through his hands, as though spurting. Pointing the gun at the wounded officer's head a moment, the killer appeared to decide his prey deserved a slow, agonizing death, rather than a quick, painless head shot.

Daniels could only watch the killer exit the hallway from his prone position.

36

Clouse had heard a gunshot echo throughout the hotel that left him wondering if Daniels had evened the playing field, or another of his friends had fallen to the killing duo.

He helplessly watched as the partner entered the atrium, with no sign of Daniels, or any other form of help left. He carried several objects, including Niemeyer's shotgun and an aged book of some sort, with a reddish ribbon protruding from its middle.

His situation paralleled the year before so closely it felt like a dream, as though entirely inconceivable. Once again he felt abandoned, left to the wolves. His gun pressed at his backside, as though to remind him of its potential help. He could only monitor everything in the room one frame at a time, like sequential security cameras in a retail store.

Zach held hostage by Joan.

Niemeyer lying perfectly still, blood oozing from his head.

A cloaked figure drawing closer, his footsteps preceding him in the form of echoes.

Jane tied up, seated helplessly on the floor with him as her only salvation.

The hotel's mammoth frame surrounding him, offering no protection, nor anywhere to hide, or even put up a fair fight.

No matter which frame he viewed, no hope peered back.

As the other killer approached, Clouse took a step back, carefully surveying the person beneath the guise of the reaper, trying to assure himself he was correct in the person's identity. He felt certain he was.

"Have you come to terms with death, Paul?" Joan asked, keeping Zach too close for him to think about anything but his son's safety.

"I'm done with you," Clouse replied, choosing to play the remainder of the game his way.

He turned his attention to the other person, now standing before him holding the shotgun in one hand, the book in the other.

"I want to see Jacob now. You owe me a peek after everything you've put me through."

"This isn't a very comfortable getup anyway," the young man said, taking off the mask to reveal a head of black hair and the snake tattoo Clouse had heard so much about. "Very hard to see, too. I almost let your two friends get the best of me," he said, looking with cold eyes at Clouse, whose lips twitched from anxiety and a building fury. He wanted so badly to take a chance on using the pistol, but he had to follow the plan to the end, even if Daniels was removed from the equation.

"Let's get down to who you really are," Clouse said evenly.

"Ah, first let's get down to disarming you. I know your friend would never let you come in here unarmed. Let me see what you have."

Clouse lifted his jacket, revealing no holster to Jacob. The young man simply smirked at his attempt to further conceal the weapon.

"Come on, Paul. I know where you have it. I saw him give it to you."

Giving in, Clouse slowly reached behind him for the weapon, seeing Niemeyer's shotgun aimed at him in Jacob's hands while his son moaned with a knife against his throat.

Realistic chances of escape were running out.

"Careful now," Jacob warned as Clouse pulled the gun from his backside, setting it on the ground softly. "Kick it over here."

Clouse obeyed.

Jacob let it jet past him without an attempt to retrieve it. After all, he was already armed.

"So you want to know exactly who I am?"

"I already do. What I really want to know is why you're involved with that psycho bitch over there."

"Well," Jacob said, forcefully shoving his finger into his hairline to help remove the realistic black wig. "For me, it was all about family, and getting my little group involved," he said, removing the wig to reveal a natural brown hair color beneath, showing Clouse exactly who he thought he would see. When the serpentine tattoo peeled off with just a hint of effort, he knew who he was dealing with, and how it was pulled off.

"Why did you conspire to do this, and let her murder your father, Ryan?" Clouse asked the son of Barry Andrews, who lie dead on the floor just a few feet away from either of them.

Any makeup, special effects, costumes, and even several various roles pulled off by one person could be explained by Ryan Andrews' experience in the theater, but several other things had yet to be revealed.

Knowledge and access to the hospital were explained, the use and access to a coroner's blade were explained, and with Joan as his partner, he could easily have gained access to the hotel and any lists necessary to track down the pieces of tile and their current owners. She had masterminded the entire scheme, and he had carried it out, but why?

"Why did I allow my father to be murdered?" Ryan repeated the question, as though he needed to truly think of the answer. The tone in his voice gave Clouse the hint that the boy, sane as he may have portrayed himself, was in the same state of mind as Joan. "See, Barry here wasn't really my dad. He just adopted me when I was an infant and lied to me for 21 years. He never intended to tell me the truth, but I found some people who would tell the truth, and they hooked me up with Joan."

"A few years ago Ryan was a sweet, innocent kid just looking for an education," Joan explained. "I certainly gave him one when the Coven introduced me to him last year after they discovered what happened to David."

"I don't believe there is any *Coven*," Clouse almost spat the words. "I have yet to see or hear of anyone except for you two, and Stephen, whom you murdered."

Ryan let out a short laugh.

"Oh, they exist. We're sort of a fraternal group who don't like public recognition. There are always eight of us, and lately it seems we've had a lot of turnover. Joan wanted in, but we were full at the time, so we settled for a working relationship. The group is talking about expansion, but you know how group voting goes. Anyway, the Coven listened to her plight and I took time out of my busy college schedule to help her."

"He's so much more creative than my husband was," Joan commented easily. "I mean, setting people on fire, stabbing them, using the scythe, sealing a person up inside a wall. It takes genius to use so many techniques. Ryan was quite a find for me, and his group."

"You two are both sick," Clouse commented with disgust. "You treat this like some sort of game where you can just knock off anyone you want, just to get your precious gems without any consequences. So, are you the leader of this little clan, Ryan?"

Ryan walked over toward Jane, casually carrying the shotgun at his side. He softly patted her head, apparently to let her know she had not been forgotten, and to keep Clouse in check.

"I'm the interim leader while our great one is away on business. And you may wonder exactly what it is my group stands for or worships. Well, we worship the Lord of the Underworld, Mephistopheles, the Devil, Satan, Lucifer, or whatever other name you may want to call him. We especially pay homage to Father Ernest, who in his own way, left a legacy for us to follow. He alone tried to show those asshole Jesuit priests the path to follow, but they wouldn't listen. And you see how many graves there are on that hill out there," Ryan finished, pointing out toward the cemetery at the edge of the hotel grounds.

"This all sounds farfetched," Clouse said. "Worshiping the devil? To what purpose?"

"You can't possibly understand, Paul," Ryan replied. "You may think we're off our rockers, but there is power you can't possibly conceive within the objects we seek. Objects this hotel has been hiding for almost a century. Objects those men, buried on that hill, fought to keep secret."

He paused a moment deliberately for emphasis.

"But we have a member who figured out what they were hiding, and even their weak religion cannot stop us from fulfilling our destiny as a collective group."

Clouse had often wondered how so many graves appeared during the few decades the Jesuits owned the hotel, but simply figured many were advanced in age, dying of natural causes. He could not believe otherwise.

"Those priests died of natural causes," Clouse said. "I don't know where you get this bullshit from, Ryan, but you're wrong on all counts."

"No, you're wrong! If we had time, I would fill you in on the entire story, but it's probably best kept within the confines of my group anyway." He shook part of the black robe, letting some cool air reach his skin within. "So while we're being so forthcoming, how did you figure it out, Paul?"

"Joan was easy once she kidnaped Zach from the school. A teacher managed to show me a picture with part of her in it, taken at the zoo."

"I always hate photos," Joan said, as though sincere. "They never catch you in the right light."

"No, I don't suppose they would show you as a nutcase murderer, would they?" Clouse deduced aloud.

With no response, he decided to continue his story.

"I figured you out from the computer program you two used to teach my son that tunnel system," he told Ryan. "I remembered using that program too, and I remember how constantly annoyed I was by the theater department being so close to the building I worked in."

He looked to the fresh corpse of Barry Andrews.

"I had eliminated your adopted father as a suspect, so that left only people close to the hospital, or working there. So, I had Mark do some checking on you, Ryan. Turns out you're minoring in architecture. What an interesting combination you've picked if you wanted to go nowhere in life, or you were simply fueling your knowledge for a project of revenge. We also found out your room-mate from last year, Rudolph Stephen Tenney, was listed missing a few weeks ago by campus police. Guess with a name like that I would have gone with my middle name too."

Clouse paused, glancing over toward Niemeyer, who still appeared dead or unconscious. He prayed one of his friends was somehow alive to help him momentarily.

"Just too many coincidences with the hospital, the cutting blade, and McCabe's investigation into the diving equipment, which I'd imagine you hadn't purchased that long ago. Turns out your entire family took diving lessons last spring, so you probably had a good enough alibi, but you weren't taking any chances, were you?"

"One can never be too careful," Ryan replied, apparently impressed by Clouse's detective work. "I worked awfully hard to pack that state trooper away only to have you two pricks dig him out."

Clouse shrugged, as though to apologize.

"Your father had an alibi, so we figured someone close to him might be behind the killings, especially with his girlfriend conveniently getting axed."

"Don't call that son-of-a-bitch my father," Ryan ordered. "My real father showed me the truth, showed me what I had to do to claim what was rightfully mine."

Clouse paused a moment, taking a few steps to one side.

"So what is your real motivation in this?" he had to ask Ryan.

"My real motivation was to find these jewels for Joan, eventually obtain the deed to this property, and live a happy existence with the occasional ceremony to worship my dark lord and carry out his wishes with my group. You can't begin to understand the power we've already unearthed, and that's just the beginning. We make quite a difference in society, as you can already tell. Everyone in the Coven has a professional job. Lawyers, doctors, teachers, you name it, we've got it. Well, we don't take to firemen or cops too well, as you might guess."

He looked to Joan, who returned a sinister smirk.

"But you gotta admit, this place makes one hell of a church, doesn't it?" he asked, looking up to the grand dome, six stories above them, the stars in the sky visible through its thick glass. "Hell, I could start my own convent here. This place is already a temple for evil, and there's room for improvement. And I have you to thank for putting it back together, Paul."

Clouse looked to both Joan and Ryan, one final question burning inside his mind.

"So where are these jewels I keep hearing about?"

Ryan looked to the book on the floor, then in the direction of Joan and her hostage.

"Seems your boy isn't very good at following orders," Ryan commented. "He said this book was all he found in the tunnels. Swears it. If you like reading about some bullshit account of Father Ernest, it's a great read, but when you're looking for something, for a quick way to get rich, it's a waste of fucking time."

Clouse began to realize the significance of the Father Ernest theme in more ways than one. Not only did Ryan aspire to dress and possibly act like the priest, but Ernest's actual past may have prevented the finish to his plan. The priests, or someone, may very well have found the jewels decades earlier and finished the job, leaving only a book behind.

"So someone beat you to it?" Clouse asked.

"Or your boy is lying," Ryan countered. "Little kids like to take things for themselves and keep secrets. I know I certainly did," he added, drawing a double-edged knife from beneath the cloak. He set the shotgun down, sliding it over to Joan. "Let's see what truths the boy tells when I cut his daddy up."

Clouse felt tense throughout his body. The time to bring the ordeal to a close had come, and he felt unprepared. He stripped off his jacket, letting it fall to the floor behind him as he defensively circled the Coven's temporary leader, ready to defend himself alone.

"One wrong move, your boy dies," the younger man warned before thrusting the knife at Clouse.

Dodging, Clouse simply stepped aside, wondering how long he could avoid being cut. Another slash missed him, then Clouse caught the knife, knocking it loose before Ryan used it. Ryan looked at Joan for a moment, as though he might actually tell her to harm the boy, but seemed to realize he might need Zach healthy for other reasons. He refocused his attention on Clouse with a visual warning not to prevent any further injury to himself.

For his trouble, Clouse received a knee to the stomach, then a barrage of fists striking everything from his jaw to his ribs, then his kidneys. For Zach's sake, he did not dare fight back after knocking the knife away, which served as his first and only act of defiance.

Ryan openly delighted himself in knocking the firefighter around, toying with his prey. Clouse found nothing respectable in how a person beat another senseless in a one-sided battle. He knew this was the same person who snuck up on others, launching a scythe into their guts before they could possibly defend themselves.

Nothing respectable whatsoever.

Clouse felt blood drip from his nose, and an open cut on his jaw, as his body fell to the floor, staggered by a body blow from Ryan. The younger man picked him up, launching several more fists into his abdomen, nearly causing Clouse to vomit from the hunched position he was held in. After half a dozen fists, he let the firefighter fall to the floor where his body naturally wanted to go. Taking a slow, deliberate walk toward the knife, Ryan turned to see Joan holding Zach hostage before staring at Clouse.

"It's too bad you really can't fight back," he said, bending down to pick up the knife. He was ready for the kill, now that Clouse was too battered to retaliate against an easy death. "Once you're gone, and we're done with your boy, who knows what we'll do with him."

"Mother fucker," Clouse addressed him between heaved breaths, lying on his back. "If you hurt him in any way, you will die."

"You're not in much of a position to make threats," Ryan said, standing over him, knife in hand.

Poising himself, Ryan pointed the knife's blade down at a battered Clouse. He prepared to launch the knife downward, into his adversary's chest, relishing the moment.

A gunshot suddenly rang through the atrium, catching everyone by surprise. Like everyone else, Clouse perked up to see where the shot had come from, and where it landed.

To his surprise, Joan let out a strange moan, her knife arm falling away from Zach as her eyes slowly rolled back in her head and her arms, followed by her body, went limp. She slumped to the floor in a heap, nearly taking the boy down with her.

Blood trickled from her back as the knife fell several feet from her body. Zach scurried away from the dead woman in a frenzy, rushing back to Jane, knowing his father was too close to the killer to protect him.

All eyes looked behind Joan's position, seeing Daniels standing at the door, a pistol held at his side. He walked in with a limp, due to the stabbing of his calve muscle. He drew close enough to protect Clouse if necessary, and to assess the situation for himself.

"You died," Ryan said, positive his eyes were not failing him.

"You're not the only one who can act, asshole," Daniels replied, holding up his wrists to reveal two slit plastic packs along the inside of each wrist. Both were lined with red where fake blood had spewed upon contact with small blades pressed against their sides. "Kind of an old professional wrestling trick," the officer said with a grin. "That gun you and I were fighting so viciously over was filled with blanks, son. Some good timing and a little fake blood, and you weren't too hard to fool."

He held his firearm up for the murderous young man to see.

"This one doesn't have blanks."

Clouse stammered to his feet, backing away from Ryan toward his friend.

"Might want to drop that knife," he told the young man.

Ryan obeyed, a smile crossing his face.

"So what are you going to do now? Kill me?"

"Actually," Daniels said, looking to Clouse who was recovering from his beating. "I think it's your turn, buddy," he said, implying that his friend should give some of what he had received.

"Suits me fine," Clouse said, launching a fist into the younger man's stomach, then another across his jaw.

He picked Ryan up, launching several more fists into his abdomen with vengeance on his mind. Not for himself, but for everyone he could never speak with again.

"This is for Kenny, and Rusty, and Dr. Smith," he said with a name for each thrust to the gut.

Ramming a knee into the younger man's sternum, he heard a painfully forced exhale from the killer. Clouse finally threw Ryan several feet further into the atrium, ready to tend to other priorities.

"Keep an eye on him," Clouse told Daniels as he walked over to Niemeyer.

His friend had not made a sound during the entire ordeal, lying motionless on his back. Clouse approached cautiously, checking his friend like he had so many patients on first responder runs. Though a certified EMT through his department, Clouse had reservations about handling his own friends, afraid he might screw something up.

"Come on, Tim," he said, kneeling beside his friend. "You're too dumb to die on me," he said, about to feel for a pulse.

"I heard that," Niemeyer said through the intense pain that came with regaining consciousness. "I'm only dumb because I followed you into this."

"Where does it hurt?" Clouse asked after a brief chuckle, beginning to examine his high school pal.

"Everywhere, but I don't think anything is broken."

"You're lucky you have so much padding, Tim," Clouse added with a bit of humor since his friend could do little about it.

"Just wait until I get my shotgun back, Paul. Then we'll see who's funny."

Clouse slowly felt around his friend's head, trying to discover if Niemeyer had any spinal or head injuries beyond a mild concussion. A large bump protruded from the construction worker's head along the back, but he doubted Niemeyer had suffered any severe injuries.

"Lie still," Clouse ordered, taking precautions. "You might have a spinal injury, and I'm not taking any chances until we get some paramedics here."

"I'm fine," Niemeyer insisted, trying to rise from the ground.

"Down," Clouse said, pushing lightly on his friend's chest to keep Niemeyer on the ground. "This is no time to be macho."

"Okay, okay," Niemeyer reluctantly agreed.

Clouse turned momentarily to see if everything was still safe.

Daniels kept an eye on Ryan while he untied Jane and Zach, letting them ease away from the killer, who kept amazingly still. He seemed to expect Ryan to make a final attempt at fleeing, or possibly charge him. Neither he nor Clouse envisioned bringing a murderer of such proportion into custody without further struggle.

"So where is your little faction when you need them?" he asked the young man.

"If you heard me talk about that, then you heard me say this was my project," Ryan answered. "Don't worry, regardless of what happens to me, you'll be hearing from them."

"I'm sure," Daniels said, turning his back momentarily to see Niemeyer's condition.

In the brief second or two the officer turned, Ryan charged him from behind, knowing the exits were all too far away for a clean escape. Confrontation was the only way he might still attain victory, no matter the cost.

To Daniels, the sound of footsteps, Jane's shriek, and the sight of Clouse desperately pointing, flooded his mind simultaneously, alerting him to Ryan's movement. Instinct, and previous experience told him the young man would attempt to flee, so Daniels turned deliberately, ready to fire across the atrium if necessary. He seemed to have no idea Ryan was already on his feet when he turned.

Ryan had already launched himself at the detective as everyone, including Clouse, watched helplessly.

Clouse saw the gun leave the officer's grip as the young man knocked it free. Daniels' legs would not allow much close quarters action, and Ryan sensed it. He knocked the recovering officer down by punching at one knee. As Daniels fell to his back, the wind knocked from him, he felt a fist bury itself in his jaw, then two hands clasp around his neck, throwing his head repeatedly back against the carpet, and concrete floor beneath it. His consciousness quickly wavered, but he felt the weight atop his body leave, along with the hands across his windpipe.

"You've done enough damage," he heard Clouse say as Ryan stood to confront him.

He backed the young man across the atrium a bit, but read the insanity in the younger man's eyes, positive Ryan would charge him, or dash toward the nearby exit Clouse had backed him to.

Glancing behind him, Ryan seemed to defy running, wanting another chance to finish the job and kill Clouse. His body rocked back and forth, as though he was prepared to attempt a tackle of his larger adversary, despite the firearm aimed at his chest.

"I'm not leaving here without claiming a life," Ryan muttered, prepared to charge Clouse for his final stand, apparently confident his father would carry out the remainder of the plan.

He began reached toward his backside, perhaps for a weapon, causing Clouse's hand to quiver as it held the gun, forcing the man to make a decision he had never made before.

To murder, or not?

"Maybe it's time *you* die," the firefighter finally said, firing a shot into the younger man's abdomen, sending him stumbling back until he hit the floor, laying motionless.

"Not bad," Daniels said as Clouse walked back to check on him.

"A little low," Clouse confessed, looking over the bruises on his friend's face. "You're not very good at this conflict resolution stuff, are you?"

"Hey, I'm getting a little better. I'll take a stab wound and a good beating to paralysis any day."

"Damn," Clouse said under his breath, looking up from his friend a moment.

Daniels seemed to already know what had happened.

From the spot where he fell, Ryan had disappeared altogether, most likely scrambling out an atrium entrance. This time, however, a blood trail left something to follow, and Clouse knew he had clipped the killer sufficiently.

"I'll be right back," Clouse said before storming out the exit door in pursuit.

"No!" Jane called, worried for his safety with good reason.

"I'll be fine," Clouse insisted, not wavering from his pursuit one second, and not turning to see any of his friends or family, fearing he might change his mind.

He followed the blood trail to the front of the hotel where it led outside. Thunder echoed in the distance as lightning illuminated the sky outside. Without fear of either, Clouse stepped outside, into the storm, looking around for any sign of Ryan. The wind howled around him, and rain smacked his face and neck mercilessly as wet droplets found their way inside his shirt, pressing into his chest like cold, stiff fingers.

A small trail of blood seemed to lead outside, then dissipate with the puddles and crashing rain drops. Any drips of blood were quickly washing away, leaving him nothing to follow. The weather showered him with rain and cold, reminding him of why intelligent people remained indoors. He took one last look around, certain Ryan had run off to die somewhere, rather than face the humiliation of being arrested. He probably felt defensive about his group, not wanting the police to divulge any information from him.

Insanity caused people to do strange things, Clouse decided.

"Anything?" Daniels asked as he returned to the atrium.

"No. I don't think he'll make it far, though."

Niemeyer sat up at this point, indicating he would be fine after some pain relievers, and everyone else seemed all right in Clouse's eyes. He walked over to his fiancee and son, taking them both into a much needed hug.

"You okay?" he asked Jane. Her reply came in the form of a weak nod. "I'm so sorry you had to go through this."

He looked around the room, keeping his arms wrapped around Jane. All the death, the remaining nightmares to relive night after night, and the wounds they had all suffered left him wondering. Somehow the answers Joan gave him seemed to make sense, but there was something about Ryan Andrews that remained a mystery. He wondered exactly what had prompted the young man to commit serial murder. He also questioned where the Rexford jewels had gone, and why a diary was left in their place. Clouse planned to read the diary soon, and learn what he could about the hotel's past.

"Want me to call the police?" Daniels asked, walking over to Clouse and his family.

"Whenever," the reply came.

Clouse felt no interest in talking to the police again. Nor did he want to leave such a moment of serenity, now that resolution had finally come.

He hoped tranquility might finally enter his life on a more regular basis, but so many questions burned at his mind, and Clouse wondered what price he needed to pay for peace of mind. He may have inherited Smith's fortune, but even that money would not buy him happiness and a normal life if things weren't fully resolved.

"Is it over, Daddy?" Zach asked, drawing close to his father.

"Yes, Zach, it's over," Clouse replied with absolution in his voice and a gnawing at his soul.

37

A week later, Clouse finally left his house to meet Daniels and McCabe at the state trooper's favorite pub for a drink one evening. Things looked up as more answers came to light, but several unanswered questions plagued the three men.

"There's been no sign of Ryan Andrews," McCabe said, now in his third day of regular duty after being incarcerated inside the hotel basement.

Apparently he and Russell Hinds had formed somewhat of a guarded friendship, even after the irregular way in which they met. McCabe promised the security guard a night filled with booze and women whenever he felt up to it. Being divorced, with the typical frame of mind that accompanied men in law enforcement, Hinds accepted.

"I don't think he could have survived that bullet wound if he didn't check into a hospital," Clouse noted. "Without surgery, there's no way he could have gotten that bullet out of there."

"I agree," Daniels said. "But that boy certainly is crafty. There's no telling what tricks he might have had up his sleeve. If he wasn't lying, there might have been a doctor in that group of his who did a private surgery."

"We did find Mrs. Landamere's stash of tile pieces," McCabe boasted, taking a gulp from his beer mug. "Man, they must have had about two-hundred of those things in their basement, and most of them were useless."

"Actually, they were all useless," Clouse said. "It turned out one of the priests moved the jewels in an attempt to keep them out of the wrong hands. That diary they found was pretty interesting reading."

"What else did it say?" Daniels asked.

Clouse sipped from his second beer bottle, thinking a moment.

"It was kind of odd for a journal, because the entire time I felt like the writer was still keeping secrets. And to be honest, I never did figure out exactly who the writer was. It briefly mentioned some odd troubles with Father Ernest, and how the priests came to regret buying the hotel after some time. Strangely, the journal ends, talking about how the jewels must be hidden, and leaves off, like there's another edition to follow."

"Is there?" McCabe inquired.

"Well, this one was listed number three, so there are obviously others, but I don't know where. Did anything like that show up in your search of the Landamere property?"

"No, but we were just searching for the tile pieces and some notebooks with relevant facts. They probably overlooked everything else."

Daniels had managed to convince authorities he had not used his police credentials in any way during the past week, to keep his job secure. Clouse knew he had also visited Susan, and discovered his prognosis looked good. He planned to finish rehabilitation and rejoin the force, hopefully taking little time to earn his spot in the investigative division back. With his life back to normal, he had taken the week off to enjoy his son a bit more, knowing he would be able to help Curtis with his own first steps.

"So what are you going to do?" the officer asked McCabe.

"I'm transferring to the north end of the state, and getting back on the road," the trooper said, as though he felt disdain for his current assignment. "Up there you just deal with speeders and the occasional horse and buggy, not serial killers. About the most excitement I'll get from now on will be searching cars for drugs near Gary."

"You'll miss your bars," Daniels said.

"I'll be near Chicago, Mark," McCabe replied with a chuckle.

He turned his attention to Clouse.

"And what are you going to do with your newfound fortune?" the trooper asked the firefighter, already knowing what Daniels had planned in his near future, since the man had informed them both early on.

Clouse sighed. Indeed, what Harold Simms told him at the funeral was true, and Clouse stood to inherit a net worth of a couple billion dollars.

Perhaps.

"Probably nothing for quite some time. It seems I'm going to be held up in court over some new injunctions, and it may be awhile before they figure out exactly what Dr. Smith owed the government. In the meantime, I'll go back to my job after I spend a little more time with my family."

"Did you ever figure out anything about Ryan Andrews' background?" Daniels asked McCabe.

"No. It seems he was left at the hospital's emergency room entrance as an infant and Dr. Andrews was the one who found him. No one had any clue who his original parents might have been. To be honest, I can't understand how that boy could be so indifferent about Joan slitting his father's throat, then disown the man completely. Something really wrong must have happened there."

"And there's been no trace of the group he was talking about," Daniels stated. "If he wasn't lying, it sure is a secretive bunch."

Clouse took another sip of beer, noticing the bottle felt warmer. The conversation was keeping them from drinking.

"I asked Zach if he checked every tunnel of the hallowed resort when he was down there, and he seems certain he did. If that journal is accurate, someone beat them to the jewels, and they murdered a lot of innocent people for absolutely no good reason."

"There's no *good* reason," Daniels commented. "And I don't see why they couldn't have accomplished their objective without killing anyone?"

"Because there's no revenge in that," Clouse noted. "Joan had it in for you, Mark. When you shot her husband between the eyes, she just snapped."

Daniels closed his eyes a few seconds, most likely reliving the experience from the year before by the painful look on his face.

Back then, the answers came clearer in the end. This year, something seemed to be missing from the whole puzzle. Granted, the investigation was not fully shut, but it was winding down. Clouse knew Daniels planned to work with McCabe in finding what few answers remained to be discovered, and hoped they succeeded in finding them.

At least until the trooper moved away.

"Guys, I need to get out of here and see the soon-to-be wife and kids," Clouse said, standing from the table.

Both nodded a farewell as he left a few dollar bills on the table and headed for the door.

Outside, the weather threatened snow with a formidable cold wind that forced Clouse to immediately zip up his jacket. He looked around at the leaves swirling in the air, and saw a bleak day around him, like so many others he had just experienced.

Strangely, his dilemma felt unresolved, but the only thing to do was wait. Stay home, protect his family, and wait for answers. He headed across the parking lot, feeling determined to put his life back together and take the positive things he had left, and make them work. He would play the waiting game, be patient, and take what life offered him, not worrying about the future, or who might come after him. Each day the demons fell a bit further behind him.

And that's where they belonged.